Con

Preface to volume I (revised edition) 1

List of selected characters 3

King James I(VI) Simplified Family Tree 8

Prologue 11

Chapter 1 : Destiny or Will? (1685-1702) 21

Chapter 2 : Fascination (1702-1703) 50

Chapter 3 : Leaving the nest (1703) 70

Chapter 4 : First step: Hamburg (1703 – 1704) 88

Chapter 5 : Pride and Music (1704-1706) 109

Chapter 6 : A Saxon in Italy: I am Giorgio Hendel (1706 – 1707) 136

Chapter 7 : A Saxon in Italy : Margherita (1707) 162

Chapter 8 : A Saxon in Italy: I am in love! (1707 – 1708) 179

Chapter 9 : A Saxon in Italy : between opera and love (1708) 205

Chapter 10 : Operatic London (1708-1709) 231

Chapter 11 : A Saxon in Italy : An opera composer is born (1709-1710) 239

Chapter 12 : Roads to London (1710) 260

Chapter 13 : A Saxon in London : Triumphal début? (1710-1711) 280

Chapter 14 : Uncertain future (1711-1712) 321

Preface to volume I (revised edition)

Born in 1685, Händel spent most of his life in 18th century Europe, where many countries were not yet nations but regions. I would like to stress that when I mention Germany, Italy, Holland or America, it is to indicate the region and not the nation. The dates are used as recorded at the time. As Britain stuck to the Julian Calendar (Old Style, the new year starting on 25 March) and did not adopt the Gregorian Calendar (New Style) until 1752, they were eleven days behind the rest of Europe. However, for clarity's sake, the years mentioned are used not as recorded at the time, but as adjusted to the New Style. I have not delved deeply into the details of the War of the Spanish Succession, so the historical background may appear simplified. However my intention was to imagine how Händel, a musician facing its consequences, saw the politics of the time. Also, the history of the House of Hanover is very complex and I could not go into details. And the story of inheritance by Ernst August, the father of the future George I, is very complicated and lengthy. The same is true for my explanation of the electorate and elector and of Hamburg and the Hanseatic League. I am guilty of simplification and humbly beg pardon from historians!

Queen Anne and her friend Sarah, Duchess of Marlborough, called each other by nicknames. However I did not use them to avoid confusion. Again, for historians it could be frustrating for this inaccuracy and I humbly beg pardon. And very often aristocrats possessed more than one title. The future King George I's mother, Sophia, was born Princess Palatine, and by marriage became Duchess of Brunswick-Lüneburg, and was known as Sophia of Hanover, Duchess Sophia, or Dowager Duchess Sophia when she became a widow. Handel's patron in Rome, Francesco Ruspoli was Marquess of Cerveteri, then Prince of Cerveteri, and also Marquess of Riano and Count of Vignanello. Handel's future patron in London, Richard Boyle, was 3rd Earl of Burlington and 4th Earl of Cork, and known as Lord Burlington, to name just a few. I tried my best to be clear and use just one appellation, or two, to avoid confusion, but again I beg pardon to the reader if I failed to be clear enough.

I use the term 'resident' as was used in the 18th century, as the title to John Wych in Hamburg, or Christoph Kreyenberg in London. 'Resident' was the term used to indicate diplomat, rather than 'ambassador' which carried much less importance, not far from 'merchant'.

I would like to give some detail about the buildings and places in London I mention. Kensington Palace was called Kensington House before George I made improvements. However, to make it simple I decided to call it Kensington Palace throughout. The Queen's Theatre on Haymarket no

1

longer exists. It is approximately the place occupied by Her Majesty's Theatre on Haymarket today. When I mention the Queen's Theatre or Haymarket, I am talking about the same place, as called in either way in Handel's time. The same thing applies to the Theatre Royal on Drury Lane. The London residence of Richard Boyle, Earl of Burlington, called Burlington House on Piccadilly, is currently occupied by The Royal Academy of Arts. The buildings on each side did not exist yet, however, the façade of the house is quite well preserved.

I tried to be accurate with the historical facts, but sometimes I have taken the liberty to change slight details to serve the narrative. The rest is my imagination.

This volume is a kind of introduction and I am conscious that there are too many characters. However, to tell the first twenty-seven years of Handel's life, where from the small town of Halle he goes around Germany, then Italy and finally London, it is impossible to limit the story to ten characters. Some of them might seem irrelevant to Handel's life. And I have included Johann Sebastian Bach. Händel and Bach were born in the same year, just 26 days apart. It is a fact that they never met, and they hardly knew about each other. However, to talk about Händel and his time while ignoring Bach seemed to me impossible, and even an insult to the history, for they are considered two giants of the Baroque era today. Those characters all have roles to play in Händel's life, directly or indirectly. So I added a short list of characters, and also a simplified family tree from James I (VI). I hope these will help the reader to not get lost too much, and I ask you to be patient and wait for other volumes to see how all that unfolds!

List of selected characters

The dates are taken from various sources, which do not always agree. I chose the ones that seemed more accurate.

Ansbach, Caroline of, *see* Hanover
Ariosti, Attilio (1666-1729), Italian ecclesiastic and composer working for the court of King Frederick I in Prussia.
Bach, Johann Sebastian (1685-1750), German composer, Händel's junior by 26 days.
Bavaria, Violante of, Duchess of (1673-1731), wife of Ferdinando de' Medici.
Bononcini, Giovanni (1670-1747), Italian composer, widely reputed by 1705 in Europe.
Boschi, Giuseppe Maria (1675-1744), Italian bass singer, husband to Francesca Vanini-Boschi. Sang in *Agrippina* and *Rinaldo*.
Boyle, Richard, Earl of Burlington (1694-1753), Anglo-Irish nobleman, also architect, patron of arts.
Brandenburg, Frederick III, Electoral Prince of, then Elector of, then King Frederick I in Prussia (1657-1713), husband to Sophia Charlotte of Hanover.
Brandenburg, Sophia Charlotte (1668-1705), Electoral Princess, then Electress and also Queen in Prussia, *see* also Hanover
Brunswick-Lüneburg, *see* Hanover
Brydges, James (1674-1744), son of Baron Chandos, a music enthusiast.
Burlington, *see* Boyle
Buxtehude, Dietrich (c.1637-1707), organist at the Marienkirche, Lübeck
Caldara, Antonio (c.1670-1736), Italian cellist and composer, house composer to Francesco Ruspoli in Rome, succeeding Handel.
Cerveteri, Marquess of/Prince of, *see* Ruspoli.
Churchill, Sarah née Jennings (1660-1744), Countess of Marlborough, then Duchess, wife of John Churchill, 1st Earl of Marlborough, then 1st Duke of Marlborough, childhood friend of Queen Anne.
Cibber, Colley (1671-1757), actor-manager, playwright and Poet Laureate.
Collier, William (c.1687-1758), lawyer, MP and theatre manager
Corelli, Arcangelo (1653-1713), Italian violinist and composer, employed by Cardinal Ottoboni
Durastante, Margherita (fl.1700-1734), Italian soprano singer, worked with Handel in Rome under Francesco Ruspoli's patronage. Her surname is

sometimes spelled Durastanti.
Farinel, Jean-Baptiste (1655-1720), Konzertmeister at Hanover, husband to Vittoria Tarquini.
Granville, Mary (1700-1788), future Handel's faithful supporter, still a little girl in this volume.
Grimani, Vincenzo (1653-1710), a cardinal, diplomat and librettist, wrote *Agrippina* for Handel.
Händel, family:
  Georg (1622-1697), physician, father of Georg Friederich
  Dorothea, née Taust (1651-1730), mother of Georg Friederich
  Georg Friederich (1685-1759), Georg and Dorothea's son, composer, Kapellmeister of Hanover
  Dorothea Sophia (1687-1718), Georg and Dorothea's daughter, married Michael Dietrich Michaelsen
  Johanna Christiana (1690-1709), Georg and Dorothea's second daughter

Hanover, house of:
  Ernst August, Duke of Brunswick-Lüneburg (1629-1698), husband to Sophia, Georg Ludwig's father.
  Sophia, Duchess of Brunswick-Lüneburg (1630-1714), granddaughter of James I, Georg Ludwig's mother
  Georg Ludwig (1660-1727), Duke of Brunswick-Lüneburg, Elector of Hanover, Ernst August and Sophia's son, future George I
  Sophia Charlotte (1668-1705), Ernst August and Sophia's daughter, Georg Ludwig's sister, wife of Frederick I in Prussia, *see* also Brandenburg.
  Georg August (1683-1760), Electoral Prince of Hanover, Georg Ludwig's son, husband to Caroline of Ansbach, future George II.
  Caroline (1683-1737), Electoral Princess of Hanover, wife of Georg August future Queen Caroline.
Haym, Nicola (1678-1729), Italian cellist and composer.
Heidegger, Johann Jakob (1666-1749), theatre manager.
Hill, Aaron (1685-1750), author and theatre manager.
Keiser, Reinhard (1674-1739), German composer and director of the Hamburg Opera House.
Krieger, Johann Philipp (1649-1725), German composer, court composer at Weissenfels.
Manchester, Earl of, *see* Montagu
Marlborough, *see* Churchill
Mattheson, Johann (1681-1764), singer and composer at Hamburg Opera House, later known as a theorist. Händel's friend in Hamburg.

Medici, house of:
    Cosimo III (1642-1723), Grand Duke of Tuscany
    Francesco Maria (1660-1711), brother of Cosimo III, once cardinal
    Ferdinando (1663-1713), Grand Prince of Tuscany, Cosimo III's eldest son
    Ana Maria Luisa (1667-1743), Cosimo III's daughter, *see also* Palatinate
    Gian Gastone (1671-1737), second son of Cosimo III, Grand Duke of Tuscany, succeeding his father
    Violante (1673-1731), Grand Princess, wife of Ferdinando, *see also* Bavaria

Michaelsen, Michael Dietrich (1680-1748), lawyer, husband to Händel's sister Dorothea Sophia.
Montagu, Charles (c.1662-1722), 4th Earl of Manchester, diplomat and statesman, friend of John Vanbrugh.
Nicolini [Grimaldi, Nicolo] (1673-1732), singer, alto-castrato.
Ottoboni, Pietro (1667-1740), a cardinal and Vice-Chancellor, and patron of music in Rome, famous for his weekly concerts at his functional palace La Cancelleria in Rome where Arcangelo Corelli was the orchestra's director.
Palatinate, Ana Maria Luisa (1667-1743), wife of Johann Wilhelm, Elector Palatine.
Palatinate, Sophia of the, *see* Hanover
Pamphili, Benedetto (1653-1730), a cardinal, also poet and librettist, patron of music in Rome; sometimes the ornamental spelling Pamphilj is used.
Rich, Christopher (1657-1714), lawyer, theatre manager.
Rossi, Giacomo (fl.1710-31), poet and librettist settled in London.
Ruspoli, Francesco Maria (1672-1731), a Roman nobleman, patron of Händel in Rome, Marquess of Cerveteri and then Prince of Cerveteri, Marquess of Riano and Count of Vignanello.
Scarlatti, Alessandro (1660-1725), Italian composer.
Scarlatti, Domenico (1685-1757), Italian composer, son of Alessandro.
Steffani, Agostino (1654-1728), Italian ecclesiastic, composer and diplomat.
Stuart, Anne (1665-1714), Queen of England, Scotland and Ireland.
Swiney, Owen (1676-1754), theatre manager
Tarquini, Vittoria, soprano singer, wife of Farinel, mistress of Ferdinando de'Medici
Taust, family:
    Georg (1606-died before 1685), pastor
    Dorothea (1651-1730), Georg's daughter, see also Händel
    Georg, pastor (1658-?), Dorothea's younger brother

Telemann, Georg Philipp (1681-1767), German composer, Händel's lifelong friend.

Vanbrugh, John (1664-1726), architect, playwright and theatre manager, creator of the Queen's Theatre on Haymarket.

Zachow, Friedrich Wilhelm (1663-1712), organist and composer, Händel's music teacher.

King James I(VI) Simplified Family Tree

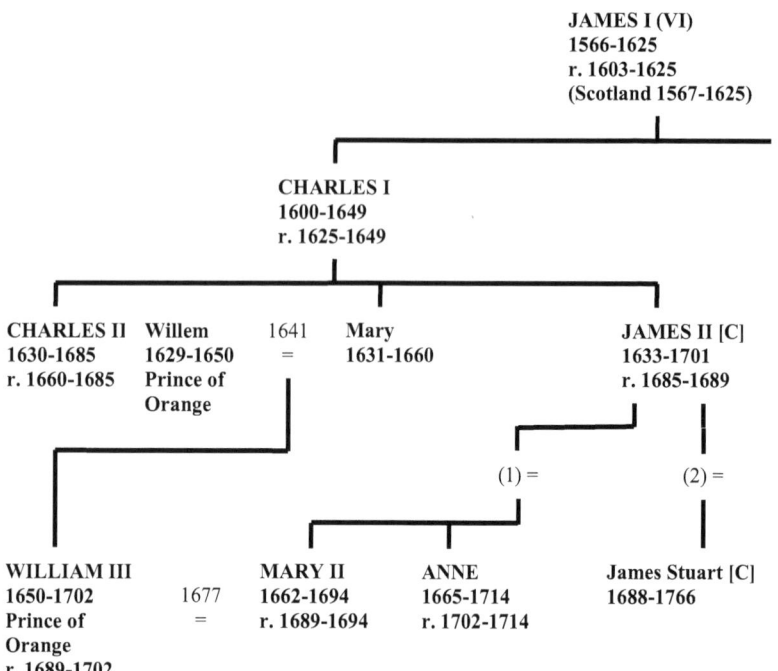

NOTE: [C] indicates Catholic

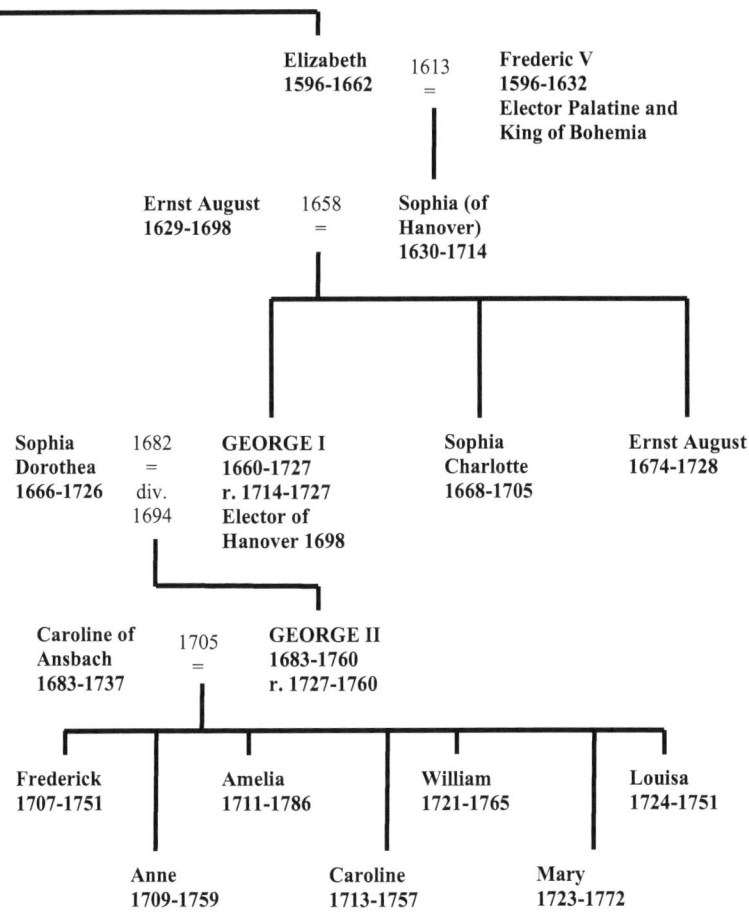

Prologue

Halle, January 1683

Halle is a small town in the middle of Germany, not far from Leipzig. At the time, Germany was a federation of the ruling princes and a part of the Holy Roman Empire, and the city was involved in war several times, changing its ruler according to shifting politics and treaties. It saw relative stability for nearly forty years, beginning in the 1640s, under the administration of Duke August of Saxony. However, with his death in 1680, the city of Halle fell to Brandenburg, as designated by the peace treaties of Westphalia, signed in 1648. The Saxon court left Halle for Weissenfels, leaving the city to become part of the Duchy of Magdeburg, an annexe of Brandenburg-Prussia. In 1683, just a few years into the new identity, people still considered themselves Saxon, and were quite reluctant to call themselves Prussians.

Pastor Georg Taust was walking back to his parsonage, which sat just beside his church of St Bartholomew in Giebichenstein on the outskirts of Halle. It was still day, but the winter lights of January were weak, and the sun behind the thick clouds would fall below the horizon soon. The news he had just received left him perplexed. He did not know whether to rejoice or worry.

He stopped and looked up at the parsonage. The house looked unchanged; however, the absence of his wife and two of his children taken by the plague two years before could still be felt everywhere. Once a family of seven, it was now reduced to him and his remaining three children, Dorothea, Anna and Georg. He gently massaged his aching lower back as he opened the front door.

Dorothea Taust looked up from her book as her father entered the house.

'Father, are you all right?' she asked, frowning slightly.

Pastor Taust did not reply. Instead, he walked over to where she sat by the fire. The simple but comfortable interior was warm. It was still bright enough to read without candlelight. Her father sat down in front of her and took her hands in his as he passed on the extraordinary news.

'What?' Dorothea Taust stood up abruptly and stared at her father. Her dark eyes were wide open. She did not notice that the book she had been reading fell to the floor.

Dorothea was not of the kind to faint easily – and she did not – but her knees gave way. Pastor Taust quickly caught his daughter in his strong arms and lowered her into the chair.

Thirty was in fact quite old for a woman to be unwed. Dorothea had seen her cousins get married at sixteen and give birth at seventeen or eighteen. That was the way it was in those days. She was almost old enough to be a grandmother.

'But, Father, I am too old...'

'I know, my daughter.' Then he corrected himself quickly. 'Well, old, but not too old.' He picked up the book from the floor and placed it gently on her lap.

'And...I like...reading,' she said looking down at the book.

This was quite a handicap for a woman. Women were better off illiterate so as to serve their husbands and children with nary a question. It was not a good thing for a woman to be educated and have opinions.

'He knows that, and he knows that I allowed you to be so.'

Dorothea did not know what to say. At her age, having refused all proposals that had come her way, she had been quite certain she would stay with her family, unmarried. That had been her choice. Now a sixty-year-old man was asking for her hand and it seemed she had no choice after all.

'Dorothea, I am happy to keep you with us, but it is not a bad thing to get married and have your own family,' said Pastor Taust. 'Of course, I will not force you.'

'My own family...' she whispered. She could not imagine herself being a mother.

Pious, calm and reserved, Dorothea Taust liked her quiet life, and most of all, she loved her father, who allowed her to study and to do what she liked.

Her father knew that by allowing her to be her own tutor, he reduced considerably the chance of his daughter finding a husband. It was their mutual inclination not to follow the convention. He loved his daughter more than the idea of her getting married.

The suitor, a surgeon, was not a stranger to her. She had met him on several occasions, along with her father, when she was helping people with illnesses or injuries. The memory of the plague was still fresh. Dr Händel had worked assiduously to help the diseased, without stopping, even when his wife and one of his sons succumbed. She felt respect for the man who was one of the most well-reputed doctors in the country, who nonetheless never let an opportunity pass to be good to the poor. Respect, that was all. She could not imagine that old, severe-looking man as her husband.

'Father?'

'Yes, Dorothea.'

'Do you like Doctor Händel?'

He looked at his daughter. 'Yes, I like Doctor Händel. He is a good man. He's never refused to help my people, even when he knew that he would never be paid,' he said calmly. 'And I trust him. I know I can count on him.'

At that moment, Pastor Taust realised why he had been called to visit the doctor instead of the doctor coming to him to make his offer. The old surgeon did not want to come to invade their sphere, out of respect. Doctor Händel wanted to give Dorothea space to breathe and think. Then the pastor felt tightness in his chest and winced.

But Dorothea did not know what to think. She could not feel the affection for the old surgeon that was needed for a good marriage. At the same time, she knew that her father was getting old and that her younger brother Georg would soon get married and have a family. He is to succeed his father as a pastor. Since the death of her mother, it had been upon her to manage the household with her sister Anna. But what would happen once her brother had a wife? Her home would not be her home anymore. She was certain her brother would not reject her, but she would become unnecessary. Her brother's future wife would run the household. What to do? Would she and her sister become servants for her younger brother's family - cooking, cleaning and looking after their children?

She stared down at her book and stroked it. The room had become dark, and only the light coming from the fire enabled her to see the contour of her book. It was time to light the candles.

On 23 April 1683 Pastor Taust duly inscribed her daughter's name along with Doctor Händel's in the marriage register of his church.

Hanover, September 1684

114 miles north-west of Halle was Hanover, residence city of the Duke of Brunswick-Lüneburg on the River Leine.

The summer palace of Herrenhausen was buzzing. The constant flow of drapers, dressmakers, goldsmiths, silversmiths, furniture makers – all imaginable kinds of craftsmen – kept the servants busy. They were all engaged in preparation for the wedding of Sophia Charlotte of Hanover, the only daughter of Ernst August and Sophia, Duke and Duchess of Brunswick-Lüneburg, to Frederick III, Electoral Prince of Brandenburg.

Sophia Charlotte's mother, Duchess Sophia, was standing in front of the window overlooking the gardens. It was still early but the gardeners were already working. She was transforming the gardens of the palace to make them like the ones at Versailles she had admired so during her visit five years earlier. So far, the project was going well, and she was looking forward to the completion.

Duchess Sophia, born as Sophia of the Palatines, was one of the grandchildren of James I of England and the youngest daughter of Frederick V, Elector Palatine, and Elizabeth Stuart. As her father had been forced into exile after losing the Battle of White Mountain as King of Bohemia, she was born in The Hague. Educated but poor, her future at birth did not look particularly bright. She had declined to be the wife of Charles Stuart, her first cousin in exile, who was now Charles II of England. She had been far from romantic when young, but she disliked the idea of being used to reinforce Charles's claim to the throne.

When she'd married the fourth son of the Duke of Brunswick-Lüneburg, she had just wanted a solid marriage. As they had known each other for some time, and had even corresponded, there was friendship and affection. However, her marriage proved to be more than a success. It was a marriage of love combined with dynastic success. She was one of the most intelligent, cultured and well-connected noblewomen in Europe. She was not stunningly beautiful, but her intelligence and wit made her engaging and attractive. As a granddaughter of James I, she was in the line of succession to the British throne. Her husband had succeeded in enlarging considerably his dukedom. And they were blessed with six sons and a daughter.

The marriage of her oldest son, Georg Ludwig, two years earlier, had been arranged as a vital part of her husband's plans. She had been against it, but was won over by her husband, whose ambition was to elevate the duchy to the level of electorate, securing and consolidating his father's dukedom. Her son was happy to marry his young and beautiful cousin. A boy was born the previous year and the couple seemed on their way to producing more children. Duchess Sophia loved her husband, and as a mother, she wished all of her seven children to be happy. Her eldest son married away, she worried about her only daughter's happiness in marriage. Her daughter, aged sixteen, was going to marry a man widowed once and eleven years her senior.

'Mama, you asked for me?' Sophia Charlotte called, waking the duchess from her daydream.

'My dearest daughter, I have to tell you something,' Sophia of Hanover said to her daughter, a little nervous. There was little time left to spend together, and she felt her duty as a mother pressing her.

'What is it, Mama?' Sophia Charlotte asked merrily.

They were in the duchess's bedchamber. Chocolate was brought in. It was a very private place, so Sophia Charlotte knew the matter was quite serious but not official. She'd inherited intelligence from her mother, and God had also given her a most delicious and infectious smile. She was the sunshine of the family. Mother and daughter were seated side-by-side on a large settee upholstered in the French style with its wood frame richly sculpted and gilded. Still in their dressing gowns, they faced each other.

'You are going to marry a man who has already had a wife.'

'Yes, Mama.'

'I have to tell you that…though he is widowed…' She hesitated and took her daughter's hands, anticipating a shocked reaction.

Sophia Charlotte smiled and finished her mother's sentence. 'He keeps a mistress?'

Sophia of Hanover, astonished, opened her mouth, but no words came out. Her daughter laughed.

'How...but...how...who...'

'Oh, it's Görgen.' She still called her oldest brother by his nickname.

'Georg Ludwig?'

'Yes, Mother.'

'That chatterbox...' Sophia felt frustration invading her mind. She had been worrying about how to tell her daughter for nothing.

'No, Mama. He just wanted me to know so I wouldn't be dismayed. He wanted to protect me,' Sophia Charlotte interrupted again, jolly as always. Inside, however, she was careful. She did not want to talk about her father's mistress, as she knew her mother's suffering.

'I see...but...' The duchess saw her daughter's point. Her son was everything but a chatterbox, and she knew it. He saw it as a duty as an older brother of the young bride-to-be to ensure she'd know what was awaiting her.

'Well, he told me that it is quite common. Some men just get a mistress to imitate the Sun King.'

'Louis XIV is a model, for good and bad...'

'And he told me quite a lot about men, Mama. That was useful, as I don't know very much about them.' She chuckled.

'You are too young to know-'

'Mother, I am sixteen, and I am getting married,' she said in a serious tone, though her eyes were still laughing.

'You could have been the queen,' the mother sighed.

'Mama, France is too far, and I do not want to be so far away from you. If I go there, I will not see you anymore. And...'

'And?'

'Well, I was eleven. I don't really remember.'

'True, the Sun King thought you were too young. He was desperate for his son to have heirs as soon as possible.'

'Mama, how old were you when you married Papa?'

The duchess hesitated, and then she decided to be honest and open. 'I was twenty-seven, nearly twenty-eight.'

'Why did you wait so long, Mama?'

'Well, I did not want to marry the man who became Charles II of England.'

'See, we are both failed queens!'

The duchess laughed. 'As you might have realised, it is not easy to find a suitable man.'

'I know. Too old or too young, too powerful or too poor, everything perfect with the wrong religion...'

'And the effort wasted by Signor Steffani...' said the mother, referring to another failed plan to marry her daughter to the son of the Elector of Bavaria.

'He is a good man, Signor Steffani. I like him a lot, and what a musician he is!' the young Sophia exclaimed.

'The young prince was more suitable for you, about the same age, a very able man, and...powerful.'

Munich was twice as big as Hanover. And an alliance with such a powerful electorate would have been beneficial for the ambition of the duke. But the negotiations dragged on and came to naught. After all, Munich concluded that the alliance did not bring benefit to them. Still, a firm friendship was made with Munich's envoy, Agostino Steffani.

'Mama, I didn't want to go so far. Munich is far too... and they are Catholic,' Sophia Charlotte sighed, 'like the French royal family.'

Her mother straightened herself. 'Now that you know your future husband has a mistress, my dear, I have to tell you about men, from our side.'

'I suppose what you have to tell me about men is very different from what my brother told me.' She looked at her mother with a witty smile.

'You are young, beautiful, well educated, and intelligent, but that is not enough.'

'To be a wife?'

'No. To keep a man. It is not the question of wife or mistress. You must use all your power, wittiness, and humour to keep him with you.'

'Not easy, I suppose,' Sophia Charlotte responded instead of asking her mother how she had fared.

'Not too complicated though. Men are a bit like dogs. You make them want to stay with you.'

'Oh, Mother!' Sophia Charlotte shouted in shock. 'Is that how you treated father?' She immediately regretted saying it.

Duchess Sophia ignored her daughter's reaction. 'You will agree with me later, I'm certain about it. But still, there is a problem of...' She hesitated.

'Yes, Mother?'

'Physical desire.'

'Well, I have to tell you, Mother, that I know nothing about it.'

'You will be his new wife. Then he will get used to you and might start looking at other women.'

'I know. Görgen told me. It is often the case in arranged marriages.'

'It happens very often when the wife is expecting a child. A man needs a woman; it is physical. But there is one simple way to calm him down and so prevent him from...'

Sophia looked at her daughter, took a deep breath, and said, 'Well, if your husband wants you, never refuse. And make it happen in the morning – every morning, if possible – so he is empty for the day. Then the dog will be calm.'

Sophia Charlotte's jaw dropped. Her eyes wide open, she whispered, 'Görgen did not tell me that.'

Sophia did not tell her daughter that she had obtained much of this useful information from her niece, Elizabeth Charlotte, who was married to Philippe I, Duke d'Orléans, the younger brother of Louis XIV, through their extensive correspondence.

A week later, on one fine morning in late September, Sophia Charlotte was ready to leave Hanover, accompanied by her parents, to become the Electoral Princess of Brandenburg. The long train, carrying her bridal trousseau, would be escorted by the prestigious Osnabrück guards' regiment 'the Parrots', headed by her brother Georg Ludwig in the regiment's green-and-red uniform.

'You look splendid, Görgen,' said his little sister.

Georg Ludwig beamed. Having recently come back from the siege of Vienna, covered in glory, married, and newly blessed with a son, he looked just perfect. And he was very fond of his little sister.

'Take care of us, Georg,' said his father. 'If we are attacked and stripped, we are quite fucked.'

'Husband!'

Sophia Charlotte laughed. Her brother smiled and said, 'In that case, why don't you all go stripped already to give the bandits no chance?'

'Are you certain you don't want to stay in Berlin with us, Brother?' asked the young bride-to-be.

'No, I will come back here as soon as possible. I have to keep the estate while you are having fun.' He just wanted to be with his wife and their baby son.

'I count on you, Son.' Duke Ernst August smiled. 'Let us go.'

Everything seemed perfect. Their eldest son, Georg Ludwig, was happily married, and the lineage seemed assured with the child born the previous year, a healthy boy. Still, Sophia's mind was not perfectly at peace. She knew that her husband was planning to announce a big change in succession law, from the existent ultimogeniture principle of dynastic succession to the new primogeniture, after their return from Berlin.

Ultimogeniture meant the youngest male child would inherit his father's title. As the duke was the last of four sons, he duly inherited the title of Duke of Brunswick-Lüneburg and a quarter of his father's estate. His ambition, combined with the extraordinary and unexpected deaths of two of his elder brothers, who died without heirs, and an arrangement made with the remaining brother, allowed him to reunite the whole dukedom of his father, once divided by inheritance. Now that he had reunited all his father's estate, he wished to preserve and consolidate it. Also the duke had always wished for his eldest son, Georg, to succeed him and he groomed his son from a young age. The duke was now in his early 50s and knew that his health was deteriorating, and his youngest son was only ten. Primogeniture, giving an exclusive right of inheritance to the eldest son seemed the best solution. The duke's ambition now was to elevate his dukedom to an electorate, and having a large estate was an important requirement for any candidature. Being an elector would mean that he would be, in German prestige and rank, immediately below the emperor, and above other ruling princes – dukes, landgraves and margraves. And it was recognised in international diplomacy that being one of the members of the electoral college of the Holy Roman Empire carried great prestige, as their function was the election of the emperor. Sophia loved her children, and she worried about the impact and the consequences. She had little hope that all six of her sons would accept it easily.

Isfahan, February 1685

It was a very cold February evening in the Persian capital. Court astrologer Larvandad was hesitating. The prospect of staying warm at home was tempting, and due to his age, nobody would blame him for doing so. But this kind of clear night was ideal.

'Father, are you going to the observatory?' his daughter asked. 'It is cold.'

'I know. I won't stay long.'

'Make sure to ask for help to go up and down, Father.'

'I will, Firouzeh.'

'Promise?'

He smiled. 'Yes.'

She looked unconvinced.

'I promise you, my dear. I cannot stay here when the sky is so clear.' He looked into his daughter's blue-green eyes, after which she had been named Turquoise.

Seeing Firouzeh sigh and smile back, resigned, Larvandad felt a pang in his heart. His only child had been widowed young and had come back home to look after him when her mother died. She refused to remarry. He was grateful to have her with him, but he wished her to be happy. 'I am happy with you, Father,' she would say. But he was getting old. What if he died tomorrow?

His study was on the top floor of the highest tower of the palace. Being the oldest of the court astrologers, Larvandad had been granted the best-situated room. It was warm. The fire was lit systematically in the evening whenever the sky was clear. It was a circular room with a small balcony. In the centre stood a large, rustic desk with a chair in front. This was a strange sight in Persia, but Larvandad had become used to this European furniture when the prince, worried about the old man's back pain, had given the order to have the low table and cushions removed. A boy servant was keeping a watch on the fire. Larvandad arrived in a chair carried by two strong slaves. He pushed aside the thick carpet to go out onto the balcony. The air was stingingly cold. He looked up. *Good.* Conditions were excellent for observation. Larvandad did not take long to come back from the balcony.

Muttering 'What is that? What is that?' the astrologer started rummaging through all sorts of scrolls and bound documents. He pulled away a few and started perusing them. Soon he was immersed completely.

Firouzeh burst into his study.
'Oh, Father! You are here! I was so worried,' she said, breathless.
'Firouzeh...but...'
'It's past midnight!'
'Oh, is it?' He looked at his daughter, puzzled. Behind her, the prince was coming up the steps.
'Prince Husayn, I am sorry.'
The prince was tall and slim. While Firouzeh was still panting from climbing up the steps, the prince's chest was calm inside his rich robe.
'Firouzeh, you drag your father home, and I will go back to entertain my guests.' He stopped at the door and looked back.
'Larvandad?'
'Prince?'
'You gave me an idea of how to get rid of my guests.' He grinned, showing a set of impeccable white teeth. 'I'll tell them you saw a bad omen.'
Larvandad raised his eyebrows.

A month later, Larvandad was preparing himself to pay a visit to a fellow astrologer first thing in the morning.
'Father, you have a visitor,' said Firouzeh.
'Good morning, Larvandad.'
'Gushnasaph, good morning. I was going to visit you!'
'Did you see it? Looks like a new star, but I am not certain...' said Gushnasaph eagerly, not noticing his colleague's invitation to sit down or Firouzeh waiting to withdraw to prepare tea.
'Yes, I did,' said Larvandad, taking his friend's elbow gently to make him move and sit. 'First, one last month, and then another last night. Strange...'
'Yes, it is strange. Two, very close and very bright. Very strange. But they do not look menacing.'
'No, not at all.'
They looked at each other, puzzled.

In October that same year, another astrologer joined the conversation.
'Larvandad, meet my pupil. This is Hormisdas.'
A young man bowed to the old man. He was tall and fit and looked more like a soldier than an astrologer. Larvandad invited his colleague to sit down and then sat in front of him across the low table. Gushnasaph motioned to Hormisdas to sit beside him. The young man obliged, placing himself slightly behind his master.

'Did you see it?' asked Gushnasaph.

'Yes.' Larvandad nodded.

'The third one…'

'Yes, the third one.'

'That's quite extraordinary.'

'Yes, it is quite extraordinary,' repeated Larvandad.

They were interrupted by Firouzeh bringing in a tray of tea. Larvandad looked at Hormisdas, who was watching Firouzeh.

'What does the young man think?' asked Larvandad.

Hormisdas went slightly pink, and he said shyly, 'Oh, it's…they…they are beautiful!'

The two old men looked at each other and laughed.

'So you like them,' said Larvandad, smiling.

'I feel quite happy about them. But what are they? Just new stars, or something else?'

'I have no idea,' the two older men said at the same time.

Chapter 1 : Destiny or Will? (1685-1702)

Halle, February 1685

Dr Händel decided that the baptism of his second child with Dorothea, his second wife, should be conducted at his house. The church was within easy walking distance, however such an excursion in February would have been foolish with a newly born infant. He did not want to take any risks after the death of their first child. So at one day old, Georg Friederich Händel was baptised and duly registered at Liebfrauenkirche, having three godparents. The mother, watching her baby wriggle when the water was poured, smiled with reassurance. Her second son was healthy with lots of life, while her first one had been born with no vitality and lived only a few hours. Dorothea's only regret was that she could not show baby Georg to her father, who had died shortly after her marriage.

Dorothea was resting. With her baby duly baptised and protected by God, she felt she could relax. Pastor Taust was visiting his sister. He thought she was beautiful.

'So the baby is in good health?' The pastor touched softly the tiny hand of the baby, fast asleep.

'Yes, and he is a good boy.' She smiled at her young brother.

'You look happy, Sister.'

'Yes, Georg. I am happy. I am.' She looked at her brother who was becoming a spitting image of their father.

A wet nurse came in to take the baby to feed him. The brother and sister were left alone. He took her hand in his.

'I am so glad to see you happy.'

'Brother?' Dorothea looked in her brother's eyes.

'Yes?'

'I did not know that marriage could bring such joy.'

'Sister…'

She looked at her brother and knew what he was thinking. 'You can talk to me. I am not afraid.'

Pastor Taust looked at his sister. 'So you overcame the death of your first child?'

'Yes, I did. A year ago, I thought I would never heal again. I thought I would spend the rest of my life mourning. I spent days and days weeping. It pained me so much that God gave him only a few hours to live…'

'I know. I was worried.'

'You know what helped me recover?'

'Tell me, my dear.'

'My husband told me that he had seen many deaths in his life, and that he had learnt that after weeping all the tears, you have to start thinking of what the dead would wish for the living. Weeping all the time would not make the dead happy in heaven.'

'True.'

'But for a baby, it is different. A baby is so small that it cannot think, so it is up to the mother to think for him, for his happiness in the other life. A weeping mother cannot make her baby happy.'

Pastor Taust just listened.

'I saw Mama, my sister and my brother die, and then Papa… but it was different for my baby. You know, Brother, Georg told me that in some countries, they say that the dead baby carries a pot on the way to heaven. The pot contains the tears of the mother. The more tears the baby collects, the heavier the pot would be and the harder it would have to struggle to reach heaven.'

'I see…'

Dorothea looked at her brother and said, 'Georg, do not worry. I hope my dead baby is happy in heaven. The more I am happy, the more the baby will be happy. And my Georg Friederich is a beautiful and healthy baby. He makes me happier every day. And I hope he will live longer, much longer for himself and his brother.'

Dorothea enjoyed looking after her baby. She poured all her love and care to the little creature who was blessed with good health. She even wanted to do what was given to the wet nurse to do. She just loved being with him. She treasured the time spent alone with her baby. What she liked most was to walk to the border of the forest on a fine day and sit at the base of a big tree for a while to talk or sing to her child.

Shortly after her brother's visit, she was sitting against a large tree, her favourite one, with her baby. It was a sunny and warm day in May. She did not realise that she had been followed from her house by a woman, a Gipsy.

The woman approached Dorothea and said softly, 'Madam, are you Doctor Händel's wife?'

Dorothea jumped. The Gipsy woman had approached her noiselessly, and besides, it was extremely rare to see a Gipsy in that part of the country. She was young, had very pale skin, which contrasted with her dark, curly hair framing her face, overflowing from the shawl she was wearing. She was very pretty. Her dark eyes were gentle.

'Sorry, I surprised you, madam. Are you Doctor Händel's wife?'

Dorothea composed herself quickly and said, 'Yes, I am.' She looked up to see the Gipsy woman staring at her baby.

The woman softly touched the cheek of the baby with her forefinger, making her bangles tinkle gently. She was completely absorbed, and muttered in a low voice, 'It is a boy. He was born under a very bright star. No, he is the star. He will be remembered and loved by the whole world.' Then she made a little start. She was back to reality and noticed the puzzled gaze of the mother. 'I am sorry... he is such a beautiful baby. I am sorry. I wanted to thank Doctor Händel, but he is very busy. I could not find him alone, so I thought perhaps you could thank him on my behalf.'

'Yes...?'

'I am not alone. We arrived in this part of the country a while ago. I was sent to see if all of us could come to spend some time nearby, but it is very hostile here. Once, I was surrounded by a band of frightening men, and Doctor Händel came and told them to leave me alone.'

'I see.'

She produced a small pouch from her pocket and handed it to Dorothea.

'This is dried herb. You make tea with it, and it is good when you have a fever. It will help your baby. I put some seeds in there as well, if you want to grow some yourself.'

'That is very kind of you, but-'

'Your husband told me that if I made it known that I could heal, I would be burned alive, that the prince dislikes us Gipsies. He told me not to come around.'

Dorothea looked down at the pouch in her hand. It was made with a thick black fabric embroidered richly with colourful threads. 'Thank you,' she whispered, stroking the pouch.

The woman was looking at the baby again, and she whispered, 'I will see you again.'

Dorothea looked at her baby, fast asleep. Then she looked around. The Gipsy woman was gone.

'A Gipsy woman?' The surgeon looked at his wife, 'oh yes, I do remember. She was young and dark. Wasn't she?'

'Yes, Husband,' and Dorothea showed the pouch.

'She was very attractive, so a few men got a nasty idea.'

'Oh dear...'

'This must be thyme,' Dr Händel sniffed the dried herb, 'yes, it helps, but it is more efficient mixed with cinnamon to calm down fever. But cinnamon is very expensive.'

'Cinnamon? What is it?'

'A spice, imported.'

'Imported...' Dorothea could not imagine where the spice came from.

The books taught her that ships travelled to cross the sea, but she had never seen the sea.

The baby was in fact very healthy. He was hardly ill, to his mother's relief, as her husband disliked to see his family unwell. A sister, Dorothea Sophia, was born when Georg Friederich was two and a half, still too young to be conscious of what it meant. When his second sister Johanna Christiana was born, he only remembered a small creature always crying and stinking of milk, and grown-ups busy looking after her. He thought the creature was quite repulsive. He was nearly five then. Though he loved his mother, his father was a distant existence. He hardly saw him for he was always out looking after his patients. The boy remembered clearly that when his father was back home, tired, his mother was tense, pouring all her attention and effort to look after her husband. She made all her children greet their father, welcoming him back home, and the ritual had to be impeccable. Then she would make them retire to their room, taken by the nurse. Immediately she would order the supper to be brought while she undressed her husband, making him relaxed. She would eat with him if he was not too late. Otherwise she would sit to keep him company.

Sometimes Dr Händel was away for a few days. He went in a carriage with luggage, wearing his best suits.

'Your father is away, to attend the duke, Georg,' his mother used to say proudly.

Georg noticed that on top of being proud of his father, his mother smiled more. She was chatty and cheerful and that made him happy. The tension was not there and everyone in his household looked more relaxed. He never felt unhappy with his father. He loved his father, but most of the time, his contact with his father was through his mother.

'No, Georg, later, your father is tired now,' she used to say when young Georg wanted to ask a question.

'No, not now, your father is busy. We must not bother him. You have to wait,' she said when the boy wanted to say good-night.

'Your father will not be happy, you'll have to wait a few days,' she said when Georg wanted to request something, 'just not now.'

The situation changed when young Georg started to go to school. Dr Händel chose the Gymnasium, a free but academically demanding school in Halle. There was no condition for admission, but with no garanty for remaining there. So the old surgeon wanted to know about Georg's study and also about his friends. His son had to be academically bright. However, soon, Dr Händel was questioning himself about the choice of the school.

One day, he arrived home and heard a keyboard playing. He frowned. There were no musical instruments in his house. Then the sound stopped and he found himself greeted by his wife and children. He looked at them one by one. The two girls seemed too young to play. His wife? No, she does not play.

'Is that you, Georg, who was playing music?'

'Yes, Papa,' the boy smiled, expecting to be praised.

He looked at his wife and asked, 'Where is the instrument from?'

'Oh, I asked my brother to bring it. It belonged to my mother but nobody is playing now, so-'

'Then take it back where it came from.'

'Husband?'

'Dorothea, I need to talk to you.' Dr Händel went into his study.

Dorothea followed him and closed the door behind them, leaving the children puzzled. The surgeon turned to her abruptly.

'Explain.'

Dorothea did not know what her husband wanted to know.

'Why you brought the instrument?'

'Oh, because Georg wanted it.'

'Why?'

'Well, because he wanted to play.' Dorothea looked at her husband, still not certain where he wanted to go.

'Why does he want to play?' Dr Händel could feel his patience running out. Back home, the only thing he wanted was to be undressed and then relax.

'Because he likes music, Husband.'

'Music!' he shouted, exploding. Then he glanced at the door. He heard someone gasp. He lowered his voice, 'how, how has he come to like music?'

'Oh, it's the headmaster, Mr Praetorius, Husband.'

'Praetorius?'

'Yes. I told you he came to talk to you several times, but you were always away.'

'So he came to talk about music?'

'Yes, to tell you that Georg is showing interest. Mr Praetorius thinks our son is very talented,' Dorothea said proudly, smiling, thinking to be approved.

Dr Händel only then realised the reason for these visits. He thought the headmaster came to discuss his son's academic level.

'I will go to see Praetorius, tomorrow morning. In the meantime, you get the instrument out of here.'

'But it's just a small spinet, Husband. It will not take roo-'

'I told you to take the damn thing out!'

Dorothea lowered her head. 'Yes, Husband.'

The young boy was back in his room. He heard everything. He clenched his teeth to not cry. It was not the shock of seeing his father's anger, but to see his mother being blamed. He felt guilty. All that because he played the spinet! The happiness of playing and to see his mother smiling was crushed at once. He felt desperate, and guilty at the same time. He did not want to be the cause of his mother's suffering, but he craved to play music.

'Doctor Händel!' Johann Praetorius got up and beamed. 'How nice of you to come to see me here. I wanted to talk with you, but each time, I was unlucky.'

The old surgeon did not smile back. 'Mr Praetorius, I want to have a word with you.'

'Please do sit down, Dr Händel,' the headmaster continued to beam at him. 'By the way, I thank you for attending the pupils. It is really kind and generous of you.'

'My pleasure,' he said dryly. Since his son started at the school, the surgeon made it a routine to visit the school once a week voluntarily, to attend injured or ill children. It was more for a practical reason, to stop spreading contagion by early diagnosis, especially the smallpox.

'I have the pleasure to announce that your son is showing an exceptional skill in music, Dr Händel.'

'So you are encouraging my son to play music.'

'Yes. Anyway music is part of the curriculum, as you know, and-'

'Mr Praetorius,' the surgeon interrupted, 'I want you to know that my son will not play music.'

Johann Praetorius looked at the man sitting in front of him, not understanding.

'I want you to stop encouraging my son to play music. No. I want you to ban music to my son, as I imagine I cannot make you ban music from the school.'

'Oh...'

Johann Praetorius let himself sink in a chair, exhausted. After two hours of confrontation neither of them could get their way. Only a compromise was achieved to the dissatisfaction of both.

'Dr Händel, I really do not understand why you are so against music.' Praetorius was losing his patience. As a music lover he was encouraging every pupil to take an interest. And still after more than an hour of talk, nothing was being achieved.

'Music is just for amusement. My son needs to study before amusing himself. And, being a musician is not a proper profession.'

'But your son is still too young to think about his profession in the future. In the meantime, why can't he enjoy music?'

'Enjoy? I never enjoyed anything in my life. I struggled, I fought, I worked hard, harder than anyone.' The old surgeon felt anger growing, 'Let me tell you, Mr Praetorius, I was a son of a coppersmith. You can imagine the effort I had to make to be in my position today.'

'I know you are a reputed physician, with all my respect.' Praetorius bowed low, politely but slightly cynically, 'and, as a reputed physician you should know that music nourishes the spirit? You are more aware than anyone that the healthy body goes with a healthy spirit?' The headmaster was convinced that the music made his pupils happier, and happier pupils improved their academic performance.

Dr Georg Händel, on his way to his surgery from the school, also felt exhausted. He could not get his way. He finally accepted that his son would practice music only within the school, on condition that he maintained his academic level as before. When the headmaster mentioned the healing effect of music, he could not disagree. What worried him most was that his son was showing an exceptional talent in music. *Exceptional talent! That would lead him to be a musician! My son a musician!* He felt his bowels boil. From that day, the old surgeon frowned more and talked less to his family.

When the boy was back from school, he found no spinet in the ground floor front room. He lowered his head.

'Georg, you are back.'

'Mama, the spinet...' He looked up at his mother. His lips were shaking.

'Georg,' she lowered herself to be at her son's eye level and whispered, 'don't worry, the spinet is in the attic. But you have to make absolutely certain that you do not play while Papa is here. Can you promise?'

Young Georg stared at his mother and then hugged her. 'Thank you, Mama. Thank you.' He felt his mother wrapping him gently in her arms.

Dorothea felt guilty, but that was the only compromise she could think of. She hid the spinet in the attic. She could not disobey her husband. However, after hearing the headmaster praise her son so warmly, and seeing her son so happy to play the spinet in front of her, she could not wrench it out.

Dorothea was not the only one to feel guilty. Young Georg knew that his father was against music, and if he played the spinet, he would feel guilty. He felt that from now on he would have to live a lie to his father, and make his mother lie as well. His only hope was to prove to his father that music was not interfering in his study. Then he had an idea.

'Mama, if I improve in Latin, would Papa be happy with me?'

'I am certain he will,' Dorothea smiled.

'Even I am playing music?'

'Your father cannot be unhappy if you improve,' Dorothea avoided answering the question. She did not know the answer.

A week passed by. Nothing happened. Young Georg kept going to school and practiced music there, as agreed. The spinet in the attic was untouched, as the boy was too scared of being discovered. Not only would he be punished, but the idea of his mother also being punished was unbearable. A month passed. Nothing happened. Now he went to the attic when his father was away for a few days to attend the duke. After six months, a routine was established. The boy was still scared of being discovered, so he practiced as much as he could at school. It was just harpsichord playing and singing, but young Georg was happy. He could forget everything when playing or singing. And the headmaster continued to support and encourage the boy.

Dr Händel got used to the routine as well. His son did not play at home, and he maintained his academic level. He even improved in some of the subjects. His worries were starting to fade when the incident happened.

'Papa, I want to go with you. May I come with you, please?' Young Georg asked.

'No, you cannot, Son.' Georg Händel replied without any hesitation.

'Please, Papa.' The boy insisted.

'No.'

'Why?'

'Because I am going there to attend the duke. I am going for work. I cannot take a child with me. There is no question.'

'Please…' The boy was getting desperate. Holding back tears, he repeated, 'Please, Papa, may I come? I will not bother you.'

The old surgeon looked at his son, and asked. 'Do you know where I am going?'

'Yes. Weissenfels.'

'How do you know?'

'Because Elke told me.'

Elke, the young servant girl, was immediately summoned. She came accompanied by Mrs Händel. The girl was already tense from being summoned by Dr Händel himself. Seeing the old surgeon frowning, she sensed she'd done something wrong. It was Dorothea who broke the silence.

'Husband, what is the…'

'I asked Elke to come, not you.' The surgeon glared at his wife, and turned to the girl.

'Is it true that you told my son that I was going to Weissenfels?'

At the word Weissenfels, the girl's face lit up, forgetting her fear. 'Oh yes, Master, I did. How wonderful! You are serving the duke? Oh, how I feel proud to serve you!' the girl could not stop, 'And, oh, how beautiful it must be, the… castle? Full of flowers, lots of food, and the beautiful ladies in pretty dresses. They sing and dance all the day!' She clasped her hands in front of her and made a little jump.

Dr Händel just stared at the girl, forgetting his anger. His wife lowered her head to conceal her stifled laughter. The young Georg just watched the girl who was still in a dream.

'You can go now, Elke.' That was all Dr Händel could say. 'Now, Dorothea, you stay here. You stay as well, Georg.' He stopped the boy who was ready to disappear.

The girl withdrew skipping, forgetting why she was summoned and still dreaming about the beautiful ladies singing and dancing. Dr Händel, seeing his wife smile, waiting for the girl to disappear, frowned. 'Dorothea, you tell your son that he cannot go to Weissenfels, and you explain why. You may go, both of you, now.'

Left alone, the surgeon muttered, 'I cannot believe it, the young folk these days...hopeless!'

Dorothea, instead of explaining to her son, wanted to know the reason. Alone in the boy's room she asked gently.

'Tell me, Georg. Why do you want to go to Weissenfels?'

'Because I want to hear the music there, Mama,' the boy said very seriously.

'How do you know about that?'

'It's Master Praetorius. He told me that wonderful music is played there. Mama, I really want to hear the music there.'

'So Elke told you and you told Master Praetorius.'

'Yes, Mama. May I go? Can you ask Papa?'

'Well, Papa was very clear. You cannot go.'

'Why?'

'Because you are a child. When you are old enough, and important, like Papa, you can go there.'

The boy just lowered his head. He felt desperate. *When? Do I have to wait until I get old like Papa?* He was not ready to wait that long.

The next morning Dr Händel put on his best shirt and suit and got into the carriage parked in front of his house.

'I wish you safe journey, Husband,' said Dorothea, looking at her husband seated, 'God willing.'

The surgeon just nodded, and the carriage departed. Young Georg was nowhere to be seen.

In the evening, a surprise awaited Dorothea. She saw her husband get out of the carriage, looking grumpy, and then her son, with a big smile, jump out following him.

'To my room, Dorothea.' That was all Dr Händel said, not even looking at her.

As soon as the door was closed, the old surgeon exploded.

'This child is so stubborn!' said he, irritated. 'I told him not to come, and he still came! He started to follow my coach, running after it!'

'Oh...' Dorothea just raised her eyebrows. 'That's why I did not see him for the whole day.'

'Did you not realise until now that he was missing?'

'Well, I thought he went to the school...' She stopped there, to not reveal that her son stayed quite late at school, to practice.

'I had no choice. I did not want to leave him on the road. You never know what happens in the middle of nowhere.'

So the old surgeon had had no choice but to take his young son in his coach, heading to the court of Weissenfels, to attend Duke Johann Adolf of Saxe-Weissenfels and his family. As soon as he arrived, he summoned Karl, his son by his first wife. Karl also attended the duke, and Dr Händel told him to look after the boy, and not let him in view. Karl left his small half-brother in the kitchen with maids, as he himself was busy with his duties.

The young boy made his way to the music room where a few musicians were practicing. There he saw a harpsichord. He had never seen such a big and beautiful instrument. It was very long and was decorated everywhere. Then he remembered nothing.

He was dragged back to the kitchen, and was planted in a chair. It was Karl who pulled him from the harpsichord.

'Don't move until your father comes to collect you,' said his half-brother firmly, 'really, what the...' Then he stopped, shook his head and went hurriedly to join the duke still in the music room.

Seeing the duke still chatting merrily with the musicians, Karl let escape a sigh of relief.

While the boy waited for his father, the latter was having a difficult time. The duke had summoned him to ask him a few questions.

'I saw a young boy in the music room,' said the duke still smiling, 'and I think it is your son.'

Dr Händel felt his blood drain and could nearly feel the blade chopping off his head. 'Your Grace, I am...'

'Is he learning music?'

The old surgeon saw his head put back. The duke was not upset.

'I heard him play. He plays very well for his age,' the duke continued.

'Your Grace...'

'Who is teaching him?'

'Your Grace...' He had no choice but tell the truth. The more he tried to escape the question, the more the duke wanted to know. Soon he found himself kneeling in front of the duke, receiving a purse full of gold coins, and giving thanks.

The young boy saw his father coming to collect to him. He could see clearly that his father was in a bad mood, if not furious. In the carriage going back to Halle his father did not utter a word.

Dr Händel felt the weight of the gold coins contained in the purse wearing the duke's coat of arms. The duke had ordered the father to allow his son to have music lessons. The surgeon could not refuse. It was an order. The surgeon felt he had made a fatal mistake by allowing his son to come with him. He forgot about being glad to keep his head on his shoulders.

'Such a stubborn child!' he repeated, irritated.

Dorothea, calm and loving, replied tenderly, 'Husband, he is your son.'

Surprised, he turned to look at his young wife, who was smiling. He was still fuming, but her lovely smile made him calm down, always. He felt better. He could not resist smiling back.

'Well, then, there is no chance of the boy not being stubborn, because you are as well.' He took his wife's hands in his and kissed them tenderly. He felt defeated somehow. He could not ignore the duke's order. The latter would ask him on his son's progress each time he would visit Weissenfels. *Musician! My son a musician!* His shoulders slumped.

So Georg Friederich Händel started to have music lessons with Friedrich Wilhelm Zachow, Kantor and organist of Liebfrauenkirche, the best he could have as a teacher in Halle. Again, the surgeon was tempted to give his son a mediocre teacher, but he knew that the duke would not be happy about it. He had no choice but give his son the best the town could provide.

His only hope was that the young boy would get bored soon, or be dismissed by Zachow for lack of skill. This desperate hope was soon crushed. Not only did his son thrive, but his teacher was delighted.

'Miracle, I can only say that, Dr Händel,' Zachow would tell the old man enthusiastically, expecting a more positive reaction. Seeing him grumpy, he said, 'God chose him, Dr Händel,' not aware that he was just pouring oil on the fire.

The old surgeon had to restrain himself very hard not to explode in anger. Grinding his well-worn teeth, he said, 'And so? He becomes a musician? And then? No, I don't approve of that.' He glared at the organist.

Stunned, Zachow did not know what to say.

'Anyway when the money is exhausted, my son will stop.'

'Money?'

'Yes. The Duke Johann Adolf kindly gave him money to pay for the lessons.'

'Oh...how...' Zachow stopped seeing the old man glaring at him. It was out of the question to ask him how his pupil got the money, or how much.

'Mr Zachow, where are you from?' He asked, without realising the mistake he had just made.

'I am from Leipzig, Dr Händel.'

'What is your father's profession, Mr Zachow?

'An organist.'

'I see...' Dr Händel saw no reason to keep talking.

Watching the old surgeon leave, Zachow's brain was working very hard. He absolutely needed to know how much money the boy got from the duke. This would help to determine for how long the boy could have lessons with him. And besides, he was curious to know. *How could a young boy get such an award?* He struggled to think of things other than music. To go to ask Mrs Händel in her house was out of the question. Too risky, and a man did not visit a woman, unless she was his betrothed, for a very short period under her parents' supervision. *Who? Who can I ask?* The only person he could go to see easily was Mr Praetorius at the Gymnasium. So he went. However, apart from having a wonderful conversation with the headmaster, Zachow got nothing as information. The only hope was what little he was told.

'The duke? Well, I guess if it's from the duke himself, it is enough to pay lessons for a few years?'

Dr Händel felt frustrated, again. It was a waste of time to try to reason with Zachow that music was not a decent profession. The compromise he'd achieved with Praetorius was in vain now. He had to think of a new plan now. Again, a compromise was needed. He would accept his son studying music, but, BUT, he would have to have another profession besides. He would have a proper profession and keep music for pleasure, and no more. Thus the old surgeon started to introduce this idea to the young boy, slowly but surely. He would not stop. Everyday, if possible, he would reason with his son that there were much better choices for his career than music.

'Do you want to starve to death, Georg?'

'No, Papa. I don't want to starve to death.'

'Then music is not a good choice.'

'Would I starve to death?'

'You might not, only if you are very very talented, and surpass anyone in your way. You can live only, only if you are the best, the best of the best. Can you be?'

Georg lowered his head. He was not certain to be the best of the best, but saying no would mean the end. All he could do was to keep quiet.

'Answer.'

'I don't know, Papa.'

'If you don't know, that means you would not be.'

It was this constant pressure under which young Händel lived at home. He felt suffocated. By contrast, with his teacher he felt happy. He could breathe freely.

Things changed when Dr Händel fell ill. It was not the first time since his second marriage that he had become seriously ill. When the young boy was four and his sister two, the old surgeon was dangerously ill, and he feared for his life. He remembered his wife getting exhausted and paler every day from nursing him. But he recovered, so well that the following year another child, a girl, was born. However, this time, he felt different. At the beginning, it felt just like a cold. He just felt tired. Then it lingered. He had a temperature, not too high, just above normal, but it refused to go down. He could feel his body sinking under it. Sensing his death approaching, he had summoned his son to his bedside.

'I am sorry, my son, I will not see you grow up to be a man,' Georg Händel had said as he looked his son in the eyes.

The young boy, not knowing what to say, had taken his father's hand in silence. It was moist.

His father had continued, 'I wrote a letter for you. You will open it when you reach fourteen. You will be growing fast, and you will see a lot of change in your body. I will explain all so you will not be confused. There will be many things that you would not dare ask your mother.'

'Yes, Papa.'

'Georg, I repeat. You shall get a proper profession. Law would be good. Lawyers are needed, by wealthy people, and you will not starve. But again, you have to excel.'

'Papa?'

'Yes, Georg.'

'Why cannot I excel in music then?'

The surgeon looked at his son and shook off his hand abruptly. He thought he had convinced his son to be a lawyer. He now realised he had not succeeded, despite his continuous effort. And now, he did not have enough strength left to start all over. He would not die satisfied. Feeling drained, he asked, 'Can you be the best of the best in music then?'

'Yes, Papa, I shall be the best. Better than Mr Zachow. I promise, Papa,' the boy said, impassioned. He just wanted approval and nothing else. It was a desperate pleading.

'How can you be so certain?'

The boy swallowed, lowering his head. Seeing his father not flinching at all, he felt that he would live feeling guilty for making music for the rest of his life. He would never be free from that guilt.

'You may go now,' he said dryly. He watched his son leave the room. Ultimately, he had failed. The gulf between him and his son was to remain. He lost the battle. He was going to die soon and his son was going to live as long as God wished. Then there was only one thing he could do. He sighed deeply and whispered, 'Well, I'll have to write another letter. God give me strength.'

The large house on the corner of Kleine Klausstrasse and Kleine Ulrichstrasse had been very quiet for three days. A small number of visitors, including relatives, doctors and priests, had been allowed inside for just a short period. The winter that year had been colder than usual and the days darker. From the mid-afternoon, candles were needed. In one room, the candles were kept lit all through the nights. Pastor Georg Taust visited his sister as much as he could to support her. On 11 February 1697, on a bitter cold day, an old man died in the house – his house.

The boy put his hand softly on his mother's shoulder and said, 'Mama, don't worry. I am here. I will protect you from now on.' He felt his mother's hand on top of his own. Her shoulders were shaking.

He looked at his dead father's face. It just looked as if he were asleep. The boy's large and slightly bulgy pale-blue eyes, inherited from his father, were not wet. Without uttering a word, he made an oath to his father. He, Georg Friedrich Händel, would take good care of his family.

Though he had known his father was old and ill, the actual death was something he could not anticipate. He just could not imagine that his father would not get up anymore. At the same time, he was scared to imagine the dead man opening his eyes.

His father, Dr Georg Händel, died at seventy-five. In those days, when an average lifespan was around fifty-five years, he was considered extremely old. His mother wept silently at his side. The young Georg stood next to her. He would be twelve years old in just a few days. His two little sisters sobbed uncontrollably, clutching their mother's skirt. The older sister was in shock and did not understand. The youngest one was just under the influence of the grieving environment.

The large house where the Händels lived got busy at once. People started to arrive to pay respect. Dorothea Händel received them, staying beside her husband's body. The children, including young Georg, found no space to stay. They were gently led to one of the rooms by their uncle, Pastor Georg Taust.

'Uncle, what happens now?' Georg Friederich asked.

Pastor Taust knelt in front of the three children. He was at their eye level, and said softly, 'Well, first, we have to bury him so he can rest in peace.'

His father's death eventually brought the boy into contact with another side of the family. His father's children by his first wife, now all grown-up and married, arrived. Georg Friederich knew just one of them, Karl, whom he had met two years previously in Weissenfels. For the young boy, his family consisted of just his parents, his two young sisters, and the servants. If before, just after his father's death, he had felt like the only remaining male, responsible for the family, now he felt weightless and insignificant. The funeral was conducted by Pastor Taust his uncle, with his mother. He was just a child, grief-stricken and useless. While among those relatives whom he had never met, young Georg Friederich was shocked to see people chat, get merry, and even laugh in his house. In his house! They just talked and chatted as if the dead man were still alive and active. Questions like 'Is Papa going and coming back?' and 'Oh, is he staying here?' and 'When would Papa get dressed?' only made the little boy more and more confused. He could not understand that it was just about the practical matter of where the body was to be prepared for burial and dressed properly in formal attire - in situ or taken away and returned home. He wanted to shout aloud, 'Stop! Papa is dead! You don't know that?' But for the young boy who had never encountered death in his life, it was a spiral of enigma. He was too young to realise the way of grown-ups to process grief.

Then his father's body was put in a coffin and taken to the church for the service. The church was filled with people from the town and around. Sitting with his remaining family in the front row, he whispered to his uncle sitting next to him.

'Uncle, was Papa famous?'

Pastor Taust looked at the boy and whispered back, 'I don't know, Georg. But he treated and healed lots of people. They are here to say thank you and farewell.'

After the service the coffin was carried out, on several men's shoulders, and put on a hearse waiting in front of the church. Only then did young Georg realise that his father would never come back. Now blessed by God, his father was going to rest forever.

The young boy had never been to the town's burial place, the Stadtgottesacker, on a hill outside Halle. As he walked behind the coffin that lay on the hearse pulled by horses, he noticed people on their doorsteps bowing, paying tribute to his father. The hearse got out of town, and began going uphill. Then he saw long walls emerging in front of him. As he looked up to his uncle walking beside him, Pastor Taust nodded.

'This is the cemetery, Georg, your father's resting place.'

Nearing the cemetery, Georg Friederich saw a single storey building with a roof. Going through the gates, he heard people talking about crypts and starting to whisper as they advanced into the cemetery. Inside, the young boy found a large, square ground. Paths were laid out, spreading from the centre of the square towards the four sides and four corners, forming a star-like shape. All of these paths were linked by another path that surrounded the square. He looked around and saw arcades bordering the square, with each arch separated by walls, making a row of empty alcoves, open only to the square. His group advanced, taking the central path to the other end.

'Straight ahead,' said Pastor Taust.

They walked slowly, whispering discreetly.

'The second to the right,' said Pastor Taust.

Now they were walking alongside the alcoves. Then George Friederich saw. In each alcove there was an opening in the ground. Some of those openings were covered with stone or metal slabs, but the others were just left open, revealing the crypt underneath, filled with coffins. This was an eerie sight. The people fell silent. The noise of the wheels echoed. The young Händel, who was holding his little sister's hand, felt her grip tighten. He looked down and saw the frightened look in Dorothea Sophia's eyes. Behind him, he could hear his youngest sister, Johanna Christiana, struggling to walk.

'Mama, I'm scared.'

'Don't be scared, Johanna. It's all right. Nothing will happen,' said her mother reassuringly.

The horses halted. There, in front of one of the alcoves, two men in black were waiting. The stone slab was put aside to reveal an opening. Pastor Taust exchanged a few words with these men in black, nodding. Georg Friederich saw candles lit in the crypt underneath, and also two coffins. They belonged to the first wife of Dr Händel and one of his sons, taken by the plague.

'Mother,' muttered a middle-aged woman, one of young Händel's half-siblings, looking at one of the coffins. Then she placed her hand on the coffin containing her father, now placed beside the opening, ready to be lowered. 'Goodbye, Father. Go to join Mother,' she said, fighting back tears.

Now the two men in black were busy putting cords beneath the coffin. Georg Friederich felt a hand on his shoulder. He looked up to see Karl.

'Take this, Georg,' he said, handing the boy one of the cords placed beneath the coffin. 'It's time to say farewell. We shall place Papa in the crypt.'

The boy just nodded. He heard a few muffled weeping sounds from the people gathered there.

'Are you ready?' Karl looked warmly at his young half-brother.

The boy replied with another nod.

A week after the funeral, the young Georg Friederich walked to the lodging of his music teacher, Friedrich Wilhelm Zachow, at the marketplace across the street from the Liebfrauenkirche. As he walked through the narrow streets lined by shops, he saw that nothing had changed. In his mind, after his father's death, nothing would be the same. It was true for his own life, but he only just realised that, apart from that, life in general would continue just like before. As he passed in front of the glassmaker, stocking-maker, and wig-maker, he breathed the same smell and heard the same noise. He'd thought he would never smile again, but now and then he found himself smiling, even laughing, and felt ashamed. He had been outraged to see people talking and laughing at his father's funeral. Now it seemed less shocking. Time was an excellent healer.

He had an important message for his teacher. Now that his father was dead, he felt he had to stop having lessons. He did not want his mother to struggle to pay the fees. He did not talk about it to anyone. That was his own decision. He felt devastated, but he thought he had to accept the fate. Lessons at the school were free, so he might be able to continue, but maybe he would have to give those up as well, and start working, to support his mother. He felt the weight of being an only male of the family.

Zachow was at home when Händel arrived, seated in front of the harpsichord. He was still young, in his mid-thirties, but already going grey. And his calm and composed personality made him seem older.

'I am sorry for the loss of your father.'

Händel did not know what to say. He saw his teacher smile.

'If someone says this to you, which will happen very often from now, just say, "Thank you." That is, say that to the people you don't know very well. Now, with me, you can say how you feel.'

'I feel sad, sir, but…'

'Relieved as well?' Zachow was not the only one to know that the young boy's father was not happy about his son learning music.

'Yes, but…'

Zachow looked at his young pupil. 'Tell me, Georg.'

'Well, sir, I came to say goodbye.'

'What? Are you going away?' Zachow felt a chill go down in his spine. He was not expecting to lose his best pupil so soon.

'No, sir.'

'Then why?'

'I cannot pay for the lessons anymore.'

'Oh, so the duke's money is exhausted now?' He felt his blood draining. The moment has come.

'Duke's money?'

'Yes, the money given to you by the duke.'

'The duke?' Young Händel was at a loss.

Zachow realised that his pupil was not aware of the money. 'Oh..er..well…' he just bubbled, not knowing whether to tell the truth, or not. Hiding it from a child was easy, but then the teacher thought it was important to let his pupil know that there was a benefactor. So he told the young boy the little he knew.

'No, I did not know about it,' whispered the boy, stunned. But that explained everything. He had thought it strange that his father had allowed him to have music lessons with the town's Kantor, but he could not ask why. He just could not. He feared that if he asked the reason his father might change his mind.

Zachow watched his pupil digesting the news. Now recovered from the first shock and feeling warmth coming back to his body, he said, 'Anyway I will continue to teach you.'

Georg Friederich looked up. He opened his mouth, but Zachow continued.

'Instead of paying me, you will help me from now on. It is an exchange,' he said with a smile. 'Of course, you will continue to copy for your study, but you will have to do more for me and assist me more in the church.'

He saw the young boy's eyes brighten. 'Are you ready?'

'Yes, Master,' Händel said, proudly. He felt a little grown up.

He hurried back home and asked his mother, who told him the whole story and showed him the purse, empty.

'How long has it been empty, Mama?'

'Not so long. Your father was ill, so he did not realise it.' His mother shrugged, smiling to him, 'don't tell anyone, promise?'

The congregation of Liebfrauenkirche did not take long to realise that now, very often, the organist playing was not the one they had nominated but his very young pupil. The senior pastor knew, but as no complaints came, he left the matter as it was. In fact, the pastor was rather pleased. He could not suggest to Zachow that he shorten his lengthy organ playing and cantatas but he could easily ask the young boy to do so. And the boy would do it so skilfully that nobody would suspect anything, not even the composer. Now Zachow introduced his pupil to the violin. When the teacher was at the organ, the young Georg was at his side playing violin, to the delight of the churchgoers. He continued to copy music by Krieger and other composers for himself to study, but now he also had to copy his teacher's music for the choir, as well as other things for the teacher's use. His hands ached from copying, but the young Händel was happy. He was much more involved now, and not just as a pupil. He was making music.

Despite the financial difficulties they experienced after the death of Doctor Händel, the whole family was much more relaxed. The pressure was gone. Dorothea had to dismiss most of the servants and had to manage the finance of the household by herself. Still, she could now openly encourage her son to study music and ask him to teach her young daughters, thus saving the money for the fees. The spinet was now out of the attic. Receiving both financial and emotional support from her own family, the Tausts, she could keep the house and give her children a decent education. Pastor Taust volunteered to give basic lessons in German to the girls, and also give support to the young boy in Latin.

Georg Friederich felt, once again, useless. When he told his mother of his intention to give up school and start working, he was met with laughter. He felt humiliated. He was only a child, and nothing else. He lowered his head, teeth clenching and trying not to cry. Then he felt his mother embracing him.

'Georg, listen,' his mother said, hugging her son, 'do not worry about money. It will be all right.'

'Are you certain, Mama?' He looked up, to see Dorothea smiling.

'Yes, I am. Thank you, Georg. But…'

'But?'

'If I need your help, I will ask you.'

'Promise, Mama?'

'Yes, I promise, Georg. Oh and…'

They were interrupted by a servant girl coming in quite abruptly. It was Elke. She was one of the very few Dorothea kept.

'Elke, I am busy now. Could you wait outside?' her mother said gently but firmly.

'Yes, madam!' She went out merrily.

The young boy looked at his mother, and asked. 'Mama, why did you keep Elke?' In his opinion, she seemed quite useless.

His mother whispered, 'Oh, she is a bit stupid, but good-natured and honest. I like her.'

Georg Friederich was quite certain she would not have been retained if his father had made the choice.

'So, where were we?' his mother said, 'oh yes.' She rummaged in her pocket and handed a coin to her son, 'here is the fee for Mr Zachow.'

'Mama, you don't need to pay Mr Zachow.'

Dorothea stared at her son, 'But your lessons…'

'I made an arrangement with Mr Zachow, Mama.' The boy smiled, feeling a little useful.

'Arrangement?'

'Yes, Mama. I am helping him now, so you don't need to pay him anymore.' And the boy hugged his mother. He did not see his mother's teary eyes.

Georg arrived home one evening to find his uncle on his weekly visit. Pastor Taust kept his habit to give support to his nephew's study and also to give his nieces the basic education.

'You are late, Georg.'

'I am sorry, Uncle,' said the boy, embarrassed.

'Are you back from the Gymnasium?'

'No, Uncle.'

'Where have you been then?'

'Church, Uncle. I was playing the organ for the evensong.'

'You should not be late for your lessons.'

'I am sorry, Uncle.' The boy lowered his head.

'Did you translate the text in Latin I gave you last time?'
'I could not finish it, Uncle.'
'Georg...'
'I am sorry, but I did not have enough time.'
'Georg, I do not accept that as an excuse.'
'But-'
'Georg, your education is as important as your music. Do not say you didn't have enough time. Take the time to do it.'
Young Händel looked up at his uncle who gazed back at him.
'You do not agree, I see. Then let me explain,' said Pastor Taust calmly. He ignored his nephew's frustration. 'I know you love music and you want to be a musician. I am aware that now you are much more involved and are playing the organ in place of your teacher. I do not know how far you can go, but you are talented and ambitious, so I guess you will push yourself as far as you can. You will travel and meet people. If you do so, the knowledge of several languages will be very important, Georg. You speak German, but you must speak the good German so that people will recognise that you are educated. Anyway, it is important that you are able to communicate in several languages. Now, you can ask me questions.'

The young boy swallowed and said, 'Uncle, which is the most useful language if it is not German?'

Pastor Taust laughed. 'It depends. French is the language used at most of the courts.'

'French?'
'Yes, Georg.'
'Is it difficult?'
'It is not easy and is very different from German.'
The young boy was pensive.
'Georg?'
'Yes, Uncle.'
'Shall we start the lesson?' Pastor Taust indicated the two little girls, who were now chasing each other around the table.

So the young Georg Friederich's life continued between the school, his teacher Zachow's instruction at his house or church, and home. The spinet was not enough for him anymore, so he spent more time playing the harpsichord at school to practice. It was the time when his body started to grow fast. He had been rather thin and small for his age, but he felt hungry all the time. The food never lacked, but the more he ate, the more he wanted to eat. His mother was surprised about the change in her son's appetite, but soon she was preparing bigger portions for him.

For the first year since his father's death, Georg Friederich was still worried, and felt insecure about the finance of his mother, but seeing no radical change in his household, he started to feel better, and worry less. After commemorating the first year of his father's death, his life was as before, minus his father. It was regular and peaceful.

It was early morning of 23 February 1699. Georg Friederich Händel was hardly awake when his mother came in to sit at the end of his bed.

'Happy birthday, my son,' said the mother softly.

The boy sat in his bed, rubbed his eyes and looked at his mother. He could see white hairs appearing among her dark-brown tresses.

'Thank you, Mama,' said the birthday boy, smiling.

'I have something to give you. This is not a present.' She produced a sealed letter. 'This is from your father.'

'Father?' said the boy incredulously.

'Yes, your father. He wanted me to give it to you when you reached fourteen.' Dorothea stroked the letter. 'He knew he would not see you today.' She placed the letter in her son's hands. 'I will see you downstairs.' She got up and was gone.

Young Händel stared at the letter in his hands. He traced his father's handwriting with his forefinger. Then he felt warmth wrapping around his shoulders and heard a soft voice. *Happy Birthday, Son.* He pressed the letter against his chest and whispered, 'Papa...' A single tear rolled down his cheek and landed on his hand.

On his fourteenth birthday, accordingly, he was given the letter, written by his father before he died. It was a long letter covering everything the dying man, as a surgeon and a father, could think of. The young adolescent was at first quite shocked by some of the contents of the letter, even disgusted. But soon, he realised it was giving answers to many questions the boys his age asked themselves. Händel thanked his father silently.

Two years had passed since his father had died, and the memory was slowly fading. He could not remember his father's face very well anymore. And the tense atmosphere in which he lived was now past, forgotten.

The life in Halle continued as before, and young Händel was getting more and more involved in music-making. When he turned fifteen in February 1700, he made a little decision; to start learning French.

A month later, while Händel led his regular life in Halle, Johann Sebastien Bach started his first long journey. Born a month later than Händel, and not far from Halle, his birth and upbringing had nothing in common with Händel's. He, contrary to Händel, had been born into a musical family, so for him, music was not only accessible but rather inevitable. From the very beginning he was expected to be a musician. But he was poor. He had been orphaned at age ten and went to live with his oldest brother in Ohrdruf. Thanks to his sweet soprano voice, he was accepted into the prestigious St

Michael's School in Lüneburg.

So, on 15 March 1700, with his friend Georg Erdmann, who was awarded the same scholarship, Johann Sebastien started the lengthy journey from Ohrdruf to Lüneburg, covering more than 250 miles, mainly by foot. The boy was used to walking long distances, simply because most of the time he could not afford to pay for the transport. His spirit was high. Though his feet hurt from long hours of walking, his thoughts were on the organs he could play. His father had taught him harpsichord and violin, but his uncle had introduced him to the organ. That was the boy's favourite. *I love playing the organ*, he thought. *Pity it needs someone to blow the bellows to make the sound come out.*

'Are you not worried, Johann?' Georg Erdmann asked.

'A little, but I am happy. I cannot wait to try the organ and go to the music library.'

'Apparently, the library is massive and has many manuscripts. I am worried.'

'About what?'

'Well, we will be with the sons of rich people with fine clothing and shoes. Look what we look like!' The young Erdmann stopped and stared at his dusty old shoes and worn clothing.

Johann Sebastian considered and said, 'We shall sing as much as possible, in every choir possible, and save our pay so we can get new clothes and shoes.' The young Bach was confident.

'Yeah, you have a fantastic memory. You can remember everything, so it will not be so difficult for you to deal with many scores. But it's not the same thing with me, Johann,' his friend replied.

Johann Sebastian smiled. It was true. He could remember everything. He just could not forget. But it was partly due to his training. Paper was expensive, and he could not afford to copy down too often. He had to memorise as much as possible.

'Georg, your voice is unique, so beautiful that you can make the toughest heart melt. You should be proud of that. They can have fine clothing and shoes but what you have is God's gift.'

'So is your memory.'

Well, yes and no, Johann Sebastian thought.

Contrary to Händel, Bach had no idea that a musician was not always considered as a proper profession. He was born into an extensive musical family and that was all he knew. His father was a professional musician as were all his uncles. However, being poor, his concern was about how to make the day, to practice and eat. The scholarship removed the worry of feeding himself and gave him the opportunity of perfecting his skill as a singer and player. There was no doubt for young Johann Sebastien that he would be a musician. He was just following the path laid in front of him. His focus was to perfect his art, and get a post somewhere.

Young Händel's mindset was more complex. Though the death of his father removed the tension between them, the pressure was still working in his mind. He knew that his father wished him to be a lawyer. So, after Gymnasium, he would go to university to read law? It sounded dreadful. He told himself that he still had time, to not worry for the moment, but this thought was eroding his mood. Then he had an idea, a brilliant idea!

Nearing the end of his secondary education, the topic was brought up, naturally. And young Händel was prepared. That was what he thought.

'No, Mama, I will not go to university,' said the boy, determined.

Dorothea, surprised, stared at her son. 'But...why? You know very well that that was your father's wish, and...'

'But, Mama...' the boy made a pathetic face, 'as much as I want to, we cannot afford it. I cannot sacrifice you and my sisters for me.'

'Oh...that...' His mother sighed and smiled. 'I am sorry to make you worried, but there is no need to be so. There is no problem. You can go to university.'

Young Händel gasped and stared at his mother. His plan was not working. 'But Mama, how... I know we are poor.'

'Oh, my son, we are not that poor.' Dorothea laughed. 'Do not worry about money.'

The boy felt desperate. *So am I going to university? If I do, I'll have less time for music!* Then he said, 'Mama, are you telling me that to not make me feel bad?'

The boy just refused to believe what his mother was telling him. He saw his mother being uneasy, not willing to talk about money.

Seeing her son unconvinced, Dorothea Händel decided to ask for help. So Pastor Taust, their uncle and brother, was summoned to explain the situation.

'Georg, there is no worry about money. Your mother sold your late father's practice, so she can afford to pay for your university fees, and will not struggle because of that.'

Young Händel just stared at his uncle.

Pastor Taust put his hand on the boy's shoulder and said, 'I know you want to do music, only music, but, after all, having another profession is not a bad idea.' He smiled. 'Let me explain. See, your mother struggled to sell Dr Händel's practice. Well, it was complicated, and that's why she could not sell it just after his death. And, also, there was the problem of the licence to sell wine, which was given to your late father, and not to your mother.'

'Licence? To sell wine? In the tavern?' he asked. A part of the house contained a tavern.

'Do you remember when your father was ill, very ill? Maybe not. You

were still very young and your second sister was not born yet.'
'I remember that. Mama was worried.'
'Yes, she was. We were all worried. And I believe it was caused by the problem of that licence. I will only say that it was complicated, very complicated.'
'I did not know all that...' young Händel said, feeling ashamed. His world was what he saw and lived every day, not beyond. He had no idea how his mother managed to keep everyday life going.
'And, I helped her. We used lawyers. We had no choice. We needed lawyers to sort out all that. Do you understand?'
'Yes, Uncle.'
'Your mother is well aware of what you want to do, and she is not against it, unlike your father.'
'Yes, Uncle.'
'Then we both realised. Maybe your father's idea is a good one. If you become a lawyer, you will not struggle financially. We absolutely needed lawyers to sort out the licence, and to be able to sell your father's practice. And we had to pay quite a lot of money. We witnessed all that. With music it's less certain. First of all we do not need music to survive. So why not both?'
He did not know what to say.
'We both felt, after all, that your father was not wrong. So why not? You can continue music but you shall have a profession that guaranties your life.'
Silence. However, he was screaming inside, *my plan is not working!*
'Your mother loves you, Georg. The only thing she wants is your happiness. I know you are happy with music. But, what if you are struggling to feed yourself? Would you be happy?'
The adolescent knew he had no choice.

On 10 February 1702, Georg Friederich Händel, now a young man of nearly seventeen, was getting ready for his first day at the University of Halle. As he went down, he was greeted by his mother.
'My son, you look wonderful.'
He was dressed in his dark-green coat with matching waistcoat and breeches, which was the new fashion. His outfit was simple and discreet, made of good-quality material. His blond hair was simply tied back. Tall and slender, he was stunningly good looking in the simplicity of his suit, and his mother knew it.
'And the green suits you so well,' she added, smiling at her son tenderly. 'Your father would be so proud of you.'
Georg Friederich smiled back, kissed his mother's forehead, looked in her eyes, and grinned. 'Mama.'

'Yes?'
'I'm taller than you.'
She laughed.

The first day was just registration, and after signing the registry, he was shown around by a fellow student who was dressed discreetly and who wore a wig. Händel, wigless, felt he was entering an adult world. When he was told about extra activities, he immediately asked whether a music club existed. He was suddenly filled with hope. There was no music club. His heart sank.

A few hours later he was walking back home briskly to keep himself warm. It was a cold day in February. His feelings were mixed. He felt he had fulfilled his father's wish, and that was duty. Did doing his duty make him feel happy? He was not sure. His pace slowed down, and then he stopped and changed direction towards the cemetery.

Standing in front of the family crypt, he whispered, 'Papa, it's done.'

Then he went through the inscription, engraved in the stone slab covering the opening of the crypt, mentioning his father's occupation: valet, physician-in-ordinary and official surgeon to the Duke of Sax-Weissenfels and to the elector of Brandenburg.

'Brandenburg?' Händel started. He did not know about that. He always thought his father served the duke only. He considered briefly, and headed to the parsonage of his uncle, Georg Taust, in Giebichenstein, on the outskirt of Halle.

'Oh, you did not know?' Pastor Taust said, surprised, 'I thought you knew.' He raised his eyebrows and smiled.
'No, I didn't.' Händel did not smile.
'Well, you know now.'
'How? Why?'
Pastor Taust just looked at his nephew.
'I thought you serve one ruler, not two.'
'Oh, that,' his uncle laughed, 'well, it's simple, and it was political.'
'Political?'
'Yes, political. Let me explain, Georg. Once, Halle was part of Saxony, and your father served the duke. That you know.'
'Yes, Uncle.' Again, Händel felt diminished. He was not made aware of it because he was a child!
'Then, two years before you were born, Halle became part of Prussia, and that was the reason the duke left Halle and went to Weissenfels.'
'Oh...but then my father should have served the new ruler, no?'
'There was no such rule, and the duke wanted to keep your father. And then he started to serve the Elector of Brandenburg. That's why he went to Berlin.'
'Berlin? He went to Berlin?' Händel stared at his uncle.

'Yes. That's when he would be away for quite a long time - Berlin is not exactly next door.'
'Oh...'
'Well I assumed you knew.'
So those long absence of a week or more were to go to Berlin! That's when he could play the spinet without worrying.
'I always thought he was off to Weissenfels.'
'You were a child, and we did not think of telling you. Well, why should we explain to a child about the political situation?' Pastor Taust said, realising that his nephew was not a child anymore, and that he had the right to know.
'Time passed so quickly, Georg. For me, you are always my nephew, but I must treat you as an adult now. I realise it. I am sorry.'
'Uncle, you don't need to apologise,' Händel felt uneasy, 'I am still a child because I don't wear a wig.'
Pastor Taust burst out in laughter, and stopped abruptly, seeing his nephew feeling humiliated. 'Do you really feel like a child because you don't wear a wig?'
'My fellow students wear wigs...'
'All of them?'
'I did not check all of them, Uncle.'
Pastor Taust laughed again. 'Georg, wearing a wig does not make you an adult.'

The wig shop was on the way to Zachow's lodging, and Händel passed in front of it nearly every day. It was not something he was interested in, so he used to pass by without noticing it. Now, it was not the same thing anymore. It was something he had to think about. Still, because he was so used to walking past, it was hard for him to stop and go in. Nonetheless, he slowed down, stopped and pushed the door, triggering the bell to ring. The door felt incredibly heavy.
'Good afternoon, sir. How can I help you?'
Händel was facing a medium-height, friendly-looking man. Jean-Christophe Lefèbvre was a wig-maker and owner of the shop. The young client saw the man looking not in his eyes but just above, at his natural hair.
'Um...' Händel was hesitant.
The man smiled and said, 'Before anything, may I ask you a question, sir?'
'Of course,' said Händel, puzzled but happy to break the silence.
'Are you here to sell your hair or to get a wig?'
Händel stared at the man. Of course, to make wigs, they need hair! That had never crossed his mind.
The man continued, 'I see you are here to get a wig. Sorry for my question, sir, but I find your hair so beautiful. It would make a wonderful wig,

and I just could not resist taking a chance. *C'est mon métier.*'
Händel, still stunned, asked, 'Really? How much would I get if I sold my hair?'
'How about five thalers?'
'Five thalers?'
'This is because your hair is not very long. If it were very long, with the quality and colour of your hair, I would happily give twenty thalers.'
'Twenty!'
The man laughed, amused by Händel's reaction. 'Can I suggest one thing, sir?'
'Yes?'
'Keep your hair and do not wear a wig. You really don't need it.'
Händel's jaw dropped. 'But...'
'I know, sir. Are you a student?'
'Yes, just enrolled.'
'I see. You came here because your fellow students are wearing wigs.'
'Exactly!'
The man shook his head. 'It is just the convention, sir. You don't need to follow it.'
Händel looked at the man. 'You speak like my father.'
'Did he...'
'No, he did not wear a wig. He had a lot of hair for his age, but he always said you should not do like others just because you feel you should.'
'He was quite right, sir.'
Händel smiled. 'You are strange. You are a wig-maker, and you're telling me to not wear one?'
'Well, I could persuade you to sell me your hair and make you wear one. I could do double business. But sir, you look so good with your natural hair, you should not spoil it. You are young. Enjoy your hair. Of course, if you keep your hair, you'll have to take care of it, which is more work than taking care of a wig. But...'
'But?'
Lefèbvre shook his head. 'I would not like to impose my opinion, sir. If you wish to have a wig, I'll make one for you.'
The bell rang, and another young man came in. He nodded to Händel and the shopkeeper. Händel saw him go straight inside the shop. He was not wearing a wig.
'This is my son, sir.'
'I suppose you said the same thing to him?'
They both laughed.
'Come back anytime, sir. You will know when it is time. I'll be very happy to make one for you.'

While Händel decided not to get a wig, a belated birthday present came unexpectedly. It was late March, a month since he had enrolled at the University of Halle to study law. He had just been appointed as a temporary organist for the Calvinist cathedral, Domkirche, in Halle. There would be a year-long gap before the newly appointed organist could take his place, following the death of the previous, so the post had been offered to Händel with a reduced salary of fifty thalers in addition to free lodging in Moritzburg, a fortified castle nearby. He had been known as Zachow's unofficial assistant organist, and his virtuoso playing was acknowledged in town, and word was slowly spreading around.

I am an organist! I have my church! I have my lodging, a place on my own! And I will be paid; I will have a salary! Though the young Händel was perfectly happy to live with his mother and two little sisters, this gave him an air of freedom and independence. It seemed the door to a new world was just opening in front of him. The authorities knew the Händels were Lutheran, and the cathedral was Calvinist. Trust and tolerance, but more of the sign that music went beyond belief even in a small town of Halle.

Georg Friederich's mother did not miss the difference of mood in her son. She thought fate was helping her son's passion. The organist of the cathedral was a respectable post. *My late husband should be proud of his son,* she thought.

'But how about your study?' asked Dorothea.

'I will keep studying, Mama,' he replied, 'It's not a heavy duty. I don't have to be at the church all the time.'

'I see.'

'And, if I cannot fulfil my duty, for some reason, I can always ask someone to replace me from time to time. Of course, I will try my best to avoid that.'

'Do you know who to ask, Georg?'

'Mr Zachow, for example.'

'Your teacher?' Dorothea looked up in surprise.

'I am certain he will be very interested to play a different organ, Mama,' he laughed, 'but, as I said, I will try to play every time I am supposed to.'

Dorothea was amazed to realise how her son had matured, talking of his teacher like a friend. 'And, how about the lodging? Are you going to live in Moritzburg?'

'I don't know, Mama,' said her son. 'It's just for a year. Is it worth it?'

'You don't have to, but don't feel embarrassed if you want to move out, my son,' said Dorothea. 'We are very happy to have you here, but maybe, sometimes, you'll want to have a place of your own where you can entertain friends. I don't know…'

Händel did not know what to say. Suddenly it became a reality. His mother was right. He was happy at home, but now he could be on his own.

He had never left his home before. The thought was somehow overwhelming.

Dorothea, seeing her son confused, said, 'Georg, you don't have to decide now.' She took his hands in hers. 'Give it time.'

'Thank you, Mama,' he smiled, 'Mama?'

'Yes, Georg.'

'I love you, Mama.'

'I love you too, Georg.'

Händel did not move out.

Chapter 2 : Fascination (1702-1703)

London, 23 April 1702

There was excitement in the air in England's capital on this day. The printmakers had been busy making hundreds of cheap prints, to be sold on that day. It was a sunny day and people were gathering around Westminster Abbey, hoping to have a glimpse of the new queen to be crowned.

In one room at Westminster Hall, Anne Stuart, wearing a big wig, was getting ready.

'Where is my husband, Sarah?' Anne asked.

'He is already at the abbey waiting for you, Anne,' Sarah, Countess of Marlborough, replied mechanically, busily looking around.

'Oh...I wish he were here,' Anne whispered, and regretted it. She knew that her childhood friend and confidant Sarah would disapprove.

'Would you like your husband to be brought here, madam?' the Duchess of Somerset asked with more kindness.

Anne saw Sarah roll her eyes. 'I thank you, Duchess, but I think I have to go now.'

Elizabeth, Duchess of Somerset stepped back to look over the dress and said, satisfied, 'You look splendid, madam.' She then turned to Sarah, smiling. 'N'est-ce pas, Countess?'

Though honoured to be one of the ladies to attend Anne on this special day, Sarah was not happy. The Duchess of Somerset was much younger than her and yet was the one in command. *Just for being a duchess*, Sarah thought, irritated, ignoring the fact that the duchess was the one most suited for the situation - calm, confident and in control nicely but firmly. Sarah felt humiliated to be inferior in rank, and was determined to use her close relationship with Anne to advance her status socially and politically.

Anne's golden robe was richly embroidered with jewels, and the petticoat was decorated with bands of gold and silver lace between rows of diamonds. She wore an elaborate wig woven with golden ribbons and diamonds. Literally covered in diamonds, she shone like a goddess. The Duchess of Somerset, helped by the Countess of Marlborough, wrapped Anne in royal robes. Her shoulders were wrapped in an ermine cape. The crimson-velvet train was lined with ermine and bordered with gold lace. Anne started to walk slowly, struggling in pain and trying to keep her balance, with her swollen and weak legs supporting her large body. Still, she felt a sort of elation. She'd waited a long time, going through uncertain periods and even fearing for her life. Behind her, she heard Elizabeth, Duchess of Somerset, instructing four women, including Sarah, in the positions they would have to carry her train. She winced in pain, as her rheumatism was particularly bad on the day.

In the early afternoon of 23 April 1702, St George's Day, the crowd saw a long procession of clergymen, a marching band, numerous aristocrats in their best suits, and the children's choir followed by the queen. Carried by Yeomen of the guard on an open chair under a canopy, Anne arrived in front of Westminster Abbey, the six yards of train floating behind her being managed by the Duchess of Somerset and her companions. Anne got out of the chair, and immediately four richly dressed women led by the Duchess of Somerset spread her train neatly. Anne walked in slowly, followed by the five women holding her train. Welcomed by the organ playing, she felt all the attention focused on her by the crowd squeezed in the abbey. She hardly remembered the Archbishop of Canterbury planting the crown on her head, or the sermon delivered by the Archbishop of York.

When she emerged from the abbey, she was Anne, Queen of England, Scotland, and Ireland. *It is strange*, she thought. *I've never had an ambition to be a ruler, but here I am, a queen.* The crowd was cheering, and the noblemen were throwing coins to them. The crowd was shouting loudly, 'God save Queen Anne! Long live Queen Anne!'

Anne felt a soft touch from behind and heard her husband whisper, 'Smile, Anne. Smile.'

Anne relaxed at once, and her spontaneous smile made the crowd cheer even louder.

'Are you all right to walk?' her husband asked.

'Yes, I am,' said Anne, 'I feel much better now. It's done.'

'Let us go to the banquet, Anne. I'm starving,' said her husband, George, Duke of Cumberland.

Now she had to resist laughing. She left the abbey on foot and crossed to Westminster Hall, where the traditional coronation banquet was waiting for her. She decided just to enjoy the day, but she knew her reign would not be easy.

Though Anne had been happily married for nearly twenty years to Prince George of Denmark, there was one problem. They had no children. Anne had seventeen pregnancies, but only one son survived who died two years before, aged eleven. Now Anne was thirty-seven, and it seemed extremely difficult to hope for an heir. This was a serious problem for the succession. There was not another Stuart remaining in the country. Her father, the deposed King James II, died in exile the previous year, leaving a son, a Catholic. Though there was the Act of Settlement to allow only Protestants to succeed to the British throne, the direct descendent of James II posed a serious threat. As the law now established that her successor would be a Hanoverian, this triggered a serious protest. For many, the idea of bringing a foreigner to put onto the throne was not easy to accept.

Another problem was political. When Charles II of Spain died childless in 1700, the succession immediately triggered a conflict, as Austria and France both claimed the Spanish throne. As part of an alliance against France, with the Dutch Republic and Austria, England was now in a war, which Anne inherited from her predecessor, William III.

'Anne,' her husband whispered, 'the toast.'

Anne woke up from her thoughts. The traditional champion on horseback was in front of her, to combat anyone who denied the new monarch's right to the crown. She smiled to her champion and raised her glass. All the guests raised their glasses to her. She smiled at her friend Sarah, Countess of Marlborough, seated a little further away beside her husband the earl. *Well, first of all, I will have to reward them. Without their support and protection I would not be here today. Dukedom?* she thought.

Halle, May 1702

'Are you Händel?'

A young man approached as Georg Friederich was coming down from the organ loft after the service at the Domkirche. The man was of medium height. His dark hair was tied back, and he bore a friendly smile.

'I am. And you are?' asked Händel, intrigued.

'My name is Georg Philipp Telemann. I came from Leipzig to hear you play,' he said.

Händel looked at him, 'Leipzig?'

Telemann smiled. 'Yes, Leipzig. I heard about you, and I wanted to meet you.' He saw that the young organist had no idea that his organ playing had been noticed and had started to attract attention.

Händel smiled back. There was something reassuring in this young man standing in front of him. 'I am Georg Friederich Händel. Welcome to Halle.' He extended his hand.

The two young men found themselves talking in a nearby tavern. Händel was surprised to see how easily he could talk to someone whom he had just met.

'Are you an organist as well?' asked Händel.

'Not really. I play the violin, lute, flute and keyboard, quite well, I believe, but organ is not my strongest.'

'But that's a lot! I play the violin besides harpsichord and organ, but that's all.'

'Your organ playing is fantastic. I liked it a lot.' Telemann smiled.
'Thank you. But I still ask my teacher to go through my compositions before playing in public.'
'Who is your teacher?'
'Zachow. Do you know him?'
'Not personally, but I think he is from Leipzig.' Telemann looked at Händel. 'May I call you Händel, since we are both Georg?'
'Good idea. So shall I call you Telemann?'
There was something very comforting in Telemann's demeanour and Händel felt he could trust him. After discussing current music, they started to talk about their life.
'You too?' Händel stared at Telemann.
'Yes. That's why I am in Leipzig. I am reading law there.'
'My God...I thought I was the only one to study law beside music. Where are you from, Telemann?'
'Magdeburg.' Telemann stared at the stein in his hands, 'I could have come here, to the university, but I thought Leipzig would be far enough from my mother.'
'Oh. Why do you say that, may I ask?'
'She took away all my instruments and forbade me any music at all.' He looked in Händel's eyes to see the reaction.
'Oh God, that was my father!' shouted Händel in disbelief. He then looked around and lowered his voice. 'But he had to accept that I would get a music teacher, by order of the Duke of Saxe-Weissenfels.'
'We have a lot in common then,' said Telemann, raising his eyebrows. 'How about now? Did you convince your father?'
'No, not at all. He died five years ago. And I am certain he is still not convinced.' Händel looked up to the ceiling and crossed himself.
'My father died when I was four. My musical passion comes from my mother's side, but she is the one against it.' Telemann looked at Händel, grimacing. 'It is typical of the...'
'Typical of what?'
'Well, the in-betweens.'
They were interrupted momentarily by the maid taking away their empty steins quite abruptly. Telemann politely ordered two more ales. Seeing her going away, he resumed.
'See, we are not of the nobility, the ruling people, and not totally of the ruled people like...' And he indicated with his eyes the maid disappearing in the kitchen, 'We both belong to that category between the two. Didn't you know that?' Then he asked, 'how old are you?'
'Seventeen.' Händel looked at Telemann. 'Well, I never thought about that. In fact, you are the first to tell me that.' He always saw servants in his house. He knew some of them were very poor. He also knew that his father

served rulers. Then, at school, the Gymnasium, he saw some very poor boys. But he never thought beyond it. After all, he grew up in a relatively well-off and very protected environment.

Telemann looked at Händel still deep in thoughts. He waited a moment and said casually, 'I'm not surprised. Nobody wants to talk about it but it is there as a reality. And within this category, there are ranks, many of them.'

'Yes... I suppose so...'

'See, being a musician is not a proper profession for my family or yours. It's a dubious job.'

'Why? Is it dubious to be an organist of a church? I thought it was respectable.'

'It is, but you have a post, and that's it. No more.'

Händel looked at Telemann, still not understanding.

'You see, the best a musician can do is to enter the service of a duke, a prince, a king...'

'My father was in the service of a duke.'

'But he was not a servant. What I want to say is that your father was needed. He could not be easily discarded like a dairymaid.'

Händel just nodded. Telemann continued.

'A musician is not really needed, he will be just a servant, and he will need permission to do anything, to go somewhere, and it is not guaranteed that the permission would be granted. There is more chance of it being refused. Serving a court or church, it will be the same.'

'I see. So we should be lawyers.'

'Or surgeons, like your father,' Telemann added, 'do you see? We all need doctors. We all fall ill at one point, and even die from illness. Doctors are needed. Lawyers, well, we might never need one, but you never know.'

'My family used lawyers. They had to.'

'Why?' Then Telemann added quickly, 'Oh, you don't need to tell me if you don't want to.'

'It was about a licence to sell wine.' Händel did not mention the sale of his father's practice.

'I thought your father was a surgeon,' Telemann raised his eyebrows.

'He was, but a part of our house contained a tavern.' Händel clearly remembered that his father's wrinkles between his eyebrows were deeper when talking about the licence, with his mother looking worried. Then, he shook his head. 'Never mind!'

They looked at each other and just laughed.

'Never mind,' Händel repeated, feeling more relaxed with the second stein of ale. 'Tell me more about opera. I want to know.'

'Of course.'

'Come to Leipzig. I'll introduce you to the Collegium Musicum I

reformed,' Telemann said, walking beside Händel from the tavern.
'Reformed?'
'Yes. It was founded by Mr Kuhnau, but it became just a name. There was nothing going on.'
'Is he the one who made you come here?'
'Well, he complained to the city council that I was stealing the choir members for my opera, making them neglect the church. So the city council suggested to me that I leave the city for a while. Not a long time though...'
'Are you staying here?'
'No, I'm on my way to go to see my beloved mother' – he grinned – 'just to remind her that I am still alive and reading law, as she wanted.'
'The students must miss you in Leipzig.'
'No, they are busy singing in churches under Kuhnau. I don't know if they are enjoying it.' He looked up at Händel, who was taller. 'Mr Kuhnau does not know that he did me a huge favour.'
Their eyes met. Händel did not know how to react.
Seeing Händel embarrassed Telemann kept talking. 'But I will not thank him. He just wanted to get rid of me. He is narrow-minded, or just jealous? I don't know.'
'Tell me more about the Collegium Musicum.'
'Well, it is an organisation to give public concerts. It mainly exists to encourage people to be interested in music. It is not professional, and I am recruiting student musicians now.'
'Recruiting by yourself?'
'Yes. And it is an excellent opportunity to play my own music.'
'And you're director of the opera house as well. You are remarkable. I admire you.'
'Oh, it's my turn to be embarrassed!' Telemann laughed.
'I'll go to Leipzig,' said Händel, determined. 'I have to.'

So Händel made his very first trip on his own, to Leipzig. Warmly welcomed by Telemann, he was shown everything his friend could think of. However, what most impressed the young organist was the opera, as his knowledge of performing music was limited to church music.
'So, it's a play combined with singing, accompanied by an orchestra?' Händel said, mesmerised in front of the stage where Telemann was rehearsing.
'I would say that it's a singing play.' Telemann raised his eyebrows, looking at his friend.
'So the singers need to act as well?' For Händel who knew the singers at church, this was something beyond belief.
'Yes, so it's more demanding for the singers.' Telemann smiled, 'Unfortunately the orchestra is quite small here. Well, as you can see, I have

to do with what I can get from the students.'
'I would say, if organ is the king of the instruments, opera is the king of the kings!'
Telemann laughed. 'Enough for today. Let's go to have a drink.'
Händel felt comfortable with Telemann. Since the death of his father he was the only male of the family. He felt he'd found the brother he never had.

Time flew, and Händel had to go back to Halle, where his duties were waiting.
'You are welcome anytime in Halle. I want you to know that.' Händel weighed his words as he bade farewell to Telemann. 'Unfortunately, Halle has less to offer than Leipzig.'
'But they have you!' Telemann laughed. 'May I stay in your lodging then?'
Händel's face lit up at once. 'Of course! With pleasure!'

'Opera?' Zachow stared at Händel.
'Yes, opera. Where could I go to see it?' Händel asked his teacher after his life-changing experience in Leipzig.
'Did you see one? I did not know that opera was played in Leipzig.'
'Telemann is trying to mount one but it's very small and simple. He can only use students.'
'I see. Did you like it?'
'Yes, and I want to see more. The true opera, the more complete one. Where can I see it?'
'Where there is a court, but…' Zachow hesitated.
'But?'
'As it is played at the court, you cannot go there and ask admission. You need to be introduced.'
'I see.' Händel considered. 'How about Weissenfels? I have my half-brother there.' He remembered the day he had followed his father on his way to Weissenfels on foot.
'Are you close enough to ask him?'
'Well, I think the duke will remember me.'
Zachow looked at his pupil. 'Are you talking about Duke Johann Adolf, Georg?'
'Yes.'
'Well, he died a few months after your father. Did you not…'
'What?!'
No. He did not know. No word came from Händel's open mouth. The duke was dead, the one who had persuaded his father to allow his son to study music. It was all thanks to him. Händel still remembered the purse bearing the duke's coat of arms, given to his father. With this, to pay for the music

lessons, Zachow entered his life. *Maybe it was a command, when I think back on it.*

'I am sorry you didn't know about it.'

'He was still young...' Händel remembered the duke looking much younger than his father.

'Yes, he was. His son is now the duke.'

Händel pondered on this. It was not that easy now, to approach Weissenfels. His half-brother Karl was still serving the court. However, he had not seen him since their father's funeral. He could feel his confidence dwindling.

'Georg, try. Just try. Krieger is there as the Kapellmeister.'

'Krieger?' Händel raised his eyebrows.

Zachow smiled. 'Yes, the very Krieger whose music you copy from time to time. Yes, Weissenfels, he is there. But...'

'But?'

'Ah, it is a pity. The court of Hanover produced fabulous operas, but that's when you were still very small.'

'Did you go there?' Händel saw his teacher become dreamy.

'Oh, yes, yes. It was like a heaven. That Maestro Steffani-'

'Steffani?'

'Yes, Steffani. Agostino Steffani. If you hear his name mentioned, be attentive. Remember that name, Georg.'

'Steffani.' Händel nodded.

'Oh, I cannot believe it, Händel!' Telemann exclaimed in excitement. 'Weissenfels! Krieger is there! But I knew that Kuhnau would never do anything to introduce me there. Your half-brother is there! Oh my God!'

Händel was amazed to see his friend's reaction and was glad to do something for him. Telemann was giving him a lot, and he always felt unable to return his generosity.

'So you agree to come with me? Good. I'll write to Karl.' Händel beamed. Then his expression changed, 'Oh...one thing...'

'What is that?' asked Telemann.

'Do you think I need to wear a wig?'

'Well, yes, I think so. We will be visiting a court. We have to look respectable.'

'I will order one.'

'And I will order more paper,' said Telemann enthusiastically.

'Paper? Why?'

'Just in case Krieger lets us copy his music. You never know.' He rubbed his hands one against the other, grinning.

'So, you've been there when you were a child?'

'Yes,' Händel looked up at the castle through the gates, 'but I hardly remember.'

'Georg?'

Händel turned to see a middle-aged man looking at him. It was Karl, his half-brother.

'You've changed a lot, Georg,' Karl said fondly, 'I can recognise you only by the pale blue eyes of my father.' And he gave a smile, which faded away quickly. 'I am sorry, Georg, but it will be difficult to see an opera now.'

The two young men looked at each other.

'The duke changed his plan, and will not be back soon.'

Händel's jaw dropped, but no words came out.

Telemann looked at his friend. They were thinking the same thing: *but we came all the way just for an opera!*

'I am sorry. The hunting is apparently good, and the duke wants to stay.'

This was the reality. At a court everyone was at the mercy of the ruler, and there was no alternative. This caused a serious problem, as they were expecting to be invited to stay. If the duke were there, they were quite certain to impress him with their playing and get the invitation. Now without the duke, there was no one with that power.

'But, surely, there will be rehearsals?' Telemann asked.

Karl saw his half-brother's face lit up. 'Well, I think, yes. But you will have to persuade the musicians to do it. As the duke's date of return is not determined, they are in no hurry.'

'Is Mr Krieger here?' Telemann enquired.

'Yes, he is,' said Karl, and saw hope in the two young men.

The two friends looked at each other again, and smiled. It was up to them to make their way now.

By now, Händel and Telemann were close friends. Telemann, four years Händel's senior, was kind and generous with a good sense of humour. Though physically very different, they both felt like brothers, sharing the same passion. They visited each other and wrote to each other as much as possible. Händel moved out of his family house and settled himself in Moritzburg, the fortified castle in which a lodging had been allocated to go with the post of the organist. It was just a few minutes' walk away from his family house, which he continued to visit.

'Berlin?' Dorothea said, raising her eyebrows.

'Yes, Mama, Berlin. I want to visit the court. Do you think I need a new suit, or will the one I have do? Do you think-' Händel stopped. His mother was still staring at him. 'Mama, are you…all right?'

'Do you want to go to Berlin, Georg?'

'Yes, Mama.' Händel added, 'Don't worry, Mama, I'm not moving there. The court of Berlin has a permanent orchestra, and they play opera there. Opera, Mama! I have to go there. I absolutely have to go!'

'But you did not see it in Weissenfels. The same thing might happen.'

'I saw the rehearsals, Mama. But not entirely. It was interesting, but we could not stay there just to wait for the duke's return to see it complete.'

Händel pursed his lips. 'This time, I want to see it, and I want to stay as long as necessary.'

Dorothea just kept staring at her son. Then she stood up, went out of the room and came back. Händel saw something in her hand.

Still staring at her son, she handed him a letter. 'This is from your father, Georg.'

It was Händel's turn to stare at his mother. 'Again?'

Dorothea smiled. 'Oh, it's not to you. See? It's addressed to Frederick III, Elector of Brandenburg.'

'But, Mama...'

'Your father knew you would not give up music. He told me to give this to you when you decided to go there.'

Händel felt his eyes getting hot. 'Papa...'

'Yes, my son. He loved you.' She looked at him tenderly. 'But you will return?'

'Yes, I will.'

Dorothea sighed in relief and smiled. 'How about your friend Telemann? Is he going with you?'

'No, Mama. He is too busy taking care of his opera house and dealing with his enemies.'

'Enemies?'

'Clerics, Mama. They don't like opera. They think it makes the people come less to the church. Ridiculous.'

Händel had witnessed, in one of his stays in Leipzig, city councillors interfering with Telemann's music-making, on behalf of the church.

She said nothing, but a shadow was cast in her mind. *Does my son like something the church does not like?* This was not good.

Lutzenburg, Outside Berlin, Summer 1702

Händel waited in a small dark room in the palace. He was restless, pacing around nervously. The letter of introduction he presented was addressed simply to Elector Frederick of Brandenburg. But the elector was now a king and Händel knew it. *What if I am just kicked out?* Five years had passed since the death of his father. *Would the king remember my father?*

Frederick, Elector of Brandenburg, had crowned himself Frederick I, the first king. Though with the consent of the Holy Emperor, due to the objections from the Polish-Lithuanian Diet and also out of respect to the region's historic ties to the Polish crown, Frederick decided to call himself "King *in* Prussia", instead of "King of Prussia". The coronation took place the previous year. He was now forty-five. Seventeen years before, when he was still Electoral Prince, he had married, for the second time, Sophia Charlotte of Hanover. It proved to be a happy marriage. Since her arrival the palace had been a merry place with lots of music.

'Your Majesty, a young man presented himself with this letter.' The valet presented a sealed letter on a silver plate.

The king looked at it and looked at the valet, who nodded, confused. *So, it is someone who does not know that I am now a king.* He looked at the letter again. The handwriting looked familiar; there was something old and severe about it. The king took the letter and opened it. Out of curiosity, the king received the visitor quickly. The young man was extremely good-looking and well dressed with an air of confidence. And, there was no doubt. Frederick I recognised the very pale blue, slightly bulging eyes of the late court physician, Georg Händel. The king was rather glad that his visitor was not rebuffed at the gates.

'So you are the son of Dr Händel.'

'Yes, Your Majesty. I am sorry my father did not have time to correct your title.'

The king laughed. He liked the boldness of the young man. 'Show me your skill then!' He turned to the valet and said, 'Ask the queen to join me in the music room.'

His wife, Sophia Charlotte of Hanover, arrived quickly and, seated beside her husband, watched the young man play the harpsichord. Aged thirty-four, she had been very active in transforming the court's mood to echo that of her parents', intellectual and cultural. Music was given a special attention and she was very keen to keep a permanent court composer and orchestra.

The death of their first son a few months after the birth was a terrible blow, but their second son, Frederick William, was a healthy boy. The couple would have wished for more children, but they let nature decide, and they lived in harmony. The king was in love with his wife, to the point of forgetting the existence of his mistress, and the queen was grateful for her husband, who allowed her to have the life she wanted. And, there was a happy addition to the family. Caroline of Ansbach had arrived at court six years earlier. She was the daughter of the queen's late friend Princess Eleonore of Saxe-Eisenach who, at her death, designated the queen as her daughter's guardian. The young woman was treated as a member of the family.

Led to the music room, Händel saw a big harpsichord, like the one he had seen at Weissenfels, and he felt his nervousness melt at once. He was so focused on playing that he did not see the king and queen looking at each other and smiling. After displaying his virtuosity on harpsichord, the young visitor was welcomed to the court. Though his background was far from poor, everything was beyond imagination to the young visitor. The palace, the court, the orchestra, the theatre – it was all far from the regular and frugal life he led, between the church, University and his lodging in Halle. It was just another world. *Telemann was right. I have to be careful not to lose myself.* Queen Sophia Charlotte took a liking to Händel, and it was she who took him around and introduced him to the court composer, Attilio Ariosti.

'Nice to meet you,' said the Italian in French with a heavy accent. He wore a dark-brown cassock, under which Händel could guess was a skinny body. His arched eyebrows and prominent pointed nose made him look like a bird of prey, but his dark-brown eyes were gentle and warm.

'He was a Servite Friar, Mr Händel, and now he is a deacon,' said the queen.

'Yes, Your Majesty.' Händel nodded without understanding the meaning of either *Servite* or *deacon*.

'I snatched him from the church in Bologna, and now he composes operas and cantatas here in Berlin.'

'It is my honour to be snatched by Your Majesty,' said the priest, smiling, and he bowed.

The queen laughed. 'Oh, Maestro Ariosti, I hope you are happily captured here.'

'Did the young man meet Maestro Bononcini, Your Majesty?'

'No, not yet.' She turned to Händel. 'Maestro Bononcini is *de passage* here in Berlin. He is a guest of honour. He is composing an opera for us now.'

'Opera?' Händel's eyes brightened.

'He is giving lessons to Caroline right now, I think. Mr Händel, you will meet my Caroline. She just returned from Ansbach. She is so lovely.' The queen smiled tenderly.

Händel, seeing her smile, thought Caroline was her daughter.

Caroline of Ansbach was now nineteen, two years older than Händel, but she looked sixteen. Quite tall with blond hair and dark-blue eyes, she was stunningly beautiful. Discreet and intelligent, she was enjoying fully the liberal and cultivated court presided over by the queen. Though orphaned young and with just a small fortune, she belonged to a branch of the House of Hohenzollern, and she was now a strong candidate to be wife of Archduke Charles of Austria, the future Holy Roman Emperor. Her manner was easy and quite informal, and Händel fell effortlessly into conversation with her.

'Is the queen your relative?' Händel asked, guessing that she was not the queen's daughter.

'No, not really. She calls me Niece, and I call her Aunt, but we are not related. My late mother and the queen were close friends, so my mother appointed the queen to be my guardian just before she died.'

'I am sorry to hear of the loss of your mother.'

'The queen treats me as if I were her own daughter, so she is my mother now.'

Händel did not know what to say. All he could do was to smile.

'The king informs me that your late father was a very famous surgeon,' she said with excitement. 'Do tell me the story of the boy who swallowed a knife.'

Händel just stared at Caroline, with his eyebrows high.

'I heard it from the king, but I want to hear it from you. Maybe you know more?' Caroline's eyes were bright.

Händel was amazed to see how a miracle story could survive and travel so far.

Giovanni Bononcini was the opposite of Ariosti. His full face was oval with a large forehead. Impeccably dressed and wigged, he was outgoing and smiling. Everybody was easily charmed by his friendliness. Already well known in Italy, he was now in the service of Emperor Leopold I in Vienna with a large salary. He had brought with him a male and a female singer. The male singer was very tall with extremely long limbs. With his small head and his fat, short body, from which four thin limbs protruded, he looked like a giant spider. Both singers followed the composer everywhere and seemed to worship him.

'I could have stayed there in Vienna, but because of the war, they had no heart to enjoy my music fully. So, I took leave,' Bononcini said with a sigh.

War? What war? This was the first time Händel had heard of a war. The succession war triggered in 1700 by the death of Charles II of Spain without heir was spreading, slowly but steadily, all over Europe.

If Ariosti kept his manner as a servant towards his patrons, Bononcini used his fame to make them glad to have him. It was subtle but perceptible. As a guest, Bononcini was not employed in Berlin. Though Händel liked Ariosti more than Bononcini, the latter's position was more prestigious. Ariosti seemed happy to have Händel nearby and had been generous in letting the young virtuoso copy his music, but Bononcini was busy chatting with nobility and giving their daughters music lessons. Händel found himself unable to get near him. Bononcini seemed particularly pleased to hear people talk about his opera *Il trionfo di Camila (The triumph of Camilla)*.

'Is it that famous, his *Camila*?' Händel asked Ariosti.

'Oh, yes, very much. It was first played in Naples, I believe, in 1696. That was six years ago, and since then, every city in Italy has wanted to play it.' The composer looked at the young man. 'You are very young, so maybe

you don't understand?'
'Not really…'
Ariosti smiled. 'An opera is a very expensive thing. But, if it's a success you can make a lot of money. When it was presented for the first time in Naples, it was a big hit, really big. So they made a lot of money, and then hearing of the success, other cities wanted to play it. First, to introduce the public to the most recent and successful opera, and make money at the same time. So it went from one city to another, and another, and another…'
'That much?' murmured Händel in disbelief.
'Yes, it is true. I get news directly from Italy.' Ariosti looked at Händel directly. 'And I am quite certain Bononcini came with the score.'
'I'd love to hear it…' *Or at least see the score*. But he knew there was little chance of one or the other happening. There was no question of asking for permission to copy his music, or even to consult the score.

The king saw Händel often with Ariosti, who made the young man participate in the court music-making as well. Then he had an idea.
'What do you think of that young man?' the king asked his wife.
'Oh, I think he is amazing,' Sophia Charlotte replied enthusiastically, 'I can stay listening to him improvise for hours.'
'I am thinking of sending him to Italy so we could have a wonderful court musician within a few years' time.' He did not let his wife ask the question. 'Don't worry, my dear. We'll keep Ariosti for as long as possible.' He saw his wife's face brighten up with pleasure.
'Please, do your best to let Ariosti stay. He is quite worried about going back to Italy as a traitor,' she was now serious. 'Poor Ariosti, just for working in a Protestant court.'
'Traitor? They are narrow-minded, those Catholics.' The king sighed.

Händel, summoned by King Frederick I *in* Prussia, was listening to the monarch.
'Italy is the best place to go for a musician like you.'
'I am certain Your Majesty is right.'
'I shall not waste your time. I will be straightforward.'
'Yes, Your Majesty.'
'How about going to Italy at my expense, and learning whatever there is to be learned, and then coming back here to be my court musician?'
Händel was astounded. He just stared at the king and did not know what to say. But, at the same time, pleased to realise that the king wanted him. He struggled to find words to fill the silence. And he could not make the king wait. 'I am very honoured and flattered, Your Majesty, but…' His mind was racing. He had to say something.
'But?'

'I don't know what to say, your Majesty. This is so unexpected...'

The king laughed. He even felt a father-like affection towards the young musician, little older than his own son, standing in front of him, embarrassed.

Händel tried his best to calm down, but he could not. He felt increasingly under pressure. The king could have all the time to reply, but not him.

'I have to honour my post as the organist in Halle, at least until the contract expires.' That was the only thing he could think of saying.

'When is that?'

'In March next year, Your Majesty.'

'Very well. After that, then.'

'I have another commitment, Your Majesty.'

'Tell.'

'I am studying law at university.'

'And?'

'I am very honoured by your offer. It is indeed beyond my expectations.' Händel considered quickly. He just wanted to buy time. He knew that he should not talk too much. He felt his hands getting sweaty. 'But please, allow me some time to think about it.' He looked at the king, scared to death. He might have offended him by asking for more time.

'Until when?' the king asked methodically.

'Tomorrow morning, Your Majesty.' Händel felt like a chased dog, trying to flee desperately. But he was relieved that the king did not seem upset.

'Very well.'

Händel came back to his room breathless. The pressure was too much, and his knees nearly gave way. He totally lacked court experience and wished he were ten years older. He was torn between the joy of such an offer, and dread pulling him back. However, gaining control slowly, he started to think about it. If he did not accept the offer immediately, it was just by instinct. Something was bothering him. His mind was in turmoil. He locked himself in his room to contemplate. He missed his friend Telemann terribly. He wanted to discuss and explore all the possibilities with him. It was a very good and honourable offer, and besides, he would not have any money issues. He would be introduced to the best places to learn everything in comfort. And he was quite confident that the king would be very pleased to have him back from Italy. But then? He would stay in Berlin as long as the king wanted to keep him. For how long? A lifetime? That sounded dreadful. In exchange for the financial stability, he would need permission even for a day's leave, and probably be refused. That was appalling. It looked like a comfortable prison. Of course, if he were to leave on his own accord, there would be no guarantee of a next post. And how about his fellow musicians? He was certain he would have rivals and enemies among his colleagues. Telemann already had his.

They would be too pleased to spread the rumour that he had been kicked out or invent some other damaging story. And then, where is the guaranty that the king would keep him for a lifetime? He could be kicked out for some reason, mercilessly. There could be another reason, like in Hanover, to be dismissed by lack of funding. Faced with such an opportunity, he could not rejoice. A very much coveted post of a court musician looked rather unpredictable.

If he refused the offer, he risked offending the king. But he would be free! That sounded intoxicating. He wanted to try freedom before settling down for a salaried post. It was a good offer, but it had come too early. He wanted more time, time to accumulate more experience. Yes, it was too early for him.

His mind was clear now. He sighed deeply in relief. At least, he could give himself an answer. Now he faced another challenge. How to decline the offer without offending the king?

The next morning found Händel facing the king. Feigning calm, his heart was racing.

'Your Majesty, before giving you my answer, may I have the permission to ask you a question?'

'Do.'

'Did you see my father in person?'

'Yes, I did. I do remember him very well.'

Händel felt quite emotional.

The king continued. 'He was very fit for his age. He was respected because he gained his fame through his work and not by flattering the ruling people. I am convinced the treatment he gave to poor people was the same he gave to us.'

Händel looked down and then raised his head to look into the king's eyes. This was the crucial moment. 'Your Majesty, it was my father's wish that I study law. He did not agree with me being a musician in the beginning. Then, as I wanted to pursue music, he wanted me to have another career beside music.' Händel's voice was shaky. 'I did not know that before he died he had prepared the letter I gave Your Majesty. He knew that I wanted to pursue music.' The pressure was unbearable now. What if the king explodes in anger? He clenched his fists. 'Your Majesty, I am really honoured by your offer, but...' He looked down.

The king, seeing Händel with his voice shaking and clenching his fists, thought the young man was fighting tears back. 'You are going back to Halle, then?' the king interrupted.

'That was my father's last wish... Your Majesty.' He struggled to squeeze out these words.

'I see.'

Händel lifted his head slowly and to his relief saw the king smile sadly.

'My father knew my wish, so I should respect his in return.'

'You are loyal,' the king said, and handed him a piece of paper. 'Here, I want you to have this.'

Händel realised it was the letter of introduction he had given to the king. He looked at the monarch. *Have I done the wrong thing? Is the king upset after all?*

'Don't think I am offended. No, you are welcome here whenever you want to return. I just want you to have a piece of your father. I am a father myself, and I know what it feels like. He loved you.'

He did not remember how he got back to his room. However one thing was clear. By refusing the king's offer, Händel could not stay in the court anymore. He had to leave as soon as possible.

Frederick was in his study when his wife came in. Sophia Charlotte could not wait anymore. He raised his head from the documents and smiled.

'I suppose you want to know.'

'Yes, I do.'

'Well, we will not have him.'

'Oh...' The disappointment was obvious on her face. Then she listened attentively to what Händel had said to her husband, and said, 'Well, we cannot force him, then.'

'No,' he said quite in a matter-of-fact way, and then he raised one eyebrow. 'If it is true, then he is very loyal to his father, but...'

'But?'

'But if it is not, he is a very good actor.'

'Mr Händel, you are leaving us.' Sophia Charlotte looked tenderly at the young musician, packed and ready to go.

'Yes, Your Majesty.'

'This is a letter for my mother in Hanover introducing you. If you go there, go to see her. She will be very happy to meet you. I am telling her all I know about you.'

'This is very kind, Your Majesty,' said Händel, bowing.

'I really regret that you are not going to Italy, but, well, maybe it is destiny. Take care of yourself, Mr Händel, and we shall meet again.'

What she did not tell Händel was that she had not mentioned his refusal of the offer in her letter. She was kind not to, but she decided to not tell him so he could enjoy the suspense. *This is the price for your refusal, Mr Händel,* she thought and smiled to herself.

On the way back to Halle, Händel stopped at Leipzig to report to Telemann everything he saw and what happened.

'What is your opinion? Do you think I am wrong?' Händel asked, anxious.

Telemann considered a while and then said without any emotion, 'Well, it is your decision, Händel, so stick to it.'

'It was so unexpected. I did not know what to do, but accepting it now seemed too early to me.'

'Too early?' Telemann looked puzzled. 'You are seventeen now. It's not too early to get married and have a family. No, it is not too early. I would agree if you were nine.'

Händel laughed.

'There is more. Tell me,' Telemann said.

Getting serious, Händel said, 'I want to see more and learn more before committing myself.'

'You don't want to be groomed to be his court musician. So, what did you tell the king, exactly?'

'I just said that it was my father's wish that I study law and that I intended to honour his last wish.'

Telemann, narrowing his eyes, whispered, 'You used your father, who cannot say a thing now, to escape?' He smiled. 'I think it was a very good idea. You cannot just say no to a king, I suppose. A deathbed promise is a good excuse.'

Händel sighed with relief. 'I know what I want. I first want to go to Hamburg. My final destination is Italy, and I want to go there on my own. I am not ready yet, so I want to spend some time in Hamburg beforehand.'

'Why Hamburg?'

'I asked Ariosti. He told me that I should go there.'

'How about Bononcini? Did he tell you anything?'

'Oh, I could hardly talk to him. I was lucky if he recognised me.'

Telemann raised his eyebrows, then smiled. 'You will like Hamburg. There is a fabulous opera house there. The biggest in all Europe. Can you imagine?'

'I cannot wait.'

'When are you leaving?'

'As soon as I can.'

'Very well. I will miss you though... Oh, and stop at Hanover. It's on the way. It is always useful to meet people and make acquaintances. Don't miss the chance to introduce yourself there.'

'I don't know if I should give them the letter.'

'Why?'

'Well, what if the letter tells of my refusal?'

'Oh, I see.' Telemann considered. 'You cannot say that you are going to Hamburg, then.'

'Do I have to pretend I'm just visiting?'

'It might create a vicious circle of-'

'Lies. I don't like that.'
Telemann put his hand on Händel's and said, 'Don't lie, but also don't give away too much. That's the only thing I can advise.'

Back in Halle, Händel's life resumed as before, between Domkirche, University, Zachow and his home. However by the spring of 1703 his decision was made. He would go to Hamburg. And he would leave the University of Halle without graduating.

Dorothea busied herself. Her son was leaving. He needed enough clothing for summer and winter. She made his shirts. She bought him stockings and ordered shoes, boots, gloves, and a hat. *What about a sword? He will need one.* Then she remembered that her late husband had one he had never used, even to go to court. It had been given to him by Duke Johann Adolf of Saxe-Weissenfels when he was made Honorary Surgeon.

'Mama, I am sure. Don't worry about the winter coat.'
'But you need one, my son.'
'I know. I will order one in Hamburg.'
'Then I will give you some money so–'
'Mama, did you forget? I had a salary. I was paid.'
'I know that, but that is not enough to–'
'Mama, I swear. I will be fine.'

Dorothea was sewing buttons on her son's coat. Very carefully and thoughtfully, she sewed them one by one, making sure they were securely attached. She heard footsteps. She turned her head and saw her son coming in.

'Mama...' His expression was grave.
'Georg...' She looked at her son. Fighting back her emotion, she said cheerfully, 'My son, you look as if you were going to attend a funeral.'
'Mama, I am sad to leave you. Will you be all right?'
'Of course I will be fine.' She smiled. 'You already left home, so I know what it is like.' She got up, folded the coat carefully and handed it to her son. 'Here, your coat is ready. I sewed on buttons from your father's coat. He will be, in this way, with you and will protect you.'

He took his coat and checked the buttons. They were in metal, roughly made and large, far from nice.

'And take this.' She took a small pouch from her pocket.
He looked at the pouch on his palm. It was very exotic, a small pouch made of thick black fabric decorated with intricate embroidery in many bright colours. He looked up and asked, 'What is this, Mama?'
'It's dried herb. It is very good when you have a fever. Just infuse a bit of that in a hot water. You are robust, so I think you will not need it very much, but take it anyway. It might be useful.'

'Is this yours?'

'No. It was given to your father, but now I think it's time for you to have it.'

'By whom?'

'Oh, it's a long story, but it was a Gipsy woman.'

Händel said nothing and delicately put the pouch in his inner pocket.

'Mama, I will write to you as often as possible, and-'

'My son,' she interrupted. 'Do not worry about me. Think of your life. Just let me know from time to time that you are well. That's all I need to know.' Now she was fighting back the tears.

Two girls entered the room, Dorothea Sophia and Johanna Christiana. They ran to their big brother. He lowered himself and took them in his arms.

'Brother, you are leaving us,' said the younger one, Johanna. She started to sob and buried her face in her brother's chest. She was of a very sensitive nature.

'Do not worry about us, Brother. We will take care of Mama,' said the elder, Dorothea Sophia, who was much like her mother, calm and down-to-earth.

'Will you write to us, Brother?' asked the younger girl, lifting her face.

'Yes, I promise.'

'Will you tell us everything?'

'That I cannot promise.' Händel smiled.

'Are you going to meet lots of people?'

'I hope so.'

'Oh!' Johanna nearly jumped, her face bright with excitement. 'Maybe you can find us husbands then!'

Händel laughed. Dorothea, watching her children, felt her heart melt.

Now that her son was ready to leave the nest, Dorothea's mind was filled with memories of the past. They flooded her thoughts, making her stop whatever she was doing to daydream. She had decided to get married not for affection but rather for practical reasons. Was it a good decision? She would say it was a right decision. Was it a happy marriage? She was not unhappy. Was she happy to have children? Yes, more than happy; of that, she was certain. And her son, stubborn like his father, was now a young man filled with hope and ambition. He is ready to leave his nest to explore the world, to grow bigger.

Chapter 3 : Leaving the nest (1703)

Venice, Spring 1703

In his palace on Gran Canal, standing in the doorframe of the reception room, Senator Agostino Marcello sighed. His eldest son, Alessandro, was busy rehearsing for the evening's concert. Alessandro was nearly thirty and showed no sign of wanting to get married. He was not interested in politics and spent his time making music and discussing literature. It was the best occasion for presenting his new compositions, and he took the weekly concert very seriously. That was the reason Senator Marcello had pushed his second son Benedetto to study law. Still, the love of music ran through the blood, and Benedetto too was a skilled keyboard player and moderate composer. The very musical Marcello brothers were known in Venice.

Not far from his palace, the senator's wife, Paolina, was comforting a little orphaned girl.

'Do not worry, my dear. I will take care of you.'

The little girl, dressed in black, was weeping silently, clutching her nurse's hand.

'Madam, it is very hard for her. She is only six, and she never knew her mother,' said the nurse.

Paolina knelt in front of the girl and gently took the girl's other hand. 'Your nurse will stay with you,' she said.

'Oh, madam! You are so generous!' The nurse put her free hand on her chest.

The girl looked up at the stranger kneeling in front of her.

Paolina said to the nurse, 'She never knew her mother, and now she has lost her father. I cannot take you from her.'

'Faustina, we are staying together!' The nurse smiled at the girl, who smiled back timidly through her tears.

'I will take care of you. I will be your mother,' said Paolina. She stood up, still holding the girl's hand. 'Now, let us go.'

The little girl, between Paolina and her nurse, looked up and asked, 'Where?'

'Home.'

'How is the girl?' Senator Marcello asked his wife.

'A little shaken. But her nurse is staying with her, so she will be all right.'

'Poor thing.'

'Yes, it is very sad.'

'Bordoni never recovered from the death of his wife. His daughter survived, but it did not give him much joy.'

'He must be happy to have joined his wife now.'

'And you, my dear, are you happy with this? Am I imposing this little girl on you?'

'Husband, I am very happy to have her. She will be the daughter I never had. I'll give her time. Poor thing! She is so small. She is six but looks like four.'

'Thank you, my dear.' Agostino took his wife's hands and kissed them tenderly.

'What is this rubbish?' Alessandro Marcello shouted in horror. There was a second harpsichord placed in the music room beside his own.

'You are up early, my son,' a voice behind him said.

'Father,' turning quickly he pointed the second harpsichord, 'what-'

'Good morning, Son.'

'Oh, yes, good morning, Father. How are you today?'

'This belongs to Faustina Bordoni. You do not touch it, and you do not comment on it. Understood?' his father said firmly. His father's tone was harsher than usual.

Alessandro was intrigued, but he could not stop himself being playful. 'Only if you tell me why, Father.' He beamed, smiling ear to ear like a Greek mask.

His father did not smile back. 'Faustina is the only child of Francesco Bordoni, who died recently. His wife died at childbirth.'

'Oh, yes, I heard of Bordoni. He was very ill.'

'Not anymore. So, Faustina will be staying with us. She plays the harpsichord, and this is hers. She is very attached to it.'

'But this is not good quality, Father. It's rubbish.'

'That's your opinion. For her this is the most beautiful thing in the world.'

Alessandro felt selfish and ashamed. 'I am sorry, Father.' He knew that the harpsichord would remain where it is.

'So, you will be teaching the little Faustina from today on,' said the father in a matter-of-fact way.

'What?' Alessandro jumped. 'But...but, Father, I'm not a teacher. I am... I am a-'

'You can do it.'

'Can't she have a teacher? A proper teacher, appropriate for a little girl?'

'You are here.'

'Ah, you don't want to pay for tuition,' said Alessandro, getting desperate.

'I can. That's not the problem.'

'Then why?' he nearly shouted.

'Because you have time, plenty of spare time!' Having spat that, Senator Marcello was gone. He loved his two sons, and there was nothing wrong with them loving music, but just for pleasure or a pastime. Seeing his eldest son devoted only to music was a source of irritation.

Faustina woke up and did not recognise the place. No one. She sat up in her bed. Her eyes wide open, she looked around. As she started to panic, her nurse came in.

'Good morning, Faustina. You slept a lot. You were tired.' She placed the tray on a small table and kissed the girl's forehead.

Everything came back – her father's death, the funeral, people taking furniture from her house, leaving the empty house with her nurse. Faustina burst into tears. She could not stop. Her nurse sat on the bed beside her, took her in her arms and rocked her gently. The nurse was also weeping, silently.

'So he left nothing?' Alessandro looked at his father.

'He did nothing after his wife's death and just accumulated debts. The creditors took everything and sold the house. I oversaw all that. There is a little amount of money left, but that is not enough for a dowry. Not at all. She will have to earn her living.'

'So how did the harpsichord escape?'

'Oh, that,' the father looked at his son, 'the nurse hid it in a neighbour's house. She said it was an order of Bordoni to keep the harpsichord for the girl.'

'I see…'

'I hope this will make you see that harpsichord in a different way, Son.'

Alessandro just pursed his lips.

It was Alessandro's younger brother, Benedetto, who befriended the little girl. Alessandro lived in his intellectual world and enjoyed it, leaving no room for a child.

'The little girl is gifted, you know, Alessandro,' Benedetto told his brother enthusiastically.

'Good for her. You know she is penniless, so that might help her to earn her living,' the elder brother spat it with contempt. He was still not happy to see a poor-quality harpsichord intruding the music room, his sanctuary.

'And she loves everything in music. I think she needs a proper singing teacher,' said Benedetto, ignoring his brother's attitude.

'Oh, excellent, so how about a dancing teacher for the little girl as well?'
'Mother is teaching her – well, they are just playing with it for the moment.'
'Mother? I cannot believe it.'
'Well she is very happy to have a girl in this house, you know. I've never seen her so happy.'
'How do you know?'
'I accompany them on harpsichord while they dance.'
'Oh that's very good, Brother. The good boy of the family,' said Alessandro cynically.
Benedetto, seeing his brother's lack of interest in the girl, left him in his bitterness, rolling his eyes.

The weekly concert at the Marcellos' palace continued as usual. The people hardly noticed a little girl attending with her nurse. At first, the pair stood discreetly against the wall behind the last row of seats, among servants accompanying the guests. Soon, Paolina Marcello noticed them and made them take seats in the last row.

One morning, after the concert, Alessandro stopped dead in front of the music room. He heard his music coming from inside, played on a harpsichord. It was the music that had just been premiered at the concert the previous evening with a chamber orchestra. He looked through the crack in the door, which had been left ajar, and to his astonishment, he saw the little girl at her harpsichord. *So my brother was not making it up. The girl is gifted.* He felt guilty for talking about her so disdainfully. He looked around, leaving noiselessly, and came back plodding. The harpsichord stopped playing. Alessandro pushed the door and entered.

'Er, I think you are Faustina,' he said, uneasily.
The girl stood up, bowed lightly, and said timidly, 'Yes, I am.' She seemed about to go, and Alessandro panicked.
'Oh, no, don't go!'
The girl stopped dead, frightened. He was mumbling now.
'Oh, sorry, don't be scared. I did not mean it. You don't need to go; that's what I wanted to say.' Alessandro tried to calm not the girl but himself. He'd never felt as embarrassed as he was now. The young women and beauties did not impress him, but he found himself tongue-tied in front of a little girl, to his own humiliation. However he forced himself to gain control. He absolutely wanted to ask the girl one thing.
'You are Faustina Bordoni, aren't you?'
The little girl nodded.
'My name is Alessandro. I think you know Benedetto, don't you?'
Another nod.
'Well, I am his older brother. Now, can I ask you a question, Faustina?'

Another nod.

'What is the music you were playing?'

'I heard it last night,' she said in a voice nearly inaudible.

'Did you like it?'

'Yes.' Another nearly inaudible reply.

'I composed it.'

She looked at Alessandro for the first time. The fear was gone. 'It is beautiful,' she said, more confidently.

'Oh, thank you,' said Alessandro, embarrassed, cursing himself silently for blushing.

Florence, Palazzo Pitti, May 1703

Palazzo Pitti was a gloomy place, only a remnant of its past glory. It was inhabited by Grand Duke Cosimo III de 'Medici, his eldest son Grand Prince Ferdinando, and his son's wife Grand Princess Violante of Bavaria. The grand duke had grown up under the heavy influence of his mother, Vittoria della Rovere, who had had an unlimited appetite for power. He had married, aged nineteen, Marguerite Louise d'Orléans, the eldest child of Gaston, Duke d'Orléans. When he succeeded his father in 1670, aged twenty-eight, the war between his mother and wife started. After five years of conflict, manoeuvres and plots, his wife left him for good. That was nearly thirty years before. Under his mother's imposing presence, he had been just a puppet. Her death nine years earlier had finally made him free, and alone. Still, despite being devout and spending hours in prayer, he was not a peaceful man.

The grand duke's son, Ferdinando, was very often away, preferring to spend time in different properties, including his favourite villa in Pratolino. He despised his wife, and the marriage was barren. Violante of Bavaria had been nearly sixteen when she arrived in Florence fourteen years earlier as a wife of the future grand duke. She lived secluded in the vast palace, abandoned by her husband.

'That's enough! That eunuch has gone too far!' shouted the grand duke. His face was red, and his fat body seemed to swell with anger.

Marquess Luca Casimiro degli Albizzi had never seen the grand duke in such fury. He tried to calm the old man down in vain. 'Your Excellency should not—'

'He shall not continue in this way!' the grand duke yelled, stomping. Then suddenly, he slumped in his chair like a deflated balloon.

'Your Excellency!'

Albizzi and the valet rushed to the duke in distress. The marquess

dispatched the valet to inform Princess Violante.
'Grand Duke, shall I…'
'Where is he now?' the grand duke asked, regaining strength.
'With the Grand Prince, in Poggio a Caiano, Grand Duke.'
'Make that singer come back to Florence immediately. He will pack and will leave Tuscany as soon as possible. He is banned. He will never set foot in Tuscany for the rest of his life.' The grand duke looked up at his master of the household. 'Take care of this, Albizzi.'
'It will be done, Grand Duke. Leave it to me.' Then he asked, hesitating. 'Does the grand duke have any message for the grand prince?'
'No. He can stay where he is. Just bring back that bastard. This is my order.'
Princess Violante rushed in. 'Grand Duke! What is the matter?' Quickly acknowledging Marquess degli Albizzi, who bowed to her and left, she knelt in front of her father-in-law and took his hands. 'I asked Dr Salvi to come immediately, Grand Duke. I'll take you to bed.' She nodded to the valet nearby.
Though blamed for not producing any heir for the family, Violante remained loyal and was a silent supporter of her father-in-law. She understood his frustration more than anyone and swallowed it with dignified silence.
Marquess Albizzi dispatched the messenger to Poggio a Caiano and was returning to the grand duke's bedchamber.
Princess Violante came out. 'The grand duke is fine. He has calmed down now. Dr Salvi is with him.' And she was gone. She made absolutely no attempt to learn what had happened.
The marquess watched her back as she returned to her apartment. She was very thin. Even her light dress seemed too heavy for her. Her forearm looked like a twig that could be easily snapped. *Poor woman. All that because of her husband's scandalous behaviour.* He shook his head, and pushed the door.
'Ah, Albizzi.'
'Your Excellency, I have dispatched the messenger. He will bring back the singer as soon as possible.'
'Good. Now, what shall I do with that castrato?'
'You have to be careful with him, Grand Duke. You don't want him to talk.'
'True.'
'Does Your Excellency have any idea?'
'He must not perform opera anymore. No contact with other singers.'
'Shall I leave, Grand Duke?' asked Dr Salvi.
'Stay, Salvi. I want your opinion as well.'
Within a week, the castrato Francesco de Castris was exiled from

Florence and given an apartment in the grand duke's palace in Rome, as well as a pension, a private coach, and an allowance to order two suits a year. He had been the highest-paid musician in the history of the Medici court.
Grand Prince Ferdinando was not affected by the loss. It was rather a good riddance. *That castrato was getting too much power.* He was interested now in a very beautiful Venetian soprano, Vittoria Tarquini. The coast seemed clear for the new conquest.

Halle, Early Summer 1703

Far from the Italian commotion, life in Halle was calm and constant. Händel was ready. He was walking slowly from his house towards Liebfrauenkirche to the lodging of his teacher, Friedrich Wilhelm Zachow. He took the normal route, going through narrow streets lined with shops. There was little change – always the same smell and same noise. He still enjoyed the noise from the glassmaker, the fragile high-pitched, bell-like tinkling noise. The shoemaker always used his small hammer to mark the rhythm and sing while nailing, always slightly out of tune but otherwise in fine voice.

'When?'

'Tomorrow morning. I will take the stagecoach to Hanover first.'

Zachow looked at his pupil, now a handsome young man. 'You will be fine, Georg. You will do well. Only...'

Händel looked at his teacher, puzzled.

Zachow hesitated, breathed in, and said, 'Only be careful of things that might get in the way – in your way, I mean.' Seeing Händel lost, he continued, 'I mean women. Look, Georg, don't be entrapped by a woman. Can you imagine if you are caught by one and–'

Händel laughed. 'Oh, do you think I am not strong enough to...'

Zachow rolled his eyes, realising that his pupil was still a virgin. 'Georg, you have not experienced a woman yet.'

Händel stopped laughing. His jaw dropped, and he went pink.

It was the first time Zachow had seen his pupil blush. He felt uneasy, but he continued, 'I don't particularly like to talk about it, but it is important, Georg. Be careful. If you are stuck with a woman and a child, your career is over.'

Händel just looked at his teacher, lost.

'Let me explain. You are a healthy young man, and you will experience women, sooner or later. Do you know what it means?'

Händel kept blushing, going from pink to red, incapable of uttering a word. He just felt all his blood going to his face.

Zachow was getting increasingly uneasy, but he cared for his pupil. Not any pupil, a genius. God chose him. 'Georg, I've seen, in my life, young musicians fall in love when they were just starting their career.'

'Yes, Master,' Händel could just squeeze out a whisper.

'They were young, delighted to discover the passion. Young people's passion. Do you understand?'

The young man just nodded, without looking at his teacher. He was not certain he understood, but he sometimes felt his heart pounding seeing a beautiful young woman of his age.

'What is the consequence? A girl becomes pregnant because of that passion.'

Händel did not know how to react. He just felt terribly embarrassed. He just wanted to escape, even by jumping out of the window.

'I've seen with my own eyes, Georg. Or the girl is abandoned, or she forces the young man to marry her,' Zachow signed heavily, 'are you following me?'

'Yes.' Another whisper.

'I don't think, if it were you, you would abscond, abandoning the girl in question.'

Silence.

'Then, what happens? You will have to support a wife and a child. You have to work.' Zachow looked at his pupil in the eye. 'You are going to Hamburg. You will be free. You won't have your mother to keep an eye on you. Imagine you fall in love, and make a girl pregnant.'

Händel felt his face burning hot.

'Then you would not be able to go to Italy anymore, to take your chance, unless you have a lot of money and you can support your family and still go travelling. That is not your case. Am I right?'

'Yes.'

'Then you would be stuck. You would have to get a post somewhere and work, to support your family.'

'I understand,' said Händel, nodding. Now it was clear.

'Be careful, Georg, I beg you. Just one wrong move and you will wreck your entire life. I don't want to see that. You have a big future. God bless you and keep you safe.'

Zachow tenderly watched the back of his pupil leaving. He did his best to teach Händel in his capacity. Coming from a musical family in Leipzig, he had a vast knowledge of all forms of music. He was a thinker and an extremely able man. His post at the Liebfrauenkirche was far from fulfilling his capacity and ability. The only thing missing in him was ambition, and he knew that his pupil had what he lacked. He still felt worried. He had known his pupil for a long time, since childhood. Since the death of his father, the boy, then aged twelve, had been helping him a lot, playing the organ in his place, copying in his place, in exchange for the fees. Apart from going to school, and then to university, he spent all his spare time for music-making. For the last six years he had practically no contact with his fellow adolescents, to hang around, joke about the girls, and so on. He had no time to mingle with them. He had had no adolescence. Hamburg will be the place where he will have his belated adolescence! Zachow could only pray.

The landscape was moving slowly past the window of the stagecoach taking young Händel from his native town of Halle to Hanover. This was the first step of the trip. Now he was on his own. Suddenly he realised that the independence he enjoyed in Halle had nothing to do with what he was going for now. In his hometown he had the lodging given to him by the church, but he could go to see his family anytime he wanted. Hamburg was not next door. It was at least a four-day trip without any stop. The landscape changed gradually. It was not the same green anymore, and the sky looked different. He felt alone in this world. His father's image came back. Händel took out the letter from his inner pocket. It was the letter given on his fourteenth birthday. It contained lots of practical advice. Now that he would not have his mother nearby, he thought the letter would give advice in case of illness or injury. He read it again, slowly, page by page, stopping from time to time to contemplate the landscape. The letter had concluded with a story:

> Allow me to tell you a story. Once I saved a small boy. He was badly injured in the forge of his father, who was a blacksmith. The father was poor and could not pay me. I took care of his son and did not ask for payment. I knew he could never afford it. A few months later, he came to see me to thank me and tell me that his son was well, and he brought me six metal buttons. He'd made them with scraps he'd saved. As a blacksmith and not a goldsmith, he would have had to make a huge effort to make such a small thing. He said that he had sprinkled them with holy water. I thanked him. I was really touched. I asked your mother to sew them on my coat. She thought they were ugly and too big. I did not

> *tell her the story; I just insisted she do so. I treasured those buttons. They made me feel good. May God protect you, Son.*

Those buttons were now on Georg Friederich's own coat. They looked less ugly.

The stagecoach stopped at Magdeburg, the birth town of his friend Telemann. Händel got out to stretch his legs and tipped a stable boy to look after his luggage, as advised by his friend. He looked around and felt vulnerable. Suddenly he missed his hometown. In Halle he knew where he was, could recognise the streets, houses and shops, and he had his family. From now on he was heading to the unknown, alone. It was daunting.

'Are you ready, sir? We are leaving,' said the coachman, making Händel start.

'Yes. Off to Hanover!' said Händel jollily, 'I cannot wait.'

'It's a long journey, sir.'

Händel just smiled.

It was late afternoon when Händel finally arrived in Hanover, so he just secured a room for the night at the stagecoach station inn and decided to present himself to the court the next morning. While Händel was trying to guess the rank of the inn, the innkeeper was trying to determine whether the lonely young traveller was to be trusted. When Händel asked for a valet to dust and smooth his clothes and comb his wig, the innkeeper's expression relaxed at once. At least the young man seemed polite and well-bred. Soon, Händel discovered that the inn had all sorts of rooms available, from the luxury rooms for travelling noblemen with cooks and valets to the rooms for merchant travellers. Sitting alone in front of his supper was quite daunting. Händel realised that this situation would be part of his life if he wanted to travel.

'So, sir, are you here for a while?' The innkeeper was curious.

'Just for a few days.' Händel was careful.

'Visiting relatives?'

'No, acquaintances.'

'Are you a student?'

'Well, yes, but I am more of an organist.'

'An organist? Oh, I see. You are looking for a post, maybe?'

'Well, if I'm lucky, yes.'

Händel looked up at the innkeeper, who seemed satisfied.

Dressed in his best suit with the shirt with frilled cuff underneath, he set off to the residence of the Elector of Hanover, Leineschloss.

Having started as a small village on the banks of the River Leine, Hanover had become a comparatively large town during the thirteenth century, due to its position at a natural crossroads. Trade had increased the city's importance, and in the fourteenth century the main churches had been built, as well as a city wall with gates. When Georg, Duke of Brunswick-Lüneburg, the grandfather of the present duke and elector, moved his residence to Hanover in 1636, the city became associated with power, and it was Duke Georg who started the so-called House of Hanover, laying the foundation for Leineschloss, where Händel was now heading.

Händel walked towards the River Leine, leaving behind the old town with its narrow and sinuous streets. He remembered the innkeeper's astonished face when he had asked for directions to the palace, and smiled to himself.

'I have a message to bring,' Händel had said with an air of seriousness. Telemann's advice was precious. *Do not give too much information, but do not lie. Just say the minimum necessary without making them suspicious. Don't show off. Don't make yourself a target.*

After handing over the letter of introduction, he was placed in a very small, empty room. Soon after, an old priest came in.

'Are you Georg Friederich Händel?' he asked in German.

Händel stood up, and said, 'Yes, Father, I am.'

'I thought so.' He smiled, extending his hand. 'My name is Steffani, Agostino Steffani. I am – or, was – the Kapellmeister. Do sit down, Mr Händel.'

Händel sat down, impressed. He had not expected to be greeted by the composer himself. *So this is the famous Steffani.* The old composer-priest was very friendly.

'Did you come from Halle?'

'Yes. I arrived yesterday.'

'I heard about you from Queen Sophia Charlotte, in Berlin.'

'Oh...' Händel did not know what to say. *Is he aware of me refusing the offer?*

'Unfortunately the dowager duchess is not here. She is in Herrenhausen, but I dispatched a messenger already. She will be very happy to see you. So, how is the queen? Did you see her recently?'

'I saw her last summer, Father.'

Steffani lowered his voice and asked, 'Are you here to look for a post?'

'No, Father.' Händel did not say more than that.

'Oh, that's good. I am asking you this because the elector is not engaging musicians at the moment, and Farinel knows it.'

'Is Farinel the Kapellmeister?'

'No, he is the Konzertmeister. There is no more Kapellmeister. I was,

but I am now engaged in diplomacy and do not really have time for music.'
'Why are you not Kapellmeister anymore, may I ask?' Händel immediately regretted the question. It was too personal.
'Well, for several reasons.' Steffani did not look upset. 'To make a long story short, it is not a good time to spend money on music, so the elector is keeping the opera house shut.'
'Oh...'
'So if there is no opera to be produced, there is no need for a Kapellmeister. A Konzertmeister would be enough to keep an orchestra.'
'I see.'
'And I am on my way to Düsseldorf.'
'Are you leaving?' asked Händel in a desperate tone. 'But I have so much to ask you, and...and...'
'And you want to see my scores?' Steffani smiled.
Händel regretted being so quick. He lowered his head and whispered, 'If you allow me, of course.'
Steffani laughed. 'Let's get another matter sorted out first. Where are you staying?'
'At the coaching inn.'
'Right. Go back there and wait. I think you will be invited to stay here. Actually, don't just wait. Visit the churches and see the organs. You might be able to play, if you are lucky. Did you see the Marktkirche?'

Händel did not have to wait long. In the afternoon of the same day, Steffani himself visited Händel. The innkeeper led the priest to Händel's room, intrigued. Steffani spoke in French to greet the young organist. The innkeeper went down to fetch two glasses of port as requested, muttering, 'I am certain he is a nobleman in disguise. I was right. He is not just an organist...'
Händel smiled at the innkeeper as he took the tray from him and closed the door.
'I came here because I am leaving tomorrow morning. A coach will be sent for you then from the palace,' Steffani continued in French.
'Really?'
'Yes. I think you will be taken to Herrenhausen first. It is not far. It will take less than an hour to reach there. It's the summer court residence, and Dowager Duchess Sophia spends most of her time there.' Steffani paused and looked at Händel. 'Now, this is special treatment, you should know. It's because Queen Sophia Charlotte praised you so much that you are already treated as a guest. But do not forget to thank the dowager duchess for this invitation to Herrenhausen. It's very important. She's made lots of improvements to the palace, and she is very proud and fond of it. She was very much inspired by the palace of Versailles and its gardens.'

'Versailles? Did she go there?'
'Yes, twice. Try to remember what I said, can you?'
'I will not forget it, Maestro Steffani.'
'You have been to Berlin, and, like there, it is quite informal here, though it is more intellectual. Still, you should keep yourself quite formal as a sign of respect, and don't ask any questions unless you are given permission to do so.'
'Yes, Father.'
'You will see Electoral Prince Georg, the son of the elector. He is more interested in music than his father. He is not much older than you, and he will be pleased to meet you. As for the scores, ask Leibniz, the librarian.'
'Leibniz?'
'Yes, Gottfried Leibniz.'
Händel tried to brand his name to his brain. It was crucial to see Steffani's scores.
'You will see Ortensio Mauro as well, a very old court poet. He wrote all the libretti for my operas. And you will see Farinel, the Konzertmeister. He is French.'
'How about the musicians?'
'There are many French musicians there, and some Italians.'

At Herrenhausen, Duchess Sophia was busy in her favourite activity: corresponding. She was writing to her daughter in Berlin, to report about Händel's visit.

> Herrenhausen, June 1703
>
> My dearest daughter,
>
> Mr Händel came to see us on his way to Hamburg. As you described him, he is a virtuoso. We enjoyed very much hearing him play the harpsichord. Yesterday morning, we took him to the chapel so he could play the organ.
>
> I never enjoyed so much. Even your brother Georg Ludwig was impressed. As for Georg August, he is delighted.
>
> This young man is also very good-

> *looking, and I am sure he will be successful in Hamburg, both in music and in love!*

    Though the dowager duchess was happy at the surprising visit of an attractive young virtuoso, her heart was not at peace. Since the marriage of her daughter seventeen years before, it had not been the same family anymore. After returning from the wedding celebrations, her husband had announced his decision to adopt the principle of primogeniture, replacing ultimogeniture. Even if by doing this the family estate was preserved, the family was nevertheless being torn apart. Her second and fourth sons refused to accept any terms, and they both died on the battlefield, one of the many triggered by the War of the Spanish Succession. They died feeling denied of their rights, and Sophia knew it. Before leaving for the battle, they both had said to her, that it was better to die than being stripped and humiliated. Her third son, Maximilian Wilhelm, had plotted to set primogeniture aside, and this led to a serious problem in her marriage, as her husband suspected her of helping her favourite son against him. Max had been exiled after the plot was foiled, and he later converted to Roman Catholicism. For Sophia, who was a devout Lutheran, it was a terrible blow. Her son was determined to hurt, and he knew where it hurt most. Right now, her fifth son, Christian Heinrich, was getting ready for one of many battles to come. Her husband had died five years earlier, just before becoming an elector. Her eldest son, Georg Ludwig, succeeding his father, duly became elector, but he also had inherited the family conflict. His marriage had ended in disaster, and it was causing tension between him and his two children especially his son Georg August. The only consolation was that her sixth and last son, Ernst August, did not show any opposition to the primogeniture and was on good terms with his eldest brother.

    She got up from the writing desk and went to the window overlooking the Great Garden. She still remembered her children playing there. Hide-and-seek behind the statues, improvised races in the walkways – it was a place filled with laughter. In the hot summer days they spent hours in the grotto, with dips in the pond with the cascade. The happy days with all her children were gone. Now the once big family was reduced to her, her eldest son with his two children, and her youngest son. Georg Ludwig was divorced and becoming increasingly isolated. He kept a mistress but refused to remarry. He was still deeply scarred from the traumatising divorce, and he busied himself administrating to forget his bloodstained marriage. His estranged wife's name was never mentioned at court, nor was the name of her murdered lover. Still, it was there in the memory of everyone in the household like a dark cloud refusing to dissipate. Sophia's youngest son, Ernst August, now nearly thirty, showed no inclination for marriage. Her two grandchildren brought her joy, but they were now old enough to get married themselves. Her grandson Georg August's possible marriage to Hedvig Sophia of Sweden came to naught.

'Maybe I should move to England and wait to be the queen,' she whispered.

In 1701, when the Act of Settlement passed in Great Britain, she became heir to the crown, making her Queen Anne's successor. She was now seventy-three, much older than Queen Anne but still very healthy. However, she realised that she was not ready to leave her beloved Herrenhausen behind to cross the channel. The geometrical patterns on the ground made with lawns, hedges, various plants and flowers were beautiful, and the orange trees in large pots, out of the greenhouse during the summer, were placed around the central basin. Leibniz was suggesting they transform the basin into a fountain, and the idea was very attractive to her.

After his visit to the court of Hanover, Händel was going towards the stagecoach to Hamburg when he saw a young woman asking around. People were shaking their heads. He heard the woman's voice with its strong French accent.

'Ambur? Ambur?'

He smiled and asked in French, 'Are you looking for the stagecoach for Hamburg, madam?'

The woman turned, surprised but pleased. 'Oh, thank you. Yes. I am going to Ambur. Where is it?'

'Follow me, please, I am going to Hamburg too.' Händel offered the woman his arm, which she took with a smile.

The trip was entertaining and Händel was glad to have company. She was a singer. She had worked for a while in Hanover and was going to Hamburg to try her luck.

She sighed. 'I had no problem at the court. Everybody speaks French. But as soon as you are out, you have problems if you don't speak German…'

'I was there. I did not see you.'

'Oh really? Well, I was in Brunswick to see if I could stay there…Wait, were you at the court? Are you a musician?'

'I am an organist and a keyboard player,' said Händel, 'So, tell me, why are you leaving?'

'Why am I leaving? The war, Monsieur, the war!' She rolled her eyes, twitching her lips. Händel had heard vaguely of the war spreading in Europe and knew that Bavaria was allied with France against Prussia. 'The elector is dismissing his orchestra and many of the singers to reduce the cost. I am one of the last of the singers to leave.'

'How many were you?'

'I don't know. I never counted one by one, and there were always people arriving and leaving. But the elector always wanted to keep an orchestra and a composer. Now all that is gone, thanks to this damn war. You did not see the singers there?'

'Not really. I mainly played the harpsichord. I did not see Mr Farinel. He was ill. I played with some of the orchestra members.'

'Oh, that unhappy Mr Farinel. It's not funny to be married and have one's wife away with a powerful lover…' She realised Händel was staring at her. 'Sorry, just gossip.' She then changed the subject. 'Your French is good. Where are you from?'

'Halle.'

'Where is that?'

'Not far from Leipzig.'

'I see. So you speak German, of course, French, and?'

'Latin. More written than spoken.'

'You are a savant, Monsieur. I think I'll have to learn German seriously if I stay in Ambur'

'Why?'

'Why? You don't know? There is no court in Ambur. Nobody speaks French there!'

'Oh…'

She laughed. She was more mature than Händel thought. She was different from German women. She was definitely more talkative, and this air of lightness was something he found very refreshing.

'Do you know anything about Hamburg?' asked Händel.

'No. I've never been there. I have the recommendation from Monsignor Steffani, but that's all. God, he is a nice man.' She crossed herself discreetly and then raised her head. 'Did you see Monsignor Steffani?'

'Yes, I did.'

'I like him a lot. He is a nice man, really nice.'

'I agree.'

'You know, you are lucky you are not a singer.'

'Why?'

'Why? I tell you, it is a tough competition, you know, Monsieur? If you were a singer, I would scratch your face so you could not present yourself to the opera house before me!' She showed her long and polished nails. Seeing Händel astonished, she laughed. 'I will have a small nap, Monsieur, if you don't mind.'

'Not at all.'

'I regret that I cannot stay in Hanover. They liked me. Do you know why?'

'Because you are a good singer, I suppose.'

She ignored the compliment. 'Because I am not that chatty for a French girl, Monsieur.'

'Really?'

'In fact, I am chatty, but I know how to control myself. You know, we love to talk.'

'Can I ask you one more question before your nap?'

'Yes.'

'What is your name?'

She looked at him. 'Veronica. Well, my real name is Sophie, but the duchess is Sophia, so I thought I'd better change. Therefore I am Veronica. It is better if my name sounds Italian.'

The sunlight was on her side, and Händel saw the colour of her eyes – purple. She soon fell asleep, leaning her head on the corner.

Händel helped her get off the stagecoach, offering his hand, which she took gladly.

'Merci, Monsieur.' She smiled.

'You are welcome.'

'Well, I'll say goodbye to you. We may see each other again. Good luck.'

'Thank you. Goodbye, Violeta.'

'Veronica.'

In Berlin, Sophia Charlotte was perplexed. Her mother's letter, just received, was cheerful but she knew her mother's heart, and she tried to lighten her mood as much as possible with her reply. And, there was another issue. She was now considering how to bring up the prospect of marrying her niece, Sophia Dorothea, the daughter of her elder brother, to her own son Frederick William. She secretly hoped for her protégée, Caroline of Ansbach, to be married to her nephew Georg August, but the negotiation with Archduke Charles of Austria was progressing steadily. She felt powerless. Who could refuse such a match? She would be Archduchess of Austria! Still, the more she thought about it, the more convinced she was that Caroline was the one for her nephew. She did not wish to see another disastrous marriage like that of her brother Georg Ludwig.

The marriage of Georg Ludwig and Sophia Dorothea of Celle had started well. She was young and beautiful, delighted at her rise in the world, and he fell in love with her. However, she was immature, just sixteen when she married the future elector, and too spoilt and undisciplined to realise what she was getting herself into. The dowager duchess was kind and helpful, and did what she could to accommodate the young bride in life at court. Soon the young bride, by then a mother, was complaining that her husband was indifferent to her. Not only was her husband busy with his duties to the house and loaded with responsibilities, but he was also commander of the Hanoverian forces. For nearly two years he was very much absent, leaving the young wife with a baby. But this was not the main problem. She was too different in interests to make friends with anyone, including her husband. She was not intellectual, making her unable to hold a nice conversation or discuss literature or art. And she was naive enough not to realise the task of her position. The only thing she could do was dress to kill or outshine, and the more she did, the more she made herself isolated.

Caroline of Ansbach was beautiful and intellectual. She loved the company of learned men and women, and she was intelligent enough to know her position, what she should or shouldn't do. She was discreet and never sought to outshine. She was a devout Lutheran, and though orphaned young with just a small fortune, she was of excellent lineage.

The queen sighed. She would never manipulate her protégée to sway her choice of husband. It was up to Caroline herself. Still, she believed that God would decide for the best.

Chapter 4 : First step: Hamburg (1703 – 1704)

Hamburg, July 1703

Out of the coach, Händel was now alone in Hamburg. He could not stop feeling lonely. He thought of Telemann.

'When you first arrive in a city you do not know, just take a room for the first few days in the stagecoach inn where you arrive,' Telemann had told him. 'Then, the first thing to ask is the location of the main church of the city.'

'Church?' Händel had inquired.

'Of course, the church. You wouldn't ask the inn people where a better inn is in the town, would you? You ask for the church, because that is the most normal thing to ask. You get to the church and go around to see. Everything important is around the church, like in Halle or Leipzig.'

'But I'll know nobody there,' Händel, still uncertain, had said timidly.

'I knew nobody in Halle,' Telemann had said, giving Händel a reassuring, brotherly smile.

Remembering those conversations, Händel felt better. Breathing in deeply, he smiled to himself and pushed away the worries.

The next morning, Händel went straight to the main church. Inside, looking up at the organ, he felt his fingers itching. He looked around. *No, I cannot.* There were worshippers and there was no way he could sneak into the organ loft. He went to another church, to realise that it was the same situation. *Maybe one a little further from the city centre*, he thought. He crossed the river Elbe and saw the top of a church tower, and walked towards it. The heat did not bother him.

Händel was ready to climb the stairs leading to the organ loft of St Maria-Magdalena-Kirche. It was a hot summer afternoon, and the church was deserted. This was not one of the main churches, so there was a good chance he would be unnoticed.

'Are you going to the organ loft?' a voice said behind him. *Oh no! I am caught.* Turning around, Händel saw a young man staring at him. His heavy eyelids made his big eyes look bigger and quite imposing.

'Um, yes, if it is possible.' *I lost my opportunity.*

'Oh, that's all right. I thought you were going to take away my chance to play,' said the young man. He smiled. 'We can share, right?'

Relieved, Händel just nodded.

'Are you a player?' the young man asked casually.
'Yes, I am, and I cannot wait to see the organ here.'
'Let's go then.' The young man was dressed nicely and wore a small, discreet wig.

Händel felt slightly intimidated by the young man's confidence, but following Telemann's advice, he forced himself to talk rather than let silence settle in. 'Are you from Hamburg, sir?'
'I am, born and bred here. And you?'
'I am from Halle.'
'Looking for a job?'
'Um, yes, of sorts.'
They were now facing the keyboards with many stops above, all surrounded by pipes of different sizes. They looked around.
'So what do you think?' asked the young man.
'Nice. Interesting.' Händel looked around to locate the bellows.
'Are you a church organist?'
'I was.'
'Where?'
'The Domkirche in Halle.' Händel saw that the young man was not really listening.
'It will be a pity to leave here without playing such a thing,' said the young man. 'I need someone to blow the bellows.'
'Oh, I can do it.'
Shocked, the young man looked at Händel. 'You do NOT do that. Never offer to do such a thing if you want to be respected.'
Händel just stared at the young man.
'What's your name?' he asked with a hint of contempt.
'Händel, Georg Friederich Händel.'
The young man looked at Händel from head to foot. 'Händel, you ask someone to do that. Never do it yourself. It's not for you, or me, to blow the bellows. We are players. Stay here. I'll see if I can get help.'
He came back quickly smiling. 'Found a boy to do the job. We don't need two strong men just to try the organ, do we? May I?' Impatient, he nearly shoved Händel aside and sat in front of the keyboards.
Händel listened to the music the young man was playing, quite different from what he was used to playing and hearing. Then the sound faded away. A young boy poked his head from behind the rows of pipes.
'You told me for just a bit. It's over, sir.'
Händel quickly put some coins in the boy's hands. 'It's for a bit more.' The boy returned to the bellows.
'Thank you, Händel. Now, your turn.'
Händel decided to improvise a fugue on a melody from the music his companion had just played. He felt the young man's gaze as he played. He

could not see his companion's eyes getting wider and wider, and his mouth open. As the sound began to fade away again, the young man quickly went to the boy to give him more money. Händel looked up and nodded, smiling. He did not smile back. When Händel finished, the young man motioned for him to follow in silence, making Händel slightly worried. He wondered if he had done something wrong. Out of the church, the young man turned to face Händel. He extended his hand.

'My name is Mattheson. Johann Mattheson. Welcome to Hamburg.' His big smile made Händel relax at once. 'Let's have a drink. I am thirsty, aren't you?' Mattheson asked casually.

Settled in a quiet corner of a tavern, Mattheson took a watch from his pocket. 'I have half an hour to spare.'

Only after a few minutes of casual talk did Händel dare to ask a few questions to Mattheson. 'Are you an organist? In which church?'

'No, I am not an organist. I play the organ, but I don't hold any post. I am a law student and musician at the same time.'

'You too? The law?' Händel stared at Mattheson.

'Who is the other one, then?' asked Mattheson.

'Me and Telemann. Well, I think I will never go back to university…'

'And we all love music.'

'More than law,' Händel said in a whisper, lowering his head. He felt guilty of abandoning his study. He felt he was betraying his father, and especially his mother who made money so he could enrol.

As they carried on talking, Mattheson forgot the time. Händel noticed the people around them drinking quite heavily.

Johann Mattheson came back home quite late. He found a note from his mother asking him why he had not turned up for supper. He raised his eyes to the ceiling. He had forgotten completely. He and Händel had eaten and drunk quite a lot. Even feeling tipsy, he was still keen to write in his diary. The moon was shining. He did not need to light a candle.

> 9 July 1703
> Met a young man by the name of Händel. Played organ together at St Maria-Magdalena-Kirche. I've never seen such a virtuoso in my life. He is just incredible at the keyboard. He wants to learn opera, and I will help him. I am taking him under my wing.

Mattheson was up quite early next morning. He went straight to his parents' house after telling his maid that he would not need his meals today, any of them.

'Mother, I am so sorry for yesterday.' He took his mother in his arms to kiss her on the cheek.

'What happened? I hope it was not something bad.' She looked up, concerned.

'Oh no. Not at all. I was so excited that I completely forgot about supper. I am sorry.'

'If you're telling me that, it is not a woman, I suppose.' She winked.

A young girl poked her head out from the dining room. 'Mama, Johann, don't stay there. Come in and let's eat. I'm hungry.' The mother and son looked at each other, smiled, and went in.

'I cannot stay long. I came to apologise for last night and to have breakfast with you. Then I'll be gone.'

'So the excitement continues,' his mother said.

'Yes, it does. Where is father?'

'Neuwerk. He will be back tomorrow.'

'I must go.' Mattheson got up.

'You didn't eat, Johann,' said his sister.

'I think I will eat with—'

'With your excitement?' his mother said. 'What's the name?'

'Händel. He is from Halle.'

'Is he handsome?' interrupted his sister.

'Catarina,' he said, frowning at his little sister.

'A young man, I suppose,' said his mother.

'Yes, Mother. I'll bring him shortly. You'll like him.'

'Is he handsome?' his sister asked again.

He got up to go, turned back, and said, 'Yes, he is handsome, if you don't mind the birthmark on his cheek. And he is tall.'

Catarina beamed.

'You need a better lodging, Händel,' said Mattheson, looking around.

'I know. Do you know anywhere?' He meant anywhere not too expensive but did not dare say that.

'I'll ask my mother. She'll know. Leave it to me. Now, today . . .'

'Yes?' Händel said eagerly, ready to go.

'We shall visit more churches,' said Mattheson, well organised and meticulous. Though deeply impressed by Händel's ability, he wanted to know more about his background in order to decide whether to treat him as an equal or not. He wanted to do this discreetly and casually. He was far from imagining that this attitude would be the cause of a short-lasting friendship.

'Which one?' Händel asked, slightly disappointed. By now he would have loved to see the opera house. Proud and independent, he was still very young and inexperienced. He knew nobody in this city. Though he did not feel as much warmth as he had toward Telemann, this encounter with Mattheson was a real blessing. Watching his new friend consult his own list of churches, Händel decided to keep himself as obedient as possible.

Händel was discovering the city of Hamburg. He listened to Mattheson, a proud citizen of this independent city-state, as he displayed his knowledge of the city's fascinating history. The city was still one of the Hanseatic cities, with Lübeck and Bremen, clinging stubbornly to past glory and maintaining the freedom of trade. Händel felt fortunate to have such a passionate guide. The wealth of the city was based on trade and the shipbuilding industry, as it was the foremost port in the Germanic states. As a major port and trading centre, Hamburg was open to the international community, in contrast to the more inward-looking German courts, where foreign visitors were often regarded as honoured intruders.

'Oh, so I was an honoured intruder in the Berlin court?' Händel said, surprised.

Mattheson stopped to stare at Händel. 'Were you in Berlin?'

'Yes. Why?'

'How did you manage to be received?'

'Well, my late father was the court physician.' Händel tried to be as casual as possible.

'Oh, I see.' Mattheson looked away. He was now burning with questions, but his pride stopped him from asking them.

Händel soon realised that Mattheson had no idea what a princely court was like, with its protocol and code of conduct. This was the result of Hamburg being free from any subjection to electoral or princely control. The rich merchants, both native and foreign, and the diplomats made the city a curious mixture of politeness and power games. The city was a dynamic cultural and diplomatic centre. This situation did not afford the church the prestige of being indispensable.

For days, they visited churches, trying the organs and walking around. Händel was getting to know the city. Mattheson did not mention the opera house once. Händel just waited.

'I will take you this evening to the house of my father's friend. They are great music lovers, and there will be a concert. I will introduce you to them,' said Mattheson, looking at his watch.

'Thank you, Mattheson. Do I have enough time to get changed?'

That was the correct thing to ask. Satisfied, Mattheson replied, 'I'm glad you are learning. Remind me to finish early today, get changed and then come to join me. We shall go together.'

Händel clenched his jaws and felt a twitch in his temple. *Learning what? I know all that!* 'Who will be there? Any prince or elector?' Händel asked innocently, looking excited.

'No. Just a few local music lovers. Why do you ask?'

'To not make mistakes. There are strict rules regarding how to call on them, as you know,' Händel replied with an air of concern.

'Of course.' Mattheson did not look at Händel, who was beaming.
Händel changed into his best summer suit. He silently thanked his mother, who had insisted on getting him a set for the hot weather. The pale blue matched his eyes, and the silver trimming made the suit look fresh. Before going to join Mattheson, Händel quickly wrote a letter to Telemann.

> Dear Teleman,
>
> I am getting to know Hamburg, which is a fascinating city, all thanks to Mattheson. I know I owe a lot to him, and he is kind and generous, but sometimes he makes me feel I am his valet. I have to do what he tells me to do, and I still have not visited the opera house. And he has no sense of humour at all. I miss you.

They arrived together at the house in the city centre. The rich merchant received them with open arms.
'Here, Mattheson! Do come in, Maestro. Oh, this is your protégé you were talking about. Do come in. Welcome to Hamburg and to my house.' Johann Wilhelm Sbuelen was middle-aged, fat and jolly.
Mattheson went to greet Sbuelen's wife and daughter. The fat merchant was talking to Händel.
'So, what do you think of Hamburg, sir?'
'Splendid, as is your house, sir.'
The merchant laughed loudly. 'We have a few French guests this evening.' He lowered his voice. 'Their king, Louis XIV, is not nice with us Jews, you know.'
Händel was introduced to an old French couple, but before they could talk of anything, he was dragged away by Mattheson.
'Come, Händel, let me introduce you to Mrs Sbuelen and her daughter Esther. Were you speaking in French?'
'Yes. They are French.'
Händel was led to meet Mrs Sbuelen and noticed a very nice harpsichord behind her. Like a fly attracted to the light, he walked slowly towards the instrument, only to be stopped by a hand on his arm.
Mattheson laughed. 'You can have a go later, Händel. Yes, it is a very nice one.'
Nobody noticed the gaze of Esther Sbuelen directed to Händel except

her mother who frowned.

'Mattheson!' a voice called out. Mattheson and Händel turned to see a tall man, impeccably dressed.

'John! Here you are. I was looking for you. Come, Händel, you have to meet Mr Wych.'

As a free city, Hamburg attracted attention as a cultural and diplomatic centre. John Wych was one of numerous diplomats. As an English resident in Hamburg, his duty was to report back anything happening on the continent. As the War of the Spanish Succession was in full spate and seemed to be dragging on, his responsibilities were increasing. Still, in a free city with no court, he could be relatively relaxed and enjoy his love of music.

The Wych family proved to be more than beneficial to Händel, and again, Händel could not stop acknowledging Mattheson's generosity. By becoming a regular at the house concerts of the Wych family, Händel enlarged the number of his acquaintances in the city and obtained a few music teaching jobs. The citizens of Hamburg were heavy drinkers; and not only the tavern-going people. Even in those elegant house concerts, the drinks were abundantly consumed, and that habit was quickly adopted by the foreigners visiting or coming to live there.

Then Mattheson got busy working for John Wych. The latter found it useful to have a friend helping sometimes in translation, or about law. Mattheson, in exchange, got information about Britain's political situation but was more interested in the state of music. That meant free time for Händel. By now his mind was fixated on what he had not seen yet. He could not wait any longer to see the opera house.

A splendid opera house was built in 1677 at the Gänsemarkt Square, and the city supported an opera company founded in 1678 by a group of German musicians, including Adam Strungk and Johann Theile, against a certain amount of opposition from Hamburg's religious authorities. The theatre at Gänsemarkt produced a uniquely eclectic style of opera. French taste introduced elements of ballet and spectacle, and the powerful impression of Venetian lyric theatre conditioned the handling of texts and subject matter. The stage, larger than those in most other European theatres of the day, was capable of immense perspective effects. Scenic effects and spectacular scenes had become an expected part of the theatrical experience in Hamburg.

Reinhard Keiser was satisfied. He had been made director of the Hamburg opera house, the Gänsemarkt Theatre, keeping the post of chief composer as well. He sat in his new office, looking around and thinking how to improve the space. This promotion increased his salary considerably, making his lifestyle easier to maintain. And he had an idea. He'd always wanted the theatre to be open to the public – all the public, not just the privileged. Instead of putting seats in only the best places, he intended to increase the space open to public access, providing seats that would have a restricted view but would be cheaper. He wanted his theatre to be vibrant, bursting with people enjoying opera. He was not worried about the city council. They would not oppose a plan to increase the income. The problem was with the church. They would argue that it would 'contaminate' more people, taking money from the less privileged. Of course, if the less privileged spent money on entertainment, less money would go to the church. He decided to not think about it. *I will deal with it when the problem becomes a reality. What is the point of worrying now?* He got up, walked to the cupboard, and opened its doors. It was quite wide and fitted with shelves. *Perfect, I can keep some of my wigs here, and maybe a suit.* He saw his valet coming in with a glass of port on a silver tray. Keiser noticed the worn shoes his employee was wearing and looked down at his own shoes, impeccably polished and shiny like a mirror. *Maybe he needs a new pair of shoes.*

'It is time for rehearsal, sir,' the valet said.

Händel walked up the stairs to the front door. He looked up and pushed the door and found no resistance. He went inside, looked around and was speechless. The foyer was splendid. It reflected the wealth of the city. He heard music coming from far inside the theatre and made his way towards the sound. There, the musicians were rehearsing. He went straight to the orchestra pit. One of the front violinists saw Händel and looked at the conductor.

'Oh, is it time to go?' The conductor turned toward Händel. 'Oh, you're not my valet.' And he faced the orchestra again to resume rehearsing.

Händel, realising that he was not going to be pushed out, decided to stay for a while. The music played was quite different from what he had heard before. It was sometimes light, sometimes very dramatic. He sat on the corner and just listened, fascinated. He saw a man who looked like a servant approach the conductor and whisper. The rehearsal was over.

As he walked out of the theatre, a voice called to him.

'Is that you, Monsieur?'

He turned and recognised the French woman. 'Violeta!'

'Veronica,' she said, slightly irritated.

'I am sorry. It's because of your eyes…'

She stopped and laughed. 'Oh, in that case, I forgive you. You know what?'

'What, Ve-ro-ni-ca?'

'I don't know your name.'

'Georg. Georg Friederich Händel.'

'Georg, were you in the theatre?'
'Yes, I just saw the rehearsal. Are you working here?'
'Yes. I got the post straight away. I am lucky.'
'Tell me, who engaged you?'
'Oh, it's the director, Mr Keiser.'
'Is he nice?'
'Yes, he is, but his clothing is nicer. He is always dressed impeccably, and he has his own valet following him everywhere. Isn't it incredible?' She laughed.

Back in his lodging, Händel found a note from Mattheson, an invitation for a Sunday lunch in his family house. He felt the irritation and frustration towards Mattheson melt at once. He felt warmth in his heart.

'Yes, he is a nice man, he is a friend,' Händel whispered to himself, holding the note against his chest.

'Mother, this is my friend Georg Friederich Händel.'
A distinguished middle-aged woman greeted him with a friendly smile.
'My son has talked about you. Do sit down, please. We're waiting for my husband to come back home.'
'I thank you for your kind invitation, madam.'
'We were waiting for Johann to bring you here. He's talked a lot about you. Oh, this is my daughter Catarina. Catarina, this is Mr Händel, your brother's friend.'

A very young woman stood in front of him, smiling, and greeted Händel. 'I am happy to meet you, Mr Händel. My brother talked a lot about what you can do with music, but we had no idea how you looked.' She grinned, showing her wittiness.

Händel did not know what to say.
'Well, your brother said he is tall and good looking, and it is true, don't you think, Catarina?' her mother said.
'Well, Mother, I was imagining someone like…' she looked Händel up and down, making her mother frown, Mattheson roll his eyes, and Händel look down.
'Catarina, you should not-' Mrs Mattheson did not finish when the father came in, to the young guest's relief.

Soon they were led to the dining room. The food was excellent and the wine abundant, all served with ease. It was obvious that the family was wealthy.

'So, Mr Händel, what do you think of the wine?' the father asked.
'Nice. Is it French, sir?'
'Yes, indeed!' Mr Mattheson raised his eyebrows. 'Do you know about wine? You are young, though.'
'My late father sold wine.'

'Was he a wine merchant?'

'No, sir, he was a surgeon.'

Mattheson laughed. 'Explain, Händel. I did not know about that!'

This was a delicate moment. Händel quickly realised that he would be judged. He felt his hands getting moist. Concealing his nervousness, he talked casually. 'Well, my father was physician at the courts of Brandenburg and Weissenfels.'

'Brandenburg,' Mattheson repeated, quite impressed.

'Yes, and he was given the licence by Elector Frederick to sell wine from the tavern, which formed part of our house.'

'He must have been a very good physician,' said the father.

'So I practically grew up in a tavern, bathed in wine.'

There was silence. Mrs Mattheson looked puzzled, and her husband's glass stopped just in front of his mouth. Then Catarina burst into laughter.

'Oh my God. You are all so slow. He is joking!'

They all laughed. The father looked satisfied about Händel's family and renewed the invitation.

'Come back, Mr Händel. You are welcome anytime here.'

'I thank you for your generosity, Mr Mattheson.'

Being accepted in the Mattheson family was quite comforting for Händel. He still missed his family. In Catarina, he could see his little sisters. And the invitations provided him excellent, free meals. His friendship with Mattheson was going well, and they enjoyed going out and making music together.

'Händel, have you ever heard of Buxtehude, the organist?' Mattheson asked enthusiastically. It was late July 1703.

'The name is not familiar to me… Where?'

'In Lübeck.'

'Oh, Lübeck. Well, yes, I think my teacher mentioned him as a virtuoso.'

'Oh, who was your teacher?'

'Zachow.'

'Really! Lucky you.'

'I am, and he is a kind and generous man. He taught me a lot.'

'Right. Let's go back to Buxtehude. The organ of the Marienkirche is superb, and the post is free now.'

'Is he dead?'

'No. He is looking for a successor. By the way, it is not just one, there are two organs in that church.'

'My God.' Händel's eyes were widening.

'Yes, how exciting is that? And it is a very good post, with generous salaries.'

'I see . . . How do you know that the post is free?'
'My connection.' Mattheson said no more. 'So, what do you think?'
'About what?'
'The post, of course.'
'I would love to try the organs, both of them . . .' said Händel dreamily.
'But you are not interested in the post.'
'How about you, Mattheson?'
'I do not see myself buried in that post and composing only church music. I need opera!'
'But still, we could go there and try the organs . . . Now that you've told me about them, I really want to try.' Händel was already itching.

Soon Händel and Mattheson found themselves on the stagecoach to Lübeck. It was the early morning of 30 July 1703. The weather was pleasant. The torrential rain the day before had cooled down the heavy, hot air. Now the sun was out and the air dry. Though it was a longer distance than between Halle and Leipzig, the roads were much wider and in better condition.

'It's slow, isn't it?' said Mattheson.
'What? The fugue?' Händel lifted his head from a scratch of paper where he was scribbling a few notes.
'No, I'm talking about the coach. It is slow, with only four horses.'
'Can you put more than four?'
'Of course. Six, even eight.'
Händel's jaw dropped. He'd never seen a coach pulled by six horses.
'Well, in England, it is quite common,' said Mattheson matter-of-factly.
'Really? Are they that rich?'
'No, there is another reason.'
'Are they always late?'
Mattheson laughed. 'It is to escape the bandits. They are everywhere.' And he stared hard at the pigeon-seller sitting in front of them.

The man smiled, revealing his missing teeth. 'I am not a bandit,' the man said.
'You never know,' Mattheson insisted.
'I'm not. Do I look like a bandit?'
'That's the point.'
The man did not know how to react.
'I can imagine you threatening people with your killer pigeons!' Handel said.
The two young travellers burst into laughter.

Dietrich Buxtehude was an old man looking forward to retirement. He had been working as an organist and composer at Marienkirche for twenty-five years. As the city council of Lübeck gave him considerable freedom, allowing him to travel and teach, and to develop his skill as a virtuoso organist, he had been widely known throughout Germany. Though he enjoyed greatly the culturally liberal atmosphere of this Hanseatic city, he started to feel the weight of his age. He was not worried about finding a successor, as the post was one of the most coveted in the land. In fact, the candidates flocked in, but most of them were easily rejected, as he wanted someone of his level, if not better. Then there was another condition, that the successor would marry the daughter of the predecessor.

Though renowned, Händel and Mattheson found a humble and friendly old man. Rather short and plump, and getting slow due to his age, he was a peaceful man, always smiling. He showed the two young men the church and the two organs. After a short interview, he left them free to try the two organs.

'I will lock the doors so nobody can enter the church while you are here. I will come back later to let you out, and then you shall stay for supper. Is that all right?'

The two young men looked at each other. Mattheson said, 'That is very kind of you, Master Buxtehude. We were not expecting this. Thank you.'

The supper was not the only surprise.

The organist's lodging was exactly like its inhabitant: simple but comfortable and welcoming. As the two young men sat, a woman entered, bringing the food. She looked to be in her early thirties.

'Here is the food, and my daughter!' Buxtehude said merrily.

The woman glanced quickly at the two young men, and looked down shyly.

'This is my daughter Margreta. Margreta, this is Mr Mattheson from Hamburg, and this is Mr Händel from Halle.'

The woman nodded, still looking down. The two young men nodded to her in return, and saw her retire quickly to the kitchen. She was not ugly, but for the two young men, she looked just boring. Buxtehude lowered his voice and said, 'Do not worry. I think she was surprised to see two candidates at once.' He smiled. 'It is unfortunate that she is bound to this rule, but she accepts it with dignity. I think she will be happy with either of you. She is a good woman.'

The two men looked at each other, puzzled. The old man continued, 'Yes, she is a good woman. Very discreet. She will be a good wife, if you decide, of course.'

Händel stopped eating.

Buxtehude continued, 'As you may know, I did the same. My late wife was the daughter of my predecessor. It is the rule, and I was not unhappy.' He raised his glass and had a sip. 'But, can you imagine, how embarrassed she must feel now. She has to choose one of you? Of course she cannot do it in front of you!' Buxtehude laughed merrily, feeling that his daughter's marriage was nearly secured.

Händel tried to say something but could not. He just smiled stiffly and looked at his friend, who looked calm, but rather pale. Now the food tasted like sand. He quickly reached the glass to let the wine push the food down. The wine tasted like vinegar. Händel felt like a cornered dog. *What shall I do? If I knew before...* Then he felt Mattheson's elbow in his ribs.

'Can you pass me the bread, please?' Mattheson addressed Händel.

As he reached the bread basket and leaned towards Mattheson to pass it, he heard his friend whisper, 'Keep talking!'

'What?' Händel whispered back quickly.

'Anything!'

'Umm...'

'Master Buxtehude, do you ever use the two organs at the same time?' Mattheson asked in a most relaxed way.

The conversation turned to music-making, and the two young visitors kept asking Buxtehude about his music and travels he had made. The virtuoso organist seemed to enjoy talking, while Händel and Mattheson pretended to be jolly. The young men carefully diverted the conversation to music or travel when it was in danger of heading towards marriage, or women.

Buxtehude was satisfied to see both young men's passion for organ. But he needed to judge their skill by himself.

'I let you enjoy the organ today. Now, I would like to test you both. It is late. Come back tomorrow morning,' said the organist. He made it a mission for his retirement to find the best of the best successor. He did not realise yet that to combine it with the marriage of his daughter would be not so easy.

Händel and Mattheson were on their way back to the inn. They were in a state of shock. They could not remember the food they'd had. In fact they were incapable, both of them, of even remembering whether it was a cold or hot meal. They looked uncomfortable. It was Händel who broke the silence.

'Oh my God. Can you imagine?'

'No, I cannot,' said Mattheson dryly.

'Did you know about it?'

'If I had, I would have been prepared.'

'To accept, I suppose?'

Mattheson stopped, glared at Händel, and then laughed. 'Oh my God. I will kill Magnus!' he shouted.

'Magnus?'

'Von Wedderkopp.'

'You have a good connection,' said Händel. 'He did not tell you about the marriage as part of the deal?'

'He deserves a good kick in his arse, if I cannot kill him.'

Händel laughed. They reached the inn, stopped, looked at each other, and then laughed again.

'Come. Let's drink. I did not enjoy the wine. Let's start all over,' said Mattheson, rolling his eyes.

Two hours later, the two friends were singing jollily, joining other guests of the inn. They just wanted to forget. They did not remember how and when they went back to their room.

Händel woke up suddenly. It was dawn. The early birds were chirping already. He jumped out of bed and shook Mattheson.

'Quick, Mattheson, we have to leave!'

'I have a terrible headache,' Mattheson muttered.

'Come, Mattheson. Get up.'

'What is the matter, Händel?'

'We must leave now. Hurry up, if you don't want to be caught up by-'

Mattheson got up at once, pale with panic and a headache. Händel helped him to get dressed.

While the two young men, seated in a stagecoach to Hamburg, were just happy to escape, Margreta Buxtehude's head went lower. Not one but two chances to get married were gone. She knew that quite a few candidates were willing to marry her, but then her father was against, judging them not good enough to succeed him.

Hamburg, Autumn 1703 – Spring 1704

The summer of northern Germany was rather short in 1703. By September, Hamburg was cooling down quickly. It was time to go back to work and for the various entertainments to begin their seasons.

Mattheson was determined. He worked at the opera house as a singer, actor, composer, conductor, and harpsichord player. If he was not a very good singer, he excelled in acting. He was also a good composer but only second harpsichordist. Now he wanted Händel to join the theatre. Mattheson was confident in Händel's abilities. Reinhard Keiser, the director, was less so.

'Mattheson, I like you, and I trust you. But there is no post free in the theatre at the moment,' said Keiser matter-of-factly.

'Mr Keiser, you will not regret him. I can guarantee it. Just let him in, and you'll see.'

Keiser did not reply.

'I can share with him, if you'll allow me. Well, I mean, he can help me.' Then he realised that Händel would need to be paid. He knew that the money earned from teaching and playing harpsichord at the musical evenings were just enough to keep him going.

Keiser was thinking the same thing. 'It is a tight budget, as you know, Mattheson.'

'Second violin?' said Händel.
'That's the best I could do, Händel,' said Mattheson. He did not let Händel protest. 'Just get in and make your way up. I am sure you can do it.'
Händel was not convinced. 'I suppose I have no choice if I want to get into the theatre, but you know very well that violin is not my strongest suit.' He regretted having arrived in Hamburg without any recommendation.
'I know you will do better as a harpsichordist, but there are already two, Schiefferdecker and myself.' Mattheson sighed, 'To be honest with you, Mr Keiser is not willing to pay for a third harpsichordist, Händel. Just get in. It's at least a beginning.'
'That's true,' Händel smiled to his friend, 'thank you. I will do my best.' However, he was surprised to find himself enjoying being part of the orchestra. This was something he had never experienced before: teamwork. The most pleasant part was the camaraderie. He loved to be among other players, talking to them and observing how they played. And now he started to try composing arias and cantatas.

Mattheson looked up from the score Händel had given him. 'Well, first, it is too long.'
'Is it?'
'Yes. If it is part of an opera, you've already exhausted the singer.'
'Oh . . . I see.'
'And . . . it is a little bland. It is not exciting or dramatic. It is like . . .' Mattheson hesitated. He knew Händel was a proud man.
'Like? Tell me.'
'It is like a woman without a face.'
Silence.
'Let me explain, Händel. You see a portrait of a woman. She is dressed nicely and stands in front of a nice background, but her face is a blank space. You cannot see how she looks, yes? It is a lady, but no more than that.'
'I see.' Händel lowered his head.

Händel busied himself between violin playing and composing as exercise. Then fate smiled upon him.
'Händel, Schiefferdecker is ill. Would you replace him on harpsichord?' asked Keiser one morning. Mattheson was behind him, nodding. 'Normally Mattheson would replace him, but he has to sing most of the time.'
'Yes, Mr Keiser, if you'll allow me to do so,' Händel replied politely, containing his joy. *I am taking the place of the first harpsichordist!*
'Have a go, then,' Keiser said casually.
Händel knew this was a test. He was not afraid, and he could not miss this chance.

After the rehearsal, there was silence. Keiser looked at Mattheson and nodded. The players started to murmur. They were quite astonished. The young second violin player was simply incredible at the harpsichord. Mattheson followed Keiser and walked beside him. Without looking at him, he said, 'So? Was I right?'

Keiser, without stopping, said, 'Yes, you were. Once again, you were right, Mattheson.'

'Would you use him as a harpsichordist?'

'Well, that's the problem. He is way better than Schiefferdecker, but I cannot replace him just like this. And . . .'

'And?'

'Well, Schiefferdecker is very accommodating, so I can talk to him. Of course he will remain as he is, composer and harpsichordist. One question.'

'Yes?'

'Does Händel intend to stay here in Hamburg?'

'Oh, I don't know,' said Mattheson, realising that Händel was not bound to stay. He had not thought about it. It would be a waste of time to give him a permanent post if he was not going to stay.

'Would he be happy to do the sing-through with the singers, Mattheson?'

A voice stopped Händel as he came out of the theatre. He turned and saw Veronica coming to join him.

'Nice rehearsal, Georg. I liked it.'

'You behaved as if you did not know me,' said Händel, protruding his lower lip.

Veronica laughed. 'Oh, Georg, you are so naive!'

'Naive?'

'Of course, you are!' She lowered her voice. 'Be careful, Georg. Avoid creating unnecessary gossip.' She looked around and continued in a low voice. 'A young harpsichord player talking privately with a singer in a friendly way?'

'Do I have to ignore you for the rest of my life then?

'Oh...' Then she laughed. 'See, Georg, you are now known to everyone, after such a rehearsal, so it won't attract attention if we talk openly in front of everyone.'

'But...'

'Listen, Georg. I am telling this for your sake. Be careful with the singers. They just love to gossip and spread rumours. Not all of them, but most of them.'

'I see.'

'And, don't forget. We singers travel much more than orchestra members. Like myself, I moved from Hanover, and people want to know

about Hanover.'
'So you told everything you know?'
'I am not that stupid, Georg.'

Händel thought, now that he was recognised as a harpsichordist, things could only get better. He had to face the reality that the theatre was controlled by the city council, consisting of not-so-music-loving people.
'The season is over? But we are only at the end of November, Mr Keiser. What about...' Mattheson looked astonished.
'Well, it's the order of the city councillors. I can do nothing.'
'Does that mean the theatre is closed?
'No. The theatre is open, but we cannot play operas anymore. The opera season is over.' Keiser suppressed his anger. 'That's fine, but I'll go,' said Keiser calmly.
'Where?'
'It is not your problem. I'm going. I cannot stay here if I cannot work. Is that clear?' said Keiser, getting irritated.
'How about the theatre, then?' asked Mattheson.
'Ask the city councillors. They could come and dance on the stage. But it is not my problem anymore!' he shouted. Then his shoulders slumped. 'I am sorry, Mattheson.'
'Mr Keiser, I understand your anger, but we already ordered the scenery and the costumes. It is a considerable expense.'
'Well, the city councillors will take care of the bill, I suppose.'
'So it's the church?' asked Mattheson, hesitating. 'Do you think they protested and threatened the city council?'
Keiser nodded. 'Why don't they transform the theatre into a church, then? The clerics will be delighted, and the city councillors too!'
Mattheson did not know what to say.
'I've had enough.' Keiser sighed deeply. 'Church. Always the church getting in the way!'

'Are you leaving as well?' said Händel, horrified.
'What's the point of staying here?' said Mattheson. 'Keiser is right. Why are we to be punished by the church? We did not sin.'
'The theatre...'
Mattheson looked at his friend and said placidly, 'Händel, you stay, and let's see how it goes. Schiefferdecker is here as well. Try your best.'
'And what about you, Mattheson?'
He put his hand on Händel's shoulder and said, 'Be there and be patient. The church cannot control the situation. And don't worry about me.'
Händel looked at Mattheson, puzzled.
'The people need entertainments. The church cannot provide that, so...'

'So?'

'Just wait and see. The people will protest.' Mattheson smiled. 'I will remain here in Hamburg, and I will keep an eye out. I am now the tutor of Cyril Wych, John's son, and I am getting busy.'

'How is Cyril? He is a good boy but not interested very much in music.'

'I know. At least it gave you a bit of income, Händel.'

Thank you for reminding me of your generosity, Mattheson!

Mattheson was right. The dissatisfaction of the people was growing bigger and bigger, and the city politicians could not ignore the pressure. Händel found himself caught between Keiser and the city councillors. He realised how complex it was to run a theatre and keep it open. It depended on politics when there was no court. In a place like Berlin or Hanover, it depended on the ruling king, elector, or prince... Which is better? He did not know. Still, the difference between Hanover and Hamburg was obvious. While he was in Hanover, the orchestra was being dismantled slowly; the entertainments were still going on in Hamburg. However, the musicians were worried about their salaries being honoured. Meanwhile, the singers, on short contracts, started to leave.

Prince Gian Gastone de' Medici arrived in Hamburg. It was the end of December 1703. He was miserable. He was suffering from the disastrous marriage imposed on him by his father, Grand Duke Cosimo III de' Medici. And he was stuck in the North, far from his beloved Tuscany. The winter here was cold and wet, making his misery worse. *It could be cold and wet in Florence, but at least there I would have the company of Violante, my lovely sister-in-law.* His only consolation was drinking. Gambling was now impossible, forbidden by his father, and even the emperor, who was related to his wife, was keeping a close eye on him. He was in Hamburg just to escape his hostile wife, who liked the country and hated courts. Gian Gastone struggled to cope with life in the little Bohemian village. His wife was unpredictable and prone to outbursts of rage. Gian Gastone, her second husband, wondered why her first husband had died so young, at twenty-four. When the prince married her, she was twenty-five and already very fat, and her bad temper and size grew year by year. Any hope for reconciliation was now lost. He could not stand his wife anymore. Once handsome and refined, he was now fat and ugly. Nothing could make him happy. However, just being away from his wife was a relief, and he was feeling relaxed. Still young, at thirty-two, he felt tired, consumed, and worn.

'Concert?' he looked up at Rinuccini, who was following him everywhere to keep an eye on him.

'Yes, Your Highness. A nice house concert. You should go.'

'Oh, if you want me to,' said Gian Gastone without showing any interest.

'Very well, Prince. I will accompany you,' said Rinuccini, ignoring Gian Gastone rolling his eyes.

The concert proved to be very interesting for the bored Italian prince. His interest in music was revived, just as it had been when he was in Florence, where his older brother Ferdinando organised concerts and operas. And he recognised the exceptional skill of the young man called Händel.

'You are a talented young man,' Gian Gastone told Händel, already drunk and feeling easy. 'My brother is a big music lover. If you go to Italy, you should go to see him in Florence.'

'I thank you, Your Highness.'

'Oh yes, he loves music' – he lowered his voice – 'more than his wife.' He nudged Händel and smiled. Ignoring Händel's confusion, he continued, 'I like her, Violante. She is my friend. She is a good woman.' He lowered his head. His entire body looked as if it was wrapped in melancholy.

Händel was struck. This Medici prince was not so bad looking, but the sadness he was carrying in him made him look miserable despite his fine clothing. The only time he smiled was when he was offered a drink. He drank continuously, and still he looked more and more unhappy.

The new year of 1704 began in confusion at the opera house in Hamburg. Keiser was still away, but by now Händel knew of another reason for his absence. The creditors were getting nervous and once raided Keiser's office in the theatre. They found only a worn-out wig left behind. Despite being a very able man, composing, rehearsing and dealing with the city councillors with little sleep, his high living was always exceeding his earning. The city councillors were struggling to contain the public's frustration, which was turning to anger, for making the theatre dormant. The musicians were still unpaid and growing more and more worried. The singers had gone to seek employment elsewhere.

It was a cold morning in February 1704. Händel sat at his desk, which was placed in front of the window, and, instead of composing, wrote a letter to Telemann.

> Hamburg, February 1704
>
> Dear Telemann,
>
> I warmly congratulate you for your appointment as the organist of the Neuekirche. Your talent and years of effort have now been

> recognised in Leipzig. I cannot imagine how Kuhnau can keep himself calm about it. Now he cannot call you an 'opera man' anymore and complain to the city council!
>
> I am now finishing the oratorio, The Passion according to St John, to be performed on Good Friday. This is my very first oratorio, and I have to confess I am quite nervous.
>
> Things are still not clear about the opera house here. Keiser is still away, and now Mattheson is thinking of leaving Hamburg. He wants to visit England.

By March, the pressure was getting too high. After Easter, if there was no entertainment available, the city councillors knew they would be in serious trouble. Then they realised that Keiser was away and the singers had left. Opera was not possible. So they allowed the operas to be played, leaving it to the theatre managers to soothe the public.

'What? We can play operas now?' Händel nearly jumped.

'Yes. The city councillors know that you have no Keiser or Mattheson,' said Johann Sbuelen. 'Have you been to the theatre recently, Mr Händel?'

'Yes. The orchestra is there, but there are no singers.'

'I can inform some of them. I was keeping in touch. If we can get even one, then . . .'

'Yes, then we can perform just a few extracts, in concert style.'

'Can you manage it?'

Händel stopped. Johann Sbuelen, a powerful influence at the Gänsemarkt was suggesting that he do the job. 'Well, I will ask Mr Schiefferdecker, but I am confident we can.'

'Very good. I will let you inform Mr Schiefferdecker.'

I have to get Mattheson back. He cannot go to England.

> Dear Mattheson,
>
> I am writing to you this day, 18 March 1704.
>
> I have no doubt you are having a very

> *good time in Amsterdam, but you have to come back. You are needed here in Hamburg. The opera house cannot function properly without you. You have to finish your Cleopatra and play it here! I am certain you can do it without Keiser.*
>
> *Your most humble servant,*
> *Händel*

Mattheson, the letter just received in his hand, sighed. He was thinking of going to London. He was curious to know the state of music there, and see it for himself. Also he knew, from John Wych, that there was a project of building a splendid theatre, funded by subscription by a group of noblemen, and that the theatre would be designed to play operas. However, at the same time, he wanted to complete his opera and play it in Hamburg. Finally, things seemed to move.

'Oh well, London has to wait. My opera is more important,' he said to himself, smiling, 'and, I have to help Händel.'

Händel was developing an increasing attachment to the theatre world. He liked the camaraderie of the orchestra members, and though challenging, he tasted the joy of achievement in putting together the orchestra, singers, dancers, and stage. Italy was still his goal. It was the only place where he could think of going if he wanted to perfect his skill as an opera composer. Opera had been born in Italy, and he wanted to see its powerful mother. At the same time, he was getting more and more curious about London. Lots of travellers from England, on their grand tour, stopped at Hamburg, as they could not go through France, England being opposed to France in the ongoing War of the Spanish Succession. And they brought fresh news to John Wych, the British resident.

'But, Hamburg first,' he said to himself. 'I have to get Mattheson and Keiser back, and put the theatre ready for operas again.'

Chapter 5 : Pride and Music (1704-1706)

England, Spring 1704

More than five hundred miles away from Hamburg, a ship from America was approaching the British coast. The air was cold one early morning in March 1704.

On the deck, Thomas Coram stood beside his wife. He looked at her and smiled. His wife smiled back with apprehension. She was from New England.

'Don't worry, Eunice. It will be all right. After all, we are all humans. There is not very much difference. I'll do my best to go back to America as soon as possible.' Thomas Coram was not convinced but tried to reassure his wife.

Eunice Coram gently rested her head on her husband's shoulder. He was the only person she knew in England.

It was ten years earlier when Thomas Coram, full of hope, got into a merchant ship headed for Boston. Still very young, at twenty-five, he was instructed to set up a shipbuilding business in New England. Crossing the Atlantic was a hazardous experience, but the young man was not afraid. He was determined to reach the New World. England at the time was at war with France, and French privateers targeted the English merchant fleet, causing considerable losses of ships. For protection, merchant ships depended on naval escorts. Charles Wager, then a young naval officer, was in command of the *Samuel and Henry*, an armed ship escorting a merchant fleet to Boston.

The merchant ship carrying Coram was on the Downs waiting for the naval ship to arrive to form a convoy. Coram was on the deck and saw the naval ship approaching. Then a small boat carrying an officer was lowered down, and it approached the merchant ship. A young officer presented himself to the captain, but that was not his only reason for coming over.

'There is a small leak in the hull. America is a long way off, and I want to make sure it will not cause further damage to the ship. Otherwise I will have to go back and repair it,' Charles Wager told the captain.

That's when Thomas Coram volunteered to go and have a look. Charles Wager was open-minded. It was easy to refuse, as there was already a technician on board, but he was curious to see how much the young man knew. After all, the technician was not a shipbuilder. Charles Wager was impressed by Coram's knowledge, competence, and confidence. Coram saw for the first time an armed naval ship, made to fight. What impressed Coram most was the discipline, and the air of pride and dignity above all. Compared to his merchant ship just a few miles away, it was another world.

Once arrived safely in Boston, they met again, and the friendship was solidly established.

Gravesend was in front of them, bursting with activity. Thomas Coram was back in England after ten years spent in America, and there was only one person he knew and could trust.

'Thomas! You're here!' Charles Wager was delighted and puzzled. 'What a surprise! I thought I would see you in Boston.' He was in uniform, impeccably clean, and his head was topped with a neat short wig. Coram, in his worn-out and unwashed clothing, felt embarrassed.

'I need your help, sir,' Coram said bluntly.

'Tell me. What do you need?' asked the officer, as blunt as the visitor. 'And do call me Charles, as before in Boston, please.' It was not difficult for Wager to see that Coram was not at ease financially.

'I need a lodging for me and my wife, Charles.'

Charles Wager considered and then said, 'Thomas, I will give you someone to help you. I will be leaving for the Mediterranean next week, and I am very busy. I am sorry.' He was indeed busy, but he would have happily accompanied his friend in searching for lodgings, and catch up with all the news. But at the same time, Charles thought that his presence might embarrass Coram. It was obvious that this was not a glorious return, and his friend was looking for a modest lodging.

'Thank you, Charles.'

'I want to see you. I will call you in before I go.'

Three days later, Charles Wager was in the lodging of the Corams. It was very simple but clean. After a simple meal, Eunice Coram left the two men alone and retired in the kitchen.

'So, Thomas, would you tell me? You don't have to if you do not wish.' Though delighted to see his old friend, Charles Wager knew something was wrong. Coram had gone to New England to work there and stay. *So why is he here now?*

Coram looked at Charles Wager. Despite the difference of social rank, they shared the same human qualities: honesty and industriousness. They liked each other by instinct. The friendship was a solid one.

'It is not pride, but I do not like to complain. Let me just say that I was treated badly,' said Coram with a hint of bitterness. Then he told Wager what happened.

Charles Wager listened. As a natural diplomat, he knew he was having only one side of the story, but it was obvious that Coram was a victim.

'Everything was going well, even when I moved from Boston to Taunton,' said Coram.

'Taunton?' Charles Wager stared at his friend, 'did you start shipbuilding on a river?'

'I know,' Coram smiled, 'it was daring, very daring, but I knew what I was doing. And, it worked.'

Charles Wager could see clearly that the early settlers were jealous of an outsider being successful. By mutual silent agreement they ousted and stripped the newcomer, who moments before had been immensely wealthy. Carefully he asked, 'Did you lose everything in your business?'

'Yes, I did.'

'Any debt?'

'Quite a lot. I have no choice but to honour the contracts.'

'My God . . .'

'I will honour and clear them. As soon as possible.'

'With your experience and knowledge, I have no doubt you will.'

Coram made a little smile and said, 'They took everything from me, but they did not manage to take my knowledge. And then...'

'Then you will go back.'

Coram beamed, filled with hope. 'Yes, I will.'

'Thomas, I do not want to disappoint you, but you must wait and see how this war will go, because...'

Coram's smile disappeared at once. In a heavy tone, he asked, 'Do you think we'll lose New England?'

'I hope not. Well, probably not, but you never know.'

'You are right, Charles. But I hope it will end soon.'

'That's what we all want, including the queen.' Charles Wager stood up to leave. Coram accompanied him to the door. The naval officer looked in Coram's eyes and pulled a silver watch from his pocket. 'This is war, Thomas. I might not return. I want you to have this, in case I do not return.'

'I hope you are wrong, Charles.'

Coram's hopes were to be half fulfilled. Charles Wager would return, but the war would last longer than anyone could guess.

In London, people were not yet worried about the ongoing war. There was a gathering in Haymarket, not far from The Mall. It was a small group at first, but then it attracted curious passers-by. More and more people were stopping to see what was going on. Thomas Coram happened to be one of the passers-by, but he was not interested in the growing crowd. His mind was focused on how to sort out his enormous debts, and as usual, he was walking briskly. However, he had a glimpse of the group of people dressed in rich clothes, their hats over expensive and elaborate wigs. *A group of nobles*, he thought. They were not really part of his world, and at that moment, he had no idea he would deal with them twenty-five years later.

A middle-aged man advanced to the corner of a plot of land. He was remarkably handsome, wrapped in a magnificent suit, following John Vanbrugh, architect and playwright.

'Your Grace, here, please,' said Vanbrugh, indicating a small hole prepared for the purpose. Then he addressed the group gathered for the occasion, 'Gentlemen,' he said merrily, 'we are here today, to lay the cornerstone of the new theatre. May this be the new beginning, to bring more opportunity to the playwrights and enrich the theatre world with new adventures!'

'Hear, hear!' a few of his friends cried jollily, at which John Vanbrugh smiled. He took the stone from his valet and handed it to Charles Seymour, 6th Duke of Somerset, who was one of the subscribers. The stone bore the date of the ceremony: '18 April 1704'.

This was the beginning of a project, launched by John Vanbrugh himself by way of subscription the previous year. After going through litigation, he finally secured a plot of land to build a new theatre on Haymarket. With more than thirty subscribers with 100 guineas each, obtained mainly from his friends and acquaintances, it was a quite easy start, and Vanbrugh felt comfortable. He had a clear idea to create a magnificent theatre, never seen before in London.

The next day, several newspapers reported on the little ceremony, making it public knowledge. Immediately it met with adverse publicity from both the anti-theatre lobby and potential theatrical competitors. This was to be expected, and John Vanbrugh was prepared. All throughout the building works, he would not admit anyone into the site except when invited and accompanied by Vanbrugh himself.

The theatre Vanbrugh would create had a few purposes. As a playwright he wanted the theatre to provide a new base for the actors. As an architect, he had a plan. Though he'd never travelled to Italy, he had lots of friends and acquaintances, gentry and aristocratic, who saw the real opera there, and he observed them discussing enthusiastically what they'd seen. In London, to the general public, opera was more of a play with music and dance. The songs and music were introduced at the beginning, during the interval, and at the end to make the plays more entertaining. That was all. There was no doubt about the eventual arrival of genuine Italian opera in London. It was just a question of timing, and he was certain the audience would be enticed. He wanted his theatre to be more than just one of the theatres in London. He wanted the opera to be played there, and he wanted to be the first to introduce such novelty to the public.

Hamburg, Autumn 1704 - Spring 1705

In September 1704, Hamburg was still deprived of Reinhard Keiser who was in Weissenfels enjoying the position of visiting court composer. However Mattheson was back from Amsterdam. Immediately he busied himself with getting the singers back.

Händel stared at the man standing in front of him, Friederich Christian Feustking, librettist of the opera house. It was October 1704.

'Are you certain, Mr Feustking?' Händel looked at the librettist, incredulous.

'Yes. Mr Keiser said it is for you.' He handed the libretto to the still stunned Händel. 'Mr Keiser is still in Weissenfels, and Mattheson is busy finishing his *Cleopatra*. So this goes to you.' The librettist was ready to go but then stopped and said, 'Mr Keiser wants it ready by December so it can be played in January.'

Händel looked at the bundle in his hands. *Almira*. It was the libretto Keiser commissioned from Feustking for his own composition for the Hamburg Opera. However, the conflict between him and the town councillors got in its way. Keiser, seeing no end to the conflict, abandoned the project, and adapted his opera *Almira* for court use, making it shorter and smaller in scale, and went off to Weissenfels. In order not to waste the costumes and scenery already prepared at the theatre, the councillors gave order to complete the opera and play it. And the task was given to the young novice.

Händel was elated, but soon realised that he was not experienced enough. He felt overwhelmed. Composing just a few fragments for exercise had nothing to do with composing an entire opera. He struggled. He had no choice but to ask Mattheson for advice. Keiser was still away.

'Is it you again, Händel?' Mattheson said with a hint of contempt. Though he had agreed to review Händel's composition, he did not miss the opportunity to make the young composer feel inferior. While Händel could teach Mattheson quite a lot about counterpoint and harmony, he was just a beginner opera composer, and Mattheson secretly delighted in seeing his friend swallow his pride.

Händel brought Mattheson the music scene by scene and listened carefully to the advice given. There were so many details to remember, as so many things happened at the same time. The pleasure and excitement of composing a real opera were superior to the humiliation. Still the pressure was there, and he felt stressed all the time. Händel was asking advice from Telemann and Steffani as well. When the opera is complete, Keiser would review it, and then it would be judged by the public. Händel was excited and terrified at the same time.

Working with the librettist was another new experience. Pastor Friederich Christian Feustking had translated and adapted *Almira* from an

Italian libretto at the request of Keiser. Seven years older than Händel, Feustking looked younger than his age. He was more of a scholar than pastor, and he loved to discuss literature. Händel had heard of Feustking being sentenced to ten years of exile from Wittenberg University a few years earlier. In fact, his libretto for *Cleopatra*, written for Mattheson, contained some very unpriestlike obscenity in its comic scenes.

'Why can't it be only in German?' asked Händel, confused by the bilingual libretto.

'Well, it is a compromise introduced by Mr Keiser. Because opera itself is Italian, keeping some Italian gives it the impression of being genuine. But if it is entirely sung in Italian, the public will not understand, and the theatre will be empty after Act I.'

'I see. It is a big cast of singers.'

'I know, but alas, we don't have a castrato.'

'Castrato?'

'Yes. And we shall never have one, I think.'

Händel remembered the one he had seen in Berlin following Bononcini everywhere like a dog following his master. They called him a castrato. His physique, with extremely long limbs emanating from a fat, short body, was hard to forget.

'Is that because they are ugly?'

Feustking laughed, thinking Händel was joking. 'No. Too expensive. And above all, the church will be too happy to attack us for using such a creature.'

'But... why? It's not their fault if they are ugly.'

Feustking stared at Händel. 'Do you know what a castrato is?'

'No, not really. I thought they belong to a specific race or tribe in Italy with very long legs and arms.'

Feustking was now laughing, very loudly. Händel watched him bending forward, holding his stomach, with teary eyes. It seemed to last forever, but eventually the pastor calmed down. Wiping his eyes with the back of his hands, he asked, 'Mr Händel, how old are you?'

'Nineteen.'

'It is time you knew what a castrato is. Let me explain.' Then, again, Feustking burst into laughter. 'Sorry...'

Händel just watched the librettist laugh, and then regain control.

'Well, it's a cruel thing, but as the name indicates, a castrato is a castrated singer.'

Händel stared at Feustking, 'Castrated? A human being castrated?' He'd known about horses and that was all.

'It's to preserve the treble voice of a boy. So it has to be done before his voice breaks.'

'Oh...' Händel, again, felt ignorant.

BRIGHT STAR

The only comfort was letters from Telemann and Stefani, giving advice and encouragement. But they were not there to support him. He felt something eroding inside himself, his confidence. At the same time, his pride was getting desperate to survive.

Mattheson looked at Händel, who brought him a scene.
'Händel, there is one thing bothering me.'
'Tell me.'
'Well, I see lots of Mr Keiser in your music.'
Händel was quite astounded by this remark. 'What do you mean?'
It was Mattheson's turn to be surprised. 'What do I mean? You don't realise that? Your music reminds me of Keiser's music.'
'Oh...'
That was something Händel had not realised, but it was obvious for Mattheson. It was true that Keiser's music was a model for Händel. When one of his beautiful melodies was stuck in Händel's head, he could not get rid of it. But it was not copying. Händel considered, and said carefully, 'Maybe, but I improve it and make it mine.'
Mattheson was not happy with this reply. He grimaced.
Händel felt uneasy. For him, it was just like an exercise given by his old teacher Zachow – to copy other people's music and then transform it into his own. It was a very common practice to all who studied music. *Why is that bad?* Händel felt incapable of distinguishing other people's music from his own once it entered his brain. But it was not copying. No way. It was too boring just to copy. He had to make his own music. *But what is wrong if my music resembles Keiser's? I am paying homage to his music! Would Mattheson ever stop being patronising?*
Now that Mattheson's opera Cleopatra was put on stage, he was busy but more relaxed. 'Händel, listen. Make your music. Your own music. This is a fabulous chance you've been given. Don't spoil it.' This was true advice without any attempt at humiliation.
Händel lowered his head. He still could not agree with Mattheson. The only thing he could do was to grind his teeth. He felt he was trading his soul for Mattheson's advice.

In the evening of 5 December 1704, the audience attending the opera *Cleopatra* by Mattheson at Gänsemarkt Theatre was treated to a surprise entertainment after the performance. The crowd was gathering, and more and more people were arriving at the sides of the opera house surrounding the two young men facing each other. Mattheson was still dressed as Antony and looked furious. Händel admired him. His friend could compose, sing, act, and conduct. Who is able to do all that? He was secretly jealous. And then, finally, all the humiliation he suffered up to this point at Mattheson's hand surfaced that evening during the performance. Händel had been conducting from the harpsichord, as usual, but this time, he refused to relinquish his seat.

Ever since the production started in October, Mattheson, after having sung his part of Antony, had been used to taking the seat as the conductor from the harpsichord for the last half-hour of the opera. Each time Händel obliged, though feeling frustrated at not being allowed to finish his job, and seeing his friend adding more to his glory. At the previous performance, Mattheson, excited and ebullient from the audience's reaction, nearly pushed Händel out of the seat. So this time, Händel refused to be pushed away, staying and finishing the opera, conducting from the harpsichord.

'Händel, go, it's my turn!' Mattheson had whispered, irritated. He could not shout as he did not want to disturb the ongoing performance.

Händel had looked up at his friend, with a big smile, and kept conducting. He had no intention of giving the place to Mattheson.

The orchestra members who were close to them could see clearly what was going on, and looked at each other, feeling uneasy. Händel saw Mattheson hesitate, and retire to the backstage. That was the only thing possible in this situation and they both knew it. Händel thought that this time, he had won.

Mattheson felt insulted. It was his opera, after all, and he felt he was being thanked with kicks from Händel, for whom he had done so much. As soon as the performance was over, he dragged Händel out of the orchestra pit, and challenged him.

'Not here, I suppose?' Händel said cynically, 'let's get out of the theatre first.'

Mattheson glared at Händel, standing in front of him. He was tall, strong, broad-shouldered, and muscular, well able to defend himself. He looked calm – calm enough to think of putting his coat on before going outdoors. They both drew their swords. The crowd was watching, holding their breath.

John Wych was getting out of the opera house when he heard a commotion and saw people hurrying towards the side of the theatre. He heard the word *duel*. He told his wife and daughter to go back home and hurried towards the crowd. He managed to swim through, and when he reached the front row, he saw, with horror, Mattheson giving the fatal blow to Händel's chest followed by a metallic noise. The crowd gasped. He saw Händel on the ground, trying to get up. Mattheson threw his shattered sword to the ground and was ready to pounce on his enemy, but John Wych dipped to grab Mattheson from behind, nearly falling backwards with him.

'What is this, Mattheson?' he shouted, and glanced at Händel, still on the ground, apparently unhurt. He dragged Mattheson away, scattering the crowd and pulling the young man back. 'Not a word! Come!' Wych pulled

Mattheson, running, losing all notion of time. It seemed like a long, very long time.

Mattheson was in shock. He just followed Wych, who was pulling him furiously. Now he was realising what he had just done.

Händel was on the ground, breathing heavily. He could see the crowd dispersing. He could also hear their comments.

'What a lucky man, saved by a button!'

'I would have loved to see more, though…'

'Oh, come on! It was good enough.'

'Not too bad. An opera and a duel in one evening!'

He did not move, still reliving what had just happened. He thought his life had ended when he saw the tip of Mattheson's sword coming straight to his chest. Then, instead of a sharp pain, he felt something hard pressing hard into his body, something too big to pierce his clothing. He was pushed back, hearing a piece of metal shatter. He lost balance and fell back on the ground. He heard his own falling thud, as if it was happening to someone else, and then saw Mattheson disappear into the crowd. *Coward, he escaped!*

A woman approached Händel and then stopped. She collected the small pieces of shattered metal button and put them in her pouch. Then she approached Händel. Her voice was calm and low.

'Georg, you are stupid. Come, you cannot stay here.' She pulled him by the arm.

Händel started, still in shock, and looked up, 'Oh, you…'

'Come with me,' she said, and then she said no more.

Händel struggled to his feet, and swayed a little.

'Come,' said Veronica and started to walk, ignoring the young man still in shock and trying to get back full control of his body.

He followed her obediently. In her lodging, Veronica was busy preparing hot water. Händel just watched her. She came with hot water and clean linen.

'Here, sit down. Let me see. Are you injured?' She checked his face and started to clean Händel's hands.

'No, I don't think so.'

She removed his wig and checked his skull and neck. 'Your head is fine, thanks to the wig. Remove your coat.'

Händel obeyed. She stared at the remains of the broken button hanging loosely from the coat. Diligently, she started to tap his back gently with her closed fist.

'Do you feel any pain?'

'No.' Then Händel winced in pain when she tapped his chest.

'Remove your shirt.'

Händel hesitated but obeyed. She stared at the round bruise on his ribs.

'This is where you were hit?'

'Yes.'

She put her palm on the bruise. 'It is quite hot. Wait.' And she came back with cold water. She soaked a handkerchief in it and put it on the bruise.

'You are damn lucky to have escaped with just this. Hold the cloth. I'll make another one. You have to cool it.'

For a while, they just kept changing the cloth without saying a word. Finally, Händel said, 'Thank you, Veronica.'

'You are stupid, Georg. Do you know that?'

'But—'

'You are a stranger here. Even if he were completely wrong, the people would support him because he is from here. You are nothing. You know that?' Her voice was getting louder. 'So stupid. I cannot believe it!' She glared at him. 'They could kill you and bury you in a field somewhere, planting a tree on top, and who would realise that you were missing? Nobody. Your family might be worried not to hear from you, but when they realised that you were missing, what could they do? It would be too late! They would never recover your body!' She was shouting now. 'Never forget that. You are a stranger; you have to behave. You are nothing here!'

Händel looked at her, stunned.

She stopped. 'Sorry, I lost my temper . . .' She looked down.

'You are right. I am stupid.' He lowered his head.

'Value your life. It is not only your life; think of your mother.'

Händel felt his blood drain at the word mother. He had not thought of his mother, and his sisters. What if he had been killed? Or, what if he had killed Mattheson? Either way, he could only imagine his mother in shock and grief. When his father died, he swore to himself to protect his mother. And just now he had done something to hurt her, more than that. She might die of grief, either seeing her son dead, or a murderer. He froze in horror. Veronica's hand taking the cloth and replacing it with another forced him back to reality.

'I lost my brother in a fight for a stupid reason. You cannot imagine the pain he caused all of us. My mother became like a ghost...' She turned her head. Her shoulders were shaking.

Händel took her in his arms gently. 'I am sorry. I promise I will never again do such a thing. Never.' He tried hard to dissipate dark thoughts, and just comfort her. After all, he did not die, and he did not kill.

Veronica was weeping silently in his arms. She was smaller than he had thought. He gently kissed the top of her head. 'I am sorry.' He hugged her tightly.

'Georg, you must go now.' Veronica was shaking Händel gently. He struggled to open his eyes. He could not remember where he was. The bruise on his chest was throbbing. He saw Veronica half naked. He saw himself in her bed.

'You must go now. People should not see you coming out of my lodging. It will harm you more than me. Be quick.'

She helped Händel dress and then pushed him out. With a light kiss on his lips, she closed the door.

Outside, it was still dark, and the streets were completely deserted. The air was cold. Händel felt his cheeks cool down. *Is she really a singer or a surgeon? Oh, she might be a witch!* Then the reality came back. He stopped. *It's over. I ruined everything. I have to go*, he thought. *But go where? Back to Halle? No way.* Then he had an idea and rushed to his lodging. He set immediately to write a letter to Steffani in Düsseldorf asking for advice on where he could go, without mentioning the duel. In another letter, to Telemann, Händel told everything, and again asked for advice. *Now what to do? Just wait?* He was certain nothing would come from Mattheson from now on – no invitations for Sunday lunch – and he was not sure his post at the opera house would be maintained. *God, it was the last thing I could do, to insult Mattheson. He would do everything to kick me out of the theatre. I am stupid, more than stupid! Veronica was right. How foolish!* He was cursing himself. It was too late. At the same time, he felt he'd be running away from the situation if he left Hamburg right now. Stay then? For how long? *I'll be alone. Nobody will talk to me, and no job at the opera house? What is the point of staying?* The only thing he could do was to blame himself, in vain.

Mattheson woke up and did not recognise the place. The maid quickly got up from her chair and went out, and his mother came in shortly after.

'Johann, you are awake,' said Mrs Mattheson, her face grave.

'Mother…' He sat up and winced. His body was aching all over. He looked around and recognised his parents' house.

'Don't worry, you have no injuries. Just muscle pain. The doctor told me.'

'Mother, I am sorry,' Mattheson whispered, head down.

'Oh, yes, you can be sorry,' she said coldly. 'Really, what is this? How old are you?'

Mattheson opened his mouth only to be cut off by his mother.

'I want no excuse, Johann!'

Mattheson was stunned. He had never seen his mother shout.

'Thank God you did not kill your friend, and thank God your father is away. It is time to stop this nonsense of opera.' Again he started to reply, but she quickly showed her hand to interrupt. 'Yes, opera. It is not serious. I and your father told you so more than once. That's enough now. And you shall get a wife. I will arrange for it. It is time for you to get serious.'

Mattheson looked at his mother in horror. He saw his free, single life shattering.

'Don't say a word. And I forbid you to go out for three days.' She left, slamming the door.

Mattheson was speechless. Not only had he never seen his mother in such anger, but he was also not expecting to be confined. He was a grown man, and his mother was treating him like a child. *A wife? Mother is getting me a wife? No! It is for me to choose...* He was in dismay when he saw the door open noiselessly, and his sister, Catarina, crept in like a cat.

'I'm not supposed to see you, Brother,' she whispered. 'Mother said you should see no one for three days so you can cool down your boiling blood.' She smiled, suppressing a burst of laughter. 'And you will get married soon!'

The morning after the incident, the whole town knew about the duel and the young man from Halle, saved only by his large metal button. Händel was already nicknamed "the button man" and people were laughing about the story. Mattheson, in spite of his mother's order, got out to go to the opera house to discuss the forthcoming rehearsals for Händel's first opera, *Almira*. Walking in the streets, he could feel the gaze of the people on his back and hear the whispering behind him. He kept his head up, to show his confidence, feeling uneasy inside. The way to the theatre seemed much longer than usual. He was surprised to see Keiser, just back from Weissenfels, to check on the progress of Händel's opera.

Mattheson beamed, forgetting everything. This was a good sign, so the theatre could function as before. 'Mr Keiser! You are-'

'I just had a visit from the town councillor about last night,' said Keiser, cutting Mattheson sharply. 'You'd be banished from Hamburg if you were a foreigner.'

'Is Händel?' asked Mattheson, shocked. Though still angered, the thought of losing his friend so abruptly was unexpected.

'I am talking about you, Mattheson. You are the one who nearly killed a man.' Keiser looked into Mattheson's eyes. He continued, 'I cannot believe it. What was—'

'You know very well why, Mr Keiser. Because-'

'I see. So you chose your pride over the music?' Keiser said, smiling cynically.

'I let him finish! I did not interrupt!' Mattheson shouted, frustrated. This was not what he thought would happen, to find himself justifying his actions.

'Enough!' Keiser shouted back. 'Go home, Mattheson, and come back in three days, if you wish to. For the moment, I am not in the mood to see you. Good day, Mattheson.' He got up to escort Mattheson to the door, who followed him silently. 'Oh, by the way, it is not my order. It's the town council who ordered three days of confinement for you both.' He closed the door, sighed and looked away. 'I cannot believe it. How old are they?'

Mattheson went back to his lodging head down. He was treated as a child by his mother and now by Keiser. The doubt started to creep in. *Was I that childish?* However, he was far from being able to forgive his friend. *Händel has to stay in Hamburg. I'll make him pay for it.*

Händel did not leave his lodging. He was restless, pacing to and fro in his room, sitting down, getting up, and pacing to and fro again. Now the reality was there to be faced. He was pretty sure his first opera, *Almira*, would be performed without him, if it ever played at all. He felt bitter, but again, he could not go back in time and change what had happened. He was realising the price of his stupid pride. He sank on his bed and buried his head in his hands. Leaving Hamburg seemed the only option rather than suffering the humiliation. He did not care anymore if he ran away to escape the situation. He could only pray to be able to forget everything. Desperation was the only thing left for him.

'Händel, are you in?' a voice said outside the door. The door opened.

'Mr Schiefferdecker.' Händel got up. Seeing Johann Christian Schiefferdecker not smiling, he expected bad news.

'Are you all right?' Schiefferdecker asked with concern. 'Are you injured? Are you—'

'I am fine, thank you, Mr Schiefferdecker.'

They sat facing each other. Händel looked at his colleague, who was six years senior, but his calm and rather humble personality made him look older.

'I was just back from Lübeck,' said the first harpsichordist, to avoid going directly to the reason for his visit.

'Lübeck?' Händel raised his eyebrows. The memory of the visit with Mattheson came back immediately. He thought, at that time, that they were friends. Not anymore. He lowered his head.

'Yes, and also Mr Keiser just came back,' Schiefferdecker said, 'and as soon as he sat in his office, he was visited by the town councillor.'

'Oh, I see,' Händel lowered his head and then looked up again. 'Are you here to tell me that I am dismissed?'

Schiefferdecker raised his eyebrows. 'Oh, no, Mr Keiser sent me to check to see if you are all right, Händel.'

'Really? Is that all?'

'Well, no, the town council ordered three days of confinement for both you and Mattheson.' Schiefferdecker looked at Händel. 'You are lucky, Händel. If one of you were injured, I am sure you'd be banished from Hamburg, never to return.' He smiled.

Händel could see the kindness in Schiefferdecker. The latter had been quite indifferent to him, but never showed any resentment or bitterness towards his young colleague who intruded into his post.

'Are you bruised?'

'I am.'

'Is that all?'

'Yes.'

'You are fortunate.'

Händel grimaced. The word *fortunate* was not easy to accept.

'Yes, you are. Fortunate to be alive,' Schiefferdecker said, serious, then he made a face. 'Can I see it? Please?'

The maid was bringing the fortified wine sent by Mrs Mattheson to Händel's room when she heard a man laugh and heard footsteps coming towards the door. She quickly stepped back. The door opened, and she saw a man, saying, 'Don't go out for three days, Händel. That's the order. The people are calling you "the button man". Just stay indoors and keep yourself quiet.' The maid saw the man stop, nod to her and go downstairs.

Schiefferdecker, on his way back to the theatre, struggled to contain laughter. He was just amazed to see two young men still behaving like children, fighting over music! Back in the theatre he found Keiser calmed down. They both laughed heartily.

The two letters Händel sent were answered quickly. Steffani's letter was warming. He promised to help Händel and encouraged him to come to Düsseldorf. There the daughter of Cosimo III was living as the wife of the elector. Steffani was certain Electress Anna Maria Luisa de' Medici would write Händel a letter of introduction to her brother, Grand Prince Ferdinando de' Medici in Florence. 'But you have to come and impress the elector and electress, which I am certain you will,' said the letter. 'But, I have to tell you that you cannot count on Prince Gian Gastone. Telling them you met him does not carry very much weight. He is not close to his older brother. Electress Anna Maria is. It is much recommended to have a letter of introduction.' This gave him hope. It had been a week, and he had not gone out. He was getting restless. By now, he felt the whole situation just ridiculous. Telemann was concerned and advised him to reconcile. Händel put down his letter and shouted, 'Reconcile? Never!' Though deeply regretting what he had done, he was not ready to accept Mattheson as the winner. He just could not swallow Mattheson's domineering attitude anymore.

Schiefferdecker, normally always smiling, was frowning. The rehearsals of *Almira* were not going well. Keiser had gone back to Weissenfels again. It was obvious that Händel was needed there. The conducting score was copied for the composer's use. Mattheson was doing his best, however he was struggling to rehearse. And it was out of the question to go to see Händel, that arrogant young man, for advice. The orchestra members looked at each other, as did the singers, uncertain of what they were doing. Veronica, among the singers, watched Mattheson without showing any emotion but her clenched fists.

'Georg, what did I say? You are nothing. Remember?' Veronica observed Händel in his room.

'I know, Veronica,' Händel said, not really convinced.

'You have to learn how to suppress your pride. Just say sorry, and it will be done.'

'I know...'

'No you don't!' Veronica snapped.

Händel looked at her, surprised.

Veronica held his hands in hers and stared in his eyes. 'Georg, I am saying this for you. If you want to continue and build your career, learn to say sorry even if you are not wrong.'

Händel looked back and met Veronica's eyes. They were filled with anger. She fumed at Händel, 'If you knew how many times I've said sorry for nothing...'

'Really?'

'Yes, and then, you will see. You get used to it.' She shook her shoulders. 'You'll see. You get used to many things in life.' Then she said softly with sister-like affection, 'You don't want to come back, Georg?'

Händel looked at Veronica. It was a silly question. Veronica laughed.

'Of course you want to. Don't say a word; I can see it. Don't try to hide your feelings. It's too late. I saw it!' she said, triumphant, as if she had just discovered a mischief done by her little brother.

Alone in his room, Händel, head down, picked up the letter from Telemann, which he had not finished reading.

> ...If you are reading this, that shows your pride is fading. I know you, Händel, proud and impatient. Händel, there is something more important than your pride: first, your life and then, your music. Don't forget that. I pray for you.
>
> Your friend and brother,
> Georg Philipp Telemann

Händel was glad to have Telemann as a friend. The bond was solid. He knew his friend was right. Still, he felt a strong resistance to apologising.

It was much easier than Händel expected. Mattheson was impatient to reconcile when he realised that Händel was needed at the theatre. It was he who opened his arms to hug Händel tight. At that moment, Händel's reluctance melted. It was the morning of 30 December 1704.

'I am sorry, Mattheson,' Händel said in his arms.

'I am sorry, Händel,' said Mattheson, still holding Händel tight.

It was the music that brought them together. At that point, they both felt they were true friends, and they hurried together to rehearse at the opera house. Händel could not be happier. He realised how easy it was to apologise once the chance was offered, and he grabbed it with gratitude.

There was another reason for Mattheson to hurry to reconcile. The pressure from his mother was becoming unbearable. He had promised his mother that everything would go back as before, quickly. It cost him considerable effort to convince his mother to let him continue with music and remain single for the moment. He promised her he would get married and give her the joy of being a grandmother. He felt quite drained. All he wanted now was to reconcile, no matter how. The pressure won over pride. Meanwhile, his sister, Catarina, enjoyed very much watching them. As for his father, who was back in Hamburg, he knew everything and chose to say nothing.

On the evening of 8 January 1705, the burghers of Hamburg made their way to the Gänsemarkt Theatre. It was the premiere of Händel's very first opera, *Almira*.

'Händel, it's packed. A full house!' Mattheson exclaimed enthusiastically, dressed as Fernando, the leading role.

Händel just stared into the void. He was terrified. This was the moment of judgement. Behind Mattheson, he saw Veronica, dressed as Almira, smile and nod to him. He walked to the orchestra pit where the musicians were ready, including Schiefferdecker as second harpsichordist. Händel looked around and looked up at the stage. He then looked down to the musicians again and met Schiefferdecker's friendly eyes. He just winked at Händel, and the young composer felt his tension vanish instantly. Händel remembered nothing afterwards.

It was a triumph.

The new opera was the talk of the town now. Mrs Mattheson was particularly pleased. She thought the people had forgotten all about the duel, and her husband just smiled. Keiser was satisfied, and seeing that after ten performances there was no sign of its popularity dwindling, he offered Händel another chance with a second opera, *Nero*.

The Hamburg opera house provided a good night out at the theatre for an audience that expected an element of high art without necessarily giving that element priority, and which offered spectacular scenes and dancing. Händel was learning, applying, and adapting the style in which he had been trained. Some of the ornate elements he incorporated may have reflected French influence, which perhaps Händel did not even recognise, since it had been integrated into the common musical habits of northern and central Germany.

A noble traveller on the grand tour who attended the opera was, however, quite shocked by the melting pot: two languages, the juxtaposition of French, German, and Italian styles of music, ballet sequences, and abrupt shifts between near tragedy and satirical comedy. *If this was the Hamburg school, I am glad this was the first and last time I attended*, wrote the nobleman. *The opera was composed by a very young man. He is only nineteen, but some arias are beautiful.*

Agostino Steffani, who was keeping an eye on Händel, was worried. He knew the Hamburg style of opera; it was just confusion. *Händel has to leave as soon as possible. He cannot be contaminated by this mess. His talent cannot be wasted in Hamburg. Italy, Venice, that's his place, and I will do anything in my power to help him.*

By February 1705 Händel's confidence with the success of his very first opera, *Almira*, was fading. He thought he had mastered the technique, and that it would get easier and easier. No, he was struggling with the libretto of *Nero*, written by Feustking. Something was not right. It should have been much easier, now that the libretto was entirely in German, but he could not find inspiration. This time, he was quite determined to not ask advice from Mattheson, but he needed someone's opinion. Who to ask? Keiser was still away. Schiefferdecker? Write to Telemann again? Then an idea struck him. He rummaged through his small collection of music and pulled out what he had copied in Hanover. Steffani's music! He went through some cantatas and arias. Then he found a wordbook Ortensio Mauro had given him of Steffani's opera *La liberta contenta (The happy freedom)*. Mauro's text was poetic, rich in mood, expression, and temperament. Then he had another idea and went to see Schiefferdecker.

'Feustking? Yes, I know him a little, just as a librettist,' said Schiefferdecker. 'Why?'

'Hmm, is he... in trouble? I mean, does he have rivals?'

Schiefferdecker smiled. 'Are you not aware? There is a war going on. Feustking against two of his colleagues.'

'Oh, how fair! Two against one?'

'Well, he has the brain to confront two of them together, I suppose.'

'Has that been going on for a while?'

'Yes, it started with *Almira*.'

So it was obvious. Feustking had been too busy to concentrate on the libretto. It was more important to defend himself. Händel had no choice but to do his best with what he had been given. The muse refused to smile upon him. Tunes did not come flooding to pour on the score. *If only I could choose the librettist*. Then he started to accuse himself for not being able to handle a libretto, any libretto. *I should be able to deal with any kind of libretto.* Still he yearned to have a librettist like Mauro. This wish he would have to wait a long time to see granted. He went through a painful process of squeezing out tunes, and it took longer to complete *Nero* than *Almira*. *Nero*'s reception was lukewarm, and he knew why. It ran for three nights, and was interrupted by Lent, luckily. It was just a fortunate coincidence to conceal its failure. Händel was determined to revise it, but Feustking refused to revise the text, saying that he would not be paid for it.

'Would it be so? I really need to revise *Nero*,' said Händel to Mattheson.

'Feustking is right,' Mattheson looked at his friend, feeling sorry. 'It's for Keiser to decide, and he is not here.' And he knew that Keiser would not give Händel another chance. Failure was a failure. There was no mending.

'Oh...'

'You will be paid – not as much as Keiser, but I did my best to negotiate for you,' Mattheson said.

'Thank you, Mattheson.' Again, Händel had to acknowledge his friend's generosity and kindness.

The failure of his second opera was a blow in two ways. He wanted his success to continue, and with the success get paid better. He had never changed his mind about going to Italy. He'd been saving as much as he could, but it was far from being able to fund his travel to the motherland of opera. Italy seemed still far away.

'Händel?' Mattheson saw his friend looking low.

Händel made a little start. 'Oh, yes... So, did you hear from Mr Keiser?'

'Not really. I suppose he will be back after Easter.'

Keiser was in fact back in Hamburg after Easter 1705. By then, the opera company had once again run into difficulties. Beset by financial problems and an unstable relationship with the Hamburg citizenry, the theatre did not reopen after Easter.

It was obvious that *Nero* could not be played. It would only increase the losses. Keiser commissioned a libretto, *Octavia*, from Feustking. It was a remake of *Nero*, sharing several characters. Keiser did not ask Händel to compose anymore, nor did he ask Mattheson. Keiser had to do his best to regain the public attention. So Händel returned to his post as harpsichordist, but his mind was not in the theatre anymore. A recent letter from Stefani urging him to go to Italy made him restless. His mind was all Italy and nothing else. He longed to go to the source of opera and learn the authentic style. He knew he could not achieve that by remaining in Hamburg.

Now he accepted more teaching to increase his earnings. This task was challenging, as he lacked in one essential quality for teaching: patience. And he saved more, to get ready. No more drinking with his colleagues, no more hanging around.

Händel left the house of one of his pupils, upset. He turned the corner, looked around, and started to shout.

'Oh my God, she is stupid and lazy! She never remembers what I taught her the last time! Stupid, stupid, stupid!'

'You should not say that in public like that,' a voice said behind him.

'Mattheson!'

Mattheson was smiling. 'I suppose you are talking about your pupil.'

Händel sighed, 'Yes. She is pretty, but stupid. Do you know what she did?'

'Tell me.'

'I gave her a sarabande to learn, and I played it for her, so she knows what it is.'

'And?'

'Instead of listening, she started to dance, laughing! I am not an accompanist!'

Mattheson laughed. 'I see. She looks quite hopeless.'

'I want to save money, but it is so hard to contain my anger.'

'You are short-tempered,' said Mattheson dryly, as usual.

'I admire you. How can you stand a stupid pupil and not lose your temper?'

'Well, it is not difficult for me, I just don't take it too seriously. But for you, I think the best thing is to just imagine that you are teaching a few coins and not a human being.'

'I can try, but...'

'But?'

'Difficult . . .'

'Then imagine the pupil is Italy.'

Händel sighed.

'Oh, by the way, did you know that Schiefferdecker is gone?'

'Schiefferdecker?'

'Yes, and guess where.' Mattheson looked amused.

'Um...I don't know... to a court somewhere?'

'No, Lübeck. He went to Lübeck, Händel,' and he started to laugh.

'Is he...'

'Yes. And, by extraordinary coincidence, as soon as he was gone, there was one to replace him here!'

'Oh, who is it?'

'One called Graupner.'

'Graupner? Is it Christoph Graupner?' Händel nearly shouted in excitement.

'Yes. Do you know him?' Mattheson asked, astonished.

'I met him in Leipzig! What a small world!'

In Lübeck, Dietrich Buxtehude accepted Schiefferdecker, the first harpsichord player at the Hamburg Opera House, as his assistant. After Händel and Mattheson's visit, Buxtehude still could not find his successor for another three years, to his frustration. Then a young virtuoso appeared. Johann Sebastian Bach walked 140 miles from Arnstadt to hear him and meet him. The young man was brilliant, and the old organist was finally satisfied. As Bach stayed months in Lübeck, Buxtehude assumed that the succession was assured. Then the young man disappeared at once, just after he was introduced to the organist's daughter, Margreta. Only then did Buxtehude realise that his daughter was an issue. He was getting old and his daughter was getting impatient. He had no choice but to compromise. As Schiefferdecker was willing to marry his daughter, he would train him as much as he could until he died. He knew there would be no retirement.

If Händel was disappointed by *Nero*'s failure, he was delighted to learn Telemann's new appointment.

> Sorau, June 1705
>
> Dear Händel,
>
> As I told you, I was invited by Count Erdmann II of Promnitz at Sorau to become his Kapellmeister a year ago, and much to Kuhnau's frustration, my resignation was only accepted by the Leipzig authorities two weeks ago. So I hurried myself to leave, and here I am in Sorau.
>
> The count is two years older than myself. He inherited his father's vast estate two years ago, and that was the reason I was invited. Now the count will be married soon, and the palace is quite upside down in preparation. I am busy composing for the celebration.
>
> Here, French music is played most, and I am excited to study Lully and Campra. The

> court spends six months in Pless during the winter, and I cannot wait to hear the local music there!
>
> Your humble servant and brother,
> Georg Philipp Telemann

Ansbach, June 1705

Wilhelmina Charlotte Caroline of Brandenburg-Ansbach, known as Caroline of Ansbach, was still in shock. The premature death of her spiritual mother, guardian, and friend, Sophia Charlotte, Queen *in* Prussia, four months before was still a painful memory. The lively court disappeared at once with the sudden death of the queen. The king was too distressed to keep the court as before, and she found no space to stay. Her desire, her only desire was to follow the queen, as she expressed in a letter she had written to Leibniz, librarian at the court of Hanover, who had been a regular at the queen's court in Berlin.

Back in Ansbach, devastated, she was considering entering a convent. She had lost her father when she was three and her mother when she was thirteen. It was Sophia Charlotte who welcomed her at the Berlin court, gave her education, and most importantly, gave her security. For the first time in her life, she had felt loved and had found happiness in the lively intellectual environment. She had been loved by Sophia Charlotte as if she were her own daughter. The young girl's lively mind had been perfect for development in this court, which attracted many scholars, including Gottfried Leibniz.

'Caroline, you cannot stay indoors like this,' said her brother.

'Oh, Wilhelm Friedrich, I have no joy in life,' said Caroline, still in mourning dress. She was asking herself what was the purpose of life. She felt empty.

Her younger brother, Margrave of Brandenburg-Ansbach, was fond of his sister. In his early childhood, when insecurity dominated, his sister was there, like a rock, to comfort him. Now he felt it was his turn to protect her, and at the same time, he wished her a happy marriage. He was certain that her beauty and intelligence deserved it. She was a devout Lutheran, and her faith prevailed over her chance to marry Archduke Charles of Austria, the future emperor. She finally chose to not convert to Catholicism, and turned down the proposal.

'Sister, tears do not suit you,' he said softly, 'and I think the late queen would be unhappy to see you like this.'

Caroline gasped, her eyes wide open. She stared at her brother, looked away, and then nodded. She had not thought of it in this way. She was just drowning herself in the grief. *It's true. She loved me, and she always wished me happiness. I am not making her happy by being miserable.* The recovery began.

Prince Georg August of Hanover was visiting Ansbach under the name of Monsieur de Busch. This was planned by his father, Georg Ludwig, Elector of Hanover, who was anxious to find him a wife. He did not wish his son to repeat his unhappy, arranged, and loveless marriage. He wanted his son to meet Caroline first without any commitment. Caroline was six months older than the young prince, but she looked younger. Also, it had been the elector's late sister's last wish. The elector still remembered vividly. On her deathbed, Sophia Charlotte had wanted to see her older brother in private.

'Görgen,' she called him by his nickname, 'please consider. She is really a lovely girl, intelligent and discreet. I've always hoped for this union.'

Georg August was immediately smitten with the beauty of Caroline. Edmund Poley, the English envoy to Hanover, was accompanying the young prince incognito and saw it at once. He smiled to himself and thought, *Well this was quick!*

Though the electoral prince thought his disguise was perfect, Caroline's vivid intelligence was not fooled. Despite his perfect French, she knew immediately that the young man was not just a travelling French gentleman. However, she did not try to identify him. *If he is serious, I will know soon*, she thought. She was right.

'Sister, guess who that Monsieur de Busch was,' Wilhelm said to Caroline excitedly.

'He is not French, I am sure. I think he is German and quite highborn. Am I right?' Caroline replied, suppressing her curiosity.

'Well, I just received an official introduction from the court of Hanover.'

'Hanover?'

'Yes, Hanover. He is Prince Georg August, the heir of the elector, and he is also third in line to the British throne.'

'British throne . . .' Caroline whispered. It sounded like the far end of the world.

'Yes. He is the grandson of Sophia of Hanover, who is the granddaughter of James I of England.'

'Oh, so he is the nephew of my second mother.'

'Exactly. What do you think?'

'I liked him, but is he . . .'

'Yes, he is protestant. Lutheran, like us and your second mother. So?'

She did not answer. Her second mother's nephew. Is that why she felt something familiar? She felt destiny drawing her towards Hanover.

The marriage contract was concluded by the end of July 1705. On 22 August 1705 Caroline arrived in Hanover, accompanied by her brother the margrave, and in the evening, she was married in the palace chapel of Herrenhausen. She was twenty-two years old. Her suite was modest, reflecting the small state of the Principality of Ansbach compared to the electorate of Hanover. However, her husband and his family welcomed her simply and warmly. The elector wanted a happy marriage for his son, not a business transaction.

Sophia of Hanover was still dressed in black. She saw Caroline of Ansbach getting out of the carriage and liked her instantly. 'My daughter loved you as her own daughter. I am so happy that you are now my granddaughter,' said the dowager duchess, opening her arms to Caroline.

Caroline knew that because of her grandmother-in-law's welcome, she would not be looked down upon despite the smallness of her dowry. Also, she knew that to strengthen her position, she needed to produce an heir as soon as possible.

Hamburg, Early Summer 1706

The decision was made. *It is time*, Händel thought. He also remembered his father's letter about travel, recommending he do it during summer when the weather was dry, the days longer, and the roads easier. *Avoid traveling in the winter unless absolutely necessary. The roads could be flooded and impossible to drive, wasting time and money.* He had no time or money to waste.

Now he needed to get ready. The Hamburg Opera kept undergoing crisis. It was marked by financial insecurity, personal and political quarrels and vigorous pamphleteering, causing the decline in public interest. He had composed another opera, a quite substantial one, *Florindo and Daphne*, but did not know if it would ever be performed under the circumstances.

'Shirts?' Mattheson looked at his friend.
'Yes, shirts. I need more shirts. How can I get them?' asked Händel.
'I don't know. Normally, it's the valet's job, but I don't have one,' said Mattheson. He had now been secretary to the British resident John Wych since January, and Händel knew he was very much attracted to Wych's daughter.
'So who is doing your valet's job?'
'My mother.'

'Oh…' Händel lowered his head. 'Then, I don't know what to do. I cannot ask your mother to be my valet.'

Matheson laughed, and said, 'I am sure she will be very happy to help you, or my sister will. She has a fondness for you.'

Mrs Mattheson was very diligent.

'You will need at least two types of shirts, Mr Händel. I heard the summer in Italy is horribly hot, so you will need muslin. How many do you need?'

'Hmm, I don't know, madam.'

'How many do you have now?'

'Twelve.'

'Are they all worn? Do they need repair?'

'Some of them.'

'So, you keep those old shirts for travelling and for everyday. Then you will need six in cambric and six in muslin. Oh, I forgot one important question. How old are you, Mr Händel?'

'I am twenty-one, madam.'

'Twenty-one! You look younger than that. Well, so you are fully grown. That's easier.'

Händel did not know what to say.

Mrs Mattheson continued, 'How about the suits? Do you have enough?'

'I think so, madam. It's just the shirts. My mother took care of those, so I had no idea how to get them.'

'Oh, good. Do you want me to get the fabric for you, or do you want to come with me, Mr Händel?'

'I'll come with you, madam.' He did not want Mrs Mattheson to feel used like a valet.

What Händel thought would be an hour errand turned out to be much more complicated. Mrs Mattheson suggested he get some lace for neck cloths and cuffs as well.

'You are going to Italy. You will attend the courts, won't you?'

'I suppose so, madam.'

'Then, you must look refined. It is nice just to be clean and simple, but the court is not the same thing, I believe.'

'I see. I'll need the shirts like the ones Mr Keiser wears.'

'He does not need that here, Mr Händel. There is no court. It's rather pretentious, in my opinion.'

Again, Händel did not know what to say.

Mrs Mattheson continued, 'And he has a valet. I don't know how he can pay, feed, and clothe a valet with his salary. Now, Mr Händel, we have everything we need for your shirts. I'll take you to my seamstress. You can go to a tailor to make your shirts, but it will be much more expensive. I have a very good one I use, and very reasonable. You will be satisfied, Mr Händel.'

'I thank you, madam. Do I need to come with you?'

'Of course. You need to be measured. Not like a tailor would, but she needs to know some measurements.'

'Yes, madam.'

The seamstress was a middle-aged, good-natured, plump woman. She welcomed Mrs Mattheson and Händel.

'You bring me a handsome young man. That's dangerous, you know, Mrs Mattheson.'

'Greta, we have no time for this. Mr Händel is busy.'

The seamstress laughed, 'I see. I just need to measure the round of the neck, the length of the arms, and the length of the shirts he wants.' She busied herself around Händel, who stood like a scarecrow. She also agreed to mend Händel's existing shirts, which Mrs Mattheson had suggested.

Händel came back to his lodging tired. This was something he'd never done before, and he realised how time consuming it was to prepare for a long stay away from home. He had been living away from his family for three years, but it was still his homeland. Now he was heading for a land where everything was different. For how long? He did not know. A year? More? It was exciting but daunting at the same time. He was going into the unknown. One thing was certain. He would not come back until he had mastered the art of composing operas.

Now he was busy checking the list. Paper, ink, stave-ruler and candles for composition. Hat, gloves, wig, powder, cravat, shirts, suits, travelling coat, stockings, shoes, boots, and sword to get dressed. Passport and money. He lacked only letters of introduction which he hoped to get in Düsseldorf. Getting ready, he felt resistance to sever links with his country and the Protestant lands. His mind was swaying between the sadness of leaving his native lands and excitement for the future. However, he felt an irresistible draw to Italy. Now with first-hand experience of the theatre, he felt more comfortable challenging the homeland of opera.

He'd managed to save two hundred ducats for the journey, and he was planning to stop at courts on the way, to display his skill.

'So you are going, Händel,' said Mattheson.

'Yes.'

'That's sad…'

'Really? Why?' Händel asked jokingly.

'I cannot try to kill you anymore.'

They looked at each other, and laughed.

'I have to, Mattheson. It's the best place. Opera is my life, and I go for the best.'

'I see. You got the bug.'

'Bug?'

'You are right... so Lübeck is out of the question?'

'I never considered it seriously.'

'Since you saw his daughter.'

'No. Well, that helped, of course, but I just wanted to try the organ. I never wanted to be buried in a job like that. No. And...'

'And?'

'You told me that Schiefferdecker is there now.'

'Yes, he is Mr Buxtehude's assistant now.'

'Then the post is taken, I suppose?'

'Well, yes...'

They looked at each other, thinking the same thing.

'How about Esther Sbuelen?' Mattheson asked.

'What are you talking about?'

Mattheson did not insist. 'You want big.'

'I want everything, and what's the form of music having nearly everything at the same time? It's opera.'

'That's the bug. And you want big.'

'I like the human voice. I cannot sing like you, and I envy you. The human voice is... unique. There are no two voices the same. And when it is a beautiful one, God . . . I have to make music for the voice, accompanied by instruments and scenery, and—'

'So you want big.'

Händel looked at Mattheson and said placidly, 'Of course I want big. What a question.'

They laughed.

'Don't forget London, though, Händel. Italy is your next step, but consider London. You will make money there, like many artists. There are more foreign artists in London than native ones.'

'Do they play opera there?'

'Well, according to Mr Wych, there are two opera houses now.'

'Two? Really?'

'Yes, and one of them played an opera called Camilla recently.'

'Camilla? By Bononcini?' Händel stared at Mattheson, incredulous.

It was Mattheson's turn to stare at his friend. 'Do you know about Camilla?'

'People were talking a lot about it when I was in Berlin. Well, Bononcini was there, but I did not hear the opera.'

'Oh...' Mattheson felt ignorant. His friend was better informed than himself.

'But I wonder how they got the score,' said Händel.

'Oh, probably from the travelling musicians. It's a good way of getting extra money. With an entire score of an opera, you can get a good amount.'

'I see. How is your English?' Händel was not really interested. He could not think beyond Italy just now.

'I am doing well, I hope.'

Händel told nobody about the serious advance he had from Esther Sbuelen. She was good-natured, pretty and he felt attracted to her. It was only the words of his teacher Zachow that stopped him. *Just one wrong move and you will wreck your entire life.* The wrong move was tempting, but he knew what was his priority right now.

During the three years he spent in Hamburg, he had acquired more experience in life. Compared to the very protected setting in Halle with its strong protestant traits, Hamburg offered much more gaiety and also vice. Händel faced, for the first time, the real boisterousness of youth. That experience was now part of him.

Händel knew his Italian was still not very good, but he did not care. What he needed was practice. He needed to be bathed completely in Italian, and the only way was to go there. *And yes, I am going there!* He remembered what Mattheson had said: 'If you want to perfect your Italian, place yourself in an Italian family. Do not seek German families there. You'll end up speaking German all the time.' That was typical of Mattheson. He had no idea that Händel would probably live amongst the Italian nobility. And he did not tell Mattheson that he was going to Düsseldorf first, where Agostino Steffani was waiting to introduce him to Elector Johann Wilhelm II of Palatine and his wife. Now aged twenty-one, the young composer's mind was filled with excitement, leaving little space for his mother. However, he did not forget to write to her.

In Halle, Dorothea Händel, with the letter from her son, went to the church. Italy sounded like the end of the world, so far away. She prayed for a safe journey. *He will be remembered and loved by the whole world.* The young Gipsy woman's voice resonated in Dorothea's memory. *So would this be the beginning?* she wondered. She could only pray for her son's safety.

Chapter 6 : A Saxon in Italy: I am Giorgio Hendel (1706 – 1707)

Florence, Palazzo Pitti, Summer 1706

Marquess Luca Casimiro degli Albizzi, master of the household, stopped Antonio Salvi in the corridor and greeted him warmly. Though born in the same year, they looked very different.

'Good day, Dottore Salvi. Are you here for the grand duke or the grand prince?' asked Luca Casimiro casually.

'The grand duke, Marquess,' replied the tall, thin man.

'Right. I shall see you later then.'

Salvi watched the back of the short and fat master of the household walking away from him.

Antonio Salvi was visiting Grand Duke Cosimo III, not as a court poet but as a court physician.

'I am fine, Salvi, but I am concerned,' said the grand duke.

'Would Grand Duke tell me?' asked Salvi.

'It's Violante.'

'Is she unwell?'

'Well, no. But . . .'

'But?'

'Salvi. She is not producing any children! It is a desperate situation for the family!'

'Grand Duke, I do understand your frustration.'

'Is she barren?'

'How long has she been married to the grand prince?'

'Since 1688! She was not even sixteen when she arrived here! Now she is thirty-three!'

'Eighteen years of marriage... I do understand your concern, Grand Duke.'

Everybody knew the reason, even the grand duke himself. Prince Ferdinando was indifferent to his wife. When he married the young girl of fifteen from Munich the marriage was probably consummated, just as a duty. Although they both loved music, Ferdinando found nothing attractive about Violante. She, on the contrary, had fallen in love with her husband and was determined to remain his wife. Still, she was miserable for being ignored.

'She is a lovely girl – well, not a girl anymore.' The grand duke sighed.

'You should not lose hope. Pray to God. A miracle can happen.'
'Miracle? Do I need a miracle?'
'The French king Louis XIV was born after twenty-three years of marriage.'
The grand duke stared at his physician. 'Twenty-three years... how do you know?'
'It is well known in France. So the Sun King himself is considered God's gift, or a miracle.'
'Well, Salvi, you give me hope. Yes, I will pray.' The grand duke smiled. 'If my wish is fulfilled, I will build a church, a splendid one to beat the cathedral!' the aging ruler exclaimed, with his face radiant, filled with hope.

Dr Antonio Salvi felt a pang of guilt as knew that the miracle would not happen. The grand duke was right; it was indeed a desperate situation. All three children of the grand duke were childless, and there was very little hope of the birth of an heir. The grand duke's second son's marriage was another disaster. And his daughter in Düsseldorf was also childless. Salvi thought it was destiny.

However, the grand duke was not ready to give up. He would chivvy his daughter-in-law from now on, but there was no guaranty as his son was always away from his wife. Now it seemed the only hope, the real hope, would be his brother, Cardinal Francesco Maria.

Francesco Maria de' Medici was enjoying his life and was far from imagining his life being completely torn apart by his older brother. In his Villa di Lappeggi near Siena, inherited from a relative in 1667, he maintained his personal court. He had put all his money and effort into renovating the house and making the gardens a spectacular display of his taste. Banquets, parties and entertainments were held. He shared the love of music with his nephew Ferdinando, the grand prince. He kept promoting a castrato, Giovanni Battista Tamburini, who, when young, was probably the cardinal's lover. The cardinal ignored the signs of illness and carried on with his immoderate and immoral lifestyle.

Düsseldorf, Summer 1706

'Mr Händel, I wrote a letter of introduction to my brother-in-law, Ferdinando de' Medici, in Florence, and my wife's letter is with it,' said Elector Palatine Johann Wilhelm.

'So my brother cannot miss my letter,' said the electress, laughing. She smiled at her husband, who smiled back.

'I thank you very much, Your Highness.' Händel bowed to the elector. Then he repeated the same thing, bowing to Anna Maria, seated beside her husband.

'It was a real pleasure to have you here, Mr Händel. Do come back,' said the elector, weighing his words.

'I cannot find enough words to express my gratitude for the generous hospitality, Your Highness. It will be my pleasure to return here.'

'You are welcome at any time, Mr Händel,' said the electress.

This was Händel's first court experience since Berlin. He was more at ease, and did his best to entertain the elector and his wife.

A voice from behind stopped Händel. 'Oh, let me say goodbye!' He saw Valeriano Pellegrini, the favourite castrato of the elector, coming towards him. 'Are you leaving for Italy?'

'Yes, I am.'

'My country! Are you going to Rome?'

'That is my intention.'

'I was a choirboy at the Sistine Chapel... That was a long time ago.'

'How wonderful, the Sistine Chapel!' Händel exclaimed.

Coming from Rome's Sistine Chapel meant first rank provenance. However the singer was simple, just enjoying being spoiled by the elector, without becoming arrogant.

'You must be busy. I will not detain you more. I just wanted to wish you a safe journey.' He took Händel's hands in his.

'Thank you, Signor Pellegrini.'

'I really enjoyed singing with your accompaniment. You are amazing,' said the castrato, smiling. 'We shall meet again. I am sure we shall.'

Händel looked up at the tall and thin singer. Pellegrini was the second castrato he had met. This was a precious experience, as he realised that in Italy, a castrato was a crucial element in an opera.

'Of course, Signor Pellegrini,' the young composer smiled.

'So?' Agostino Steffani asked.

'Yes, I got what I wanted, plus a purse full of money,' said Händel, beaming.

'Good. I told the elector it would be more practical to give you money than a piece of jewellery.'

'Thank you, Father.'

'I hope it will cover the trip until you reach Munich. I wrote you the letter of introduction to Elector Max Emmanuel there. I first served his father. I grew up in the court of Munich, so you will be received warmly.'

'That's why your German is so good.'

'Thank you, but I remain Italian in my heart.'

'I will stop at Munich, Father, and do my best to please the elector.'

'Now, I have written to Count Antonio Maria Fede in Rome about you.

This is my letter of introduction for you to him. With this, you will be able to access important people in Rome. He is well connected. You are armed now. But I have to warn you. The political situation is quite unstable. You are going to Florence first, I suppose?'

'Yes, Maestro.'

'Observe the situation from Florence before heading to Rome. Try to inform yourself as much as you can.'

'I cannot thank you enough, Father.'

'It is really fortunate that you are going on your own.'

'Father?' Händel did not understand.

'Think. If you were going there paid by the elector of Hanover, or the Palatinate, you would be regarded as an enemy.' Seeing Händel puzzled, he continued, 'Remember this: Italy is divided into various city-states, principalities and duchies, and they are mainly pro-French, and the northern German states are against France. I am talking about the ongoing War of the Spanish Succession.'

'Oh . . .' Händel was not convinced. This war was still far away from him. He knew of it only through word-of-mouth.

'So you proved to be right by refusing the King in Prussia's offer.'

'What?' Händel gasped. 'How did you…'

Steffani laughed but did not explain. 'In Florence, try to see as much as you can. And the grand prince has his private theatre in Pratolino, just outside Florence.'

'A private theatre? Just for him?' said Händel, incredulous.

'Yes. Try to go there, Pratolino. Now I have to tell you, Prince Ferdinando has a strong character, rebellious against his father the grand duke. And he is a libertine.'

'Oh.'

'I have to warn you, Mr Händel, that the grand princess, his wife, is Duchess of Bavaria, and she is the sister of Elector Max Emmanuel in Munich. But she is not loved by her husband, quite the contrary. That's why I did not write the letter of introduction to her. You have to be careful to not upset the grand prince.'

'I see.'

'The princess loves him, but he does not love her. It is known that he talks of her as being too ugly and too dull.'

'Do you know why?'

'I think that it is a way for the prince to rebel against his father for the arranged marriage. No more than that.'

'I am sorry to hear that.'

'I am sorry too. She is a lovely girl – well, now she is a mature woman.'

Steffani looked at Händel with a serious expression. 'Now, is your bruise gone?'

'What… are you…' Händel gasped, again.
Steffani laughed. 'I am a diplomat. I have informers everywhere.'
Händel lowered his head, ashamed. So he would have to carry this for the rest of his life?
'I see. Maybe the mark is gone, but it is still hurting in your mind,' said the priest.
'Yes, Father, I must confess. I regret, really and truly. If I could go back in time…' he whispered.
Steffani took Händel's hands in his, and said, 'You are young. Be careful, and don't forget the lesson you learnt from it.'
'Yes, Father. It was a lesson. A big one.' Händel felt the warmth of Steffani's hands.
'Now, go with God's blessing. I pray for you.'
'It is all thanks to you that I can go to Italy, Maestro Steffani,' Händel knelt and kissed his hand.
'Perfect! You do it very well to greet the cardinals,' laughed Steffani.

Dear Telemann,

    Just arrived in Florence and took a room in Il Cervo, just next to the cathedral. I was very well received in Düsseldorf, thanks to Steffani. I owe him everything. He is a really generous person. I was very much welcomed in Munich by the elector, who was eager to know about Steffani's welfare. The court of Munich is splendid, and the musicians are happy to work there. They are well treated and respected. The journey was long but not too bad, thanks to the good weather.

    I just sent the letter of introduction to Grand Prince Ferdinando. I will visit the churches around while waiting and try to sneak to the organ loft, if possible.

Your most faithful servant,
Georg Friederich Händel

BRIGHT STAR

Florence, Autumn 1706

Alessandro Scarlatti was bitterly disappointed. Grand Prince Ferdinando de' Medici had no intention of taking him on as his court composer. He had been trying for years. Antonio Salvi was the Medici's family doctor, court poet, and librettist, and he was well respected and loved. The prince used Giacomo Antonio Perti as a composer, but the latter was based in Bologna. There was no permanent composer at court. That's what Scarlatti had been hoping for. He had been composing operas for five consecutive years for the grand prince and he had delivered each one in person. And, each time, the grand prince made allusion to hiring him. He believed it, but now he thought he had just been used. The prince received the score of the commissioned opera, *Il Gran Tamerlano (The Great Tamerlan)*, paid the composer, and that was it. Scarlatti was not even invited to conduct. He was just a supplier of music. The prince himself conducted at Pratolino. Scarlatti did not want to try or wait anymore. He'd had enough.

'Ten scudi!' he uttered in disbelief. That was not even the price for a small cantata. He had supplied a full opera and delivered it to the prince himself. Scarlatti felt humiliated. All he could do was write to the prince to thank him, give him some ideas about the music, and try to get more money.

'I am not doing this for you, Prince. I am doing it for my music,' he muttered between clenched teeth. This was enough for him to give up the idea of being in the prince's service. 'There is nothing to do in Florence,' he said, and looked around the shabby room. 'Now I will focus on Rome and Venice for commissions.' He sighed deeply and started to pack. He stopped at hearing the bell from the church nearby, and shook his head. He could not even have the courage to attend the Sunday mass. He was certain to blame God.

Not far from Scarlatti's modest hotel, the grand duke was giving his arm to the grand princess to escort her to the chapel of Palazzo Pitti. It was Sunday morning. It could not be more awkward to see the very fat and very thin figures walking side by side. The grand princess was, as had become the habit, wearing a narrow hoop so she could stay close to the grand duke and hold his arm.

'Dottore Salvi told me that the French king was born after twenty-three years of marriage,' said the grand duke, walking beside his daughter-in-law.

'The Sun King?' Violante looked at her father-in-law, who was looking straight ahead.

'Yes.' Before entering the chapel, the grand duke stopped and faced his daughter-in-law. 'Princess, let us pray. There is still hope.' He smiled.

Violante's heart sank. She would love to satisfy her father-in-law, but she knew it was impossible. Within a few seconds, she felt anger growing and the strong desire to shout at him, 'Well, tell your son, not me!' However, she managed to suppress all emotions, smile shyly at her father-in-law, and nod. The grand duke looked satisfied.

Händel looked up from the window of the carriage approaching Palazzo Pitti. The palace was colossal and in a rustic style, built of stone. From far off, Händel could see its severe and forbidding appearance. Now as he approached, it seemed impressive. However, behind this projection of power, there was something gloomy. The vast front courtyard was completely deserted. Händel felt uneasy, but he brushed his feeling off, blaming it on the grey sky. This was the place where the Medici family had been living for generations. Elector Johann Wilhelm's recommendation had been effective. Grand Prince Ferdinando replied quickly to summon him. This would be the first court experience in Italy. He felt apprehensive. The very first thing would be to display his harpsichord playing skill, as usual. Apparently the grand prince himself is an able player. *Could I impress the grad prince?* There was another reason for Händel to be nervous. In Munich he had been given a secret mission from the elector.

The carriage stopped at the main entrance, and a servant came to open the door. Another one led the way inside. Händel was left in an empty room with just benches against the walls. He looked around and up. The walls were painted with outdoor scenes, and the ceiling was painted as a sky. Footsteps made Händel turn, and he saw the double doors flung open.

Another servant in livery appeared and led Händel to the first floor by a monumental staircase. Händel made a huge effort not to look around. Everything was huge, and he felt small. *This is not a human place; it is for the giants*, he thought. Going through the large and long corridors seemed to take forever. Eventually they stopped in front of a double door, and the servant announced him. The double doors were opened from inside.

The grand prince was in his study. Middle-aged, elegant, and handsome, Ferdinando de' Medici was seated at his desk. He looked very relaxed. Händel recognised the letter of introduction on the desk.

'You impressed my brother-in-law and my sister, Mr Andel,' he said in a quite lazy tone, 'and Agostino Steffani likes you a lot.'

'I thank you very much, Your Highness, for your kind invitation.' He looked in the prince's eyes and bowed lightly.

'You must be tired, Mr Andel. Have a good rest, and I will see you at dinner,' said the grand prince, without moving. Then he addressed his valet standing nearby. 'Take care of Mr Andel, Marco, would you?'

'Yes, Your Highness,' said Marco.

The valet led Händel to a room on the second floor.

'This is your room, sir.'

'Thank you.'

'Do you have your luggage with you, sir?'
'No.'
'Where are they, sir?'
'At the inn by the Duomo, Il Cervo.'
'I will make sure they are brought as soon as possible, sir.' Then he was gone.

Händel had watched in confusion as the valet disappeared. The latter had shown absolutely no emotion, with his face like a mask. Then Händel realised and was quite surprised. *I am a house guest already!* The letter must have been quite flattering for him to be accepted without any display first.

Händel was not unfamiliar with palaces, but Palazzo Pitti was beyond his imagination. The scale was quite inhuman. The ceiling was so high that he felt small and insignificant. *It is not the time to be impressed,* he told himself. *It is time to impress.* Händel still felt uneasy. No instruction came. He knew that he could not explore the palace without permission. He could only guess that he would not be summoned to play until dinner time. His luggage was brought quickly, so he just busied himself going through the scores he had copied in Düsseldorf and brought with him.

After hours left alone in his room, Händel was following a servant, at last. He could hear a harpsichord playing and a woman singing somewhere. *Very nice voice,* he thought. The servant stopped in front of a room and waited until the end of the piece before opening the door. Händel saw the grand prince himself at the harpsichord and a woman beside him, surrounded by an entourage.

'Here is the Saxon! Come in, Mr Andel. Come in and meet Vittoria,' said the grand prince.

Vittoria Tarquini was her name. *Probably in her late twenties,* Händel thought. Of medium height and slightly chubby, she was stunningly beautiful. He was quite impressed to see how different she was from Caroline of Ansbach. Both were blond with blue eyes, both stunningly beautiful, and still, very different. Vittoria was wearing a blue dress that matched her eyes, and her blond, fluffy hair was decorated all over with small, white flowers. It gave her the air of a fairy. But Händel's attention was on the harpsichord.

'Prince, you have a nice harpsichord.'

'And you have nice fingers to play, I suppose.' The prince laughed and got up. 'It's your turn.'

'Prince, do you have any preference?' Händel asked, seated in front of the harpsichord. That was the right thing to ask.

Prince Ferdinando looked pleased. 'I'd love to have an idea of the opera played in Hamburg. My brother, Gian Gastone heard one, but I think he was drunk as usual.'

People surrounding the harpsichord laughed very discreetly. So Händel decided to improvise and make a medley from the opera *Salomon* by Keiser.

It was the very first one he had heard in Hamburg. Prince Ferdinando was attentive, and Keiser's French style seemed to please him. When he finished, the prince clapped. The others followed.

'Bravo, Maestro! So, what was that?'

'It is from the opera *Salomon* by Keiser, Your Highness, Reinhard Keiser.'

'Is he the director of the opera house in Hamburg?'

'He is, Your Highness.'

'Interesting, very interesting, and quite different.'

The doors were flung open, and a richly dressed woman entered. Händel, imitating everybody, stood up and bowed. Violante of Bavaria was pale and thin.

'Princess, meet Mr Andel. He came from Hamburg,' said the grand prince.

'Hamburg, that's a long trip,' said the grand princess in German. Her eyes were bright with curiosity.

'Mr Andel, this is Grand Princess Violante, Duchess of Bavaria.'

'It is my honour to meet you, Your Highness. My name is Georg Friederich Händel,' Händel replied in German before quickly repeating it in Italian.

The grand princess smiled. 'Did you stop in Munich, Mr Händel?'

'Yes, I did.'

'You saw my brother?'

'Yes, Princess.'

'You'll have to tell me all about it, but not tonight. I feel quite tired.'

'Are you not dining with us, Princess?' asked Ferdinando.

'No, Prince. With your permission, I'd like to stay in my room.'

'As you wish, Princess.'

Händel saw others bow again, and did the same. When he lifted his head, he saw that Vittoria was still bowing very low. She was the last to lift her head, looking down.

'Let's eat, and you can tell me more about the opera house in Hamburg, Maestro,' said the grand prince jollily. 'By the way, your name is Endel, not Andel? Princess pronounced it Endel.'

'It's closer to Endel but with an *h* sound, Prince.' *Oh how my name is mutilated, with Italians unable to pronounce h*, he thought.

The grand prince was not listening.

Vittoria sat to the left of the grand prince, who indicated that Händel should sit on his right.

'Mr Saxon, you are the guest of honour.'

'I thank you, Grand Prince,' said Händel bowing, and he sat. 'I feel extremely honoured.'

Prince Ferdinando was merry. 'You know, Mr Saxon, Vittoria was the star of our last opera at Pratolino.' He placed his hand on her right hand. 'You just missed it.'

'May I ask which opera, Prince?'

'You answer, Vittoria.'

'It was called *Il Gran Tamerlano*, and I was Asteria.'

'May I ask who composed it?'

'Scarlatti, Alessandro Scarlatti. Do you know him?' asked the grand prince.

'No, Prince,' Händel replied. He had never heard his name in Hamburg, Hanover, or Düsseldorf. He felt ignorant. *Well, that's why I am here*, he thought.

The next day, Händel was shown some rooms by Marco, still devoid of any expression.

'The grand prince asked me to show you the *sala dei cimbali* and to tell you that you are welcome to play all the instruments there and elsewhere,' said Marco, 'and you are welcome to walk in the gardens.'

'Please thank the grand prince for me.'

Then he was left alone again. This was disturbing. *What to do? Where is the grand prince?* This was not the first time Händel had stayed in a palace as a guest, but he had never been left to his own devices. Normally a work was suggested quite quickly, and it kept him busy, meeting the singers and instrumentalists. *Where are they? Nobody?* The palace seemed deserted. At least he was now free to look around. Not knowing what to do, he just went to the music room to try the instruments, and there he forgot the time. The collection was wonderful. He was in the midst of an improvisation when he was interrupted abruptly by a servant.

'The grand prince is asking for you, sir.' The man nearly pushed Händel from the music room.

'Ah, Mr Saxon! Come! Come to see my new acquisition!' said the grand prince excitedly. He looked quite different from last night. He did not look indolent anymore.

Händel found himself in a large room with walls covered with paintings. A few servants were busy removing several paintings from the wall. The grand prince himself was deciding the place of the newest addition to his collection. It was rather a small painting compared to the others, representing the Virgin seated in the centre with the Christ-child under a baldachin.

'Look at this masterpiece, Maestro. Isn't it wonderful?' The grand prince was all smiles. 'I never thought I would be able to get a Raphael!'

Händel looked around and realised that the paintings were placed symmetrically. The grand prince was trying to find a place for this painting.

'I think it must be in the centre, the place of honour. I could not touch it. It would be a crime to cut it to fit into a frame.'

Händel observed the frames. They were all the same.

'Oh, be careful! Don't touch the canvas! Careful. Yes, there. Maybe a little higher. Let's see.' He walked back a few paces to contemplate. 'Higher. Yes, there.'

Händel was amazed to see the grand prince show such enthusiasm. He was looking at one of the paintings when the grand prince said, 'Maestro, you seem interested. Let me show you more. Come with me.'

Rome, Autumn 1706

If Ferdinando de' Medici in Florence seemed quite happy to have a guest musician to distract him, in Rome, Francesco Maria Marescotti Ruspoli was deeply satisfied.

He had just inherited not one but two important properties not far from Rome, Vignanello and Cerveteri, as well as the title of Marquess of Cerveteri. Aged thirty-three, married, and wealthy, he was a dynamic young man. His love of music, however, was no doubt bigger than his political ambition. The two properties would bring substantial income, increasing not only his wealth but also his grandeur. He could now enlarge his musical establishment and get a house composer.

The superintendent Fabio Cavalcanti came in to interrupt his daydreaming. 'Marquess, you asked for me?'

'Yes, Fabio. Have you inquired about Maestro Scarlatti?'

'Yes, Marquess. After he left Naples, he was very much between Florence and Rome, trying to enter the service of Grand Prince Ferdinando. But I think he is not hoping for it anymore.'

'Oh? Do you know why the grand prince is not having him?'

'I tried to find out. It seems it's just the grand prince's caprice.'

'That's rather unfortunate. Where is the maestro now?'

'Here in Rome. He's been working for Cardinal Pamphili and for some churches as well.'

'I cannot steal him from Pamphili . . . Oh, and how about Signorina Durastante?'

'She accepts the invitation and will be able to come at the end of the year or the beginning of next year.'

'Very good, Fabio.'

'One more thing, Marquess, if I may.'

'Of course, Fabio.'

'I heard that Grand Prince Ferdinando is hosting a young virtuoso harpsichord player from Saxony at the moment. He composes as well.'

'Young?'

'Yes, Marquess, very young.'

'That's why, probably. With that young Saxon, he is hoping to have two for one.'
Fabio looked puzzled.
Francesco Ruspoli smiled. 'The grand prince is known to have a big taste for lovers, both male and female.'
Fabio's jaw dropped, but no word came out.
The marquess laughed. 'It's Florence, and he is a Medici. Try to find out more about the young Saxon, Fabio.'

Florence, Autumn 1706

'It's time to go. Pratolino is waiting for us!' Prince Ferdinando said jollily, and his entourage clapped in approval.
'How about the *Sassone*, Your Highness? Are you taking him with you?' Vittoria asked.
Grand Prince Ferdinando looked at her sideways and dryly said, 'No,' and nothing more. *He does not bow low enough*, he thought.
Vittoria shrugged. *I just ruined his mood.*

'Mr Saxon, I will be off to Pratolino. I'll be hunting. There is no reason for you to come, as the opera is over now. You shall come with me next year, in September.'
'I thank you, Grand Prince, for your generosity.'
'You are free to stay as long as you wish. The grand princess will be happy to take care of you.'
'Grand Prince, you are most generous.'
'Will you wait for my return?'
'I would like to leave, with your permission, Grand Prince.'
Prince Ferdinando looked surprised. 'Leave? Where?'
'Rome, Your Highness.'
'Rome! Well, good luck Mr Saxon. I might see you next time converted.' He burst into laughter. *He has contacts. Maybe he is not so low born for a musician*, he thought. He was used to seeing visiting artists stay, trying to get a permanent position.
Händel did not know if the grand prince was just mocking him or if he was hiding his surprise for not asking to stay.
Händel was not disappointed by not being included in the entourage going to Pratolino. He had just received an invitation. Francesco Ruspoli, Marquess of Cerveteri, was inviting him to Rome. This was exciting. He was quite bored in Palazzo Pitti. Prince Ferdinando was not showing very much interest in him. Händel was mainly playing the harpsichord to entertain the grand prince and his entourage. He was not asked to provide substantial

music, just some light music, not even a cantata with basso continuo. Still, he had been asked to stay. This was not what he wanted. He wanted big. He wanted to compose opera. And, now, without the grand prince, he thought he could at last accomplish the secret mission. He felt relieved. During all his time at the palace he had hardly seen the grand princess. The grand prince and his wife lived a separate life apparently. And by now he was certain that Vittoria was the grand prince's mistress, living with him publicly. He felt uneasy about it, as he thought a mistress should be the shadow figure.

As soon as the grand prince was gone, Grand Princess Violante summoned Händel. She was waiting in the gardens accompanied by a middle-aged lady.

'Mr Händel, this is Barbara. She came with me from Munich.'

Händel bowed to the woman, and she nodded without looking at him. Händel and Violante walked side by side with Barbara following behind. They talked in German, which made both of them feel more comfortable and at home.

'I hope you do not mind walking. I was thinking of receiving you in my apartments, but it is so nice out here.'

'It is, and the gardens are splendid.' Händel looked around. Both sides of the alley were bordered by impeccably trimmed hedges.

'I am sorry you were not invited to go to the Villa di Pratolino, Mr Händel. It is a beautiful place.'

'Is it where the grand prince has his own theatre, Your Highness?'

'Yes. And Pratolino is his most loved place. He goes there every autumn.'

'Oh, then I guess it is not the only place?'

Violante laughed. 'No. But Pratolino gives him two of his most loved activities: opera and hunting.'

'And what are the other places, may I ask?'

'Well, normally he spends the spring in Poggio a Caiano. He keeps a troupe of comedians there. Then in the summer he goes to Villa Imperiale.'

'So he spends only the winter here in Florence?'

'Well, he goes to Leghorn, where he pays for operas to be played.'

'Oh, God. So he is always away.'

'He wants to avoid his father. Did you see all those priests and monks surrounding the grand duke? He hates them all.'

Händel felt uneasy, not knowing what to say.

'I can accompany the grand prince if I want to. He invites me each time, but I decline most of the time. I think he is happier without my presence… and the grand duke is lonely.' She looked at Händel. 'Tell me, Mr Händel, how is my brother?'

'He is well.'

'Did you see his wife?'

'No. I was told she was away.'

'Well, they cannot stand each other.' She lowered her head, sighing. 'It is a pity my brother could not marry Sophia Charlotte of Hanover.'

Händel wanted one thing done before anything. 'Your Highness, I have something for you,' said Händel, still walking and looking straight ahead. 'I was given this from your brother, the elector, with the strict orders to give it to you directly.' He produced a letter from his jacket and handed it to the grand princess without looking at her.

She stopped, facing Händel. She pressed the letter to her chest and smiled. 'Thank you, Mr Händel. Oh, poor you! You've been waiting for this moment since you arrived?'

'Well, it was not easy, and I was getting anxious. So...'

'So not being invited by the grand prince was not too bad.' She laughed. 'You could accomplish your mission, at least.'

'That is true, Your Highness,' said Händel, smiling.

They resumed walking. 'Tell my brother, if you see him again, not to worry. I have some true friends.'

Händel could feel how isolated she was in this Medici world. She was lonely.

'I walked here a lot with Gian Gastone. I miss him.'

'I saw him in Hamburg, Your Highness.'

She stopped, surprised, 'Oh, did you? How is he?'

'Well, he does not look well. He drinks a lot.'

Violante sighed. 'I know, poor thing. His life is just a hell. Do you know about him?'

'Not very much, Princess.'

'Poor Gian Gastone, he was ignored by his father and lived a lonely life here until I arrived. We became friends. Then he was forced to marry. That was nine years ago, and it was a disaster. His wife bullies him, and he is miserable.'

'I see... He was on his own in Hamburg.'

'He escaped her.' She looked down. Sadness was emanating from her. She was not only sorry for him. They shared the same fate of an unhappy marriage and isolation. Raising her head, Violante changed the conversation. 'So you came all the way from Hamburg?'

'Well, from Düsseldorf.'

'Oh, Düsseldorf!' Violante nearly jumped. 'Did you see Steffani, then?' she asked, her eyes bright.

'Yes, Your Highness.' Händel saw excitement in her eyes. Of course, she grew up in Munich while Steffani was there. He could see that she had a great fondness for the old composer and priest.

'Oh, tell me, tell me, is he well?' She asked a lot of questions about Steffani, but did not mention her sister-in-law at all.

Without Ferdinando, Grand Princess Violante was more relaxed. She made sure that Händel could see operas and play the organ in the churches, and she had Händel meet other musicians at her service. With the grand princess, the evenings were often spent playing music, with singing, in a very pleasant environment. Händel was often invited to share the midday meal with her. When the weather was fine, she ordered the table set in the garden. Sometimes Antonio Salvi joined them.

'Mr Händel, have you met Dr Salvi already?' asked the grand princess in an easy and friendly manner.

'Doctor? I thought you were...' said Händel, looking at the man.

'Well, I am a poet and librettist, but my first function is to tend the family as a physician.' Salvi smiled.

'I see,' said Händel, looking in his eyes. 'My late father was a surgeon.'

'Oh, really?' said the grand princess, excited.

The conversation then turned to how Händel grew up having a court surgeon as a father, and he told the story of how his father retrieved a swallowed knife from a young man. He secretly thanked his father for such an entertaining story to tell.

Violante listened fascinated. This was one of the most delicious moments she'd had. She felt happy.

'After the meal, I shall take you to the *sala dei cimbali*. Mr Cristofori will be there to tune the instruments. You will like him,' said the grand princess happily. She loved music and was an able player. Händel did not understand why Prince Ferdinando was so indifferent to his wife.

Grand Princess Violante herself introduced Händel to Bartolomeo Cristofori. He was a rather short and skinny middle-aged man. He was very happy to show Händel his inventions, and after that, he bombarded the young musician with questions. He was very curious to know what was going on outside Florence.

'Mr Cristofori, are you happy with your accommodation now?' asked the grand princess.

'Yes, Your Highness. Thank you. I am fine now. It is much more calm and pleasant,' replied Cristofori with a smile.

Violante turned to Händel and said, 'Mr Cristofori was at Uffizi, but it was too busy and noisy. The place is used to house craftsmen now.'

Händel discovered that Grand Princess Violante had her own activities, setting up plays and even operas. She knew how to build her own life. And she was kind and generous to him. She had shown him all the scores she possessed and allowed him to copy freely. This was a very nice surprise. From that moment, Händel concentrated on studying and copying. The grand princess even arranged for the young composer to have enough paper and ink. He could not be more grateful. The grand princess' calming presence was like a spot of sunshine within the palace.

Händel was busy copying when he heard a voice outside his room. He raised his head to see the door open and Antonio Salvi coming in.
'Am I interrupting you, Maestro Sassone?' said Salvi.
'No, not at all. How can I help you?' said Händel, intrigued but quite happy to see the physician and poet.
'The grand princess told me you were too busy to come to dine with us today.'
'Yes. Sorry, I just wanted to finish copying.'
'I do understand. I just wanted to tell you that you made the grand princess very happy.'
Händel did not know what to say. He just stared at Salvi.
Salvi continued, 'You guessed that the grand prince has a mistress living here.'
'Yes, I did.'
'The grand princess suffers in silence,' he sighed. 'When I think that he dared to introduce his mistress to the court...' Salvi looked at the young man. 'Well, it is not to tell you this that I am here. No.'
'Do you think I am ill?'
Salvi laughed. 'I think you are a perfectly healthy young man, body and spirit.'
'Thank you, Dottore Salvi.'
'Do you have any plans for the near future, Mr Endel?'
'I am going to Rome for the moment, but . . . my intention is to learn Italian opera, to be an opera composer.'
'I thought so.'
Händel looked at Salvi, surprised. 'How do you know?'
Salvi laughed. 'It is not that difficult to guess, Maestro. You get excited when the word opera is just mentioned. I am happy you could see some here.'
'Yes. The grand princess took me to the Cocomero Theatre.'
'So what do you think?'
'Very different.' He did not go into details, but the *opera seria* (serious opera) was new to him. Serious opera meant no comic scenes, which meant dramatic and mostly tragic. And the *opera seria* was well on the way to standardisation. The division between aria and recitative was firmly established, the latter accompanied almost throughout by continuo and only on rare occasions and for special effects by the full string orchestra. The vast majority of arias were in *da capo* form. Having seen the opera seria, he was not certain he could produce such a thing. It was very different from what he composed in Hamburg.

Salvi looked at Händel. 'Now, I will be very honest with you. You are talented. Florence is not the best place for you. You should go to Venice.

That's the place for you. The opera is played all year round, and there are several theatres.'

Händel's eyes were bright with excitement.

Salvi continued, 'And Grand Prince Ferdinando is a capricious man. He chooses his musicians not according to ability. I saw how he treated Scarlatti.'

'Oh... is he...?'

Salvi sighed. 'Alessandro Scarlatti. When I think that he provided operas for Pratolino for five years... and they are masterpieces. I provided the libretti twice. With this, obviously, Scarlatti hoped to be the court musician, to be employed. Nothing. The prince just used him. And I will not be surprised if Scarlatti was left unpaid.'

Händel just stared at Salvi. That sounded dreadful. But just now, he was not worried about the payment. Being housed meant no expense, so he could just think of training himself. Before being paid, he needed to perfect his art. And having libretti at hand would be a good exercise. *He is a librettist! How can I ask to see his libretti? And maybe he knows where the scores are kept.*

'Oh... is it possible...'

'I think he will do the same to you if you stay here. Another thing, Mr Endel. In Pratolino, it is the grand prince who conducts the opera, not the composer.'

'What?' Händel nearly jumped, 'How...?'

Salvi laughed. 'I think I've given you enough reason to not stick to the grand prince.'

Händel nodded. 'Yes, I understand.'

Dr Salvi was urging him to get out of Florence as soon as possible. It was pleasant to stay in the palace with the grand princess's company, but it was time to move forward. There was nothing more to learn in Florence.

'So you are going to Rome.'
'Yes, Princess.'
'Where in Rome, may I ask?'
'I received an invitation from a marquess, but...'
'But?'
'Maestro Steffani gave me a letter of introduction for Count Fede.'
'Then you must go there first,' said the grand princess decisively.
'May I ask why, Princess?'
'Certainly. The marquess should know that you have contacts and that you are not jumping on his invitation.' Violante looked at Händel and said, 'It is the same everywhere – a power game. Let the marquess ask for you.' She let escape a witty smile.

Winter was advancing fast. It was time to move before the rain made the roads unpractical. While Händel was heading south to Rome, Alessandro

Scarlatti was on his way to Venice. He was hoping to make enough money there to not worry for a while. Cardinal Vincenzo Grimani knew the situation and was generous enough to commission two operas from him. Scarlatti was quite confident. Though the preparation took time and the schedule was delayed, he was more than happy with the cast. There would be that fabulous castrato Nicolo Grimaldi, called Nicolini, and the soprano, another virtuosa, Diamante Scarabelli. His operas were to be played in San Giovanni Grisostomo Theatre, the best in Venice. There was everything to attract a large audience.

Rome, Late 1706 – February 1707

It was the end of 1706. After spending nearly a month at Count Fede's palace, Händel was now heading towards another palace, the one occupied by Francesco Maria Marescotti Ruspoli, Marquess of Cerveteri. Händel had already made acquaintance with a few notable people. He was glad he had followed the advice of Grand Princess Violante.

Händel arrived at Palazzo Bonelli by the carriage sent by the marquess. The Piazza dei Santi Apostoli was flanked by Palazzo Odescalchi and Palazzo Colonna, which faced each other; Palazzo Bonelli stood at the far end between them. The façade was square and symmetrical, with the entrance in the middle. Compared to the austere exterior of Palazzo Pitti, it looked more friendly and inviting. Once inside, what struck Händel was the lack of formality. Upon entering the palace, the first noise he heard was the laughter of a child. Following a servant to meet the host, he saw a troupe of children led by nurses crossing the corridor.

Francesco Ruspoli was in the back garden, having a discussion with the gardeners. Young and not so tall, he looked fit. He saw Händel and came to greet him.

'Maestro Sassone. Welcome!'

Händel bowed. *So I am il Sassone, the Saxon*, he thought. Since he had arrived in Rome, he had been called *Sassone* more than anything else.

The young marquess grinned, showing his impeccable set of white teeth. 'At last! You made me work hard to get you extracted from Count Fede. I hope he was not keeping you prisoner.' Seeing Händel speechless, he just laughed. 'Let's get to business, Maestro. This is my superintendent, Fabio. If you need something, he will take care of you more efficiently than me,' said the marquess.

'Marquess, I don't deserve such compliment.' Fabio Cavalcanti bowed humbly.

The marquess ignored him and continued, 'And this is the head gardener.'

The gardener removed his hat and smiled, showing his not-so-complete set of teeth. Händel nodded slightly and smiled.

'You see, Maestro, we came to this palace just a year ago, and we are trying to make it a home.'

'Marquess will be surprised this spring,' said the head gardener.

'Come, Maestro, let me introduce you to the marchioness. Oh, Fabio, make sure the maestro meets Angelo Valeri as well.' He led Händel inside. 'You will not see her very often, as she is expecting.'

'Congratulations, Marquess.'

'Oh, thank you, but I am so used to being a father now. See, this is my eighth child.'

'Eighth?' Händel stopped on the spot.

The marquess ignored Händel's surprise. 'Oh, one thing, Maestro. I am very sorry, but I am putting you in my old palace for the moment. It will be better for you. We are not yet organised, and the children are not sorted out. You will be much calmer there. And it is just a few minutes' walk from here.'

'Marquess is very generous,' Händel bowed.

'Let's go to see my wife,' Ruspoli led the young man to a large room.

The marchioness was resting on a chaise longue. When the doors were opened, Händel and the marquess were pushed inside by the troupe of children arriving. The nurses shouted after them, 'Stop, children, stop! Don't push!'

Ruspoli just laughed. 'A little rough welcome from my children, Maestro.'

The marchioness smiled. 'I am sorry for this mess.' She looked around fondly at her children. 'It is impossible to get orderly and tidy... I hope you understand, Mr Endel.'

Händel bowed, thinking, *She is trying to call me by my name, at least.* 'Is this correct? You are Mr Endel and not Andel?'

'Händel, in German, Marchioness, but I am very happy with Endel,' Händel replied, giving up any effort to correct the pronunciation.

'Well, children, greet Papa's new guest. Mr Endel, these are my children, I will present them from the eldest. This is Isabella; she is eleven. And this is Bartolomeo; he is ten. Giacinta is eight, and this is Vittoria. Margherita—'

'Mama, I'm Teresa!'

'Oh, sorry my angel. See, Mr Endel, they are twins. So, Teresa, where is Margherita? Oh, here you are. And this is Anna.'

The marquess was surrounded by his children, and he was lifting them high, one by one, as the children shouted, 'Higher, Papa, higher!' or 'It's my turn!'

Händel felt dizzy.

Händel was given an apartment in Ruspoli's old palace with a valet attending him. Everything was completely different from his Florentine experience. The marquess was young, energetic, and jolly, even childish sometimes, and what Händel most appreciated in the personality of his new host was his openness. If Prince Ferdinando was like a dark forest, the young marquess would be a sunny meadow. Händel was never left alone. The marquess made sure Händel joined his table when he was at home. Otherwise, he always joined the house musicians. It was like the time when he was part of the Hamburg opera house. He enjoyed the gossip and was surprised to realise how well informed the house musicians were. This was possibly due to the singers, who travelled extensively from one place to another all over Europe according to their engagements. They were all aware of the Florentine court: Prince Ferdinando's immoral conduct, Princess Violante being left alone, and the grand duke's desperation to get an heir.

The year 1707 started for Händel in the household of Francesco Ruspoli, which was like a merry storm.

'Are you still lodged in the old palace?' asked Domenico Castrucci, who was the oldest of the house musicians.

'Yes, I am.'

'Do you have Matteo with you? Is he all right?'

'Well, he is very young.'

'He is the son of Gianni, the valet of the marquess.'

'Is this the marquess's new house?'

'Yes and no. See, the old palace, where you are, is to be rebuilt. So the marquess needed another place to stay for a couple of years.'

'I see. Are you very busy?'

'Not too much during the winter. For the moment, we have just *conversazione* on Sundays, and we go from time to time to help other concerts. When the Accademia resumes its meetings in the spring, we'll be pretty busy. Rome is calm right now. Many people are off to Venice for the carnival season.'

'Venice . . .' Händel's eyes were bright. 'Is it for operas?'

'Well, it's THE place for operas. See, we cannot play opera here in Rome, so the people are waiting for carnival season, not only for operas but also to get drunk and do naughty things under the mask.'

'Has opera always been forbidden in Rome?'

'No. Not at all. It is the present pope who forbade it completely. He is terrible.' He paused, and made the sign of the cross. 'The Teatro Capranica is closed, Teatro Tor di Nona is used as a grain storeroom now, and the one at Cardinal Ottoboni's was demolished, though that was with the previous pope. I miss opera.'

'Demolished...' Händel whispered. He did not know that the ban was that rigorous. That meant there was no possibility of seeing even one. 'So the only thing we can play is concerts?' he enquired, 'and, there are not even Sunday concerts right now. Why?'

'Well, first because it is new year, and the marquess is waiting for Signorina Durastante to arrive. Do you know her?'

'No. Is she a—'

'Singer, soprano.' Castrucci looked at the Saxon. 'Tell me, Maestro. Your name, is it Endel?'

'Well, it's a German name, Händel.' He laid stress upon the *h*.

Castrucci stared at him. 'What the hell?'

Händel laughed. 'I am happy with Endel, Signor Castrucci.'

'People will call you Sassone, or maybe just Maestro.'

Händel considered. 'Signor Castrucci, do you think I could surprise the marquess with your help? I have an idea.' He felt the only thing he could do was to keep himself busy.

'Why not. I'm sure he would appreciate it.'

They did not dare to ask burning questions of each other. Händel wanted to know how much Castrucci was paid as an employed musician. Castrucci, in turn, wanted to know if Händel intended to seek a permanent position. They both felt they needed to get to know more about each other before broaching these personal questions.

'Let's eat first, Maestro. Then afterwards I'd like you to play the harpsichord, if you'll agree,' said Francesco Ruspoli.

'It will be an honour to do so, Marquess,' Händel replied politely.

'Good. The marchioness might join us once all the children are in bed and all settled down.'

'My lord, if I may, I'd like to play with two of your house musicians. I have composed a trio.'

Ruspoli was delighted. 'Oh, in that case, I'll insist the marchioness join us. Thank you, Mr Endel. It is nice of you.' He did not expect the benefit of a house composer so soon, and could not wait for Margherita Durastante to arrive, and yes, she was on her way to Rome.

Everything seemed easy and natural. There was no stiffness between the patron and his subjects. Händel could not be more grateful to be part of this carefree environment.

Händel was summoned by the marquess one morning.

'Maestro, you are invited to play the organ of the Basilica di San Giovanni in Laterano. I just received a word from Cardinal Pamphili. Do you know him?'

'I met him at Count Fede's, Marquess.'

'Oh, I see.'

Francesco Ruspoli was amazed at the power of the cardinal. To let a

Protestant into a Catholic church – not just any church, but the pope's own sanctuary – and let him play the organ! Then he remembered what the cardinal had said to him, jokingly: 'I crowned him. I made him Pope Clement XI.'

Cardinal Pamphili had been named the archpriest of the basilica in 1699; it was the pontifical cathedral of Rome. The organ was probably the most interesting one in the city. Benedetto Pamphili knew it, and as a music lover, he believed that it was an honour to let the organ be played by the young virtuoso, no matter if he were a Protestant.

'Are you happy, Maestro?' the marquess teased, seeing Händel smiling from ear to ear.

'More than happy, Marquess. Delighted!' This was a chance to show off his skill, and also, be able to play publicly and not by sneaking into the organ loft.

It was 14 January 1707, and the audience was amazed and delighted. Händel could not thank the cardinal enough for letting him play the organ. This made Francesco Ruspoli proud to have him as a house guest. His uncle, Cardinal Galeazzo Marescotti, was in the audience, not quite to hear the organ but rather to keep an eye on his nephew. He was there to scan the people's reactions to his nephew having a Protestant musician in his household. Moreover, he had learnt, at the last minute, that Cardinal Vincenzo Grimani was attending, and he was determined to stop any kind of communication between his beloved nephew and Grimani. While his nephew seemed to have little to no fear of the unknown, Marescotti was a worrier.

Cardinal Vincenzo Grimani was deeply impressed by the young German virtuoso. Born into one of the oldest families of Venice, one that produced three doges, he was not affected by the cold reception he got in Rome for being pro-Austria in the ongoing War of the Spanish Succession. As a diplomat, he spent nearly six years in Vienna, where he was created cardinal by the previous pope, Innocent XII. Now he was an Austrian ambassador to the Holy See. Despite Pope Clement XI's attempts to be neutral in the War of the Spanish Succession, many powerful Romans were pro-France. However, through his love of music, Cardinal Grimani maintained loyal friends among the clerics. He left the church hurriedly, at the relief of Cardinal Marescotti, just after Händel's performance. His departure was not to avoid hostile gazes. He wanted to correspond with his friends in Rome as soon as possible to share his enthusiasm. He knew he had to be discreet if he wanted to keep them as friends.

Cardinal Francesco Maria de' Medici, accompanied by Annibale Merlini approached Francesco Ruspoli, who was busy greeting and chatting outside the church.

'Monsignor! You are in Rome!' the marquess merrily greeted the short and fat uncle of Prince Ferdinando. 'How did you find the Saxon? Oh, maybe you already saw him in Florence.'

'No, I did not, and I could not wait to meet him,' replied the cardinal politely. In his forties, he looked older and tired by his lifestyle of banquets, parties, and entertainments that were not often 'correct'.

Händel emerged from the church and attracted attention from the audience. He did not notice the greedy look on the face of Cardinal de' Medici, who was quickly distracted by Merlini.

'Monsignor, you should greet your friend Cardinal Pamphili. He is just over there,' said Merlini, pulling gently the arm of Cardinal de' Medici.

'Oh, of course.' Francesco Maria scanned the crowd, and exclaimed, opening his arms, 'Benedetto, my friend!'

The two cardinals greeted each other warmly and started to discuss the young virtuoso.

Annibale Merlini let a sigh of relief. *Christ, he nearly started to lick his lips!* Merlini was Grand Prince Ferdinando's correspondent in Rome, but he believed his main task was to protect the family's reputation as much as he could. As soon as he got back home, he wrote to Prince Ferdinando about Händel and the impact he'd made in Rome that day.

As soon as Cardinal Ottoboni resumed his Wednesday concerts, Händel accompanied the marquess to the Palazzo della Cancelleria. Händel was astonished by the grandeur of the palace. *Is this inhabited by a man serving the church?* For a Protestant grown up in northern Germany, this was hard to understand.

'Is this his residence, Marquess?' asked Händel, going up the monumental staircase, not resisting looking around and up and down.

'Yes, it is. Grand, isn't it? Save your neck, Maestro. There is more to come.'

'Do all the cardinals live in this way?'

'No. This is the residence of the vice-chancellor. My uncle lives in a much more modest way.'

They reached the *piano nobile*. Händel saw a few men in cassocks hanging around, talking.

'Your Lordship!' A tall figure approached them. He bowed low to Francesco Ruspoli.

'Signor Adami. Meet my guest, Mr Endel. You surely heard about him?'

Andrea Adami rose and looked at Händel. 'So you are the famous Saxon. I am Andrea Adami, secretary to the Cardinal Ottoboni and master of the Sistine Chapel. I am honoured to meet you.' He bowed.

'I am Giorgio Frederico Hendel, it is my honour to meet you,' replied Händel as polite as Adami.

'Are you singing tonight, Maestro Adami?' Ruspoli asked.

'Yes, I am. Please, Your Lordship, this way.'

Händel followed the marquess and Adami walking side by side. *Is he a castrato? He looks like one. I will see when he sings*, he thought. He looked at them talking like two friends. This was Francesco Ruspoli's way, to never look down at his subjects. Händel felt, though there was no opera in Rome, that he would enjoy his stay, and in the meantime learn as much as he could.

They arrived in the centre of a vast, richly decorated hall. Händel saw, in the middle of the crowd, a man in a red cassock. He saw the man notice Francesco Ruspoli and walk towards him, smiling, with his arms open.

'Francesco, here you are, with your famous Saxon!' Cardinal Ottoboni exclaimed.

The Saxon was drawn, at once, into a storm of music, greetings, and food and drink.

Händel came back to the old palace exhausted. He'd never met so many people in his life. So many ladies and priests among the guests! He could only remember Cardinal Ottoboni, his castrato Andrea Adami, his master of the orchestra Arcangelo Corelli, and Filippo Amadei the cellist. Händel saw Corelli being venerated like a god, by the guests and the musicians. The maestro directed the orchestra, playing violin himself, and the sound he drew from the orchestra was something Händel never heard before. However, he made a show of his harpsichord skill to impress the maestro and the audience. It was quite overwhelming, but Händel was excited to know so many things to come. Now the lack of opera seemed not so important. And he was determined to attend these Wednesday concerts as often as possible. There was something special in the orchestra under Corelli's direction. There was no comparison with Florence, where the grand prince was the ruler and the musicians his servants. Here, the house musicians were much more respected and appreciated. The name of Margherita Durastante was mentioned more than once, and the marquess looked pleased, proud to have secured her. Francesco Ruspoli was waiting for Margherita Durastante so he could present the *conversazione*, his regular concerts on Sundays, with a young, dashing composer's music sung by a young virtuosa.

The invitation from Cardinal Pamphili did not take long to arrive. As a Great Prior of the Order of Malta, he lived in the priory on the Aventine Hill. Originally built as a Benedictine monastery, it was a composite of architectural styles reflecting the periods in which the extensions were made, including an adjoining mediaeval church. It was much more modest compared to Cardinal Ottoboni's Palazzo della Cancelleria, matching his simple personality. However, Händel was astonished by his collection of Flemish paintings. If Ottoboni's residence was a flashy show-off, the priory represented quality and intellect.

'The marquess is very sorry not to be able to come, Monsignor,' Händel

said. 'I received word from him. The marchioness is about to give birth. I pray for a safe delivery.' He made the sign of cross, and looked at Händel. 'Well, it will be a very small gathering. Maestro Scarlatti is busy in Venice, but I wanted you to meet Maestro Pasquini. Have you heard his name?'
'No, Monsignor.'
'Let's go out for a short walk. It is not too cold today.' The sun was still out on the hill.
'Have you walked around Rome, Maestro?' the cardinal asked, walking side by side with Händel in the gardens while waiting for other guests to arrive.
'Not really, Monsignor. I've visited some churches.'
'That's very good, but you have to see the Roman ruins. I am sure you will be invited to the grand palaces, but go out and see what is left of the ancient Rome.'
'Ancient Rome…' Händel had just realised that history was there in situ, not in the books.
'They are half-buried, and you will see also the dwellings of the poor. That's part of Rome.'
'Are there many here to visit those ruins – I mean the people on tour?'
'Well, the wealthy foreigners are busy socialising and sitting for portraits. Their tutors are much more interested in history.'
'I heard about English people going to Italy when I was in Hamburg.'
'They buy anything they can put their hands on and commission portraits. They feed lots of dealers and artists.' The cardinal stopped and indicated a direction for Händel to look. 'I wanted to show you this. It is very special for me.'
From the end of the garden, the dome of Saint Peter's Basilica could be seen. Imposing, it seemed to Händel to represent power more than faith.
A monk appeared from nowhere to announce that the guests had arrived. Händel was introduced to Bernardo Pasquini. Very old, in his early seventies, Pasquini was now a symbolic figure. As a keyboard virtuoso, he had played often with Corelli, and as an opera composer, he had travelled all over Italy. Now retired, he only attended the small intellectual gatherings to discuss literature and music. It was a relaxing atmosphere.
It was a fascinating evening for Händel. He listened with attention to the typical old people's talk, mainly of the past. Queen Christina of Sweden was mentioned several times, and Händel understood she was an important patron of the arts and the creator of the Accademia. He did not dare to ask what exactly this 'Accademia' was, though. He guessed it was a kind of club where the marquess, as well the cardinals Pamphili and Ottoboni, and Pasquini, were all members. And then, naturally, the subject turned to opera.
'What a pity. I miss opera,' said Pasquini turning to Händel. 'It was so

widespread here in Rome, Maestro Sassone. But Pope Innocent XII started to torture it, and Clement XI finished it off. Killed! Nothing today . . .'

'Maestro Pasquini, I heard that one theatre was even demolished,' Händel said.

The cardinal and the old composer both sighed.

'It's the one at the Cancelleria,' said Pamphili, 'and that was the beginning of the end.'

'And then the war erupted five years ago. We thought it was not our concern, the Spanish succession, but it was. And it is still going on. Then we had an earthquake three years ago, Maestro Sassone. We feel punished. What did we do to trigger the wrath of God?' The old composer looked distressed.

Händel mentioned Corelli's orchestra to change the subject. Pasquini smiled, and suggested, 'If you are interested, go to the rehearsal on Tuesday. You will see how he works his orchestra.'

'You will see, he bewitches them all,' said Cardinal Pamphili.

'What?'

They laughed, and Pasquini said, 'Mr— Oh, I am sorry. Could you repeat your name?'

'Händel.'

'Very difficult to pronounce, isn't it?' Cardinal Pamphili said, turning to the young composer. 'As you realised, we Italians are quite incapable of pronouncing *h*.'

'Mr Endel. That's the best I can do,' Pasquini said. 'Going back to Maestro Corelli, my friend Pamphili meant charisma. He uses his magic called charisma.'

Händel just smiled. *I wish I had charisma*, he thought.

That night, Marchioness Ruspoli delivered her eighth child, a girl, safely, to the huge relief of her husband. It was before term, and he had been worried. He loved his wife.

Händel came back to the old palace. Alone in his room, he muttered, 'Well, it seems that I lost an *h* and umlaut in my name.'

Chapter 7 : A Saxon in Italy : Margherita (1707)

Rome, January 1707

One evening in late January 1707, a coach arrived in front of Palazzo Bonelli. Two women, one young and another not so young, got out.

'The marquess is in the music room, Signorina,' said the servant, 'please follow me.'

Margherita Durastante and her mother followed the servant. She heard people talking and laughing mixed with harpsichord playing. She went through the door, followed by her mother. In the middle of the room there was a big harpsichord, and a young man was playing. Francesco Ruspoli was facing him, showing his back to her. Händel saw her, and their eyes met. Margherita felt her heart miss a beat. Händel looked up at Ruspoli who turned.

'Ah, here, Miss Durastante! Finally! Now we are complete!'

Margherita and her mother bowed low in front of Francesco Ruspoli.

'Please rise. Let me introduce you to the famous Saxon. Maybe you already heard about him?'

'No, Your Lordship,' said Margherita, looking down.

'And you, Maestro?'

'No, Marquess.'

'Well, introduce yourselves then!'

Händel stood up and greeted her with a small nod and a smile. 'My name is Händel. I know your name. People have been talking about you long before you arrived.'

'Oh, thank you...' she said, still looking down. She did not dare to look at Händel. She did not want him to see her tired face after a long journey.

Margherita was of medium height, neither plump nor skinny, just average. It did not escape Francesco Ruspoli's eyes, as a keen observer, that Margherita was struggling to conceal her emotions while Händel remained quite indifferent.

'Your Lordship, I would ask your permission to withdraw. The trip was long, and we are quite tired,' said Margherita. She knew that her and her mother's travelling attire was not appropriate for the music room.

'Of course, Miss Durastante. Would you and your mother join us for supper later?'

'With the marquess's permission, I would like to have supper with my mother in our rooms, please,' she said without hesitating, showing that she knew how to behave. She completely ignored her mother trying to protest.

Margherita was alone in her room. *Oh God, how handsome he is! Those pale-blue eyes! Tall and slim, but with quite strong shoulders. Oh my God!* Then she had to face reality. She knew she was not good looking. *No, he will never be interested in me. He is too handsome . . . but I have my voice. He is a composer. I can charm him with my voice. Yes, there is a chance. And a composer with a singer, it is a perfect match!* Her mind was oscillating between hope and despair. *Is he nice? Oh, he can be horrible, arrogant, and despising, because he knows! Girls fall in his arms without resisting; it is too easy for him.*

'Margherita, are you all right?' Her mother walked in from the adjoining room.

She woke from her daydreaming. 'Oh, Mama, I am fine. I am just tired. I am not very hungry.'

'Go to bed early, then. You start working tomorrow, I suppose?'

'Yes, Mama.'

Margherita was intelligent and realistic. She knew she was not good looking. Her face, with its strong jaw, was rectangular, dominated by a large nose with a pair of rather small eyes. She did not have the ambition to have a wealthy admirer who would marry her eventually. She knew she must build her career with her voice and work hard. She had been singing from a young age and had seen beautiful singers being flattered, admired, and showered with presents and flowers. But often, the outcome was not very happy. Most of the time, they were simply dumped or, in the best case, became mistresses. She knew that a singer would never be treated as an equal among nobility and gentry. At twenty, sometimes she felt old. She knew that her voice could not last forever and that she must be careful with money, not spend easily, and save for retirement. With the fee she commanded, she could easily have a maid, but she chose to be with her mother. It was a compromise, economically and socially. Her mother could help her dress and mend, if necessary, without pay, and she represented moral protection. Apart from being blunt, she was a good-natured mother.

Margherita could not sleep. She felt tired when a valet brought a note in the morning. She read it and gasped.

'Are you all right, Margherita?' Her mother asked through the door from the next room.

'I'm fine, Mama. Did I disturb you?'

'What was that?'

'I nearly dropped a pot of cream. Sorry, Mama.'

She pressed the note to her breast and closed her eyes. *Am I dreaming?*

He wants to see me! Then the other Margherita laughed at her. *Oh, poor you! It is nothing of the sort. He wants to see you for his work, that's all! But why? Apparently the cantatas are not even started... It is not for rehearsal...* Torn between hope and despair, she could not eat. She felt exhausted, and her throat was dry. This was not a good start. She dressed simply and wrapped her upper body with a thick wool shawl.

As she approached the music room, she could hear the harpsichord playing. *It's him playing!* Her heart started to beat faster. Breathing deeply to control her heart, she nodded to the accompanying servant who announced Margherita to Händel. The music stopped, and the servant pushed the door.

'*Buon giorno*, Signorina Durastante,' Händel said with an awkward accent, and he smiled. He did not notice that Margherita was pale.

'*Buon giorno*, Signor... Endel?'

'Giorgio.'

'And your family name?'

'That's more complicated. I call myself Hendel, with an *h*, but my name is Händel in German.'

That was a sound totally unknown to Margherita, this German name. She swallowed and said, 'I'll call you Giorgio, then. Call me Margherita, without *Signorina*.'

'Very well, Margherita,' Händel said automatically. Then he got up and rummaged among the scores.

Margherita was surprised by his professional attitude. *So he must be quite experienced, despite being young.* She asked casually, 'Is it far, Germany?'

'Far? Yes, very.'

'How long did it take to come here, then?'

'Oh, about two months. I could have done it in one month if I had not stopped to sleep or eat at all!' Händel laughed and, ignoring more questions to come, sat in front of the harpsichord.

'I am sorry to make you come so soon. I just want to hear your voice. Could you please sing this?' And he handed her a score.

Margherita took the single sheet of paper and touched it with her fingers.

'Is there anything wrong, Margherita?'

'This paper is different.'

Händel laughed again. 'It's from Hamburg. I hate being short of paper, so I always get more than necessary. I brought the left-overs with me from Hamburg.'

'Hamburg . . .' Margherita murmured as she stroked the paper. She sensed the pride in this young composer. *So he does not want to ask for paper and wait for it. Or is he so impatient, that he needs to have paper when he wants? Oh come on, Margherita, stop guessing!*

Her mother was quick to notice Händel.

'He is so handsome, that Saxon! All the maids are quite mad about him, you know?'

'I am not surprised, Mama.'

'What do you think of him, Margherita?'

'He is nice. Not very patient, but I can cope with that.'

'He might be a good match for you.'

'Mama!' She was caught by surprise, and did not know how to react.

'Only if you can catch him. Pity you are not very good looking...'

'Thanks to you, Mama. Thank you!' Margherita was desperate to hide her feelings. Now she hated her mother.

Her mother laughed. 'My daughter, you are intelligent, clever, and sensible, and you have a voice on top of that. You must not worry.'

Margherita was not convinced. She just felt ugly and stupid.

Now with Epiphany gone, all the New Year's Celebrations behind them, and Margherita duly arrived, Francesco Ruspoli felt ready to resume his Sunday concerts, called *conversazione*, meaning 'conversation'. Without a formal contract or even a verbal agreement, the routine was quickly established. Händel was to provide a new cantata each week for those concerts. Margherita was to sing. At first, it was just for one voice and continuo, but the marquess had a plan to expand it with borrowed musicians. He wanted to make it bigger as the season progressed and fully bloom in the Spring, to coincide with the opening of the Accademia.

Now Händel would need more paper and ink, and a copyist as well.

'Paper? Oh, that's not part of my duty, Maestro. You ask Castrucci,' Fabio Cavalcanti explained. 'Castrucci the elder, Domenico. He will take care of that.'

'Oh, all right. Yes, I will ask him. Hmm... and...'

'Tell me, Maestro.'

'How about the ink? And does Castrucci prepare – I mean, stave-rule?'

'What? Stave what?'

Händel saw that Cavalcanti had never heard those words. 'Oh, never mind, Mr Cavalcanti. I'll ask Mr Castrucci all that.'

'Did you ask all that of Fabio? I would like to have seen his face!' Castrucci the elder laughed. 'You ask anything related to music of me, Giorgio. Paper, ink, stave-ruling. I take care of the harpsichord, but I do copying as well. And I am a *cameriere* too.' He slightly raised his chest to show his pride.

'What's *cameriere*?'

'Well, if you are *cameriere*, that means your work involves more than just music. You are part of the household. My task is mainly with music, but if necessary, I am expected to do other things like...'

'Like?'

'Well, once I was asked to go to see the marquess's tailor to give him some money under the table to make him finish the marquess's suit first, jumping the queue.'

'Fabio could not do that?'

'He was doing the same thing for the marchioness's dress. There was a big ball, and everybody ordered new clothing. I am sure those tailors and dressmakers made a lot of money. I don't know why I was asked to do it. Maybe Fabio thought I was good at subtle negotiation.'

'How about your son Pietro? Is he *cameriere* as well?'

'No. He is employed as a violinist and no more.'

'He is an excellent player.'

'That's why, thank God. He is asked everywhere to play and is very busy. He cannot be attached to a household.' The father smiled proudly.

'So you do copying as well?'

'Yes. If it's a small thing like one voice and continuo, I can do it, if I'm not busy. Anyway we have Angelini. He is our copyist.'

While Francesco Ruspoli's idea was to employ Händel, the latter did not seek actively for a permanent position. On the other hand, Ruspoli's intention was not to offer Margherita a position. He wanted to see the reaction from the church first. This was the advice given by his loving uncle, Cardinal Marescotti. In Rome, women were frequently prohibited from appearing on the stage in public theatres, where the female roles were played by men, even in the times when opera was allowed. It was different for private concerts. However, the scale of concerts given by Cardinal Ottoboni meant they had a public aspect, and it was Ruspoli's intention to do the same. He wanted his concerts to be big and memorable, to be the talk of the town. The marquess could understand his uncle's worries, and he wanted to make him happy. His uncle had been there to support him since the death of his father. However the marquess was fundamentally optimistic, making his uncle worried.

Opera had been banned for nearly ten years in Rome as the pope judged it inappropriate for the Holy City. Händel quickly realised that Rome still provided an excellent training ground. He was exposed to the greatest music Rome could offer. The musical style and forms of opera were to be found at concerts in performances of the secular cantatas. Sometimes, for a special occasion, large-scale cantatas were accompanied by orchestra with several singers used as soloists. It was just a small-scale opera without staging. The Romans knew how to make a distinction without a difference.

Sunday was Francesco Ruspoli's *conversazione* concert, and Wednesday was Cardinal Ottoboni's concert. So Händel looked for other concerts of cantatas, serenatas, or oratorios to attend in one or another of the princely palaces in Rome. If he could be invited, that was fine, but he could always sneak in with the musicians he knew. Margherita was often invited to sing in different palaces, and she always suggested she be accompanied by Händel. Thus he could increase his income, have more experience, and make acquaintances. Margherita was doing her best to help him and make a special bond with her secret love. Händel just took it to be her generosity and friendship. Again, Händel could not stop himself comparing his Roman life with his experience in Florence, at Prince Ferdinando's court. While he was nearly all the time confined to Palazzo Pitti, just allowed to walk in the gardens, in Rome, he was busy going out, requested to play. One acquaintance leading to another, and the Saxon, il Sassone, was getting to be well known among music lovers.

While in one palace or another, Händel noticed quite a few foreigners as guests. They could be noblemen, gentlemen or artists, most of them being English. This was one of Rome's aspects, to be one of the destinations of grand tour. Each time he met an English person, he remembered Mattheson's words: 'Don't forget London, Händel. You will make money there.'

'Are you interested in London, Giorgio?' Margherita asked, 'you enquire a lot.'

'Yes, I am.'

'May I ask why?'

'Well, have you seen people from there, how they spend their money? They have to be immensely wealthy, buying everything they can as antiques and commissioning full-length portraits.'

'And do you want to know why they are so rich?'

'That's not the point. If they are buying, it's because they don't have those antiques over there, I suppose. If they are having their portraits made here, it's because they don't have painters to do it there, or their painters are not good enough.'

'I see. It is the same thing for music, then?'

'I heard that some nobles go back home bringing with them musicians and painters.'

Margherita felt a chill going down her spine. 'Do you want to be one of them?'

Händel smiled. 'No. Not yet. I am not ready.'

Not yet. This was not what she wanted to hear. London seemed her rival now.

'But, mostly, I want to know about the opera house there. Well, there are two, apparently competing one against the other,' said he enthusiastically.

'Opera house? Are you an opera composer?'

'Well, I composed a few in Hamburg, but I am here to learn Italian opera.'

Margherita just smiled. *He is not ready to go, yet.*

Händel liked Francesco Ruspoli's court. A bold, free spirit prevailed there. It was dynamic, not gloomy like in Florence. The marquess was young, jolly, and daring. Händel could see that he did not care very much about protocol. Very quickly he realised that Ruspoli and Cardinals Ottoboni and Pamphili were friends bound by their love of music, making rather a curious and interesting trio. The marquess was the youngest of the three, open and easy, Cardinal Pamphili was the oldest, calm, reserved and intellectual, and Cardinal Ottoboni for the grandeur with his palace and the orchestra. Händel witnessed them visiting each other quite often as they organised their concerts in turn or together.

Händel attended the concerts at Cardinal Ottoboni's residence as much as possible. The more he went to the Palazzo della Cancelleria, the more he saw that everything was done quite cheaply. Though Cardinal Ottoboni had a fine collection of great paintings, it was the opposite of Cardinal Pamphili's priory. Music there was excellent, thanks to Corelli, and Händel had a lot to learn. Still, he started to dislike those monks hanging around and trying to convert the young German Protestant to Catholicism. They were all fat and full of rich food with greedy eyes for the ladies. Händel could not resist feeling angry towards them. However, he had to hide his feelings carefully so he could enjoy Corelli's music and have easy access to the palace. Again, Agostino Steffani's advice was precious. 'Never make quick decisions if you can. Weigh everything. What is your priority? Music, your career, and your personal life are all linked together.' The Palazzo della Cancelleria was an excellent ground for learning to be diplomatic as well.

'Francesco, you have to be very careful,' said Cardinal Marescotti on his regular visit to his nephew. Cardinal Grimani's prolonged stay in Rome was making him concerned.

'That's why I am talking to you, Uncle,' said Marquess Ruspoli.

'Cardinal Grimani clashed seriously with the Holy See, more than once...'

'On the Austrian matter?'

'Exactly. He is here representing the emperor's interest.'

'I envy him to be so daring!' laughed Ruspoli.

'Francesco... the Grimanis are powerful.' The uncle frowned.

What a pity that you could not be pope, then, thought Ruspoli, but he did not say it so as to not hurt his uncle. Nevertheless, it was obvious to Galeazzo Marescotti what his nephew was thinking.

'So his presence is not recommended,' said the nephew.

'Not here in your palace. You can compromise, if necessary.'

'Ottoboni?'

'Pamphili will be more suitable.'

'Or Colonna. They are all in the same rank.'

Cardinal Vincenzo Grimani was a known music lover. Cardinal

Marescotti thought, very naturally, that his nephew might face pressure from Grimani seeking an invitation to hear the Saxon's music. It did not happen. Cardinal Grimani remained silent, to the great relief of Cardinal Marescotti.

One cold morning in early February, Händel was summoned to Ruspoli's office. The double doors were opened by the servants on each side, revealing the marquess with Cardinal Pamphili.

'Maestro, here you are.' Francesco Ruspoli smiled. 'Come in!'

Händel approached them, ready to kneel and kiss the visitor's hand.

'No, no. You don't need to kiss his hand, Maestro Endel. He is here as a friend.'

'I don't mind being kissed by a young, handsome man, even only on my hand.' The cardinal laughed. 'I am here for a favour, Maestro.'

'He wants you to compose a cantata,' Ruspoli said.

'I am most humbled by your request, Monsignor,' said Händel, suppressing his excitement. 'With the permission of Marquess...'

'Of course, Maestro Sassone.' Ruspoli did not have a choice.

'Excellent. I'll tell Grinelli to get ready. He is my copyist. He'll have a bit of work. It's with an orchestra.'

Händel could not resist beaming.

'Benedetto, I think Maestro is happy.'

'I'll send the text as soon as possible,' said the cardinal. 'I thought of bringing it with me, but I did not, just in case my request was refused.'

'Benedetto! That is impossible!' said Ruspoli, quite indignant.

The cardinal laughed. 'Oh, I just sinned. The truth is that I have not finished it yet.'

'Oh, so you are the poet, Monsignor?' said Händel, raising his eyebrows.

'Yes, I am. The title is *Il delirio amoroso* – totally compatible with my position.'

Seeing Händel incredulous, they both laughed. It was difficult to imagine *Il delirio amoroso (The Love's delirium)* being written by a cardinal.

'One more detail, Francesco. I think it will be better if Maestro came to the priory to do the work so I will be able to answer any questions and Grinelli will be nearby.' He turned to Händel. 'Is this suitable for you?'

Händel turned to the marquess for approval.

'That's fine,' said Ruspoli. 'You will have a change of scenery. Enjoy, Maestro. Just be here for my *conversazione*.'

It was obvious that Grinelli was only the excuse. Cardinal Pamphili wanted to ensure that his commission would be protected. Though he trusted his young friend, he did not know Händel, and he knew Angelini, Ruspoli's copyist, was known to be very chatty.

So Händel moved out temporarily to the Aventine Hill, to come back on Sundays for the marquess's concerts. To Händel's surprise, Cardinal Pamphili proved to be much more engaging. The latter knew many details of composing and was curious to know more. Instructions given to Grinelli, the copyist, reflected this. The cardinal even asked the young composer about the size of the paper and the way staves should be ruled. The meeting with the soloist singer was arranged even before Händel requested it. And Händel was invited to the cardinal's table each time. In the end, an unexpected bonus came.

Händel found himself in the cardinal's library. Benedetto Pamphili first showed the young composer his collection of books and then showed him the scores, nicely bound. Händel scanned the titles engraved in gold on the spines.

'I have quite a lot of Scarlatti and other Italians, but I also have French, Spanish, German . . .'

'How could you get those non-Italians, may I ask, Monsignor?'

'Through church connections, of course.' He smiled. 'Religion does not have borders, as long as it is Catholic, I mean.'

'I see. Monsignor, am I allowed to consult those scores?'

'That's why I am showing you my collection.'

'I thank you very much, Monsignor.' Händel could not stop beaming.

'If you want to, you may copy as well.'

Händel stared the cardinal in disbelief. 'Really?'

'On two conditions.'

'Yes, Monsignor.'

'You tell nobody, and you make the copies yourself.'

'Monsignor, I don't know how to thank you.' Before Händel realised it, he was kneeling before the cardinal and kissing both his hands.

This was much more precious than being paid in money or with a piece of jewellery. And Händel knew what he wanted most – Steffani's chamber duets – and he copied them himself, carefully. He knew that this would come to be one of his most precious possessions, to be kept all his life.

Händel was seated beside Margherita, sharing the table with Francesco Ruspoli. He did not notice Margherita flushed with happiness. He had returned to the household of the marquess after completing the cantata and seeing it played. Händel had conducted from the harpsichord as usual. The intimate setting of the priory made it precious, a special treat for the small number of guests, to the great satisfaction of all. This was Cardinal Pamphili's preference, a small jewel instead of a huge flower display.

The marquess made an announcement.

'Now that you are back from the priory, Mr Endel, I think it is time for us all to go to Cerveteri.'

'Cerveteri? Where is it, Marquess?' asked Margherita enthusiastically.

'It's before Civitavecchia. Do you remember, Maestro? We went there together.'
'Yes, Marquess, I do remember Civitavecchia.'
'The marchioness can travel now, and she needs rest and good air. Also, it's not too far from the sea for the children. We can make the journey in one day.'
'How exciting!' said Margherita. *Sea for the children? It's still February!* she thought.
'I will organise a stag hunt as well. But we must be back before Easter.'
Stag hunt? I will see what it's like, Händel thought. *Maybe a hunting cantata for the marquess?*
'Then from May, we will start the Arcadian meetings, so you both will be quite busy.'
Both. Margherita lowered her head, smiling.
'Is that the Accademia, Marquess?' Händel asked.
'Yes, exactly!'

Francesco Ruspoli was thinking of going back to Rome from Cerveteri when a messenger from his uncle, Cardinal Marescotti, arrived. He was advising his nephew to stay in Cerveteri, while Cardinal Grimani was planning celebrations in Rome after Prince Eugene of Savoy won his great battle over the French at Mantua and drove the French troops out of northern Italy.

'How daring!' The marquess exclaimed, the note received in his hand. *My uncle is right. Such celebrations will be very provocative. Better stay here,* he thought.

Francesco Ruspoli, his family, and his court were finally back in Rome in early April 1707. He was happy with his stay in Cerveteri. His wife and the newborn baby were doing well. The stag hunt was a big success, and he'd had the luxury of offering the guests Händel's cantata for the occasion. He wanted to stay longer, but it was time to be back in Rome to concentrate and prepare for Easter.

It was agreed with Cardinals Ottoboni and Pamphili that the Easter Sunday concert would take place in his Palazzo Bonelli and that Ottoboni would lend his orchestra, including Corelli. Francesco Ruspoli had commissioned Alessandro Scarlatti to compose an Easter oratorio. This had already been arranged before Händel's arrival, and he slightly regretted it.

Alessandro Scarlatti could not stop feeling anxious, being summoned by Marquess of Cerveteri. In his late forties, the composer was quite thin, with a long face and big brown eyes. Though he heard from other patrons like Cardinal Pamphili or Cardinal Ottoboni about young Ruspoli's openness and generosity, he could not stop being apprehensive. He still could not recover from the treatment he had received from Prince Ferdinando in Florence. He could only pray to be treated with respect. Having a commission was one thing. Being paid properly was another matter.

'Maestro Scarlatti, do come in!' said the marquess. 'Welcome back to Rome. I heard you had great success in Venice.'

Scarlatti advanced and bowed low. When he got up he found himself in the marquess's study with Ruspoli himself; his superintendent Fabio Cavalcanti; Silvestro Rotondi and Pietro Castrucci, both virtuosi violinists; and Domenico Castrucci, with whom he had already made acquaintance. There was another young man, tall and good looking.

'Maestro, shall I introduce, or have you guessed already?' said Ruspoli, indicating Händel.

Scarlatti relaxed at once. 'Marquess, is he your famous Saxon?'

Francesco Ruspoli turned to Händel. 'You are famous, I see. Introduce yourself, Maestro Sassone. You don't need me,' said the marquess, laughing.

Händel straightened himself, and, feeling his back stiff, said, 'It is my honour to meet you, Maestro Scarlatti.'

The superintendent Fabio interrupted. 'Marquess, shall I show them the place? You have to go to see your uncle, the cardinal.'

'Follow me, then. I will show you the place!' said Ruspoli merrily.

Händel walked beside Scarlatti. The famous maestro was friendly.

'You are very young, Maestro Sassone. How old are you?'

'I am twenty-two, Maestro.'

'Oh, that's Domenico's age. He is one of my sons. He is in Venice now.'

'Is he a musician?'

'He is. He is the second of my musician sons.'

'May I ask how many children you have?'

'Ten.'

Händel stopped, his eyes wide open, and whispered, 'Ten…'

Francesco Ruspoli, overhearing it, burst into laughter. 'Mr Endel, Maestro Scarlatti is stronger than me. I have only eight!'

With that, any remaining tension evaporated.

'This is the *Stanzione delle Accademie*,' said Fabio, opening the double doors. They were on the second floor of Palazzo Bonelli. It was a large room, lavishly decorated.

'This is where your oratorio will be performed, Maestro,' said Ruspoli proudly. 'I use this room for the concerts and meetings.'

Scarlatti bowed to the marquess. 'Your Lordship is too kind to show me the place yourself.'

Francesco Ruspoli laughed. 'I like to be in control, just a little. My father used to let everything fall to his superintendent and then complain that he could do better. Fair, isn't it?'

'Marquess, it is time to go to see your uncle,' Fabio reminded him.

'I know, Fabio. I'm going, now!'

Ruspoli left, leaving Fabio to deal with the musicians.

'Maestro Sassone, would you like to take part?' asked Fabio.

'Oh, you can do the second harpsichord, as I will be directing from the first harpsichord,' said Scarlatti.

'Is it a big orchestra, then? How many voices?' asked Händel, curious.

'Yes, it is a big orchestra with five voices. Cardinal Ottoboni's orchestra is joining us, with Maestro Corelli.'

Händel's face lit up at once. 'An entire orchestra? Oh, can I play the violin then?'

Everybody turned to him, surprised.

'Violin? But . . .' Pietro Castrucci said.

'Signor Domenico could do the second harpsichord. Oh, please! Of course, I cannot play like you, Pietro,' Händel said. 'I will be at the rear. Please!'

'Well, if you want to,' said Scarlatti, looking at the others for approval.

Händel was delighted. He felt as if he was back in the Hamburg opera house orchestra, with all the chat and camaraderie. He'd been hearing Corelli's orchestra, but he could not miss the opportunity to mingle with the musicians. And he knew this was the best way to live and feel Corelli's orchestra.

'Maestro Scarlatti, did you bring the score with you?' Domenico Castrucci interrupted the composer, who was looking around, daydreaming.

Scarlatti nearly jumped. He was imagining how it could be displayed.

'Oh, of course I did.'

'Well, then, would you be kind enough to leave it with me? I'll ask Angelini to make copies.'

'Signor Castrucci, before copying, do you know who are the singers? I might make some changes.'

Scarlatti was happy. After the success of his two operas in Venice, the composer was more relaxed. And now with this commission, he was hoping to save some money. Having a big family to protect was a constant worry.

Händel looked at Scarlatti, amazed. *Of course, it is better if the music is fitted to the singers!* This was something to remember. That meant experience, and he felt respect towards the composer, who was just open and straightforward. He also liked the fact that Scarlatti did not try to flatter the marquess. But for Händel, who'd had an old father, it was difficult to imagine Scarlatti as a father of a son as old as himself.

Although given the explanation that Scarlatti was commissioned before Händel's arrival in Rome, he could not stop himself from being slightly disappointed. And he disliked the idea of doing nothing. The marquess was unlikely to ask him for anything, now that he was busy preparing for the forthcoming Easter. He would have more than two weeks without any task until Easter was over. *Que faire?*

'*Dixit Dominus.* The Lord Said.' Händel murmured to himself, and signed at the end of the score, 'G. F. Hendel, Rome, April 1707'. Using the Latin text of Psalm 110, he had made something to satisfy himself and, at the same time, to show his skill to his patrons. Though quite short, it required five voices, chorus and orchestra. This was his opportunity to demonstrate his ability in writing large-scale choral works, which he had not yet had the opportunity to do. Cantatas for solo voice gave him no space for grand effects of counterpoint and block harmony, and Händel was getting rather thirsty for it. He did not care if it was played or not. *Sistine Chapel choir maybe? I want the best if played. A mediocre choir cannot master it.* Dixit Dominus happened to be the only piece of music Händel composed without commission in Italy.

On 24 April, Easter Sunday, Alessandro Scarlatti's oratorio *Il giardino di rose (The garden of roses)*, commissioned for this occasion, was performed. The *Stanzione delle Accademie* was decorated lavishly with flowers and huge, gilded candle stands. Francesco Ruspoli anticipated the opening of the Accademia and invited his fellow members, among them Pasquini. There was also a young man, dark and short, called Paolo Rolli. He was a poet. He paid little attention when the name of Händel was mentioned. He firmly believed that nothing could surpass native composers. He had to restrain himself with difficulty from laughing when he heard that the Saxon was among the second violins.

Händel was hearing the words *accademia* and *arcadia* quite frequently but paid little attention. He just focused on Scarlatti's music.

'A cantata?' said Händel, looking at cardinal Pamphili.
'Yes, Maestro, another one.'
It was Easter Monday. Händel felt as if people in Rome could not wait any longer for the end of Easter. Cardinal Pamphili himself brought the text for *Il trionfo del Tempo e del Disinganno (The Triumph of Time and Disillusion)*.
'Again, it is secular. Four voices representing Time, Truth, Beauty, and Pleasure.'
'I suppose with an orchestra, Monsignor?'
'Yes. It will be played at Pietro's palace. We all agreed to that.' *We* meant the trio, Ruspoli, Ottoboni, and Pamphili.
'When would Monsignor like me to complete it?'
'I'll give you three weeks. Is that enough?'
'Certainly, Monsignor.' Händel beamed.

In fact, Cardinal Pamphili was the only one to give him enough time. Last-minute commissions were quite frequent. Händel could cope with it, taking it as part of training, but he felt much more relaxed when given enough time.

Wednesday concerts given by Cardinal Pietro Ottoboni at the Palazzo della Cancelleria attracted foreign visitors. Known to be the best in Rome, with Corelli on top of it, it was one of the must-sees for the nobility and gentry on their grand tour. Now that the very young castrato Paolucci had joined, Cardinal Ottoboni was quite overloaded with requests for invitations. Reckoned the finest voice in Italy, Paolucci was the attraction.

Though a cardinal, Pietro Ottoboni had not yet taken holy orders. It was his great-uncle Pietro Vito Ottoboni who had made him cardinal and vice-chancellor of the church when he became Pope Alexander VIII. Young Pietro was only twenty-two then. Nepotism was rampant in papal Rome. He had been hoping to marry a wealthy woman, and even now, at forty, he was still hoping. He scanned carefully the list of people wishing to be invited, looking for a wealthy widow. His unsuccessful romances in the past provoked several shouting matches between himself and his great-uncle the pope. Now his chances were getting thin, but he was still hopeful. His obsession with self-aggrandisement resulted in an extravagant lifestyle, and despite his numerous benefices, his expenses perpetually exceeded his income. Taking in several of the late queen Christina of Sweden's musicians was one of the reasons his accounts were in the red. Arcangelo Corelli, the cellist Filippo Amadei, and the castrato Andrea Adami were employed permanently. And Alessandro Scarlatti benefitted from his patronage as well. The cardinal considered his spectacles and sumptuous banquets to be expected from a man of his position. His palace, with its large halls, garden, and even a basilica, San Lorenzo in Damaso, provided the setting. The only problem was money.

> Rome, May 1707
>
> My dear Telemann,
>
> You cannot imagine the joy you gave me upon receiving your letter. I am sorry to hear that you had to flee Sorau to avoid the invading troops of the Swedish king, Charles XII. I pray for you to get a position in Eisenach. We are about to leave for Vignanello,

> one of the marquess's properties outside Rome. It will give me a break from attending concerts in Rome. Cardinal Ottoboni's Wednesday concerts are superb, with an orchestra you cannot see anywhere else under Corelli's control. But I am really getting fed up with those priests swarming there. They show little interest in music; they only come to fill their bellies with the liquors and delicacies served. If they are not pestering me to convert to Catholicism, they are busy concealing crystal bottles or silver spoons under their cassocks! The other Wednesday, I met a French tutor accompanying two young English brothers on their grand tour. He witnessed those holy thefts and was outraged.
>
> Write to me, please. Your letters give me such pleasure, and my heart fills up with affection.
>
> Your humble and devoted servant and brother,
> Händel

It was approaching the end of May, and the sun was getting stronger in Rome. The morning was sunny. Palazzo Bonelli was buzzing with people going to and fro. Everybody was busy. Händel, Margherita, and other house musicians were ready, waiting to be called to get into carriages. Fabio Cavalcanti seemed too busy for Händel to ask him questions, so he asked Margherita.

'Do you know why the entire household is going there, Margherita?'

'No, I don't.' She turned to Domenico Castrucci. 'Signor Castrucci, do you know why?'

'I think there will be festivities, and that's why. I don't know more than that, and Fabio will tell you off if you stop him to ask any questions. Look at him.' He indicated the superintendent rushing back and forth, giving instructions and orders.

'Where is your son Pietro?' Silvestro Rotondi, invited to join, asked Domenico.
'He is gone to say goodbye to his brother. He'll be here soon.'
'Where is Vignanello?' asked Händel.
'Not very far from here,' said Domenico, 'we go north.'
'How long will it take?' asked Margherita.
'I would say about seven hours,' said Domenico.
'Quite long . . .' sighed Margherita.
'We can do it in one day, though. Just one stop will be enough.' Domenico seemed confident. 'You don't like travelling, Margherita?'
'Not really. I get easily sick in a coach.'
'Oh, in that case... let me see... Hey, Paola! Here!' Domenico shouted and stopped a maid. 'Would you bring some children's potion for Signorina Durastante? Be quick!' He turned to Margherita. 'Be assured, you will be fine. You will just sleep, like the children.' He laughed.
'Oh, thank you, Signor Castrucci. Have you been there before?'
'No. The marquess has been there several times for a short stay, but just with Fabio. Oh, here he is.'
Fabio Cavalcanti was hurrying. 'So, we are ready to go. You can get in the carriages. You are responsible for your own instruments, please. I am going to ride with the marquess, so I'll see you later at the *castello*.'
Händel saw a group of women and children getting in their carriages. The smallest of Ruspoli's children, Anna, was crying.
'Where is Mama?'
'She has gone ahead, Anna. You will see her later,' one of the nurses reassured her.
'I want Mama!'
'Don't cry, Anna.' The oldest sister, Isabella, took her in her arms. 'Mama went with the baby earlier.' She stroked her little sister's cheek.
'Why?'
'Because the baby needs to stop often.'
'Why?'
'Because she is a baby, Anna.'
'Why?'
'Because she was born only in February.'
'Why?'
Isabella put her little sister on the ground. 'I cannot do this.' She got into the carriage, abandoning her little sister.
'I want Mama!'
Margherita was watching the little drama intently as she stood beside Händel. *Oh, if I could have a family with... how charming...*
'Margherita, have you taken your potion?' asked Händel.
'Yes, I have, thank you, Giorgio.'

'I am sorry you get sick easily. Will you be all right?'

'If I don't eat before, it will be all right, normally.' Margherita smiled, touched. *How considerate he is!* 'How about you?'

'Me? No problem at all. I can eat, drink and sleep and I am fine!' Händel laughed, 'but now I feel lucky.'

'You are, Giorgio. Well, let me know if I snore!'

'Oh, Margherita!' Händel laughed.

'Margherita, are you coming?' her mother called from inside the carriage.

Margherita nearly jumped. 'Yes, Mama, I'm coming.' *Maybe it is time to get a maid.*

The train started slowly, with mounted huntsmen in the front and rear.

Chapter 8 : A Saxon in Italy: I am in love! (1707 – 1708)

Vignanello, Summer 1707

This move to Vignanello of the whole household, with cooks, huntsmen, and musicians, had a purpose. There was the feast of Sant'Antonio of Padua in Vignanello, and in this year of 1707, the 475th year of his canonisation was to be celebrated. This was the chance for Francesco Ruspoli to establish his presence and to mark the anniversary in a lavish and generous way.

The long train proceeded without any incidents. One of the huntsmen shouted from alongside the musicians' carriage, 'We are arriving soon!'

Händel looked out. He saw an imposing castle on top of the hill, dominating the surrounding area.

'Is that there we're going?' asked Margherita, pointing to the castle on the hilltop. Seated opposite to Händel, she let a sigh of relief.

'Looks like it,' said Domenico, leaning towards Händel to look through the window.

It was indeed their destination, and the carriage started to go slowly uphill.

Francesco Ruspoli greeted Händel and Margherita with a big smile. 'Welcome to Vignanello! This is the property from my father's side. My father and my uncle the cardinal were both born here.'

'Oh, how about Cerveteri?' Händel asked, and he regretted it immediately. It was an intruding question.

'Cerveteri belonged to my other uncle, my mother's brother,' the marquess replied with ease. 'My uncle Bartolomeo. He had no children, and he gave us everything, including the palace in Rome where you have been staying, Maestro. My son was named after him. Now, let me show you the garden. You are free to walk around, of course. It was my grandmother's creation. She loved it.' Francesco Ruspoli led the two inside, towards the rear of the castle. From the little balcony of the first floor, they could see the whole garden.

'Oh, how beautiful!' exclaimed Margherita.

In front of them, there was a parterre, equally divided into twelve small rectangles, with a fountain in the centre. In each rectangle, formed by hedges, intricate designs were made in smaller hedges, all different.

Händel was less impressed. He thought that the gardens of Herrenhausen in Hanover were much nicer. *It is quite boring*, he thought, *in all green and not a single flower in it.* However, he was impressed by the view beyond the garden. There, he could see the beautiful Italian landscape spreading to the horizon.

Father Benedetto Marcioni could not have been happier. His church of San Sebastiano in Vignanello would be hosting the feast of Sant'Antonio, and he had already received a large sum, partly for organising it and partly as a token of thanks from the marquess. Then the decorations and accessories started to arrive from Rome: a pair of large candle holders, a small, gilded canopy and other pious objects for display, and a thousand little prints with the image of Sant'Antonio of Padua to be distributed. Also a large painting by Michelangelo Cerruti that would serve as the new altarpiece arrived to be consecrated.

'I came to see the church and the new painting, Father,' Händel presented himself. 'I am to compose a motet for the consecration, and I would like to see the place and also the new painting, if possible.'

'Of course, of course, Signor… what is your name?' Father Marcioni was quite confused.

'Hendel, with an *h*. Giorgio Hendel, Father.'

'Signor Endel, very well. Of course you can see whatever you want to. The church is for everybody, as you know. You don't need my permission to visit the church. It is open.'

'In that case, Father, may I see the painting first? Then I will not trouble you more.'

'Of course.' Father Marcioni led Händel to a small room. He produced a key to unlock the door. 'It is Signor Cavalcanti who suggested we lock the door.' He entered the room, followed by the young man. It was dark, but the light from the small grated window high up was enough. The priest uncovered the painting.

It depicted Saint Antony above the clouds, holding the traditional lily and book, surrounded by angels and putti. Händel saw the priest make the sign of the cross. They were interrupted by footsteps approaching.

'Angelini! You're here,' exclaimed Händel.

'Just arrived from Rome. I came with paper, ink, and some of the forgotten items. Nice company to keep me entertained,' said Angelini, wiping his sweaty forehead.

Händel watched the priest and the copyist make acquaintance with lots of hand movements. *What would happen if their hands were tied?* He just enjoyed watching these jolly and chatty Italians. It was very musical, and sounded like singing.

BRIGHT STAR

On 12 June 1707, Pentecost Sunday, Händel's motet *O qualis de coelo sonus* for soprano and small orchestra was duly performed. The next day, at the Festival of Sant'Antonio, Cerruti's painting was consecrated, followed by the performance of Händel's motet for this occasion, *Coelestis dum spirat aura*. Margherita sang splendidly, to the composer's great satisfaction. Her voice was crystal clear and sounded very dignified in a church. When *Salve Regina* was played on Trinity Sunday, 17 June, Francesco Ruspoli finally felt he could relax. Everything had gone well, and now he wanted something secular. Then there was unexpected news.

'We will have a visitor,' announced Francesco Ruspoli at table.

Händel and Margherita, at the top table with the marquess, looked at each other.

'Cardinal Ottoboni will be stopping here. He is on his way to Bologna, and he is with La Bambagia.' Ruspoli looked at Händel. 'You probably met her, Maestro?'

'La Bam... what?' Händel said, puzzled.

Margherita laughed. 'You don't know she is called La Bambagia? It is Vittoria Tarquini.'

'Vittoria? From Florence?' Händel vaguely remembered her just as Grand Prince Ferdinando's mistress. 'But, why...' he stopped as he felt a discreet nudge. He saw Margherita making him a sign to shut up.

'I think I will ask Angelini to stay longer.' Francesco Ruspoli grinned. Now he could have two sopranos for a secular concert. He looked at Händel. 'What do you think Maestro? '

'As you wish, Marquess,' replied the composer, 'maybe a cantata for two voices?' He knew Vittoria's voice was in a slightly lower register, so he could compose a nice duet.

Vittoria Tarquini looked quite different. Far from the oppressive environment of Palazzo Pitti, her beauty seemed to explode in the sunny daylight of the countryside. Cardinal Ottoboni could not be happier to have his patronage attracting so much attention. Father Marcioni was not too happy to see his church full because of the presence of a beauty.

'Pietro, do you have any text ready?' asked Francesco Ruspoli of the cardinal.

'Not really, why?'

'I want to give a reception in your honour, and it will be nice to have a piece of music to accompany your text. I have the Saxon, and we have two singers. What do you think?'

'Oh, well, thank you, Francesco. Very nice of you. I can improvise something. Let me see . . . I was working on a text, but it is just for one voice. Well, yes, I think I can arrange something.'

'*Perfetto!* I'll invite my half-brothers as well!' Francesco Ruspoli beamed, nodding.

This was an excellent opportunity to invite all the dignitaries of the area and get to know them far from the church. *Maybe I can invite my uncle Galeazzo. He is more familiar with the area.* Spontaneity and affection came first for the young marquess.

'Are you in Rome now?' asked Händel, addressing Vittoria. He was sitting between Margherita and the newly arrived singer at the top table.

'Yes, at Cardinal Ottoboni's Palazzo della Cancelleria. We are now going to Bologna.'

'What do you think of Maestro Corelli?' Margherita said, leaning forward to look across Händel at Vittoria.

Händel watched the two women exchange ideas and opinions with lots of hand movements. *Really, those Italians!* Then he realised they had different accents.

'Vittoria, where are you from?'

'Venice.'

'Did you notice her Venetian accent, Giorgio? Charming, isn't it?' Margherita said.

'It must have come out. Cardinal Ottoboni is from Venice as well, so we were talking quite a lot in our dialect.' Vittoria smiled. 'It is nice to feel at home.'

Home, Händel thought, and he looked around. There was nobody to speak to in German. He thought of Grand Princess Violante. He thought he had a glimpse of what she had been going through all these years in Florence. Quite lost in thoughts, he just watched the two women in lively conversation, smiling and laughing, ignoring the man between them completely.

The weather was lovely; hot, dry, and breezy. Everybody seemed to enjoy it, especially the marquess's children. The marchioness was seen often out in the garden with them.

Vittoria, under the mask of a smile, was miserable. She knew perfectly why she had been sent to Rome to Cardinal Ottoboni: the singer Lucrezia, the grand prince's new interest. It was not the first time it had happened to her, but it was the first time since she turned thirty. Lucrezia was much younger, fresh and vivid. *Will he call me back?* She was not certain. If not, what happens? Her life was a failure. She married a much older man when still very young, seeking for fatherly affection and protection. Having lost her mother when an infant, she only remembered her father, who loved her unconditionally. When her father died, she said yes to the first man who vaguely looked like him. The man proved to be no father or husband. He did not even object to her going back to Italy, staying in his post as a Konzertmeister in the court of Hanover. Back in Italy, at her first reappearance on the stage in Venice, she met Ferdinando de' Medici. *Oh how lovely and protecting he was!* she remembered. *He presented me into the court of Florence!* At the time, she felt bathed in happiness, as it was a very daring gesture, to make a mistress accepted into the entire court. But, looking back, she realised that he wanted to get his way and nothing else. The result was that it had increased the hostility against her and the sympathy towards the grand princess. He made her believe that he loved her. However, his mood was unstable, and he could turn from a charming man into a dreadfully cold and despising man without any warning. She had no choice but to accept it. She felt like a prisoner. She was scared of him. He was a powerful man. Her career was over. She was allowed only to sing for him, in his presence. *Maybe this is the chance to get free?* She could only blame herself for falling into such a trap. She felt she had failed and betrayed her father.

You should go to Venice. That's the place for you. Händel remembered the words of Antonio Salvi. Looking over the garden from his room, he saw Vittoria, walking slowly, looking around. He decided to join her to ask more questions about Venice. Out in the garden and when she noticed him, only then did he remember that the musicians were all gossiping about Vittoria being dumped by Prince Ferdinando. *I have to be careful to not mention Florence or the grand prince.* He approached her, smiling.

'Do you mind if I join you for a walk?'

She smiled. 'Not at all. What a lovely day. And the smell!' She breathed in deeply.

'Could you tell me more about Venice? I am very curious.'

'Of course.' She smiled. 'Well, it is very different from Rome. You won't see so many cardinals around.' She looked at Händel, 'I suppose you want to know about opera, am I right?'

'Yes.'

'Opera is not forbidden. They are free to play as much as they want to.'

'That sounds like a dream to me! Did you sing there?'

'I had my début there. It was a long time ago.' Vittoria smiled, clad in the armour of acting. 'The Venetians are very independent and proud. They feel quite free. Yes, free. There are a few opera houses, and everybody can go there, as long as they pay for a ticket. Everybody. No need to beg for an invitation.'

'Hmm, that's like Hamburg.'

'Are you from Hamburg?'

'No. I am from Halle, but I spent three years in Hamburg.'

Vittoria looked up at the sky, breathed in deeply and continued about Venice. 'I love Venice, with all those canals and gondolas. Have you ever been there, Mr Saxon?'

'No. What are gondolas?'

Vittoria looked at him. 'Oh, of course, you have no idea if you haven't been there. Sorry. Gondolas are boats, flat-bottomed boats. It's easier to use the canals to get around. The streets are very narrow and impractical for carriages.'

'Canals?'

'Yes. We use canals like streets.'

'Really? Hard to imagine...'

Now Vittoria wanted to avoid talking about Venice. Seeing the young man fascinated made her homesick. It's the place she loved dearly, and as long as she remained Ferdinando's mistress, she would never see it again. Never.

'So, tell me. Which are those opera theatres?' Händel continued, enthusiastic.

'There is San Giovanni Grisostomo, and Sant'Angelo and also San Cassiano...' Then she stopped. The memory of singing in Venice and being free was now unbearable.

Händel saw her profile, and noticed her lips quivering. 'Oh...er...' Completely taken by surprise, he wavered between facing or ignoring her sorrow. Ignoring seemed too cowardly. *Don't escape, face it!* his inner voice said. 'Forgive me, are you all right, Vittoria?'

She just lowered her head. The armour of acting just fell. She was now just a lonely woman missing her hometown. She covered her face with her hands. Her shoulders were shaking.

'Do you want me to go? I am sorry...'

'It's...not your...fa..fault...' Vittoria struggled, 'I just...feel...I am lonely...'

Händel stared at her in shock. *Poor woman. She is lonely and now dumped by Prince Ferdinando. And then?* He saw the reality of those vulnerable singers. He wanted to say something but found no words. The only thing he could do was to wrap her in his arms. Then he remembered when last he had held a woman in his arms. It was Veronica, in Hamburg. *Would it end like before?* The thought crossed his mind, but he pushed it away quickly. *No, this is not right.* He just stayed in the embrace, not knowing what to do. Talk to her? Comfort her? It felt quite a long time to him, but at last Vittoria's sobbing calmed down.

'Thank you... for... comforting me, Giorgio. I felt as if I was being cuddled by my father. He was tall like you,' she whispered, without looking at him.

Then they resumed their walk, side by side, like before but in silence. It did not end as it had with Veronica, and he did not know whether to be relieved or regretful.

Though Händel felt uneasy and shaken by Vittoria's distress, she felt at peace. Back in her room, she thanked God for the peace she was given, even temporarily. Then she gasped. No, it was not God. It was that young Saxon. The way he had wrapped her, gently but quite firmly, was how she remembered her beloved father holding her. And how deep it was, his chest. This was the first time a man had given her such comfort since her father died. Neither her husband nor Prince Ferdinando offered her such warmth.

Händel avoided Vittoria as much as possible, apart from music-making. Margherita and Vittoria seemed to get on very well, and they did not stop chatting, laughing, commenting on each other's dresses, and discussing what was fashionable in Rome – just women's talk. Händel was asked to compose two cantatas, one for each singer. Marquess Ruspoli and Cardinal Ottoboni agreed that it was better to avoid putting the two singers in competition. One of the cantatas, *Armida abandonata* (*Armida Abandoned*), carried too much allusion to Vittoria's present situation, so it was given to Margherita. Vittoria was to sing *Un'alma innamorata* (*A Soul in Love*). Could she be?

Vittoria was watching Händel play the harpsichord. There was something different about it compared with other players she knew, including the grand prince. Händel's playing was full, bold and energetic. She was used to hearing sensitive, delicate, and elegant play.

'Isn't it amazing how Giorgio plays?' Margherita addressed Vittoria, making the latter slightly jump. It did not escape Margherita's attention.

'Yes, it's...I don't know. It's just extraordinary,' Vittoria avoided saying *manly*. She knew that considering Händel as a man would be the last thing she should do.

'Oh, you haven't seen everything,' Margherita wanted to make a point, 'if you haven't seen him playing the organ!'

'How fortunate you are!' Vittoria smiled to Margherita. 'But I will never see it,' she said, shrugging. She refused to admit that a tiny seed had been planted in her heart.

The weather changed. The breeze stopped, and the air became very humid. The marquess had no choice but to allow the children to play in the central basin. The grown-ups watched with envy as the children played in the water. The marquess also ordered blocks of ice to be delivered, so he could offer ice-cold wine.

'Are you not hot, Pietro?' Händel asked as he saw the violinist wigged and wrapped in a suit, ready for the concert.

'Well, I am not cold, I have to say, but the heat here is much less than in Rome. It's rather nice.'

'Really?' Händel said horrified. He thought this heat was infernal.

Pietro Castrucci laughed. 'You are not used to this weather, Giorgio. You are from the North!'

'So how much hotter is it in Rome?'

'You will see. We will be back soon, I think.' Castrucci grinned.

It was a particularly humid day. There was no wind, and the air was stuffy. No storm came to break the heat, and the night arrived as heavy as lead. Händel could not sleep. It was too hot. In the dead of night, he slipped out of bed and opened the window. No air came in. Everything was still and sticky. He looked up from the window and saw the moon shining. There was enough light. *I'm not staying in my room.* In just a shirt and breeches, he slipped out of the room, down the corridor, and outside. The same garden where he had walked during daytime looked completely different at night. He could hardly recognise it. The insects were busy buzzing and chirping everywhere. It was a little cooler, and Händel felt more relaxed. He was walking slowly, enjoying the cooler air, but soon he noticed a vague white shape far ahead of him. At first it was a small shadow, but he saw it getting bigger and bigger. He stopped. *What is it? A ghost?* The light was fading as a big cloud slowly covered the moon, and the darkness blurred his vision. The apparition was getting closer to him. He could not move. Then he realised that the figure was human; a woman, he guessed. She was looking straight ahead and stopped ten paces away from Händel. Then she pulled her scarf tight around her shoulders, crossing her forearms in front of her, came nearer and stopped in front of him.

'Too hot to sleep?'

'It's you, Vittoria,' said Händel with a sigh of relief. 'I thought it was…'

'A ghost?' She smiled. 'Don't go straight on. I came back because I heard people…'

'People? Oh, that's fine.' Thinking they would be his fellow musicians, Händel was about to carry on, but then felt Vittoria's hand grabbing his arm.

'I think they are servants – well, lovers.'

'Oh…' Embarrassed, Händel stopped, looked down and walked along with Vittoria the way he came. He was glad it was dark enough to conceal his blushing. She was in a light nightdress with just a scarf on top. Her feathery blond hair was loose, floating like a cloud.

'I thought there would be nobody here at this time.' Händel was still staring at his feet as he walked.

'You are not the only one to think… oh!' Vittoria looked up the sky.

Händel felt raindrops on his shoulders. The droplets began to come faster and faster. 'We have to hurry,' he said. They ran towards the black shadow in front of them, which they thought was the house. It was not.

'Oh, I thought it was the castle. What is it?' Handel asked.

Vittoria pushed a door and entered. Händel followed.

'It must be the orangery. Can you smell the earth?' Vittoria replied. It was completely dark.

Now it was raining, harder and harder. The sky was dark. The storm was breaking, and the lightning revealed them standing in an empty space; the orange trees, grown in pots, had been moved outside during the warmer weather.

'We are trapped here,' Vittoria said, looking sulky, 'I wanted to stay in the gardens.' Then she tightened her scarf around her again, as if she were cold.

'Do you know where the castle is?' Händel felt uneasy to be left alone with her. He was ready to go back, even in the rain.

'Not really. It's too dark to see.' She walked towards the large windows, guided by the lightning flash. The rain was pounding on the glass. She could see nothing but rainwater pouring down.

Händel did not move. He saw Vittoria standing in front of one of the large windows, looking up at the sky. Another lightning flash outlined her perfect profile and her golden hair loose on her back. He just stood there watching her. The place was filled with noise from the occasional thunder and the rain hammering on the roof. He felt alone with Vittoria in the world. It was surreal. He did not know how long he stayed there. Vittoria looked calm, just watching the rain pour down. Händel approached her slowly, stood just behind her. His hands met her hands. He felt her body leaning against him and her head resting on his chest.

When the storm was over, two figures entered the house noiselessly. They went up the stairs together. At the top of the stairs, the taller figure kissed the smaller figure passionately, and they parted.

Margherita, awake from the storm, waited for the rain to stop before opening the window of her room. The cool air entered and she breathed in deeply. Then she saw two figures running towards the castle, and smiled. *Two lovers, maybe servants. Hope they were not drenched.* She could sleep soundly for the first time since the heatwave.

Margherita saw it at once the next day. People looked refreshed and happy, but she could see clearly that Händel and Vittoria looked particularly happy - and not because of the cooler weather. She froze and went very pale. *Oh, the way he looks at her! He loves her.* It was very subtle, but her eyes were not fooled. *And she looks so happy and beautiful.* The image of the two figures she had seen returned to her, and she felt a chill down her spine. Vittoria feigned indifference, smiling as usual, but she was just radiant. Margherita felt desperate and powerless. *I cannot hate her. She is a nice woman. And I cannot compete with her.* Though heartbroken, she still could not just give up her love. The only thing left for her was to remain his friend. If she lost him as a friend, there would be no purpose in her life. She could not see her life without him; just to see him play, to chat with him, and see him smile to her. Desperate, she vowed to herself not to put herself in their way. But her heart was aching too much. Then the hatred crept in. She loathed Händel and Vittoria and wanted to harm them both. *What shall I do? Tell the marquess?* Then she collapsed in tears. She did not want to harm him, at any cost. Then she felt drained. All the effort to get closer to Händel, from the day she arrived at Francesco Ruspoli's household was, she realised, in vain, just a waste of time. In just a few days Vittoria had conquered him. Such was the unfair rule of love.

When all the entertainments were duly performed, the whole household could feel it was time to go back to Rome. Vittoria left with Cardinal Ottoboni for Bologna, to Margherita's relief.

Händel saw Margherita walking towards the superintendent's office.

'Are you going to see Fabio?' asked Händel.

'Yes, and you?'

'Same.'

They walked together. The door was ajar, and they could see Fabio Cavalcanti working at his desk. At the call, he raised his head.

'Avanti!' He got up and retrieved two small boxes from the cupboard behind him.

Händel and Margherita looked at each other.

'The marquess would like to thank you both for the performances. He is very pleased and asks you to accept these as tokens of his gratitude.'

He handed a box to each. Händel did not know what to do and just stared at the box in his hands. Margherita, much accustomed to this, asked merrily, 'May I open it, Signor Cavalcanti?'

'Of course, Signorina Durastante, please do.'

Margherita opened the box, and her face lit up. 'Oh, my God. It's beautiful!' It was a ring with diamonds. She looked at Händel and said, 'Open your box, Giorgio. I want to see it.'

Händel obeyed. It was another ring.

'Oh, how nice!' Margherita pressed her box to her chest and said, 'Do thank the marquess for me, please. Tell him he is too generous.'

'I will, Signorina Durastante.'

They were going towards their respective rooms. When they were far enough from Fabio's office, Margherita stopped and looked at Händel.

'Do you like your gift, Giorgio?'

Händel looked at her, puzzled. Margherita did not wait for him to answer her question.

'I do not like mine. It is not to my taste at all.'

'But—'

'But it is of value at least, so it is a good thing to have.'

'But—'

'I will have to wear it from time to time as long as I am staying in his house, of course.'

'But—'

'Come on, Giorgio! It's called acting! Don't forget to thank the marquess in person.' And she was gone, leaving Händel speechless.

Back in her room, Margherita felt a little hope. *I still have a chance. She is gone now. Maybe he will wake up. She is much older than him. And she might go back to the prince after all. Back in Rome, everything will settle as before.* It had been a real challenge for her. She had acted as if she were aware of nothing, but she could see that the fellow musicians sensed something. She just behaved as a good friend of both Händel and Vittoria, talking to them often. This was a plan to try to make them talk more, to extract some hints. Nothing. Not the slightest hint of the truth. Then she had considered rebelling against Händel, perhaps singing against his instructions, to provoke him. She was desperate to get an inkling of what was going on. She did not dare to do so, after all. She sighed deeply, and hoped that the stay in Vignanello would be wiped out of Vittoria's memory and also Händel's.

Rome, Summer 1707

'It's a living hell! It's too hot!' Händel shouted, out of control. He got up from the harpsichord and went to the open window.

The musicians looked at each other. They were rehearsing for the next day's *conversazione*. It was hot in Rome, and as there was no audience, they had removed their wigs and opened their shirts.

'Giorgio. How about me? I cannot remove my hair and be undressed like all of you.' Margherita pressed the damp cloth to her forehead.

There was Fabio's voice outside the Stanzione, and all the musicians hurriedly put their wigs back on. Two violinists entered following the superintendent.

'Here they are. This is the Stanzione,' Fabio said looking back. 'I am sorry, I am very busy. Could you introduce yourselves?'

'I can do it, Signor Fabio,' said Pietro Castrucci who was acquainted with the newly hired musicians. 'Welcome to Palazzo Bonelli, to the household of the Marquess of Cerveteri,' he said, addressing the newcomers. He turned to his fellow musicians, saying, 'This is Alfonso Poli, and this is Lorenzo Bononcini.' The two men smiled and bowed slightly.

'Bononcini?' Händel looked at one of them.

'Yes. You are probably thinking of my brother Giovanni?'

Händel found the man to be friendly, very similar to his famous brother, minus the haughtiness.

'Are you all right, Giorgio, not too hot?' Margherita enquired, seeing

Händel ready for the concert, wigged and wrapped in a suit. 'Fortunately, the marquess decided to start later than normal. It will be cooler.'

Händel smiled. 'Thank you, Margherita. I feel much better. I went to the barber this morning.'

'Oh, did you?'

'Yes, I did. Shall I show you?' Händel started to lift the edge of his wig.

'Oh, no, please! I don't need to see that!'

Händel giggled.

'Did you shave Giorgio?' Domenico Castrucci asked.

'Yes, I did.'

'I told you. Once you start doing it, you cannot stop, especially during the summer. Now you will survive!'

His Highness, Grand Prince Ferdinando de' Medici,

Your Highness,

As usual, the festival of Our Lady of Mount Carmel was done lavishly. This year, the Colonna family chose the Saxon, Endel, to compose the music for the celebration. Illuminated arches were erected in the surrounding streets, as before, and I attended all the ceremonies – the first vespers on 15 July and the mass and second vespers on 16 July.

I must say that the Saxon deserves to be treasured by the most powerful patrons of Rome. He conducted himself from the harpsichord, and the young Paolucci was extraordinary. Cardinal Carlo Colonna proved to be more than right to persuade the family to commission a young German Protestant.

You enquired about Paolucci. He is too young to travel on his own. He is now under

> the patronage of Cardinal Ottoboni but still lives with his parents.
>
> Your most humble, faithful, and devoted servant,
> Annibale Merlini

Grand Prince Ferdinando was not the happiest. The letter just received from his correspondent in Rome in hand, he grimaced. He could not have the castrato Paolucci, and there was nothing he could do about it. He did not like it when he could not get what he wanted. As for the Saxon, he was getting more and more famous and difficult to ignore. The prince did not like to acknowledge he'd misjudged the young composer. Then he had an idea to amend the situation. With a solution found, he now wanted to concentrate on Pratolino opera. He made Vittoria come back. Lucrezia was, after all, disappointing. She was not that good, either in singing or in bed.

Two weeks later, Annibale Merlini was to bring Händel a libretto of a full opera, arranged by Antonio Salvi. Händel was delighted but intrigued at the same time. A commission for an opera, his very first Italian opera! But why Prince Ferdinando? By now Händel was certain that the grand prince did not like him, compared to the way he was treated here in Rome. The prince's indifference was the proof of it.

'Is the opera for Pratolino?' Händel asked Merlini.

'No, Maestro. It is for Cocomero.'

'Cocomero?' Händel knew then that the commission did not come from the grand prince. The Cocomero theatre was where he went to see operas with the grand princess.

'Yes, Cocomero, Mr Endel. In fact, the commission comes from *l'Accademia degl'infuocati* at the suggestion of the prince, and he asked Salvi to provide you with a libretto.'

'I see.' *Then why did the grand prince suggest it?* Suppressing more questions, Händel smiled, and said, 'You would thank the grand prince on my behalf for his generosity.'

He decided to not question anything. *Just concentrate. This is a fabulous chance. I cannot fail.* He was far from realising that it was Prince Ferdinando's way of showing his patronage. By making *l'Accademia degl'infuocati* commission an opera from Händel, he would be the dedicatee, and it would cost him nothing. A good compromise.

From now on, all Händel's spare time would be dedicated to the opera. Between providing cantatas for the marquess's Sunday concerts and, occasionally, cardinal Ottoboni's concerts, fulfilling cardinal Pamphili's commissions, and accompanying Margherita when she sang in different palaces, Händel's life was busy. After the festival of the Carmelite order, the Colonna family had asked for his presence as well. Now it would be busier.

While Prince Ferdinando kept himself busy with opera in Pratolino, Händel was struggling in Rome. Now he was realising how different an *opera seria* was from the ones he knew in Hamburg. There was hardly room for spectacular scenes or comic characters. It was made of arias and a large number of recitatives. And how about the singers? *Well, it's called learning.* His burning question was about Vittoria. *Did the grand prince make her come back? Would she be singing in Pratolino this year? Would she be singing in my opera? Would I see her again?*

He guessed a few of the answers. The follow-up came from the academy directly. *L'Accademia degl'infuocati* was a group of Florentine noblemen promoting the Teatro Civico Accademico, the city theatre. The theatre was situated in the Via del Cocomero, or Watermelon Street, and thus was known as the Teatro del Cocomero. The academy sent him the list of the singers, five altogether. Vittoria was not mentioned. That meant no Vittoria in his opera. And it was clear that Händel was excluded from Pratolino opera. *But still, is she back with the prince? Whom could I ask? Dr Salvi?* He decided, after all, to keep himself quiet. No questions. Knowing how gossipy the singers and musicians were, he preferred to wait. *I will know once I am in Florence.*

Uncertain of the ability of the assigned singers, Händel decided to go to Florence, and prepared for his move. His opera composing was often the subject of conversation at the marquess's table.

'Would you come back here after Florence, Maestro?' asked Isabella, the marchioness, now feeling well enough to attend meals with the others.

'To be honest, Marchioness, I don't know. I think if I get enough money from my opera, I would love to go to Venice.'

Margherita struggled to hide her emotions. *He will not come back!* She could not be happy for him, unlike the others.

'Well, you are absolutely right to go there, Maestro,' Francesco Ruspoli said. 'After all, Rome is very limited, and I know that.'

'I thank you, Marquess.'

'Anyway, you are welcome back anytime,' continued Ruspoli, 'or maybe I will have to go to Venice to drag you back after the carnival season!'

Everybody laughed, including Margherita, forcing herself to join in.

The marchioness interrupted, 'No, my love, I will retain you here. You will send Fabio with that giant gardener, Mario.'

The laughter doubled. Seeing the marquess willing to get Händel back, Margherita felt better.

Florence, Autumn 1707

When Händel arrived in Florence people were still talking about the opera played at the Pratolino theatre with Vittoria in the title role. She was back in favour. It was an awkward situation for Händel. He was lodged in Palazzo Pitti as a guest of honour but spent most of the time at the Cocomero Theatre. However, whenever required, he was summoned to the prince's court to play the harpsichord on his own or with other court musicians, with or without the singers. Vittoria behaved as if she were meeting him for the first time. The presence of Antonio Salvi and sporadic sightings of the grand princess were a relief in this tense and oppressive air of Palazzo Pitti. Händel stayed at the Cocomero theatre as much as he could, even when he did not need to be there. He even thought of getting a room near the theatre, but that idea was quashed by Antonio Salvi, from whom he sought advice. 'Grand Prince Ferdinando would kick you out when he wants to, but otherwise you stay,' was the answer. A subject did not have the right to decide or choose.

'Is it ready, Maestro Sassone? Can we start printing the wordbook?' Salvi asked, entering the rehearsal room of the theatre. As the librettist, Salvi made himself available to Händel as much as he could.

'No, Signor Salvi. I have to make changes,' Händel replied, concerned. 'I would like to suppress some arias and maybe a duet.' He looked at Salvi, 'if you agree. It's just...not going well.'

'Oh, could you show me where?'

Händel indicated in the libretto, 'Here, Signor Salvi. I think this scene goes smoothly if there were no aria here, and instead put it at the end of the scene as an exit.'

They worked together for a while.

'So, what do you think of the libretto? You know it is an adaptation?'

'No, I did not know.' The composer looked up. 'Could you tell me about it?'

'Of course. The original source is the libretto by Francesco Silvani called *Il duello d'amore e di vendetta*. It was set by Marc'Antonio Ziani and produced a few years ago in Venice.'

'Oh,' Händel smiled, remembering the *Almira* he had composed in Hamburg. 'My very first opera's libretto was also an adaptation from an Italian one.'

'It's a common practice, especially when the opera was a big success.'

'Was the original libretto, I mean *Il duello d'amore*, a big success?'

'Oh yes. Rodrigo was played by Nicolini. It was his début in Venice. Have you ever heard of him?'

'Nicolini? No.'

'Try to hear him sing, and act, if you go to Venice. He is apparently fabulous. Remember his name, Nicolini, the castrato.'

'Yes I will. Nicolini,' Händel nodded. He was glad to have a friend.

'May I ask how the grand princess is, Signor Salvi?'

'She is well. She is looking forward to the opera here, Signor Sassone.'

Working with the singers, Händel realised how fragile the political situation was now in Italy, due to the War of the Spanish Succession. Most of the singers were hired from the court of Mantua where the duke was exiled for being pro-French. Mantua was now occupied by the Imperial force. One singer was from the court of Modena where the ruler was forced to flee for resisting the French force. Mantua and Modena were less than five hours apart by coach and were now in opposite positions. The singers' futures were uncertain, and two of them were planning to stay in Florence.

Händel did his best, but the very first Italian opera was a struggle. On top of it, he found no harmony in the orchestra and singers. There was no camaraderie. Though inexperienced, Händel, who knew the quality of Corelli's orchestra, was disappointed with the one he had to deal with. The orchestra was quite big, but the quality of instrumentalists was uneven; it felt bumpy compared to Corelli's orchestra that was like a strand of perfect pearls. The singers were restless, more concerned about their near future, trying to find and secure a patron. Some of them did not stop pestering Händel, pushing for an introduction to Prince Ferdinando.

With the title of the opera changed from *Il duello d'amore e di vendetta (The Duel of Love and Vengeance)* to *Vincer se stesso è la maggior vittoria (To overcome oneself is the greater victory)*, and the wordbook duly dedicated to His Highness the Grand Prince of Tuscany Ferdinando de' Medici, Händel's opera was played at the Cocomero Theatre. The premiere was attended by the grand prince and grand princess with many others from the nobility. Then the prince departed to Pratolino, as usual, for hunting. Left alone, Princess Violante went to the theatre accompanied by Salvi. Händel was now at times invited by the grand princess for a private concert or a meal when he wasn't busy at the opera. Händel conducted all the performances from the harpsichord. When the interest for his new opera started to fade, Händel knew it was time to stop and move on. It was early December.

Her eyes bright, Grand Princess Violante said, 'So this time, Mr Händel, you are going to Venice. How exciting!' she beamed, clutching her hands together in front of her chest.

'Yes, Princess.' Händel could not conceal his enthusiasm.

Seated between Händel and Dr Salvi, at a very private and relaxing supper, she was cheerful.

Händel was touched to see the princess just being happy for him. Despite being nearly a prisoner, looking after her grumpy father-in-law, and being ignored by her husband, Violante of Bavaria showed no sign of bitterness.

'Do you have any connections there, Mr Händel?'

'No, not at all.'

'Oh, let me think...'

'Princess?'

'Yes?'

'That's what I was told to tell anyone who asked the question.'

Grand Princess Violante stared at Händel, not understanding. Händel continued. 'Princess, it was Monsignor Steffani. He told me to address myself to Cardinal Grimani.'

'I don't understand.'

Dr Salvi just listened.

'Cardinal Grimani is considered to be an enemy in Rome, and it could be the same anywhere else, because he is supporting the Austrians. I was told to be careful as many Italian states support the French, though not officially. That's all. Being acquainted with Cardinal Grimani could be harmful, eventually. So I just say I know nobody,' Händel grinned.

'I see. So you *do* have a connection.'

'No, Princess.' Händel pursed his lips, nodding vigorously.

Grand Princess laughed.

'See as much as you can, Maestro,' Salvi said, 'but at the same time, be careful.'

Händel looked at the librettist, lost, then the words of Domenico Castrucci came back. Händel asked, 'Oh, the naughty things under the mask?'

'Yes, those naughty things,' Salvi said, seriously, when he found himself alone with Händel. 'Be careful. The people who don't know are easily entrapped and exploited.' He could see that the young Saxon had not very much experience in life. 'There will be lots of visitors in Venice, really crowded. Needless to say, pickpockets are there, but they are not only in Venice.'

'I know! I was pickpocketed once in Rome. And you know, Signor Salvi, I did not even realise my pocket was emptied.'

'They are very skilled.'

Händel clearly remembered when the small pouch was returned to him. Until then he had not realised it was missing from his inner pocket. At the time, he was still living in the old palace of the marquess.

'I was told to give this to you, sir,' Matteo, the young valet assigned to him had said one morning, showing the black, embroidered pouch.

Händel had stared at the pouch, rummaged through all his pockets, and realised that it was his. 'But, how... Who gave that to you, Matteo?' he had asked, still confused.

'A Gipsy woman, sir.'

'Yes, they are very skilled,' The voice of Antonio Salvi got the young composer back from his thoughts.

'But pickpockets are nothing. They are a nuisance, true, but there are more serious issues.' Salvi continued. 'I give you an example. Many people visiting Venice catch diseases, nasty ones, that sometimes are fatal. Don't be tempted. Be firm.'

Händel just stared at Salvi, speechless.

'I don't want to make you scared, but never accept an invitation from people you don't know. You might regret it terribly afterwards. I know a few people who have come back with syphilis.'

'Oh…' Händel understood. He knew that the disease was fatal, a slow painful death.

'Venice is a fabulous place for opera, but because it attracts lots of people, there are lots of not so respectable things going on behind the scenes.'

Händel felt his excitement dwindling.

'Just simple precautions, and you will be fine,' Salvi reassured the young man.

Though excited for his very first visit to Venice, Händel felt a pang of sadness. All through his Florentine stay, Vittoria was utterly out of reach. She chose the grand prince. She looked happy. The only occasion he could see her was when he was required to play the harpsichord, solo or to accompany the singers. She avoided Händel skilfully in a very natural way, so that he could not even exchange a word.

Vittoria just refused to listen to her heart. She had been Ferdinando's mistress for years now, and that was the way it should be, she repeated to herself. And she knew the best way was to let Händel go, anywhere, so he could pursue his career and not have a woman in his way. This was the only way she could help him.

Venice, January 1708, carnival

> Dear Telemann,
>
> I am writing to you from Venice. At last! After my opera in Florence, I hurried to Venice. As instructed, the first thing I did was

to go to the Teatro San Giovanni Grisostomo, to ask for Cardinal Grimani. He was not in Venice, but he left a letter for me. What a generous man! He saw me in Rome, but he kept himself discreet. In his letter, a few letters of introduction were included, and I was granted free entrance to the theatre.

I got a modest lodging to save money so I can see as much as possible. I saw the famous Nicolini sing in Caldara's opera *La Partenope*. Then I saw *Teuzzone* by Lotti. What a difference from Rome! Operas are played everywhere. Last night was *Armida in campo* by Boniventi. A young castrato called Senesino was there. He could follow Nicolini's path.

I have received an invitation for a masked ball tomorrow, so I am going to get a mask.

One thing I regret is that I could not go to Pratolino in Florence. I will probably never go. However, Antonio Salvi gave me the wordbook of the last opera played there, *Dionisio re di Portogalo* by Perti. Salvi was the librettist. Though I did not gain sympathy from Prince Ferdinando, I made some friends in Florence.

Hope you are settled and happy in Eisenach. Please write to me. I miss you, and I miss my country.

Your most devoted and humble servant and brother,
G.F. Händel

Baron Johann Adolf von Kielmansegg, Hanoverian envoy to the Serene Republic, was arriving at the reception at Palazzo Grimani. Married to the Hanoverian elector's half-sister, he was one of the trusted people of Elector Georg Ludwig. As he stepped off the gondola, he noticed Domenico Scarlatti going up the steps.

'Maestro Scarlatti!' he shouted. As an ardent music lover, he was acquainted with the son of the famous composer.

Scarlatti turned and beamed. Here was one of his admirers, the Hanoverian baron.

'Baron, how are you?'

Their identities were checked at the entrance and then they were allowed to wear masks. As they entered the reception hall, they realised it was quiet despite the crowd. In one corner, there was a circle surrounding the harpsichord and the player. They were drawn to the spot. A tall man in a visor was playing with incredible ability. They stopped and looked at each other.

The baron turned to Scarlatti. 'Who is playing?' he whispered.

'I don't know, but I can guess. It is the famous Saxon.'

'Saxon?'

'Or the devil.'

There was applause. The tall man got up, bowed, and walked away from the harpsichord. The baron and Domenico Scarlatti approached him.

'Caro Sassone,' Scarlatti said.

Händel stopped. He saw two men in front of him. Scarlatti removed his mask. Händel did the same but did not recognise the man. He did, however, see something familiar.

'My name is Scarlatti,' said Domenico.

'Scarlatti?'

'I am Domenico, Alessandro's son.' He smiled.

'Ah, that's why you look familiar!' Händel exclaimed, and extended his hand. 'Giorgio Hendel.'

'Let me introduce you to Baron von Kielmansegg.' Domenico turned to the baron, who removed his mask.

Händel saw a man about his height. He was middle-aged, and very good looking with dark soft eyes. Händel liked him instantly.

'I missed you in Hanover,' the baron said in German.

Händel, surprised but pleased, replied in the same language, 'Oh, are you from Hanover?'

'Yes, I am here as the Hanoverian envoy. They call you Saxon. I thought you were from Halle.'

'I am from Halle, so I am a Prussian, but I am known as a Saxon. I think they just call every German a Saxon.'

As Scarlatti took the place at the harpsichord with a singer, they walked away from the crowd. Händel did not realise that he had been watched and followed by a masked couple since he had left the harpsichord.

'Tell me what you have been doing here in Venice,' the baron asked in a friendly manner. 'I heard about you from Duchess Sophia.'
'I arrived not long ago. I am here to see operas, as much as possible.'
'You are in the right place then. And before here, where were you?'
'Florence.'
'At Prince Ferdinando's?'
'Yes.'
'How is he?'
'Well, Baron.'
'And before Florence?'
'Mainly Rome.'
'Ah, that's more difficult to guess. Let me think...'

They talked while abundant food and fine wine were served. Baron von Kielmansegg left Händel with a firm invitation to stay in his palace. The masked couple observing Händel looked at each other, and one of them nodded. As the woman was slowly approaching Händel, another man overtook her from behind. The woman backed away discreetly.

'You must be Mr Handel,' said the man in French.
Oh, this one can pronounce the 'h', Händel thought as he turned. 'Yes, I am, sir,' Händel replied in French. He saw a tall man, dressed very elegantly and unmasked. His face was quite long, with heavy eyelids that made him look sleepy.

'My name is Charles Montagu, Earl of Manchester. I am here as Britain's ambassador to Venice.'

Händel nearly jumped. 'Oh, Britain!'

Charles Montagu laughed. 'I see you know the name.'

'I would like to know more about London, my lord.' Händel asked, feeling easy with the wine he'd consumed.

To this Charles Montagu just smiled. 'Come to my palace tomorrow, then. I am giving a reception. There will be some of my friends and acquaintances from Britain.'

'Is there an opera house in London, sir?'

'I will tell you all that tomorrow.' He handed Händel his visiting card, and smiled, 'I will see you tomorrow.'

Händel was watching the earl going to join other people when he found himself face to face with another man.

'Welcome to Palazzo Grimani, Maestro Sassone. You arrived and were dragged to the harpsichord. I am Pietro Grimani. Let me introduce you to my family. Come with me.' The host led Händel gently, walking alongside him. 'There are a few composers and singers as well. You have to meet them.'

The masked couple watched Händel disappear among the guests. They looked at each other. The woman whispered something to the man, and nodded.

Händel came out of the palace loaded with invitations. As he was not looking for patronage in Venice and was not committed to composing, he wanted to use this respite to see opera as much as possible and make acquaintances. He was walking quite dreamily towards his lodging. Helped by wine, he felt relaxed, and walked slowly thinking of the reception he would attend the next day. Then a voice called him from behind. He stopped and turned to see a masked couple.

The woman approached him and said, 'I saw you in Palazzo Grimani. Would you like to spend some time with us if you are free?'

They were still wearing their masks, and they did not introduce themselves. Händel sensed something was not quite right. It was just instinct. He frowned.

'Oh, do not worry. We mean you no harm,' the woman continued. 'We thought we could talk to you in a quiet corner, or maybe you could come to our house?' Then she removed her mask. She was very pretty. Still, Händel was not feeling easy. He could not find out what was bothering him. Being invited to the Palazzo Grimani, they could not be unrespectable; still, this was an invitation from strangers.

The man, still wearing his mask, started to lead Händel gently by the arm. They apparently wanted to take him somewhere. Händel started to panic. Then he heard a cough. The man nearly jumped, released his grip and rushed to the woman.

'Are you all right, darling? It's the cold air.' And he tapped gently on the woman's back.

Händel stood there, staring at the couple. He knew what was wrong. The woman's voice was faked. Her cough betrayed her. He observed the woman closely. She was thin of frame and was dressed impeccably. Händel felt his heart beating fast. *What to do? How can I get out of this? Confront them?* Then he remembered the advice from Dr Salvi. *Avoid confrontation. Just escape. The narrow streets of Venice are just like a maze, very easy to get lost in. Keep calm and do not go into those narrow streets. The best way to escape, if you are in trouble, is to go to into the crowd, like at the Piazza San Marco. Then it will be impossible to find you.*

Händel forced a smile at the couple and said, 'I am going to the Piazza San Marco.' He felt his hands sweaty.

The woman smiled back. 'We will accompany you, then.' She took Händel's arm and walked beside him.

'Are you from here, Madam?' Händel tried his best to look casual with his heart pounding.

'Yes, born and bred.'

Händel was sure about the faked voice now. 'May I ask your name, madam?' His voice was shaking slightly now. *I have to get out of here. God knows what they want of me.*

'Mariana.'

Händel recognised the street leading to the Piazza San Marco. *It's now or never.* He stopped, turned to the woman, and took her hands. He looked at her rather strong hands and had no doubt.

He addressed the man. 'Enjoy carnival, Signor.' He stared at the woman. 'You've got the wrong person. Enjoy carnival, Signor.' He saw the woman's eyes widen. Getting free from the couple, he ran. He never ran so fast. He did not dare to look back. He just ran to dive into the crowd of San Marco.

Three days later Händel found himself settled at Baron Kielmansegg's palace. It was the palace leased by Elector Georg Ludwig, following the family custom to have a palace and theatre boxes in Venice. This was very fortunate for Händel, allowing him to save money and make acquaintances.

'I have to tell you, Händel, that I cannot give you the best room I have.'

'Baron, I thank you for your generous hospitality, and I do not deserve the best room. May I commit the indiscretion of asking you who will be having the best room, though?'

Johann Adolf laughed. 'It is Prince Ernst August of Hanover, the youngest brother of the elector. He will be arriving soon.'

'Oh?'

'I will introduce you, of course, but…'

'But?'

'He is not really a music lover' – he raised his eyebrows – 'just to let you know, so don't talk about music too much.'

The whole household was waiting for Prince Ernst August in the hall. Händel was standing just behind the baron. After disembarking from the gondola, the prince appeared in the hall. It was the baron's wife, Sophia, who greeted him first. She was the daughter born to the mistress of her father, the late duke. Boisterous and with a strong character, she always imposed herself as equal towards the legitimate children of her father.

'Welcome to Venice, Brother!'

'Nice to see you, Sister,' the prince said casually. 'I see you are still growing,' he said, looking up and down at her plump figure, smiling.

'Ernst! I am expecting!' Sophia shouted, irritated.

'Again!' He looked at the baron and rolled his eyes. 'What a hard worker you are. I feel lazy.'

The prince, the baroness, and the baron burst into laughter, leaving the German servants smiling and the Italian servants puzzled. Händel looked at his feet, not knowing how to behave but letting a smile escape. The prince was quick to notice him.

'Baron, is he the young musical genius you talked about?'

'Husband, I'll let you take care of my brother. I have to go to rest, because...' She glared at her half-brother. 'Because I AM expecting.'

Prince Ernst did indeed show little interest in music. However, as a natural diplomat, he was curious to know about the young German composer in Italy. As a soldier, he was now engaged in the War of the Spanish Succession alongside the emperor. With an excuse to enjoy carnival season in Venice on temporary leave, his mission was to know Italy's position in the ongoing war.

Prince Ernst was fourteen when his father, Duke Ernst August, made the change from the ultimogeniture principle of dynastic succession to primogeniture. He was fully aware of the meaning of it. He, as the last male of the family, lost everything, and that everything went to his eldest brother. Despite the opposition of his elder brothers, he decided to not follow them. Calm and not ambitious by nature, he thought it was quite fair, having known his eldest brother, Georg Ludwig, to be hard-working and serious, maybe too much, sacrificing himself to the service of the family interest. He witnessed the disastrous marriage, purely out of interest, that had scarred his brother for life. From that, he developed an idea that beautiful women were dangerous, and spending much of his time involved in battles suited him better.

Charles Montagu, 4th Earl of Manchester, was deeply impressed by the young German composer, who was incredible at the keyboard and had been spending his time under the best patrons in Rome and Florence. Arrived in Venice as ambassador, the earl was a friend of John Vanbrugh and was actively corresponding with him. Being one of the first subscribers of Vanbrugh's theatre project, he was following the progress and struggle his friend was going through. He witnessed the disastrous opening of the theatre, named Queen's Theatre, partly because the rival theatre's manager, Christopher Rich, nicked Vanbrugh's initial plan and introduced the Italian Opera in London. The war then started between Rich's Theatre Royal on Drury Lane and Vanbrugh's Queen's Theatre on Haymarket. However, Rich seemed always a step ahead. It was he who introduced a castrato, Valentini, to the London public, and then the famous opera *Camilla* by Bononcini. It was only his outrageous management that led him to lose the war. A recent letter from Vanbrugh informed the earl of the change of the opera monopoly, now given to Haymarket. His unofficial mission was to look out for singers and musicians. As an opera lover, he attended as much as he could and was now carefully approaching Nicolini. It was not difficult to find a castrato better than Valentini in Venice, but he wanted the best for the Queen's

Theatre. He was not certain about Händel. To promote Italian opera in London, it would be preferable to have Italian composers. There was a rumour that Rich was trying to get Bononcini. It seemed better to just keep an eye on that young German composer, for the moment.

Baron Kielmansegg kept Händel busy, taking him to numerous receptions. Soon Händel became familiar with some prestigious Venetian family names, like Contarini, Vendramin, and Pisani, and he was allowed to use the box belonging to the elector in various theatres. He was shocked to see masked nobles bending forward out of their boxes and crying out loud for female singers, '*Cara, cara!*' Händel thought those star female singers were often ugly, or very ugly. And he realised that the use of those boxes was not limited to sitting and watching. Venice was a very active trading centre, and the boxes were perfect for discussing business, giving privacy in a public place. The world came to Venice and maintained boxes at the opera houses. And gossiping was rife everywhere, in and out of the boxes. Händel was deeply grateful to Baron Kielmansegg and could not thank him enough. The baron gave the young composer the opportunity to see operas as much as possible and make acquaintance with the local nobility, gentry, singers and composers; Händel could also save money for the uncertain future. He still felt unsure about challenging Venice with his composition skill and would prefer to train himself more. Where? Rome? Would Marquess Ruspoli recall him? Or maybe go to Naples, and put himself under a famous teacher, like Porpora? In that case he needed money to pay for lessons. Then, a message arrived.

> Dear Telemann,
>
> Your letter filled me with joy, and I cannot congratulate enough for your betrothal. Your fiancée, Mademoiselle Eberlin, sounds absolutely sweet and charming.
>
> It is a dream to be in Venice. Opera is played every day. Caldara, Lotti, Mancia, Gasparini, Albinoni, Polani, Pollarolo...all opera composers! The private receptions I go to with Baron Kielmansegg are excellent occasions to meet them. I met Caldara, Lotti, and Nicolini, the castrato. Caldara had to

leave Mantua, due to the war. The female singers are all ugly to the highest degree, but they are all mistresses. I think they charm wealthy men with their voices, making them believe that it is a point of honour to have them in their possession.

    I heard of a composer named Vivaldi. People call him the red priest, because of the colour of his hair. He is the master of violin at an orphanage, Ospedale della Pietà, and I was advised to go to one of the concerts they give. I was told to hurry, because he might quit soon. Apparently he does not get on with the board of directors.

    I will go back to Rome soon. The marquess sent me a messenger asking me to compose an oratorio for Easter. The messenger waited for my reply, so he could to back to Rome immediately. Of course I said yes.

    My compliments to your fiancée. Write to me again. I will write to you once I am in Rome. I think this time I will be living in Palazzo Bonelli.

Your most humble and obedient servant and brother,
G.F. Händel

Chapter 9 : A Saxon in Italy : between opera and love (1708)

Rome, Early Spring 1708

'That's a very good idea, Francesco,' said Pietro Ottoboni.

In Palazzo Bonelli, Francesco Ruspoli and Cardinal Pietro Ottoboni were busy organising for the forthcoming Lent and Easter.

'So you agree, I can borrow Corelli and the musicians,' said the marquess.

'Of course. So that is for Easter Sunday and Monday.'

'Yes. So what would you do, Pietro, for Lent?' Ruspoli asked.

'Oh, I thought I could just reuse Scarlatti's oratorio.'

'*Il giardino*?' The marquess asked, remembering the oratorio played at his palace the previous Easter.

'Yes.' The cardinal looked to his friend for approval. 'And then I'll ask him to compose an oratorio for Passion Week.'

'Sounds good. Will you be the librettist, Pietro?' Francesco asked, feeling slightly inferior. *I wish I could write libretti like him*, he thought. Unlike his holy friends, the marquess was the only one to not be a poet.

'I will. And you have the Saxon to compose a new oratorio.'

'I do. I want something grand.' The marquess beamed.

'Who is the librettist?' The cardinal asked, curious.

'Capace.'

'How exciting!' Cardinal Ottoboni exclaimed, hiding carefully his apprehension. *Oh, I will have to do my best.* He will inevitably be compared to one of the best poets in Rome, Carlo Sigismondo Capace.

Francesco Ruspoli was in his office with the superintendent Fabio and the architect Giovanni Battista Contini.

'Fabio, did you hear from Mr Endel?'

'Yes, Marquess. He accepts, and he will be back in due time.'

'Good.' He turned to the architect. 'Contini, I want it big, splendid.'

'How big does Marquess want it to be?'

'I want the stage decorated richly, and I want a big orchestra. Oh, I want the audience space decorated as well. Everywhere. I want it to be talked about as something never seen before!'

'I see. So I shall need a master mason, a carpenter, and a painter or two.

Does Your Lordship want curtains as well?'

'Yes.'

'So, a draper will be needed as well.'

'And, I want the interval hall to be decorated as well. Some surprising decoration.'

'Does Marquess have any idea of the location?'

'Well, I'm thinking of using the second floor Stanzione delle Accademie for the concert and the first floor Great Hall for the interval.'

'As you wish, Marquess,' said Contini.

Fabio, once alone with the marquess, said, 'Marquess, it will be very expensive. Is Your Lordship…'

'Don't worry, Fabio.'

Three days later, Contini was presenting his project. As he unrolled his drawings, he could sense the excitement of the marquess.

'So, the stage for the orchestra will be slightly curved towards the audience, with ranks ascending towards the back. I will need to know the number of musicians, but for the moment I put four ranks. I will place a barrier to separate the orchestra from the audience. The music stands will have curved legs and racks, if Marquess wished to have those especially made.'

'Yes, that's a good idea.'

'As you wish, Marquess.'

'Go on. That's not all.'

'For the back decoration of the stage, there will be a large painting, like this.' Contini produced another drawing. It represented a square canvas. Within the square there was a round frame in trompe l'oeil with the Ruspoli coat of arms in the four corners. Within the round frame was an angel sitting on the tomb announcing the resurrection to Mary Magdalene and Mary Cleophas, with John the Evangelist in the vicinity of a mountain and demons plunging into the abyss.

'Who is the painter?'

'It's Cerruti, Your Lordship.'

'Very well. Is that all?'

'One more thing, Marquess. I would like to show you this.' Contini produced another drawing. 'This will be hung high on an arch that will cross the full width of the room above the proscenium.'

The drawing represented an ornamented frontispiece with cornices, volutes, a cherub, a tablet, foliage, and palms. On the tablet was the title of the oratorio in four lines and forty-six letters:

BRIGHT STAR

ORATORIO
DELLA RESURREZIONE DI
N.° SIGNOR
GESU CHRISTO

Marquess Ruspoli smiled. 'Very well, Contini. Go ahead.'
'I will come back with more details, Marquess.'

Margherita saw a coach approaching and stop in front of Palazzo Bonelli. She had been watching from her windows for days. She hurried downstairs.
'Giorgio, you are back!' exclaimed Margherita, her face flushing. 'We all missed you.'
'Yes, I am back.' Händel smiled.
'How was Venice?' Margherita asked, instead of enquiring about his opera in Florence.
'A dream! I've never heard so many operas in my life, and...' He stopped. 'Margherita, have you ever sung in Venice?'
'Oh, yes, just once. I was very young then.'
'Which theatre?'
'I think it was Sant'Angelo. I had a small role.'
'That's the very first one I went to. And then?'
'Oh, that was all. I was not employed in Venice.'
'How come?'
'I was employed by the Duke of Mantua then. The production was just transferred to Venice with all the singers, and I was among them.'
'Mantua? There were several singers from Mantua in Florence. They cannot stay there anymore because of the war. Was it the same for you?'
'No. I did not stay long there. I realised that I was not ready. I wanted to have more training. Well, Venice made me realise that.'
'Il Sassone! You are back!' Pietro Castrucci came to embrace him. 'You will be busy, Giorgio. Be prepared. The marquess is preparing something big.'
Other musicians came to greet him, and soon there was a small group in the entrance hall.

Händel's Roman life resumed, lodged this time in Palazzo Bonelli.
'Viola da gamba?' Händel looked at Domenico Castrucci.
'There is a virtuoso here right now from Germany, and the marquess wants to know if you want to include the part in your oratorio.'
'From Germany? Do you know the name?'
'Um . . . I'm not sure, something like Ernesto Esse?'
Händel's face lit up. 'Hesse? Could it be Ernst Christian Hesse?'

It was. Händel had first seen Hesse in Hamburg, and was deeply impressed by his virtuosity and sensitivity, and his ability to project the delicate sounds of the instrument to the fore. *That will help to bring a truly suffering effect, and with such a virtuoso, I can put in some duets with Corelli!* He was happy to be back under the patronage of Francesco Ruspoli, liberal in any sense. It was just the right balance. Händel was protected financially, and he could enjoy freedom. However, there was one thing missing: opera.

'How nice to see you again, Maestro Hesse!' Händel embraced the violist tightly, beaming.

The happy reunion was witnessed by other musicians who could not stop being affected by Händel's happiness. Someone noticed Hesse's instrument and called the others to look at it.

'Seven strings!' one said.

'How curious,' another muttered.

Hesse laughed. 'I am a traditionalist. I suppose you cannot find such a thing here in Rome?'

'Is this from Hamburg?' Händel asked.

'Yes, indeed. It is Joachim Tielke's.'

From the first Sunday in Lent, 26 February 1708, every musician in Rome was in fact very busy, some even managing two concerts in the same day. Oratorios were played in several Roman palaces. Händel worked most of the days, to keep up with the commissions. Nevertheless, he attended concerts as much as possible. Now he had little time to attend the marquess's high table for meals.

'A *dispensatore*? What is it?' Händel asked Fabio.

'Marquess wants to give you a *dispensatore* to take care of your meals and wine, as you are very busy.'

'Oh, that's very nice of the marquess. So who is it?'

'De Golla, Maestro. His name is Francesco Maria de Golla. You will ask him for anything you want, and he will take care of it,' said the superintendent, not suspecting the consequence.

Händel was excited. A large array of instruments was provided at Francesco Ruspoli's request, enabling him to produce several novel effects of orchestra colour. It was like a dream. He had no restrictions and his requests were accepted almost automatically. He knew, however, that this was not to be taken for granted. He could have it because it was Francesco Ruspoli, and nobody else. The composition was going smoothly. Now that he had seen as many operas as possible in Venice, he had a clear idea of what *opera seria* was, and he was just applying the technique. He treated the oratorio as an opera without staging. Nonetheless, as much as his professional life was fulfilling, his heart was restless. He still loved Vittoria. He could not forget her, knowing that she was out of reach. The only thing he could do was to bury his feeling deep down, and having a busy life was helping.

Now housed in Palazzo Bonelli, apart from composing, his interest for paintings was growing. Marquess Ruspoli possessed an impressive collection. And, having seen the collection of Ferdinando de' Medici in Florence and those in several palaces in Venice, his eyes were growing more and more trained. It was, at the same time, the attraction of the opposite. While music was ephemerous, disappearing when the performance is over, a painting would remain on the canvas. And the same painting looked different, according to the light or the mood. Händel liked landscapes more than anything. Each time he looked at a painting, he would discover a detail that he had not seen before: a tree there, or a bird, a sailing boat reflected on water... And he marvelled to see what a painter could create on a flat canvas.

The virtuoso viol player Ernst Christian Hesse had been recently appointed *Kapelledirektor* by the landgrave of Hesse-Darmstadt, but more importantly, he was the landgrave's secretary of war. Under the pretext of going on a concert tour and studying Italian music, he had official business to attend to in Italy. Hesse's playing, which commanded special attention, allowed him to go anywhere, like Paris, in the middle of the War of the Spanish Succession. Also, if Cardinal Vincenzo Grimani was in Rome, it was not an accident.

Made aware of Hesse's true mission, in strict confidence, Händel realised that being a virtuoso opened horizons beyond music.

'Are you happy with it, Ernst?'
'I don't know, to be honest, Georg, but . . .'
'But?'
'Believe me, I am not the only one.'
'I know. Like Steffani.'
'Steffani and I both have official titles. But there are many musicians without any particular appointment acting as informers.'
'Hmm, I don't like to think that all the travelling musicians are spies.'
'Sometimes they don't even realise that they are used as spies, Georg.'
'Oh... do you think...?' His eyes wide open, Händel pointed to his chest.

Hesse laughed. 'No. You are not used as a spy. You cannot be, because you have no patron. You are independent, and that's very fortunate.'

So being a guest at Ruspoli's household seemed the right choice. The only thing Händel could think was to keep himself quiet and discreet, to avoid being used. *Could I escape being caught in the web?*

'So he is not your house composer, Marquess?' Cardinal Grimani asked Francesco Ruspoli.

'No, Monsignor. He is... he is a... a guest,' taken by surprise, the marquess bumbled.

Cardinal Pamphili had given one of the Lenten oratorios in his priory, and Ruspoli had not expected to see Cardinal Grimani there.

'In that case, do I still need your permission, Marquess?' Grimani smiled.

'Well, no, Monsignor... I suppose not.'

'May I ask him then?'

'Well, yes, I suppose... Of course... yes, of course...' Francesco Ruspoli stammered.

As one of the leading diplomats in the Imperial service, Cardinal Grimani was now in disgrace at the Vatican. On top of that he was recently nominated viceroy of Naples, making himself one of the principal opponents of Pope Clement XI. Thus he became someone to avoid even for an apolitical person.

'I thank you, Marquess,' Cardinal Grimani said in perfect politeness and went to seek Händel.

Francesco Ruspoli let out a sigh of relief. The idea of creating a regiment was growing in his mind more and more, to help the pope fight the Imperial force. He had just realised, by doing so, that he would make himself the cardinal's enemy.

'Naples?'

'Yes. There will be a big wedding and I was asked to find a composer. Would you do that?'

'Well, I have to ask the marquess.'

'Do, please. Are you interested?'

'I am, of course. Naples...'

'And, how about an opera in Venice?'

Did I hear opera? Händel stared at the cardinal. 'Opera?'

Cardinal Grimani laughed. 'My family owns opera houses in Venice, like San Giovanni Grisostomo, as you know.'

'San Giovanni Grisostomo...' It was the best theatre in Venice. He struggled to digest what was happening.

'And, carnival season is the best time. There are many visitors from all over Italy, so it gives an opera the chance to be spread.'

Händel felt the initial surprise being infiltrated by excitement. 'Do you have any idea of—'

'Libretto?'

'Yes.'

The cardinal pointed to himself.

'Yourself, Monsignor?' Händel felt overwhelmed. *An opera in Venice, and the cardinal the librettist? This is too good to be true. I must be*

dreaming...
    Grimani just nodded and said, 'I will send you the libretto as soon as I can.'
    Händel just watched the back of the cardinal leaving him, speechless. There was, in the personality of Cardinal Grimani, something very similar to Agostino Steffani – warmth, kindness, and generosity. However, it was not the time for Händel to daydream about his opera in Venice. It was time to concentrate on the Easter oratorio. First things first.

    Domenico Castrucci stopped in front of Händel's room. The sound of a harpsichord could be heard. He waited for a pause to call.
    'Signor Endel!'
    'Avanti!'
    Castrucci entered.
    Händel was in his gown with a bonnet on his head.
    'Giorgio, I am here to ask you about the quantity of paper you need.'
    'Oh...' Händel did not move from the harpsichord. Staring at the keyboard, he muttered, 'About four hundred? That will do for the moment.'
    'I will order it, Giorgio.'
    'Thank you. Oh...' Händel lifted his head.
    'Yes, Giorgio?'
    'Could you ask Angelini to prepare them, please?'
    'Of course.'
    Händel was back to composition, forgetting to get dressed.
    Coming out of the room, Castrucci muttered to himself, 'Holy shit! Four hundred sheets! For the moment!'

    Antonio Giuseppe Angelini was getting more and more busy. He managed to get two helpers, but now that was not even enough. Twenty-four hundred pages to copy! He'd never seen that before. This was due to the length of the oratorio and the size of the orchestra, with five singers.
    'Are you busy, Panstufato?' asked Domenico Castrucci, calling him by his nickname.
    'More than busy.' He raised his head from the paper. 'Oh, it's you. I need help. Mr Endel is going very fast.'
    Domenico talked to the house musicians. 'Panstufato is asking for help.'
    'Is he very busy?'
    'Yes, more than that. He is panicking.'

    Händel finished the oratorio *Resurrezione (Resurrection)* but did not date and sign the bottom of the manuscript. He was quite certain some last-minute changes would occur. *Just be ready and flexible*, he thought. Apprehension about the inevitable last-minute adjustments was bigger than satisfaction from completing the oratorio. He was confident about Angelini's skill, but he would make certain that the parts for the violinists were copied in a way that avoided turning the pages at the same time. He prayed for the singer's ability. The only one he knew well was Margherita.

Castrucci entered Angelini's room.

'I was asked by Signor Endel to ask you if you had finished the conducting score for him.'

'No. And I need more paper. I'll need a lot,' Angelini replied without stopping. 'Did you ask for more paper?'

'Yes, I'm waiting.' Castrucci was getting worried. He went to see Händel, who frowned.

'But I need the score for the rehearsals.'

'I know, but Angelini is late.'

'I'll go to see him.' Händel got up, still frowning.

'Signor Angelini.'

'Signor Endel,' Angelini replied without lifting his head. His helpers just nodded to the Saxon.

Händel liked Angelini's neat copying. *Very professional*, he thought. Then the copyist stopped.

'I am stuck.'

'What?'

'This is the last paper I have. I cannot go further. This is your conducting score.'

'Oh my God...' Händel felt his blood drain. 'So are we...'

'It's too hot here,' he stood up and removed his jacket.

The door opened and a servant burst in with a huge bundle, followed by another, and another.

'Panstufato! Here is your paper!'

Angelini's face lit up at once. 'Hallelujah!' he shouted, and he turned to Händel. 'I need more help, signor Endel. Can you ask anyone to help me? As much as possible.'

'Of course. I will do it now.'

Angelini removed his wig, revealing a bald head. He untied his neckcloth, loosening his shirt. 'Let's work!' He said merrily to his helpers, who were rolling up their sleeves.

Händel smiled. He really liked the jolly temperament of Italians. He went to ask for help one by one. No one refused. Even Margherita offered help, which he declined.

'I can rule the staves, at least,' Margherita said, indignant at being refused.

Händel laughed. 'Margherita, you ruling the staves! What happens if

your dress is stained by ink?'
Every hand was borrowed. Händel was even teaching a footman to trace the staves. Though relieved, he felt responsible. This was a lesson. *I should have organised better for a big work like this, and planned beforehand.* In Florence, for his opera, he did not encounter this problem, as the theatre people were used to it. Here, at Francesco Ruspoli's household, nobody knew about it.

Fifteen hundred wordbooks arrived from the printer, Antonio De Rossi, with one specially bound in Cordovan leather for presentation to the dedicatee of the oratorio, Filippo Antonio, cardinal of the Roman Catholic Church. Francesco Ruspoli inspected the specially bound copy and was satisfied. Everything was going well.

Musicians hired for the occasion were arriving, including Arcangelo Corelli with his orchestra. Händel could see that the musicians, especially the string players, were very much impressed by Corelli, the famous *Il Bolognese*. It was a huge orchestra, with over forty instrumentalists and five singers. Händel, again, felt the power of the marquess. With the arrival of four singers in addition to Margherita, the vocal cast was complete. The score for vocal parts was ready. Angelini was still finishing, but he assured Händel that all would be ready in time for the first general rehearsal. Händel gathered the singers for the sing-through. To his satisfaction there was no need to change anything. This was a good start. Three general rehearsals were scheduled instead of the usual two. This was another sign of financial power.

It was Palm Sunday, 1 April 1708. Before the first rehearsal, Händel went up to the second floor Stanzione. He stood there, looking around, speechless. There were, on the stage, four ranks for the orchestra, sloping upwards to the back wall. There were twenty-four music stands, their legs shaped like fluted cornucopias. On half of them was the coat of arms of the marquess, and on the other half, those of his wife. The back of the stage had a large painted canvas depicting the resurrection. There were damasks, red and yellow taffeta, huge candelabra, and a curtain in front of the stage. The whole hall looked like an opera stage. As Händel wandered around the hall, Fabio Cavalcanti came in, accompanied by another man.

'Ah, here you are, Maestro Sassone. Would you please try this on?' Fabio turned to the man behind him, who produced a suit in red.

'For me?'

'Yes, for the Easter oratorio. Could you just put on the gilet and the coat, please?'

The man busied himself around Händel to see how they looked. The two pieces fitted perfectly.

'You and Maestro Corelli will be wearing red, and the rest of the orchestra will be in blue, the two Ruspoli colours,' said Fabio proudly. 'Do you have a nice shirt, Maestro?'

'Don't worry Fabio. I have a very nice one with lace.'

Fabio Cavalcanti beamed. 'Very well, Maestro. Don't forget to give your shoes for polishing beforehand, please.'

Margherita came in and looked around. 'Wonderful, isn't it? Is the fitting over, Giorgio?'

'Did you receive your costume? How is it?'

'Oh, it has to be biblical, so it is very modest. No corset, no hoop, no wig. I will feel naked.'

Händel laughed. 'Well, that's good. The tight corset is never good for singing. You will shine as Mary Magdalen. I count on you, Margherita.'

Margherita loved those moments of intimacy. Working closely nearly every day, she believed she could build up a solid relationship between her and Händel, at least professionally. She wished this to last as long as possible, but she knew this was not likely. Händel would not stay forever at Ruspoli's household, and it was the same for her. One of the singers' tasks was to travel, whenever they were required. The only thing she could do was to enjoy the moment.

The first of the three rehearsals was over. The public was allowed to attend, and it was obvious. The hall on the second floor was not big enough to contain all who wanted to come. The crowd was thronging in. Francesco Ruspoli was happy about the popularity of his event, but he had to face reality.

Ruspoli was consulting the architect Giovanni Battista Contini when the master mason, Francesco Pagnaccelli, and the master carpenter, Crespino Pavone, joined them.

'Maestro Pagnaccelli, Maestro Pavone, we have to move everything to the main floor. The Stanzione is too small,' said Ruspoli.

Their eyes nearly popped out. The mason just swallowed. The carpenter gasped. They had just finished before the first rehearsal that morning.

'Marquess…' The mason could find no words.

'Can you do it?' asked the marquess, still optimistic.

'Uh… Of course, of course, Your Lordship,' stammered the carpenter, struggling to talk, 'but that will take about two weeks.'

'I need it to be done by Saturday, before the third rehearsal.'

'Oh…'

Ruspoli turned to the architect. 'Can you get more people?' Seeing their reaction, he started to realise the gravity of his request. 'Would it help?'

'Of course, I can try, Marquess…' Contini looked at the two craftsmen in dismay.

The marquess considered quickly, and said, 'Maestro Pagnaccelli,

Maestro Pavone, I do understand it is not easy, but do it for me. And do it well. It has to be done. All of you will be paid double, and you will be provided food and wine, all of you,' Francesco Ruspoli assured them. He needed to make them want to do it.

'Marquess, you are very generous,' said the carpenter. Both men bowed. The double payment was encouraging, and it would be easier to find more help.

'I count on you, Contini.'

'Marquess?'

'Tell.'

'Can I have permission to use Ascanio, the messenger boy, so I can quickly get the word around?'

'Of course, Contini, of course.'

'I thank you, Marquess.' The architect feigned calm, and bowed.

The carpenter and the mason nodded. When the marquess was gone, Contini faced the men. He felt he found himself, all of a sudden, in the middle of a whirlpool. *I need to stand firm*, he thought.

'So, first, we have to undo everything, but while doing so, you, Maestro Pagnaccelli, can start in the main hall. Get as much help as you can, please.'

'*D'accordo*, Maestro Contini,' said Pagnaccelli, and hurried to get started as soon as possible.

'Now, Maestro Pavone, first we have to take down all the damask, and then all the frames. How many men do you need?'

'Maestro Contini, we first need to erect the scaffoldings to remove all that.'

'Oh... That's true...' Contini lowered his head. This was overwhelming.

'We can do it, Maestro Contini. We'll rotate, so we won't be exhausted and risk accidents. I'll tell Pagnaccelli to do the same so we can work all through the nights,' said the carpenter, trying to convince himself.

'That's... that's brilliant!' exclaimed Contini, seeing a glimmer of hope.

'One more thing, Maestro Contini.'

'Yes, tell!'

'We'll need candles for the nights. Lots of them.'

'Oh...' Contini lowered his head again. 'Oh my God, the fixing of the canvas was so difficult, and we have to go through it again...'

All the time, Fabio Cavalcanti was witnessing the meeting without uttering a word. Now that Contini was alone, he put his hand on the architect's shoulder. 'Courage, Contini.'

'Thank you, Fabio. I need it.'

'I can get the candles for you,' said the superintendent, feeling sorry for the architect. 'Now I have to tell the Saxon,' he said, and went to seek Händel.

Contini's knees gave way. Fabio was gone. The architect was squatting, burying his face in his arms. At that moment, he wished the ground would open up and swallow him. He just wanted to disappear.

Händel was puzzled by the crowd present at the first rehearsal. That was the first time he had experienced a public rehearsal. As he watched the crowd leaving the Stanzione, Pietro Castrucci approached him.

'So, Maestro Sassone, what do you think?'

Pietro, in comparison to his father, was more outgoing, curious, and jolly. He loved listening to Händel talking about his experience.

'Are you talking about the rehearsal or the public? Why so many people?'

'Oh, that's because of' – Pietro looked around and lowered his voice – 'because of the pope.'

'Pope?' Händel just mouthed the word without uttering a sound.

'You know the pope issued a decree forbidding operas?' Castrucci whispered.

'I know.'

'Well, the pope might think that his decree is enough, but do you think the people just comply and weep?'

Händel stared at the violinist. Pietro Castrucci laughed and winked.

'We do play opera, but we just don't call it opera. It's just called rehearsal.'

'Oh… is… is that the Roman sense of humour?'

Pietro slapped Händel's back, laughing. 'I like that!'

Händel gasped and stared at the superintendent in disbelief. 'What? We just rehearsed. It was good. And you are telling me that it will not be in the same place?'

'Yes, Maestro. I am sorry, but the Stanzione is too small.'

'My God. So where?'

'It will be in the *salone* on the first floor. But it will not be ready, so you will still use the Stanzione for the next rehearsal.'

Händel just stared at Cavalcanti, and swallowed.

'I know, Maestro.'

From that day, Palazzo Bonelli became a giant beehive. The workers were there in and out, day and night. Francesco Ruspoli had to make his wife and children move out for a few days to Cerveteri.

The second rehearsal, on the following Monday, was done in the Stanzione as before, without the decoration. Still, the room was as crowded as before, if not more so.

While builders and craftsmen were working round the clock, Händel had a little respite on Wednesday, 4 April. At Cardinal Ottoboni's Cancelleria, Scarlatti's oratorio *Passione (Passion)*, on a text by the cardinal himself, was played. As Händel watched Scarlatti conduct from the harpsichord and Margherita sing, Agostino Steffani, seated next to him, whispered, 'It is the first time a *Passione* is being sung in a palace, not in a church.'

Händel looked at Steffani. 'The Holy See . . .'

'Let's wait and see.' Steffani just shrugged with a little smile. Like Cardinal Grimani, his presence in Rome was not an accident.

Margherita was busy, after the concert, surrounded by the people praising her, but she did not miss her secret love approaching.

'Brava, Margherita,' Händel smiled, 'you did really well.'

'Thank you, Giorgio.' Margherita smiled back, her heart swelling with joy. She could feel that Händel had returned to Rome as a changed man. Not the man in love as she had seen in Vignanello. Yes, everything was as before. Vittoria retook her position as the mistress of the Grand Prince Ferdinando in Florence, and Händel was in Rome, beside her, smiling to her.

'Marquess, there is a problem. Good Friday, nobody will work in the afternoon and evening. We need to keep working, otherwise it will not be finished.' Contini was pale.

Francesco Ruspoli did not seem concerned. 'Do you have any ideas, Contini?'

'Well, yes...' Contini hesitated.

'Tell, Contini.'

'Marquess, those men need to feel that they have permission to work, so if you can arrange for a priest to come along and say a prayer and give them permission to work, I think they will accept.'

'I'll arrange it, Contini. Is that all?'

'Yes, Marquess.'

'Contini.'

'Yes, Marquess.'

'Don't worry about the workers. I'll ask the priest to say a proper mass, and he will give his blessings to all of them.'

'Oh, Marquess, that will be perfect! I'll go immediately to tell them.'

Francesco Ruspoli reflected on the situation and summoned his superintendent.

'Fabio, would you go to Vignanello and come back with Father Marcioni? It's urgent.'

'Father Marcioni?'

'Yes, he is the easiest to bribe. There is no time to waste.'

'Yes, Marquess. I'll depart as soon as possible.'

'Oh, and I need some coins for me, silver and gold piasters, for tips.'

'It will be done quickly, Marquess. I'll tell Angelo.'

When Fabio was gone and Ruspoli found himself alone, he sighed.

Though fundamentally optimistic, the situation was enough to make a small crack in his confidence. To the marquess's great relief, the craftsmen and builders finished in the morning of the third rehearsal. It was fortunate that it was the Easter period when work was scarce, so they had been able to find enough people to get the job done. He did not forget to thank them all personally. However, he admitted it was too much. Too much pressure on everyone involved, including himself. He wouldn't be ready to contemplate organising another such event for a while.

The third rehearsal on Holy Saturday, which was a luxury, was done in the *salone* with the new decorations already complete. Händel marvelled. It was done as if it had been conceived for the grand *salone* from the beginning. Now without the musicians and the public, the maids were busy arranging the flowers everywhere. Händel ignored some of them smiling to him. *Tomorrow is the day*, was all he could think of.

It was spectacular. The visual effect was such that the public needed little effort to stimulate their imagination. There was no stage acting, but it was easy to visualise. A very large orchestra, all its members wearing matching wigs and suits in blue, was placed in a semicircle surrounding the large harpsichord in the centre front.

Cardinals Pamphili, Ottoboni, Colonna, and Marescotti sat together in the front row with Francesco Ruspoli and his wife, Isabella. Agostino Steffani sat with Cardinal Grimani, melting into the crowd. Steffani was impressed by the maturity Händel had achieved. It was German solidity mixed with Italian style, rich in colour and light. He was glad that Händel had extracted himself in time from Hamburg.

However, a papal rebuke was awaiting the marquess, for allowing a woman to take part in the performance.

'Francesco…' Cardinal Marescotti stared at his nephew, pale. He had rushed to Palazzo Bonelli, terrified.

'I know, Uncle,' said Francesco, embarrassed.

'You did not realise?'

'Well, I really don't understand. There were three rehearsals,' replied Francesco. 'And why just me? And, Margherita Durastante sang at the *cancelleria* before. Why am I the only one to be punished?'

'You have to be careful, my nephew.'

'Yes, I know, Uncle, but—'

'I know, but it is Easter.' Cardinal Galeazzo Marescotti knew his nephew was right. He once again resented the French for having interfered, stopping him from being the pope.

When Pope Innocent XII died in 1700, Cardinal Marescotti had been one of the candidates to succeed. However, the French presented a veto against his election to the papacy, putting the end to his ambition. He was

then over seventy and it was his last chance.
'Do you know who?' his nephew asked.
'It's Cardinal Paolucci.'
'Ah! I am not surprised. That rascal… Fabio tells me that each time he comes in here, he eats and drinks an enormous amount and he nicks the silver spoons!'
'Tut, tut, Francesco.'
'Nice way to offer thanks for the hospitality!'
'Please, calm down, Francesco.'
Francesco looked at his troubled uncle and started to understand. Maybe the pontiff wanted to turn a blind eye, but he could not ignore Cardinal Paolucci's complaint. Maybe it was just for the principle. Francesco Ruspoli took his ageing uncle's hands in his.
'Uncle, I am sorry for this, but I am sure the Holy See will forget all about it very shortly.'
'Tell me.'
'How about an army?'
'An army?' Cardinal Marescotti stared at his nephew.
'Yes, an army. A fully armed brig was not enough, even with a cantata as a bonus, so an army this time.'
'When I think that you expressly went to Civitavecchia with your Saxon to present him the papal fleet…'
'I liked the cantata, Uncle, but it did not work. That's fine. Let's see what happens with a regiment, a Ruspoli regiment!'
Cardinal Marescotti smiled. 'Without the cantata?' Now he was glad for his nephew's optimism.
'No cantata, but the army will be led by an Amazon on horseback – naked, of course.'
'Francesco…' *No, I was wrong. He is too optimistic*, he thought.
'Just kidding, Uncle.' Francesco Ruspoli giggled, ignoring his uncle's frowning.

'Signorina Margherita, I am sorry, you cannot sing tomorrow.'
Margherita froze in fear. 'Marquess, is there any problem with my singing?' She was whispering, pale.
'No, no, not at all. You were splendid, but the pope is not happy.'
'Oh my God.' Margherita went from white to red. 'The pope?'
'Do not worry, Signorina Durastante, you will not be punished.'
'You will be punished, Marquess?'
Ruspoli shrugged. 'The punishment is that you cannot sing tomorrow.'
Margherita pressed her hands against her chest.
'Do not worry, Signorina Durastante. The pope cannot do more than that. He does not want my gifts to stop coming.' He laughed and then stopped

abruptly. He took her hands, stared into her eyes, and said, 'Signorina, you know, what I said is between us.'
'Of course, Marquess.'
Ruspoli was relieved to see that Margherita had not been aware of the papal wrath before he told her. Margherita, on the other hand, was quite content with her acting, convincing the marquess that he was the one who broke the news.
Händel saw Margherita passing in the corridor and called her. She smiled.
'Are you disappointed, Margherita?'
She shrugged. 'I have no choice.'
'Did you see the marquess?'
'He came in person to tell me.'
'That's kind.'
'It is.' She looked up. 'Giorgio, will you be all right?'
'Well, I have to rehearse quickly with Pippo, just him and me, but I'm sure it will be all right. What a pity! You sang wonderfully. I am sure everyone was moved by your Mary Magdalen.'
'I will be in the audience.' Margherita smiled and, with a small nod, left him. Then she stopped. She came back to Händel and whispered, 'I hate Rome!'
Händel watched Margherita leave him, nearly stomping. She was right. Rome was suffocating under the pope's intolerance. Was Rome so sacred as a city? No. Those cardinals lived like princes in palaces. *They give lavish parties with fine food and wine. Those monks came in to take advantage of the food and wine and glare at women, nearly salivating!* Back in Germany, Händel's pastor uncle, despite being married and having a family, led a much more pious life, and so did his wife and children.

'Signor Endel, you asked for me?' A castrato, hired in rush, asked. He was the one to replace Margherita.
'Yes, I did. Come in, Pippo.'
'So I will be Mary Magdalen.'
'Yes. Can you just go through it?'
Händel accompanied the castrato on harpsichord.
'What do you think, Mr Endel?'
'Giorgio. Well . . . I wrote this for Margherita, for a woman's voice...'
'I am a soprano, Giorgio, and I will be dressed in Margherita's costume.'
Pippo was quite short for a castrato, so it could be convincing. Händel looked the singer up and down and laughed. 'You are quite different from Margherita.'
Pippo was blond with his eyebrows nearly invisible. 'Oh, don't worry.

I will paint my eyebrows. Not too dark, just like Margherita's and I will look like her with make-up,' said the castrato with confidence.

'Then the Holy See summons the marquess again, and…'

'No, this time he will send his guards to arrest you and me on the spot,' the castrato said. 'We will be dragged in front of the pope, and—'

'And you just lift your skirt!'

They both burst into laughter. Pippo was holding his tummy with one hand as the other wiped his tears. Händel was on the floor, fallen from his stool. A servant came in bringing a tray of wine and water and stopped dead.

'Where is my honey?' asked Pippo, ignoring the servant's embarrassment.

'Presto, Signor, presto.' The servant disappeared after nearly tripping on Händel's leg.

'Ahem, Mr Endel, Giorgio. I can lift the skirt, but I'll be wearing the breeches underneath.'

They were laughing again. They tried to rehearse but it was simply not possible. As soon as they began, one of them would start to giggle. It was contagious.

'Oh, just let it go as it is. I cannot make changes, and you cannot change your voice.'

'No, Giorgio, but I can change my wig.'

Again, they were laughing.

In the evening, Margherita found a fine brooch in her room.

'Margherita, is this from the marquess?'

'Yes, Mama.'

'He is generous.'

'It's the price of silence.'

'What?'

'Mama, it's because I cannot sing tomorrow. He is apologising.'

'How kind of him!'

'Yes, it is.'

Easter was now over, and Fabio Cavalcanti was busy with Angelo Valeri calculating the cost of the whole production.

'So, you got the bills for refreshments, the rental of the chairs, and the candles?' asked Angelo, the accountant. 'I have here all the costs for the decoration. You know, it is just for the *Resurrezione*.'

'Yes, I know. I have the bills for all that. And the marquess purchased a violoncello for this occasion.'

'How about the fees for the musicians?'

'I have the list here.' Fabio produced a piece of paper. 'Maestro Corelli, twenty scudi. Pippo, ten. Pasqualino, eighteen. Vittorio, ten. Cristofano, ten.

Matteo, eighteen. Oh and 244 scudi 50 baiocchi for the orchestra.'

'How about Angelini?'

'Thirty scudi for him.'

'And how about the presents? I know the marquess ordered rings.'

'I am waiting for the bills to come, Angelo.' Fabio watched the accountant do the sum.

'So, for the moment... oh, *mamma mia*... it is already over a thousand scudi.'

They looked at each other, speechless.

The expenditure did not stop there in the household of Francesco Ruspoli. At the end of April, another bill came in when Händel had already gone to Naples for his commission.

Angelo Valeri entered the marquess's office with a piece of paper. He saw Fabio Cavalcanti beside Ruspoli.

'Marquess, I would like to have a word about the Saxon.'

'Is that about paper?'

'No, Your Lordship, it's about the food. I just received a bill for his food – thirty-eight scudi and seventy-five baiocchi, Marquess! In just two months, nearly forty scudi!'

'Oh my God,' said Fabio, 'that's two months' fee for a top singer.'

'Well? You cannot ask him for the food back,' said Ruspoli, 'it's already digested and gone.' He just shrugged.

Angelo was not comfortable. 'Marquess, I know he had a friend with him, but still... it's the quantity. It's enormous, Marquess. You could feed an entire regiment! How could he eat so much?' He did not get any reaction from Ruspoli. 'So does Marquess agree to pay?'

'Do not worry about the bill, Angelo. He was a guest. And I hope he will come back, with or without a friend.'

'He might *not* come back, Marquess?' Fabio enquired, a little surprised.

'I asked him to come back, but he's gone to Naples, so...'

'How about employing him then, with a salary? It would be cheaper,' the accountant asked.

'I would love to, but this Saxon is larger than a *cameriere*. He will not accept. That I know.' He turned to his superintendent. 'Fabio?'

'Yes, Marquess.'

'I have to do a bit of politics now. It's time to think about the Ruspoli Regiment.'

'Regiment?'

'Yes, a true regiment. You can ask Angelo how much you need for food,' said the marquess, 'so when the Saxon returns you'll pay the food for two regiments!' And he laughed heartily.

The Naples Händel saw was a kingdom under Spanish Habsburg control with the viceroy sent directly by the empire. Once Europe's second largest city, Naples had been a major cultural centre, attracting numerous artists, philosophers and writers. Music played an important role and several conservatories were founded from the 16th century. Alessandro Scarlatti had been once *maestro di capella* to the viceroy. The reason for Händel's visit was to provide a cantata for the wedding of Tolomeo Saverio Gallo, Duke of Alvito, to Beatrice di Tocco, Princess of Montemiletto. The commission came from the bride's aunt, Aurora Sanseverino, patron of arts and poet, who was also the member of the Arcadian Academy. Händel arrived in the city in a festive mood, and produced *Aci, Galatea e Polifemo (Acis, Galatea and Polyphemus)*. Dazzled by the Mediterranean light and cradled by the local dialect, Händel would have loved to stay, but he had to go back to Rome as soon as the cantata was produced. He was needed by Francesco Ruspoli, who was the host of the Arcadian Academy, and one of the duties was to provide music.

Back in Rome, Händel was taken aback. The difference from Naples was everywhere. The air felt different; people were different; everything was stiff in Rome. Being busy was a good diversion.

'So this is the famous *Accademia*?' Händel asked Margherita.

'Yes.'

'Do you know exactly what this Academy is, Margherita? I've heard of it many times, and I cannot really figure it out.'

Margherita shook her head. 'No, Giorgio. I don't know what it is. I know that the marquess is a member, as are his friends the cardinals, but apart from that, I know nothing about it.'

'Oh.'

'Why don't you ask Domenico Castrucci? He should know more.' Margherita was just happy to be near Händel, to have a chat and work together. 'We shall be busy. The marquess looks to be enthusiastic about the *Accademia* meetings.' But what happens after the summer? She did not want to think about it.

Francesco Ruspoli felt stimulated, and he looked forward to these meetings. The planning started.

'A Christmas cantata? Now?' Händel stared at Ruspoli in his office. He had just been asked to compose a Christmas cantata for one of the meetings.

'Yes, Maestro,' said Ruspoli who turned to Cardinal Pamphili for help.

'Maestro Endel.' Pamphili smiled at the stunned Saxon. 'It is quite logical to celebrate Christmas in summer, and not just because it is too cold for us to do it outdoors in December.'

Händel just stared at the cardinal.

'Our meetings are held outdoors, always,' Francesco Ruspoli added.

'The bible tells clearly that the shepherds were sleeping outdoors when they saw a bright star.'

'Yes, Monsignor.'

'So it could only have been in summer if the shepherds were able to spend the night outdoors.'

That's true. Why did I not realise that before? 'But, then why do we celebrate Christmas in winter, Monsignor?'

'Ah, that's a long story, but to make it very short, it was a compromise.'

'Compromise?'

'Yes. To make it easier for the Romans to assimilate Christianity, they decided to make it in late December, when they used to celebrate Saturnalia.'

'Saturnalia?'

'Yes. It was one of those pagan festivities. They celebrated it by eating and giving presents. So it looked like just a change of the name.'

Marquess Ruspoli interrupted, 'See, Maestro, Cardinal Pamphili is a scholar.'

'I like history,' replied the cardinal modestly.

It was Cardinal Pamphili who provided the answer to Händel. *L'Accademia degli Arcadi* (the Arcadian Academy) started as a literary gathering formed under the patronage of the exiled Queen Christina of Sweden in the middle of the seventeenth century in Rome. After her death in 1689, the academy was established in her memory, and it elected her as its symbolic head. The academy's main intention was to reform the baroque style of Italian language, with its overindulgence in ornamentation, which was the dominant Italian poetic style at the time. The Arcadians sought a more natural, simple poetic style based on the classics and particularly on Greek and Roman pastoral poetry. They were named *Arcadian* after a pastoral region of ancient Greece, and each member took a Greek name as a shepherd. The meetings were held each year during summer in a grove. They would discuss and recite poems. Music, too, played an important part.

Among its members there was a young man, Paolo Rolli. He was a pupil of one of the founders, Gian Vincenzo Gravina, who recognised his skill. So he was admitted to the Academy at a very young age, full of hope and ambition for his career. He was not particularly impressed by the music provided by a German that summer. While other members commented on Händel's music enthusiastically, he was busy making acquaintance with potential patrons.

After spending the summer in Rome composing cantatas for the Arcadian Academy and the Sunday concerts, in addition to attending various concerts himself, Händel was getting ready for the special day. It was 9 September 1708. The torrential rain the previous night had refreshed the air, and the weather was much nicer. It was still hot but dry. There was first a luncheon, which the whole Ruspoli family, including Cardinal Marescotti, attended. Händel and Margherita shared the top table with the marquess and marchioness, but the one presiding that day was their only son, the eleven-years-old Bartolomeo. At the other tables were officers in wine-red uniforms with gold braids; their hats were adorned with white feathers and white-and-turquoise cockades. Francesco Ruspoli stood up and immediately had everyone's attention.

'This is a very special day for me, my wife, and the entire Ruspoli family. I thank you, the gentlemen officers, for sharing this meal with us. As you all know, the Ruspoli Regiment will depart today to fight the Imperial army. Let us pray for victory.'

Cardinal Galeazzo Marescotti stood and said a brief prayer, then resumed his seat.

'Let's drink to my son, Colonel Ruspoli!' said Francesco, raising his glass to his son, who was also in uniform, blushing and smiling rigidly.

'To Colonel Ruspoli!' everyone shouted, even the children seated at their table in one corner.

After the luncheon, the officers were excused. Walking out of the dining hall, Margherita turned to Händel.

'Did you see Lady Isabella? She was nearly in tears when we raised our glasses.'

'Yes, I noticed. Well isn't it a bit ridiculous for a child to—' Händel was stopped by Margherita, who looked around and lowered her voice.

'Giorgio. You did not hear the rumour? The marquess did it on purpose to give his son confidence.'

'What rumour?'

Margherita looked around again. 'Apparently, he was born impotent,' she whispered.

Händel's eyes widened. 'No, I did not hear that.'

'Well, Giorgio, pay a bit more attention to what goes on around you. Rumours can be useful sometimes.' Margherita smiled. 'And did you know that Lady Isabella is expecting again?' Seeing Händel open-mouthed, she just laughed.

They arrived at the second floor Stanzione. The musicians were getting ready for the afternoon cantata. This was a small-scale one, however, a trumpeter had been added for heroic effect.

Francesco Maria Marescotti Ruspoli created the Ruspoli Regiment at his own expense, recruiting nearly a thousand men, and he was determined to make it known to the whole town. A special cantata, *O come chiare e belle* (*Oh how clear and beautiful*), was commissioned from Händel, and three hundred copies of the wordbook were duly delivered, to be distributed to the carefully chosen guests. Contrary to the usual pastoral-style cantatas, this was a heroic one. The hero, Olinto, which was Francesco Ruspoli's Arcadian name, will rouse Rome, represented by the River Tiber, to its old glory. Olinto, il Tebro, and Glory, the three singing figures, are led by a goodly star, Astro Clemente, referring to Pope Clement XI. Händel composed it carefully, as he knew that this would be probably the last one in Rome.

'Are you staying here, Giorgio? I have to go to get changed,' said Margherita. 'Oh, here comes Anna Maria.'

Anna Maria di Piedz, another soprano, was dressed like a Greek goddess. 'What do you think, Margherita?'

'Just glorious as Gloria.'

'And how about me?' asked Gaetano Ursini, dressed to represent the River Tiber.

'Is that all you can do? Just a blue cape?'

'I know, but it's not opera, so I cannot wear drapery bare-chested. And with this heat, I cannot stand a false beard.'

'I have to hurry. I'll be Olinto.' Margherita quickly disappeared to transform herself into a shepherd.

It was late in the evening. Händel and Margherita joined the entourage of the marquess outside Palazzo Bonelli to watch the soldiers leaving. Francesco Ruspoli's new regiment, after receiving the papal blessing first, marched out of Rome. It was much easier for the armed soldiers to walk during the night when the air was much cooler. The inhabitants, who had trembled at the likelihood of an assault by Austrian troops, greeted the parade with cheers. They believed – or rather, wanted to believe – that fighting the Austrians would remove the curse bestowed on Rome, with the flooding and earthquake.

Händel went for a last walk in Rome. It was mid-October. Those labyrinths of narrow streets with extremely old houses, where he used to get lost, were now familiar to him. Those streets led to vast squares bordered by fabulous Baroque palaces, abutted by Roman temples and graves, overgrown with grass. Life was not easy in Rome if you were not among the clerics or nobility. This sharp contrast was so obvious, and Händel always felt uneasy hearing of the poor dying of disease from living in appalling sanitary conditions, or by fires, easily sparked in crowded houses. And those cardinals who were supposed to help the poor lived in palaces, in luxury, passing fast in their magnificent carriages with footmen, runners, torch-bearers, and men-at-arms. Rome was hot and dusty in the summer, and it was cold, muddy and dark in the winter. Human life was not worth much in the Eternal City. All gentlemen wore swords, pistols, and daggers. Robbers and thieves were bold, despite grim punishments if they were caught. The pious objects in churches disappeared, and even wrought iron window grates disappeared. Händel liked the early morning walk. The air was cool, and that was the safest time of the day.

'So you are going, Giorgio,' Margherita looked at him tenderly.

'I am. I suppose the marquess will be concentrating on the battles, and the Arcadians' season is over now. I won't have very much to do here.'

'May I ask you where?'

'I think I will go first to Florence and then to Venice.'

'Florence? Any commission from the grand prince?' Margherita asked casually. But she could hear her heart beating furiously under her dress.

'No,' Händel looked away.

Margherita's heart sank. *He is going to see Vittoria.* 'Are you thinking of coming back?'

'To Rome? I don't think so. Rome is too religious, and with the war, it is not stable. And…'

'You did not like Rome?'

'It was great to work for the marquess, but Rome is suffocating. It is too hot, and… and I am a bit fed up with cantatas. That's the only thing we can do.' He stared at her.

'I see what you mean. Well, I'm staying as long as the marquess is paying me.'

Unlike Händel, Margherita Durastante had been formally employed by Francesco Ruspoli a few months after her arrival.

'And there is one more thing that you don't encounter. How many times have I heard that I was on the road of damnation? The road of damnation! That's because I am a Protestant. At best, I am of mistaken principles.'

Margherita did not know what to say. She just raised her eyebrows.

Händel looked at Margherita and swallowed. 'Margherita, can I ask you one thing?'

'Of course. Tell me.'

'If, by any chance, I get a chance to compose an opera in Venice, would you come to sing?'

'Oh, of course. I will, with pleasure!' Margherita said without thinking.

'Really?'

'Promise.' Margherita smiled, filled with hope. She had been desperate for the last few days, thinking that she would probably not see Händel again.

'Cardinal Grimani talked about an opera, but I have not received the libretto yet, so I cannot tell for sure. Oh… and what about the marquess?'

'I am sure he will let me go. He admires you, Giorgio.'

Händel did not answer. He just looked straight ahead. Margherita's heart sank again. He was thinking of Vittoria.

Händel knew that Rome was not the place for him. He'd enjoyed the best musical patronage that Rome had to offer and had repaid it handsomely, but this was not the environment for a permanent career. And, there was

Vittoria. Though she had chosen the grand prince he could still not forget her. He desperately wanted to see her. He wanted to know the truth, whether her heart was truly and only for the grand prince, or not. Leaving the patronage of Francesco Ruspoli without any confirmation for an opera in Venice was risky, but he felt he could trust Cardinal Grimani. Also Florence was on the way to Venice, and even if he could not see Vittoria, he wanted to get a chance to see operas in Pratolino. No. He was just using the excuse of Pratolino to go to Florence. He wanted to see her. He had to see her. With mixed and contradictory thoughts, he started to pack.

Angelo Valeri's eyebrows were raised and stayed that way for a moment. He was staring at the bill he'd just received from the ice provider. Forty-five pounds of crushed ice! *That Saxon ordered forty-five pounds of ice to cool his wine!* The Saxon was gone again, and he would not come back soon. The accountant sighed, feeling defeated. *The marquess is right*, he thought, *he cannot be an employee.*

Florence, November 1708

The atmosphere in Palazzo Pitti was tense, more than usual, and everybody looked stressed and worried. They saw Cardinal Francesco Maria de' Medici, younger brother of the grand duke, summoned very often, looking gloomy.

'What?' the cardinal started, believing he'd misheard.
'You heard me. You have to be released from cardinalate, and I already expressed my desire to the Holy See,' Grand Duke Cosimo III said coldly, not looking at his brother.
The cardinal felt his heart pounding. He knew his behaviour was not always exemplary, but nothing had happened to prompt this. Why now? 'Brother, I don't understand. Did I sin? I was always loyal and faithful to God and to you, and so I will be for the rest of my life.'
Cosimo III saw a chance. 'My dear brother, if you are loyal and faithful, that's all the more reason to abandon your cardinalate, because you are needed.' He smiled.
Francesco Maria still did not understand.
The grand duke, seeing his brother's puzzlement, continued, 'Gian Gastone is on his way back to Florence. He will never return to the North.'
'Oh, what about his wife then?'
'She is staying there.' The grand duke said it as a matter of fact.
'What about...the...marriage?'
'It's over.'

'Oh...'

'That's why you are needed now.' Cosimo III stared at his brother.

'Brother...' Francesco Maria whispered, and his knees gave way. He landed on an armchair heavily, his eyes wide open. 'You are not telling me to...'

Cosimo III de Medici showed little emotion in response to his brother's dismay. 'Yes, of course. You are the only chance now. You shall get married to produce an heir.'

This was the worst thing the cardinal could imagine.

When Händel arrived in Florence, Cardinal Francesco Maria de' Medici was trying desperately to convince his elder brother the grand duke to change his mind.

'Brother, please! Can't you see that I am too old now? And, I cannot abandon God in that way. Please!'

The grand duke was adamant. 'You are the only hope to me.'

'You have Gian Gastone. He is much younger. He could do it!'

'He is still married, even if the marriage is over.'

'You can ask for an annulment.'

'You are the one.'

Of course, the grand duke had thought of Gian Gastone, and the annulment. It was possible. But how long would it take to obtain the annulment? It could take a long time, and he could be dead by then. Time was running against him. He had to choose the quickest way.

'Brother! Please!' the cardinal pleaded desperately.

The grand duke wrapped his younger brother's hands in his and said in the most compassionate way, 'You can do it.'

'I cannot abandon God!'

'The pope is blessing your marriage,' Cosimo III's patience was running out, 'so is God, Brother.' He released his hands abruptly from his brother and said dryly, 'You may go now.'

But if the atmosphere was bad in Palazzo Pitti, outside the palace it was rather different. The rumour that the grand duke was making his brother renounce the cardinalate in order to marry him off for a potential heir was already all over Florence. People were laughing and mocking. Another rumour was that Lucrezia was back in favour, and now Vittoria was sent off to Venice.

Though greeted courteously in Palazzo Pitti, Händel sensed immediately that something was not right. It was suffocating. The grand prince, to escape his father, was again in Pratolino. Grand Princess Violante kept herself quiet, as did Dr Salvi. Händel felt the only thing he could do was to go to Venice as soon as possible. And Vittoria? Where is she? He could ask nobody. He just guessed. If she was nowhere to be seen, then she must have followed the grand prince. He wanted the rumour to be true, that she was now in Venice, but it was just a rumour. The grand duke was too distracted to grant stay to Händel. It was obvious that he could not stay in Florence. If he did it could raise suspicion. Why is an uninvited musician hanging around? Is he a spy? With heavy heart he decided to continue to Venice.

Since Cardinal Grimani had become viceroy of Naples, communication had become delicate. Händel remembered the short conversation with the cardinal in Naples.

'I will not send any message to Rome, Maestro. I am certain all my correspondence will be intercepted.'

'I do understand, Monsignor.' Händel looked at his calm but determined face, remembering how highly Scarlatti had praised him.

'The safest place will be Venice, at my theatre. If you hear nothing from me, please go to Venice.'

Having had no news from the cardinal, it was obvious he must go to Venice. He might see Vittoria. Now he wanted desperately to believe in the rumour.

Chapter 10 : Operatic London (1708-1709)

London, Autumn 1708 – Summer 1709

Owen Swiney sat in his office at the Queen's Theatre, happy to be the manager of London's opera house. Arrived from Ireland five years before, he built his career with patience. Starting in Theatre Royal in Drury Lane running day-to-day management, he mounted Bononcini's opera *Camilla* practically on his own. Educated at Trinity College in Dublin, fluent in French and Italian, his initial dream was to be a playwright. However his interest shifted slowly to theatre management. He loved the atmosphere of a theatre, to produce plays and operas to make the audience dream. He navigated through the war between the Drury Lane theatre and Queen's Theatre and got the post of manager where he wanted to be.

Now he signed, for the cast of the 1708–09 season, the first-rate, fabulously expensive castrato, Nicolini. Considered one of the century's finest singing actors, the thirty-five years old Nicolo Grimaldi, called Nicolini, arrived from Venice with Charles Montagu, Earl of Manchester. By mid-October, the castrato was in London letting the nobility and fine ladies take care of him. The Italian painters Marco Ricci and Giovanni Pellegrini were on their way to London, invited also by Charles Montagu. Their main mission was to decorate Castle Howard and also to provide painted scenes for the Queen's Theatre. It was all about a circle of friends. Vanbrugh, creator of Queen's Theatre, designed Castle Howard, the grandest and biggest private residence at the time. Its owner, Charles Howard, 3rd Earl of Carlisle, was one of the architect's friends and also among the initial subscribers of the Queen's Theatre project.

Charles Montagu was not successful in his official work as a diplomat. He had ultimately failed to persuade the Venetians to break their neutrality and join the Imperial force, Britain's ally, against the French and Spanish in the War of the Spanish Succession. However he was fairly satisfied with what he achieved in his unofficial task. Securing Nicolini made a big impact both in Venice and London. The world of opera was now aware that London was seeking to be one of the main operatic cities in Europe and was ready to offer astronomical salaries.

Swiney, with Nicolini as a key attraction, expected to open the season in a spectacular way. His future looked bright. However, he was aware that he had to be careful. The castrato's salary was a huge dent in the theatre's budget. He needed to make hit after hit. Still, he was confident. As a manager he was in control, and it was up to him to fill the theatre.

Londoners were excited about the famous castrato, but then there was tragedy within the royal family. On 28 October 1708, Prince George of Denmark and Norway, Duke of Cumberland, and husband of Queen Anne, died at Kensington Palace at 1.30 pm, aged fifty-five.

The queen just stared at her husband's lifeless body, lost. 'Why do the ones who love me and whom I love leave me?' she whispered.

She had not left her husband for days. Even for the most hardened hearts, it was moving to see the queen kissing her husband, accompanying him, nursing him until the last breath. Prince George had been seriously ill for some time amidst the mounting political pressure against him. As Lord High Admiral, he was blamed for the naval disaster the previous year in which four warships were lost off the Isles of Scilly along with 1,550 sailors. This was one of the many consequences of the War of the Spanish Succession.

The queen first refused to believe his death. When she realised that she could not defy reality, she refused to leave her husband's body. The harshness of Sarah Churchill, Duchess of Marlborough, did not help. She forced the queen to go to St James's Palace, leaving the body behind. The queen did not have any children to give her love and support. After seventeen pregnancies, the only one who survived infancy had died eight years earlier. She was alone now.

'Where is my husband's portrait? Why is it not there?' Anne walked nervously around her bedchamber, looking for the missing piece.

'Oh, Anne, it is not good for you to—' Sarah's confident voice was interrupted.

'Did you remove it, Sarah?' The queen glared at the duchess.

Sarah Churchill was taken aback. 'Your Majesty, I said it is not good to—'

'Sarah, put it back.' Anne kept glaring at her. 'I want it back immediately, Sarah.' The queen felt anger growing inside. 'This is an order, Duchess!' she shouted.

Sarah Churchill gasped. This was new. The position of power seemed reversed at once. The queen was clearly indicating that she was the one who had made her duchess, and that she was quite capable of removing the title if she wanted to.

It was Elizabeth Seymour, Duchess of Somerset, who brought the portrait back to the queen's bedchamber, which caused the flood of tears again. The duchess was calm, and she held the queen in her arms. In reality, it looked like the duchess was clinging to a massively fat woman.

'I envy you, Your Majesty,' she said calmly. Anne looked up, incredulous, with her cheeks drenched, but the duchess ignored her and continued, 'You loved your husband, and you were loved. I will never know that.' She looked away.

This remark made the queen calm down at once. It was true. It had been a happy marriage. By contrast, the Duke of Somerset was known to treat his wife with disdain and very little affection, despite that he owed his luxurious lifestyle to her.

When the duchess was out of the queen's bedchamber, she was confronted by another duchess, Sarah Churchill, Duchess of Marlborough.

'I will advise you to mind your own business, Duchess!' Sarah hissed.

Elizabeth Seymour looked her in the eye and said calmly, 'That's what I am doing, Duchess. In this time of great distress, we should all of us bring the queen comfort and peace. I believe you have a husband you love, and also I believe you have compassion, Duchess.' Then she walked away slowly.

Sarah could only stare at her back and curse her.

The mourning period was established until 14 December at noon, and all the theatres were ordered to close. This was a heavy punishment for the entertainment world.

'The fourteenth of December?' asked Nicolini.

'Yes, the fourteenth of December. That is your London début, Maestro,' said Owen Swiney and sighed. He could do nothing. The mourning period had to be respected. He could only wait. Everything was ready. He had translated the libretto of *Pirro e Demetrio (Pyrrhus and Demetrius)* by Adriano Morselli, and Nicola Haym had adapted the music by Alessandro Scarlatti, premiered in Naples in 1694. They could only wait.

Nicolini, on the other hand, was not worried. It gave him more time to get acclimatised, and the invitations for private performances did not stop coming. It would not affect the promise of 800 guineas for the season, and he would get extra income from those concerts. The weather in late October was getting cold and he already started to miss Italy's blue sky. *Get warm and focus on working,* he said to himself, *even for just one contract, with extra income, it will give me much ease financially, and I can get more presents for mama.*

It was the early afternoon of 9 December 1708. Prior to the end of the royal mourning, the general rehearsal was organised at the Queen's Theatre for *Pirro e Demetrio.*

Isabella, Lady Wentworth, sent word to Adelhida, Duchess of Shrewsbury, that she would not attend the rehearsal. Despite being told that it would be of a small scale with very few people in a dark room, she did not believe it, and she proved to be right. A great number of people turned up, already thirsty and impatient for the end of the royal mourning, to see the famous castrato.

Along with Swiney, Nicola Haym felt tense. This was a big day. Though Haym was officially the leading cellist in the orchestra at the Queen's Theatre, his real role was much greater than that. Since he had arrived in England seven years earlier, he had been very active. Beside working for Wriothesley Russell, 2nd Duke of Bedford, as his master of chamber music, he busied himself teaching, publishing, composing, organising private concerts, and obtaining scores and libretti of Italian operas. In fact, the London audience was able to enjoy Bononcini's *Camila* as early as 1706 thanks to his adaptation, filling the missing pieces with his own composition. Coming from Cardinal Ottoboni's orchestra in Rome, where he had served under Corelli's direction, he was, in fact, one of the best musicians Italy could offer. The young Wriothesley Russell, then Marquess of Tavistock, on his grand tour, had promised Haym a huge salary to leave his position in Rome and follow the marquess to London. Haym was settled in Southampton House, the Russells' London residence. Treated with respect, enjoying freedom granted by his young patron, he participated actively in London's musical life, enlarging his interests.

Now in his early thirties, Haym was developing more and more interest in opera, encouraged by his patron, now Duke of Bedford, who came back as an opera lover from Italy. Not only composing, he was now considering trying his skill at adapting libretti.

Owen Swiney was looking for Nicolini everywhere, and then he nearly walked into Nicolini's valet.

'Oh, Sam, where is your master?'

'At home, sir. He is not coming. I was sent to tell you that, sir.'

Swiney went white. He rushed to tell Nicola Haym.

'Shall I go and fetch him?' asked Swiney.

Haym considered and said, 'No. I don't think it is a good idea. Leave it to me. I will ask a lady to do that. He cannot refuse a lady's request.' With confidence he started out, then he stopped and turned to Swiney. 'You told me his valet was here?'

'Yes, he was.'

It was Haym's turn to turn white, 'Go and send him back! He is telling everyone that Nicolini is not coming, that brainless chatterbox!'

It was too late.

Katherine Tofts was annoyed. 'Am I wasting my time, Mr Swiney?'

'Madam, be patient. He'll be here. He is just—'

'Refusing to come. That's what Sam told me! Oh, that Italian!'

Swiney agreed, but seeing Margherita de l'Epine nearby, he had to be diplomatic.

The Duchess of Shrewsbury told the coachman to hurry and told her maid the reason in the coach. The duchess laughed. 'I find it entertaining!'

'Will madam persuade him to come?'

'I will. I am sure I will.' She was quite confident. Not only was she a woman, but she was also an Italian.

'Oh, Signor Nicolini, what is wrong? Are you unwell?' asked the duchess with an air of concern.

Seeing the duchess herself, looking worried, Nicolini did not know what to say. He could not sulk. He muttered, 'Oh, madam, I slept very badly, and I feel…very tired…'

The maid saw a fat and tall man come out of the house, offering his arm to the duchess. They were both smiling and talking casually, walking towards the coach. Everything looked fine.

Then it was Mrs Tofts' turn to refuse to sing. When Nicolini appeared with the costume, Katherine Tofts was back in her own dress and ready to go home. Owen Swiney, suppressing his anger and the urge to punch Nicolini and slap the soprano, repeated what Margherita de l'Epine told him.

'Madam, please. Do not take it badly.' Swiney stood in front of the singer. 'It is quite normal, apparently, for a castrato to be capricious. I ask you to be understanding and compassionate.'

Katherine Tofts glared at Swiney. 'Compassionate! How dare you!'

'Madam, please. Let me explain. You know he is a castrato. You know what he went through.' Swiney saw hesitation in her eyes.

The soprano stopped and looked puzzled. 'Well, yes, of course I know.' She did not. She was quintessentially English.

'Madam, due to the very unnatural procedure he went through, like all other castrati, he suffers from brutal changes of mood. Apparently, they are all like that, and that's something they cannot control. Don't you think we can forgive him for the price he paid for…?'

'You are telling me that he is just capricious?' she said, but the anger was gone. She just did not want her ignorance to be discovered.

The rehearsal was over, and Owen Swiney felt drained. He sat on the bench in the pit, looking at the stage in the dark auditorium. After a while, he got up, ready to go, when he noticed something on one of the stands in the orchestra pit. He thought it was a forgotten score.

'Who is that careless…' He reached the stand, feeling irritated, and realised it was not a score. He picked it up and put it in his pocket. It looked like a newspaper, but it was too dark to see. He went out and forgot it until he arrived at his lodging. Surprisingly, the forgotten paper provided Swiney with something to divert his mind from his troubles and worries. *The British Apollo*? He had never heard of it. *It must be new.* It consisted of questions from the public and their answers. A man was asking for advice, being uneasy about the drunken antics of his aristocratic friends. The paper said:

A Genteel Deportment, and Inoffensive Carriage, These the True Marks, These the Genuine Characteristic of a Gentleman . . . Unhappy They, who write themselves Gentlemen and yet owe their whole Gentility to their Coat of Arms . . . But He, who Acts and Lives the Gentleman, adds new lustre to his Birth, and Daily Blazons his Arms Afresh.

'Oh, you are right!' Swiney exclaimed to the paper, smiling. 'I cannot agree more!' He turned the page and saw an advertisement inviting subscriptions for a book called *Ottoman Empire*, followed by a list of subscribers. Swiney was quite impressed by the names, which represented wealth and power. It was quite sensational, as the newspaper itself was claiming.

'Who is the author? Aaron Hill? Never heard of him,' Swiney said to himself.

Five days later, *Pirro e Demetrio* was premiered in the Haymarket, and it was an absolute triumph. Swiney staged it carefully. He put out several advertisements for Nicolini, and the first six nights were accessible only by subscription for the pit and boxes, making it exclusive. The audience was completely bewitched by Nicolini's singing and acting. They could clearly see what a top-quality singer could do. From then on, the public would not accept a second-rate castrato, it had to be the top of the line.

John Vanbrugh, among the audience, was satisfied. From the very beginning, he had designed the theatre to be an opera house. At that time Italian opera was not yet introduced to the public in London, and he wanted to be the one to launch it. However, the public's reaction was very lukewarm. Then the rival theatre, the Theatre Royal on Drury Lane, got in the way, stripping Vanbrugh of the right to play operas, and triggering the war between the two theatres. He fought. He fought tirelessly, and finally he got the monopoly for opera in his theatre. It had been five years since he started the project, and finally Italian opera was starting to be fashionable. However, he felt tired. He could not stop feeling that the triumph came a bit too late.

At the Queen's Theatre, things seemed to have settled into a routine of operas. *Pirro e Demetrio (Pyrrhus and Demetrius)* was a huge success, carrying on into 1709, and *Camilla* was still attracting an audience. Marco Ricci and Giovanni Pellegrini provided the painted stage scenery. The theatre was armed with the strongest cast of singers, musicians, and decorators. Confident of his position and the ability of Nicolini's talent to draw the public to his theatre, in April 1709 Owen Swiney renewed the contract with the castrato for three more years. About the same time, Aaron Hill's *Full and*

Just Account of the Present State of the Ottoman Empire was published. This was possible thanks to three years lived in Constantinople, from where he visited Greece, Mecca, the Holy Land and Egypt. Hill had travelled and seen much more than any of the ambassadors or wealthy aristocrats on the grand tour. This publication was an impressive achievement for a twenty-four-year-old. With this, Hill's ambition to establish his social and literary credentials seemed achieved. Owen Swiney remembered well the advertisement. Cultivated and curious, he would have bought a copy if he had been able to afford it, but a thick volume of nearly 350 pages in a luxurious edition was too expensive. He was looking forward to the success of operas at his theatre, which would put him at ease financially.

At Drury Lane, things were quite different. As a result of role swap and Queen's Theatre getting the opera monopoly, all the actors from there were sent to Drury Lane theatre where only plays were allowed now. The actors, predictably enough, were not getting along at all with Christopher Rich, the manager. Now with the return of the actors, he just continued his outrageous management as before. The tension was mounting, but Rich just kept his way, ready to starve the actors. The final blow came when Rich ignored the Lord Chamberlain's order to respect the benefit plays. A benefit, as it was called, was a common practice to award or help actors. An evening of benefit for an actor meant that the profit of the evening went to that actor. Normally it was a special evening with special events, and the public was invited to contribute more than the price of a ticket. Christopher Rich had no scruples about promising a benefit night only to pocket all the profit for himself.

This time, Henry Grey, the Lord Chamberlain, had had enough. Though half-dormant and reluctant to make changes, Rich's outrageous behaviour was getting more and more pronounced. He could not ignore it anymore and also it was an insult to not respect his orders. After allowing the actors to support themselves, he dispatched Sir John Stanley to close the theatre on 6 June 1709 until further notice. Rich was removed as manager.

The actors were delighted. They had won.

'Finally!'

'That's the end of Rich!'

'Let's celebrate!'

Overjoyed, they immediately started to make plans. They were still on contract at Drury Lane theatre, but were allowed to self-support, now that their theatre was closed.

'Drury Lane closed? Rich removed?' said Vanbrugh incredulous.

'Yes. All that is true,' said Baron Halifax. 'You don't look pleased, John. I thought I had brought you good news.'

'Well, it is, of course. I thank you for bringing the news yourself, but…'

'But?'

'Well, it took time. It sounds like it may be too late for me. I've lost too much money in this venture.'

'I am sorry to hear that, John,' said Halifax, placing his hand on Vanbrugh's arm. 'So, tell me, how is Castle Howard going?'

Christopher Rich now realised he had gone too far. In desperation, he made his treasurer issue a pamphlet accusing the actors of pocketing fortunes, as much as £2,000. Nobody believed it. Then he attempted to sue the actors for breach of contract. This was met only with laughter. Still he refused to recognise defeat.

The Lord Chamberlain was now fully awake. Soon after removing Rich, he granted the actors permission to move out and perform plays at Queen's Theatre four days per week. This was a temporary measure until Drury Lane theatre could reopen. The actors nominated, among them, three representatives to be unofficial co-managers of Queen's Theatre with Swiney: the highly experienced and influential Wilks, Doggett and Cibber. The actors would form, in that way, an independent body within Queen's Theatre. Set free finally from Rich's clutches, they approached Swiney to suggest they remodel the theatre. The Queen's Theatre, from the beginning, had been notoriously poorly fitted for spoken drama.

'If we want to present plays, we have to do something,' said Wilks.

'I agree,' said Swiney. 'Do you think it's that the ceiling is too high?'

'Exactly,' said Cibber.

Owen Swiney knew then that the spectacular and unique feature of the theatre would be lost. However, using the theatre full-time was more beneficial, instead of presenting operas twice a week. He considered and asked the triumvirate, 'Shall I ask Mr Vanbrugh to do this?'

The three actors looked at each other. This was like asking a painter to destroy his favourite painting.

'It's delicate,' said Doggett.

'I know, but Mr Vanbrugh is still the owner, and it's his creation,' Swiney said, 'you cannot do it without his permission.'

'Can you talk to him first?' asked Cibber. 'You know Mr Vanbrugh better than all of us.' He remembered the first time he met the architect, when he visited the theatre in construction. His feeling then about the ceiling being too high was right.

Swiney considered. This was also a chance to get more authority towards the actors. He did not want to be overweighed by them in the co-management. 'Well, it's a heavy price to pay for Mr Vanbrugh,' he looked at the actors, 'but, if you can promise success and good profit, it will be easier for him to sacrifice his creation.'

Chapter 11 : A Saxon in Italy : An opera composer is born (1709-1710)

Venice, Winter 1708-1709

Händel arrived in Venice from Florence. If he had stopped in Florence after leaving Francesco Ruspoli's household in Rome, it was only to see Vittoria. Not only could he not see her, but the rumour was circulating that she was in Venice. Grand Prince Ferdinand was away, and Händel found himself unable to know whether Vittoria was with the prince, or not. Having failed to obtain permission to stay at Palazzo Pitti, he had no choice but hurry to Venice. He was, at the same time, relieved to escape the oppressive atmosphere of Palazzo Pitti, and frustrated to get no information about Vittoria.

His aim in Venice was to obtain the libretto for his opera. To his relief, the libretto by Cardinal Vincenzo Grimani had been waiting for him at San Giovanni Grisostomo theatre. Being aware of the family crisis in Medici Florence, the cardinal kept away and quiet, like everybody. The libretto in his hands, Händel then tried to enquire about Vittoria. He realised how the rumour could be either correct or wrong. Francesco Maria de' Medici's release from cardinalate seemed imminent and the news had reached Venice quickly. However, Vittoria was nowhere to be seen in Venice. And what about the rumour that Lucrezia was back in favour with Prince Ferdinando? It was Baron Kielmansegg, still in Venice as an envoy, who gave him the answer, partially.

Housed again in the palace leased by Elector of Hanover, and occupied by the baron, Händel led the conversation carefully to extract any information.

'I did not stay at Palazzo Pitti at all while I was in Florence, so I can only tell you about the rumours I heard, Baron,' Händel said.

'I suppose you heard quite a lot?' Baron Kielmansegg smiled.

'Yes. People seemed delighted to talk about the Cardinal de' Medici.'

To this the baron raised his eyes to the ceiling, shaking his head, still smiling.

'Anyway, I did not stay long. I only heard that a certain Lucrezia was in favour with the grand prince.'

'Oh, Lucrezia,' he said, 'or rather, Lucrezias.'

'Are there two Lucrezias?' Händel said, with his eyes wide open.

'Well, at least, if not three. The one Lucrezia of last year is off for sure, but there is more than one Lucrezia. That's what I heard. There is Lucrezia d'Andre and another Lucrezia. I don't remember her family name…'

It mattered little to Händel about the Lucrezias. 'And how about singers here in Venice? Any newcomers?'

'There are always newcomers. They come with contracts.' The baron did not mention Vittoria, at all. 'So, Georg. You will be composing an opera.'

'Yes, Baron.'

'Happy?'

'More than,' the composer grinned.

'But you will see operas as well, I imagine? It's the carnival season.'

No Vittoria in Venice. That was certain now. He would go back to Florence then. But, before that, he decided to see operas as much as he could.

Tuscany, Early Spring 1709

By February, Händel was back in Florence from Venice. Händel presented himself at Palazzo Pitti as soon as he arrived in Florence. Grand Prince Ferdinando was in Florence and Händel was offered hospitality as before. Bowing low in front of the prince, he felt he was ready to do anything to stay. The only reason to come back to Florence was Vittoria. She had, in fact, been with the grand prince all that time, looking fine. Händel struggled to conceal his feelings when he saw her. Exactly like when he saw her for the first time, she was singing beside the grand prince playing the harpsichord. Vittoria did not look at him. Händel, this time, was not treated as a guest of honour at supper, and sat beside a sculptor who was trying to get a commission from the grand prince. Händel watched from the other end of the table Vittoria seated beside the prince, talking, laughing and flirting. His heart collapsed, and he was ready to go when he saw another singer appear beside the prince. Then he started to see more clearly, that Vittoria was just pretending to be happy. She was neither back in favour nor in disgrace. Prince Ferdinando was playing dirty. He wanted to conquer another Lucrezia but was unwilling to let Vittoria go, putting the two women in competition. Händel accompanied them singing side by side, and saw Prince Ferdinando looking cynical and satisfied. This was not healthy. Händel felt uneasy day by day. Vittoria behaved professionally and did not let escape a drop of emotion. This was getting unbearable. He wanted to leave. But how? He was even considering leaving without the prince's permission when there was a vague suggestion that Händel might compose an Easter oratorio for Siena. He did not hesitate. He would go anywhere to escape the grand prince. He wanted to forget all about Vittoria, and to concentrate on composing his opera for Venice.

Grand Princess Violante looked better. In fact, her old friend and miserable brother-in-law Gian Gastone de' Medici was back in Florence. She was busying herself, trying to restore his health.

The commission for Siena came from the grand duke, not the grand prince. Suggested by his master of the household, Marquess Luca Casimiro degli Albizzi, and approved by the court poet and physician Antonio Salvi, the commission was aimed to stop Ferdinando's escalating outrageous behaviour. The dignity of the Medici court was at risk. However, it did not work as planned. Händel ended up in the Villa di Lappeggi, main residence of Cardinal Francesco Maria, near Siena, with Princess Violante and Gian Gastone. Then at the last minute, Vittoria was dispatched.

'Oh my God, I am so happy to be away from Florence.' Vittoria sighed in relief. 'The grand duke ordered Ferdinando to send one singer to Siena, and he just refused. It was horrible. He wanted to go to Poggio a Caiano, taking both me and Lucrezia.'

'And?'

'And the grand duke forbade Ferdinando to go to Poggio a Caiano. The grand duke wanted Lucrezia here, but Ferdinando refused.'

'And you ended up coming here.'

'Exactly!' She jumped into Händel's arms. 'I wanted to see you. I wanted to talk to you. I missed you.'

Händel just held her tightly in his arms and kissed the top of her head.

'It was horrible to have to ignore you…' Vittoria whispered.

Händel released her abruptly and held her away with his arms extended. 'So, that means you are singing my cantata. I need to make some changes. Come with me.'

Vittoria smiled. 'Music first. Of course, Maestro.'

Rome, Summer 1709

Margherita Durastante could not believe it. Händel wanted her in Venice! She pressed the letter just received to her breast. Margherita felt herself ready to leave Francesco Ruspoli's household. Like Händel, she was getting fed up with cantatas. Though opera was performed, it was under the guise of being a rehearsal, and she always felt guilty. She wanted to sing in opera openly. *Yes, I will join you, Giorgio! He wants me!* Her heart swelled with hope. Then she froze. *What if Vittoria is there? Will I be able to stand her presence?* She knew Händel had no feelings for her. He just needed a soprano for his opera. But still, there was friendship and trust between them. That was something she worked very hard to build. She lowered her head and said to herself, *Yes, I will. I will stand anything if I can see him.* She just wanted to see him, desperately. Then her practical and realistic side woke up.

She needed a contract. She would not leave the present post without securing the next.

In July 1709, Antonio Caldara became the house composer of Francesco Ruspoli, replacing Händel. If the latter was happy to remain a house guest during his stay, Caldara was more than happy to be formally employed.

Siena, Summer 1709

During the summer of 1709, there was a curious court in Siena. Gian Gastone and Violante were still there, with Händel and Vittoria. Despite the wife and the mistress of Ferdinando being at the same place, there was harmony and peace. Soon, Gian Gastone and Violante were summoned back to Florence for the wedding of Francesco Maria de' Medici.

Left alone with Vittoria, Händel could finally talk to her.

'Are you going back to Florence?'

'I don't know.'

'Then come with me. To Venice.'

Vittoria stared at Händel, incredulous, and then sighed. 'Giorgio, you are naive. You are just a child.'

'I am not.'

'Well, you are, to me.'

'Are you telling me that I am too young for you?' Händel was not bothered by her comment. 'My mother was much younger than my father, and they were happy. The difference in age is not an obstacle, Vittoria.'

'It is not the same thing!' Vittoria rolled her eyes. 'God, men are stupid…'

Händel, despite being with Vittoria, was not certain. The flood of affection he expected did not come. She kept her distance from him while not rejecting him completely. Her calming presence was a blessing, and he could focus on his opera. Yet, it was impossible to know whether she loved him, or not.

On 14 July 1709, the wedding of Francesco Maria de' Medici to Eleonora Luisa Gonzaga was celebrated. However the marriage was to be quasi-non-existent, as the young and attractive bride was repulsed by the sight of her old, fat and diseased husband, and would refuse to fulfil her marital duties.

While all of Florence was enjoying the free wine distributed to celebrate, Händel, upon receiving a letter from Halle, had to hurry back from Siena to his native land.

Eisenach, August 1709

'Händel!' Telemann opened his arms, beaming.
The two friends embraced firmly until a little cough brought them back to reality. Händel was still in his simple black mourning suit.
'Let me introduce you to my wife, Händel.' Telemann took his wife's hand. 'This is Amalie Eberlin. Amalie this is—'
'Your friend Georg Friederich Händel,' the young bride interrupted, smiling. 'I know all about you, Mr Händel. My husband talks a lot about you.' Then she turned to her husband. 'I will let you alone. I suppose you have a lot to catch up on.'

'I am so sorry for the loss of your sister, Georg.'
'I know. I still cannot believe it. She was so young...'
'How old was she?'
'She was going to be twenty shortly.'
'God... How is your mother?'
'Devastated...'

It was fortunate that the letter from Händel's mother reached her son quickly, thanks to the kindness of Francesco Ruspoli and the Medici network. Händel had hurried back to Halle to console his mother and other sister. He had not seen them since he'd left for Hamburg six years before. His little sister's words were still alive in Händel's memory. *Maybe you can find us husbands!* Poor Johanna Christiana. Why had God taken her so young?

Händel was deeply saddened to see his mother in grief. She looked as if she had aged ten years in an instant. Lost, praying and weeping silently, she sat still, lost in her thoughts. He could do nothing. He could not bring his little sister back to make his mother happy again. He saw her smile sadly to him when he arrived. He would do anything to make her laugh, but he could not. He just wanted to make her happy, but he could not. All he could do was to try to comfort her, in vain. It was painful to see. Why is God so unfair to punish her in this way? All she did was to give love to her children. Without her he could not be who he is now... Her laugh, her smile, her singing, her embrace... He was so desperate to make her feel a little better, that he nearly blurted out that he would soon be married... The only consolation was that his other sister had been married the previous year and was now expecting. The letter announcing the marriage of Dorothea Sophia Händel to Michael Dietrich Michaelsen was apparently lost.

He felt a hand on his own. He looked up, to meet Telemann's warm and compassionate look. *Yes, I have a friend.* He smiled.
'You love your mother,' said Telemann.
He just nodded. 'Tell me about you. And the duke?' He just wanted to

divert his mind from grief, even momentarily. The conversation turned quickly to music.

'Duke Johann Wilhelm is very happy to have you here, Händel. We shall treat him, shan't we?'

'Of course.' This was not just diversion.

Getting into a court was an important factor, to become acquainted with the ruler, and be recognised as an able musician. This could lead to a letter or two of recommendation to another ruler. For a travelling musician, being able to stop at a court with a recommended introduction was an advantage, providing hospitality, if accepted, and an extra income if approved of and applauded. Only a highly reputed musician like Bononcini could bypass this ritual. Händel was thinking of his mother. If he could not make her smile, he could, at least, give her financial comfort.

After escaping Poland from the hostilities of the Great Northern War, Telemann entered the service of Duke Johann Wilhelm of Saxe-Eisenach, where he became Kapellmeister.

'Tell me about your opera,' Telemann said.

Händel's face became serious. 'I am so excited, but I am so scared. Venice is big, and what if I fail?'

Telemann put his hand on his friend's shoulder. 'Händel, don't be scared. This is a fabulous chance to show what you can do. Don't let the fear overtake you. Just believe in yourself. You can do it.'

Händel put his hand over Telemann's and nodded.

'How long are you staying here?'

'I'll go back to Italy tomorrow.'

'Oh no…I thought I could go to Weimar with you.'

'Weimar? Why?'

'I heard of an organist. Apparently he is a virtuoso. His name is Bach. Did you ever hear of him?'

'Bach? No.'

'I got permission from the duke. I am excited!'

'Well, good luck. That's how we met.' Händel smiled, 'um…'

'Yes?'

'No, nothing…' he was very much tempted to talk about Vittoria to his friend, but did not dare. He would tell him when at last he was with her physically and for good.

Seeing his friend smiling Telemann asked, 'It's good news, I guess?'

'I hope so…'

Johann Sebastien Bach, after marrying, at twenty-one, his sweetheart and second cousin Maria Barbara two years earlier in Mühlhausen, moved to Weimar where he obtained the post of organist at the court of Wilhelm Ernst,

Duke of Saxe-Weimar. With a growing reputation as a superb performer, he attracted attention from other composer-performers. Independent, sometimes arrogant and confrontational, Bach did not get along well with his previous employers. However, having a wife to protect made him conscious of the responsibilities. He was determined to be compliant, get on well with the city council, not get involved in fights, and to respect his job, unlike in his previous post. He would not disappear for several months, instead of the few weeks granted, to go to Lübeck to hear the organist Buxtehude. No. He wanted to keep his post and get promoted. His wife was expecting a child.

Pratolino, September 1709

Händel left Germany immediately after his reunion with Telemann, heading for Italy. Apart from his coming opera, Vittoria filled his mind. He had to go to Florence before reaching Venice. The atmosphere at Palazzo Pitti was now unbearable after the disastrous failure of Francesco Maria de' Medici's marriage. Still, Händel had to see Vittoria. This was his last chance. The grand prince was ready to go to Pratolino when Händel presented himself. This time, the prince could not find an excuse not to invite Händel to Pratolino. Händel ignored the prince's cold reception.

Händel was impressed by the beauty of Pratolino. He could understand why the grand prince was so attached to the place. It was busy in the preparation for the forthcoming opera, making the grand prince ignore the Saxon completely. As much as Händel wanted to see the opera there, the message was clear, that he could not stay. He decided to confront Vittoria.

'Come with me, to Venice.'

'No, I cannot,' said Vittoria firmly.

'Why?'

She looked at him in amazement. 'Why? Why? What a question!' She sighed, 'you know I am committed. I am in the opera.'

'Then when you finish the opera, join me in Venice.'

Vittoria smiled sadly. 'You know very well that I am... I am...' she swallowed and said, 'I belong to him.'

'No, you do not. You are not married to him, and you are talented. We can work together and make a lot of money, and we will be very happy. And...'

Vittoria looked Händel up and down but said nothing.

'And, I received a commission. My opera will be played in Venice.' Händel took a deep breath. 'And I love you, Vittoria.'

Vittoria felt her heart melt. Though she had had many admirers and a few lovers, this was the first time she had heard someone say he loved her, from the heart. She buried her face in his large chest. She felt his arms wrap her gently.

Later, seated in the garden, Vittoria's mind was in turmoil. She regretted not being firm in rejecting him. She could not. Deep down, she knew she wanted to escape the grand prince. She wanted to be free, free from his clutches. At the same time, she felt terribly guilty for putting Händel in this situation. She was still a married woman, and a mistress at the same time. *Confess everything and beg him his pardon? That might make him give up. But he might help me to get out of here...* The grand prince is very busy and it would be much easier to escape. Deep in thoughts, she did not see someone approaching.

'Signorina,' Marco whispered.

Vittoria jumped.

'Quick, Signorina. The Grand Prince is looking for you!'

'I do not care as long as you are mine,' Ferdinando said without looking at Vittoria. They were alone in his study. 'But don't go too far. He might find himself in a ditch with a broken neck.'

She felt her blood drain and a chill run down her spine. *How? I was so careful...Someone saw us...Maybe he ordered someone to watch me.* This was not a warning; this was a threat. But she managed to keep calm.

'Is that all, Your Highness?' she asked coldly. Then she regretted it. She was taken by surprise and did not have time to act.

'Yes.' He looked at her with contempt and disdain for what she was – a mistress.

It was humiliating, but she had no time to be hurt. Händel's safety was at stake. She swallowed her pride, employing her acting skill in full. She knelt in front of him and kissed his hand.

'Prince, he is just a child. I am yours, always.' She looked at him with an angelic madly-in-love expression.

He let a despiteful smile escape, satisfied. He was sure she would not leave. She was his. There was no alternative.

She found herself in a terrible situation. She must let Händel go. He could not stay here in Pratolino. *Reject him in a most hurtful way to make him leave? He might not believe it.* She had to make him go willingly. He would refuse to go if she didn't leave with him. She must convince him that she would come later, but that they could not leave together. They'd have to depart separately and meet somewhere. This was a terrible lie, but she had no choice. She wanted him safely out of danger's way.

As soon as Vittoria was gone, Ferdinando summoned Händel. In a most jolly tone he asked, 'So, Maestro, what is your plan?'

This was to be expected. Händel looked at the prince and said with confidence, 'Grand Prince, my aim is to get a situation in my country, not far from my mother, if possible,' said Händel, not mentioning his opera in

Venice.

The grand prince, facing the talented and daring young composer, felt irritated. He smiled, and handed over a letter. 'Maestro Sassone, I wrote a letter of recommendation to Prince Karl of Pfalz-Neuburg. Go to see him in Innsbruck. He will assist you.'

This was not a suggestion. The grand prince wanted him gone.

'Your Highness, you are most generous,' said Händel. He bowed low. As low as possible. He knew he must go as soon as possible. *I have to see Vittoria. I cannot leave until I've seen her. But how?.* He slowly went back to his room. When he closed the door and turned, he found Vittoria standing in front of him, dressed as a man.

'I cannot stay long, you know, Giorgio.' Her face was grave. 'This was the only way I could get to see you.'

'But...'

'You have to go. As soon as possible. You have to,' she whispered, ready to leave his room in a hurry.

'I know.' Händel could not say more.

'Start packing, now,' Vittoria said, turning her back to him. Then she felt a hand in hers. She stopped.

'You... coming with me?'

Vittoria swallowed, and faced Händel. 'I will join you. We cannot leave together. You know that.' She felt her hands wrapped in his. She saw his face light up.

'I will wait for you, Vittoria. I will be in Venice first, then Innsbruck, and then Hanover. Join me wherever you can. I will wait for you at each place. If we miss each other, we will meet in London,' said Händel, looking in her eyes.

'I will, Giorgio, I promise. I will join you in Hanover, and we shall go to London together.' She looked back intently at Händel. 'Innsbruck will be too risky. We have to be far enough away, and I will be travelling under another name, and probably disguised.'

'I will wait for you.' He weighed every word, and then he kissed her.

He watched Vittoria leave the room, and immediately he started to pack.

Händel was soon ready.

'Grand Prince, I am here to ask your permission to leave.'

'Do you really want to go, Maestro? Already?' Ferdinando looked surprised.

'I would love to stay. You are so generous, and you have the best musicians. It is really heaven to be here.'

This was mere acting, for both.

'But you want to go.'

'Yes, Your Highness. I promised my old mother that I would get a

situation in my country, not far from her.'
'Then I will not stop you.'
'I thank you, Grand Prince.' Handel bowed.
'And, I have a gift for you.' Ferdinando made a sign to his valet who showed Händel a set of silver plates. 'They are wrapped and ready.'
'You are most generous, Your Highness,' said Händel bowing again, low.
The grand prince knew Händel could not refuse a gift. He also knew that the best gift for a travelling musician would be gold coins, rather than bulky and heavy silver plates.

An hour later, Händel was getting into the carriage. Behind him the grand prince, accompanied by his court, was there to bid farewell. This was another display of his generosity for the others to witness. Händel made a huge effort not to look at Vittoria, standing behind the grand prince.

Vittoria watched the carriage disappearing in the dust. She knew that the grand prince was observing her, but she did not care. She knew that she would not see Händel again, that she would remain the prince's mistress for as long as he wished her to be. She was, at least, relieved that Händel got away unscathed. All the promising future was in front of him. Her only future was mercy. *Giorgio, you are good. I am sorry I cannot fulfil my promise, not in this life. I will come back, and I will only live to love you. I promise. I am sorry.*

'So the great Saxon is gone,' the grand prince said, merrily as always. 'Some people might be sad to lose such a talent here, but we shall have other talented people.' And he looked at Vittoria.

She bowed to him elegantly. 'Your Highness, may I have permission to go for a short walk in the gardens? It is still warm outside,' Vittoria asked casually.

'You have all the permission you wish.'

As she reached her room, coming back from the gardens, she heard a noise coming from inside. Somebody was in her room. It could not be the maid; she leaves the door open when she comes to service the room. Vittoria stopped, retreated noiselessly, and hid behind a column. The door opened, and she saw the grand prince coming out. She saw him walk away calmly. She felt uneasy. Something was wrong. She went into her room and looked around. Nothing was changed. Then she jumped to the small box placed on her dressing table, opened it, and gasped. Her ivory comb was broken into two pieces. Her knees gave way, and she collapsed to the floor. She was pale with her eyes wide open and tears flowing down.

'Vittoria, Vittoria...' a voice called her from far away.

She was still on the floor, lost, 'Papa...'
'Vittoria, my child, my dear daughter. I am dying. I am sorry I am not leaving enough money for you. But fear not, you are talented. You can earn well with your voice.'
'Oh, Papa, don't say that. You will recover soon. Don't be pessimistic.'
'I wish I was just pessimistic, but I think it is time for me to join your mother.'
'Papa...'
'Let me give you this, Vittoria, before I go.' Signor Tarquini produced an ivory comb. 'This is the first present I gave your mother when we met, and she treasured it. She received many presents from her admirers, but she did not care. She just wanted to keep this. Sell my harpsichord. You will get a good amount of money, so you can keep going for the time being. Work hard, my child.'

'Papa...help me...' She was still on the floor when she heard her father's voice again in her head. *You are talented.* She got to her feet. She looked straight in front of her. This was not the first time she had been humiliated, but this was the first time she felt she could not accept it. She started to gather her belongings. She was hearing Händel's voice. *'I will wait for you.'* Yes, wait for me, I will join you. I love you. Then the fear crept in. *What if I fail to escape? He will be pitiless.* Then she prayed. *Giorgio, I will try my best, but if I fail, I will join you in another life. I will be there for you, just for you, to love you and only you.*

She did not go out of her room for supper. She waited until late in the night. When the whole household was asleep, she slipped noiselessly out of her room. She had not made it ten steps when she stopped. Prince Ferdinando was standing in front of her, smiling cynically.

He was alone in his study with Vittoria's lifeless body on his feet. He was still panting and quite shaken. He was not used to being challenged. He was still living what just happened. He still heard her voice. *'I do not need to justify myself, Ferdinando.'* She called me Ferdinando. How dare she to call me Ferdinando! *'God knows what you did. God will judge you.'* What was she talking about? Was she talking about that comb? It was just a comb. She is mad. *'I do not care anymore. I will get free from your tyranny no matter how.'* Tyranny? Did she call me a tyrant? I am the Grand Prince. *'I know what you will do to me. God is witnessing it, and I will accept it as my fate.'*

Her gaze had been quite imposing. She had talked from her heart, and that had made Ferdinando uneasy for a second. Now he started to feel the anger swelling inside. He looked around. Nobody. No noise. The place looked dead. He looked through the French doors opening directly onto the garden. Not too far away, he knew, there was a disused dry well. He considered. If he dragged the body to the well, it would leave traces on the grass. It would have to be carried. He opened the French doors carefully. He lifted the body to his shoulder, took her travelling bag, and started to walk towards the well.

Anna awaited her sweetheart in the bush bordering the garden. She was getting cold. *I told him to come to the big tree near the dry well*, she thought. *Why is he late?* Then she heard the cracking of branches, and Paolo appeared. They hugged each other, and then Paolo started to talk. Anna put her hand to his mouth. They heard a noise. They looked at each other, then turned towards the noise. The moon came out from behind a cloud, and they saw a man carrying something over his shoulder, something quite bulky. It looked like a body. The moon revealed the profile of the grand prince going towards the dry well. He was carrying a woman with her arms dangling. They saw it as they stood terrified and frozen. It seemed a long time before they were sure that the grand prince had gone back inside. They left in silence, shocked, hoping what they had seen was just a nightmare.

Paolo was clearing the lawn the next morning. With autumn in full swing, the leaves were falling abundantly, but the grand prince liked to see the lawn always clean. It was early morning, and the sun was rising. He was bending to collect the leaves and then froze. He could see the dry well some sixty feet in front of him. And there, with the light coming sideways, he could see the footprints of the grand prince. With the weight of the body he was carrying, his feet had sunk into the soft lawn, leaving his footsteps quite clear. The image came back in a flash. Paolo could not move. Then it was gone. The sun was behind a thick cloud, and he could see nothing. Relieved but still shaking, he collected the leaves and hurried back to the garden shed.

Grand Prince Ferdinando woke up late with a terrible hangover. He had drunk all night, going from one place to another. His valet came in, bringing a glass of cold water and a damp towel. Ferdinando emptied the glass and fell backwards into the bed. The valet gently applied the towel to his forehead.

'Marco?' He called his manservant without moving.

'Yes, Your Highness.'

Eyes closed, he said, 'Marco, I want you to arrange for that dry well at the end of the garden to be filled in.'

'Yes, Your Highness.'

'You are right. It is dangerous.'

'You heard about the little girl, Your Highness?'

'Yes, and I nearly did the same thing last night. It was dark, and I did not see it.'

'Your Highness, leave it to me. It will be done very quickly.' He left with a smile.

That was enough. Within a few minutes the whole household knew that Grand Prince Ferdinando had nearly fallen into a well because he was drunk. Marco's pleasure did not stop there. A few hours later, he saw the grand prince in a rage, ordering him to look for his mistress everywhere and to bring her back, regardless of the cost. The news of Vittoria eloping with Händel quickly circulated within the household.

The servants were delighted about the grand prince's incidents and did not stop talking about them. Except Paolo. He was restless. He met Anna's eyes and approached her.

'Anna.'

'Don't say anything to anybody, Paolo,' she whispered, nearly hissing.

'I know, but…'

'But what?'

Paolo swallowed and said, 'Come with me.' He dragged Anna to the shed. There were a few large wicker baskets full of leaves. Paolo fumbled in one of those and retrieved something.

'I found this among the leaves.'

It was a shoe – Vittoria's. Anna gasped, her eyes wide open.

Venice, Autumn 1709 – Carnival 1710

Margherita Durastante, after securing a contract, made her début in early November at San Giovanni Grisostomo as Fiordalba in Antonio Lotti's opera *Ama più che men si crede (To love more than is believed possible)*.

'You did well, Margherita, really well. I liked it,' Händel congratulated his friend warmly after the premiere.

'Really? I was so nervous, Giorgio.' Margherita smiled.

'It did not show.'

'It is nerve-wracking, Venice. You do well, and you live; you do badly, and that's the end of your career. There is no second chance.' Margherita looked into Händel's eyes.

'It is a challenging world, I know. But you know what, Margherita? It is the same for us composers, with much lower fees.'

Margherita stared at Händel and then laughed. 'I will not deny it, Giorgio. But remember, singers cannot last as long as composers.'

'That's true.'

'Are you lodged in the Hanoverian baron's palace?'

'No. He is back in Hanover. Cardinal Grimani arranged a lodging for me near the theatre.'

'How is your opera going, Giorgio?'

'I've been working on it for nearly a year, but I am making huge changes, so it's as if I am doing it all over again.'

'Are you certain about giving me the title role? Diamante Scarabelli is more experienced.'

Händel looked into her eyes. 'I wrote Agrippina with you in my mind, Margherita. I cannot change it now. Diamante will be Poppea.'

Margherita felt, for the first time, authority in Händel. He was sure of what he was doing.

'And you know what? Poppea is new for me.'

'New?' Margherita said, puzzled.

'Yes. I was quite surprised by her personality in this libretto written by a cardinal. But after all, it is for Venice. It could never be possible in Rome,' Händel said. 'I've never composed for a woman like Poppea.'

'True! I hope you are enjoying composing the arias for a seductress!' Margherita laughed. 'And how about Nerone, my son?'

'Valeriano Pellegrini will join you soon to sing Nerone. Your son will be twice as old as you.'

Margherita laughed. 'Shall I make myself a toothless old witch?' She did not dare to ask about Vittoria.

Händel saw a small group of people approaching them. 'I leave you with your admirers, Margherita. I'll see you tomorrow.'

Margherita was soon surrounded by people congratulating her. Händel happily watched her dealing with her newly acquired followers. He had no doubt, with her voice and acting skill, that she would build up a solid career here in Venice.

Margherita could not be happier. Her début was a success, and most importantly her secret love was there and she would soon be singing the title role in his opera. She had been desperate when she realised the affair between Händel and Vittoria two years before, but she felt she had recovered from the wound. And it looked just like a short-lived love. She still had a chance. *If I do well in his opera he might want to keep me. So, I must excel to make myself indispensable!* Now she could not resist dreaming of her future, following her love wherever he went, and singing in his operas.

Händel's opera's turn came. It was a big cast. Soon Margherita found herself surrounded by arriving singers. Valeriano Pellegrini was hired specifically for the production as a virtuoso from Düsseldorf with the blessing of Elector Johann Wilhelm and Electress Anna Maria Luisa. Giuseppe Maria Boschi and his wife Francesca Vanini-Boschi also came just for the production.

Gossip-addicted Francesca Vanini-Boschi did not waste her time. 'Tell me, Margherita, were you in Rome with that Saxon?'

'Yes, we both worked for Marquess of Cerveteri – well, Prince of Cerveteri now.' She clearly remembered. When the Ruspoli regiment defeated the Austrian army in Ferrara, in recognition of this victory Pope

Clement elevated Cerveteri to a principality, making Ruspoli a prince. On top of that, his wife Lady Isabella blessed her husband with a healthy boy soon after. His ageing uncle Cardinal Marescotti was in tears of joy.

'I heard he is very rich.' Francesca pulled out Margherita from her daydream.

'Oh, he is, very. If you saw the receptions he gives…'

'Quite young and attractive.'

To this Margherita just smiled.

'So the Saxon composed and you sang?'

'That's right.'

'What do you think of his music?'

'Well, I like it a lot. And you know what? I enjoyed very much singing his cantatas. They are challenging, technically. He does not let you idle in his music, but it is so good to sing. I have a feeling that he knows how we sing, as if he has been a singer.'

'Does he sing, then?'

'I've never heard him sing.'

'Is it true that he was in love with Vittoria Tarquini?'

Margherita stared at Francesca, incredulous. 'Do you know her?'

'Oh, yes. I was with her in Piacenza ten years ago, shortly before she became Prince Ferdinando's mistress.'

'Oh…'

'Did you know she is married?' Francesca continued.

'Well, no.'

'She was married very young to a French Konzertmeister in Hanover. He stayed there, and she went off to sing in various places.'

Margherita was speechless. She could not believe the speed at which gossip travelled.

Despite Francesca's gossiping, Margherita liked her, and they were talking more and more. She also liked the fact that Francesca was happily married to Giuseppe, another singer. That allowed them to work and travel together, which seemed perfect to Margherita. That was something she would love to achieve.

'London?' said Margherita, staring at Francesca.

'Yes, London. We are going there after here. It was already planned. We would like to have a go.' Francesca looked at her husband and smiled. 'It seems a nice place to make money. Nicolini confirmed it.'

'Oh yes, he is there now. But it's so far. I cannot imagine myself travelling all the way to London,' said Margherita.

'Well, there are quite a few people from London in Venice. They came all the way here from there.'

'Oh, that's why you know about London?'

'Yes, indeed!'
'How about the language? Is it very different?'
'Oh, it could not be more different from Italian,' said Francesca.
'Ah...'
'But we all sing in Italian,' said Giuseppe Boschi.
'And there is an opera house, a new one built a few years ago.'

Margherita was now certain. The cast was complete. Her only worry had been about Vittoria being included in the cast. No room for her! She was convinced that the affair was over, or rather wanted to believe. She was now considering whether to tell Händel that Vittoria was a married woman, to give the final blow to their relationship. Then she felt ashamed. *No, I will not tell him. What is the point? To hurt him?* Hurting him was the last thing she wanted to do. She decided just to enjoy working with Händel each day, like in Rome.

'You know, Francesca talks a lot about other singers, but she was not immune from gossip either,' said Antonio Carli to Margherita.

'Tell me, Tonio,' Margherita felt at ease, having worked with him before.

'I saw it with my own eyes. She was once in love with a castrato.'

'A castrato?' Her eyes nearly popped. 'Are you...certain?'

'Oh Yes. His name is Tamburini. Do you know him?'

'No. Never heard of him.'

'He was madly in love with her, and she was kind of reciprocating, but...'

'But?'

'One day, she decided to stop it. I think she received an order.'

'An order? From whom?'

'Probably Cardinal Francesco Maria de' Medici, Tamburini's patron. Well, he was still a cardinal at that time.'

'And?'

'Poor Tamburini. I saw him following Vanini in Genoa like a ghost.'

'And that was before she married Giuseppe?'

'Yes. And that was before the cardinal got married, too.'

Margherita smiled. Francesca Vanini-Boschi loved gossiping, but there was no malice in it. She liked more and more the Boschis.

Valeriano Pellegrini was then in his forties. He was merry and affectionate but wanted to be the centre of attention, a chatterbox. He was the favourite of Elector Johann Wilhelm in Düsseldorf.

'Giorgio! I knew I would see you again!'
'Signor Pellegrini!'

They hugged each other merrily, in front of the other singers, who were quite amazed.

'You know I am here with special permission from the elector?'

'I am very honoured,' said Händel, smiling.

'And I have a mission to bring back your music – the whole opera if possible, but at least arias. The elector and electress are impatient to have them. They'll be so happy to be the very first ones to get the new Venice opera score!'

And it was true. Getting a score of a new opera produced in Venice was a sign of privilege, power and influence. It was worth sending the court castrato for it.

'I am very much humbled. I'll take care of that myself.'

'You know, Giorgio, you are very much admired by the elector and the electress. They talk of you very often.'

'Signor Pellegrini, I heard you are—'

'Oh, come on, call me Valeriano.'

'I heard you were knighted.'

'Yes, I was. The elector is very generous.'

'Cavaliero Valeriano, shall I introduce you to your fellow singers? And maybe it's a good idea to start rehearsing?'

The star castrato realised only then that the rest of the cast was waiting for him to stop talking. He laughed.

On the evening of 26 December 1709, at the best opera house in Venice, San Giovanni Grisostomo, Händel was getting ready for the premiere of his opera *Agrippina*. He felt the pressure. Though he had already composed an opera for Florence, and his works were presented frequently in Rome, Venice was different. It was the place for opera and the audience was not politely gathering there to applaud. They were there to judge, evaluate and spread the news to the rest of Europe.

'Are you ready, Giorgio?' Margherita asked, in her costume of Agrippina. She could see that Händel was tense, and she could not agree more. She remembered how nervous she had been for her début a few weeks before.

'Yes, I'm fine,' he said, not so convinced. 'And you, Margherita?'

'Oh, I feel much better this time,' she indicated her Roman costume, 'last time, as a shepherdess, I was wearing very little. This time I am sure I will not catch cold!' This was just to divert Händel's mind. With lots of candles lit in the theatre, it was quite warm, even in winter.

'Giorgio!' Valeriano Pellegrini approached, 'look, am I convincing as Margherita's son?'

Margherita put her arms on her hips, and said, 'Son, I told you to not disturb Maestro!'

'Oh, I am so sorry, Mama,' he lowered his head, 'I promise, Mama, I will behave.' He hid himself behind Margherita.

Händel laughed. He felt better. He could concentrate. He had worked very hard, and this was his chance to show what he could do. He could not afford to mess it up.

Agrippina was presented for the first time in the packed theatre. The audience was thunderstruck, resulting in an electrifying reaction. The theatre resounded with shouts of '*Viva il caro Sassone!*' at every pause. It was Händel's solid German background of intellectual force in harmonic adventure and his different treatment of the orchestra, mixed with Italian lightness and refinement. But what fascinated the audience was the power of his music. Directing from the harpsichord, Händel's bold personality was reflected in his music with strength. With his ability to create a mood instantly, the audience was drawn into the opera, living in it. Even the seasoned opera-goers were astonished to see Händel's ability to express in music the innermost secrets of the human mind, both male and female.

Agrippina was the culmination of his Italian training. In this second opera, the tone was lighter and the action faster, making the characters move with clear assurance. After composing nearly a hundred cantatas, serenatas, and similar works, Händel had duly mastered the Italian style and language. His musical invention was rich and varied in melody, harmony, and rhythm. His mastery in building up tension was apparent. In *Agrippina*, Händel made it, despite the comical tone, an *opera seria*, a serious opera. Moreover, the Venetian tradition allowed him to be more flexible, freed from the rigidness that Rome required.

Only when it was over and he was bowing to the audience did Händel realise he had achieved what he was after, to be recognised as an opera composer. It was a solid cast he could count on, and the stage manoeuvres were done smoothly by very efficient staff. There was everything to give him the grounds to thrive.

Händel was more than happy with Margherita. Not only did she sing beautifully, but her acting was exceedingly good. She was versatile. Her height was perfect, not too short and not too tall. She had a pair of strong shoulders and quite narrow hips for a woman, but that was easily corrected with the costume. And it meant she could do the male roles as well, in case a castrato was not available. And her hair! Her abundant and gracefully waved hair was so beautiful that she did not need any wigs; any kind of elaborate hairstyle was possible. Her face, a pair of small eyes separated by a quite long and bulbous nose, together with her strong jaw, the lower part of which protruded, made her profile look like a quarter moon. Still, with skilful makeup, which she knew how to do, she looked splendid on the stage.

Margherita was perfectly conscious of her looks. It was also a learning process being a prima donna and attracting admirers. She made the mistake of going out of the theatre one night after the performance without any makeup. An admirer asked her where Margherita was, taking her for her maid.

The theatre managers produced *Agrippina* as much as possible, but now it was time to move on. The carnival schedule was tight. By the end of January, the production had to end to prepare for the next opera. As soon as his opera was over, Händel decided to leave. He could not wait anymore. Vittoria. He needed to be out of Italy to be able to join Vittoria.

'You are ready to go?' said Margherita.
'Yes, I am.'
'To London?'
'Yes. But I will be making a few stops on the way.'
'I see. You are ready to go but not yet for London. Take your time, Giorgio. It's a long way.'
'Are you staying?'
'Yes. I have a contract, and this is the place to build up a career. Then I will be able to ask for big fees.' Margherita laughed. 'I will resume working with Maestro Lotti soon. He is the composer of the season.' She looked into Händel's eyes. 'Giorgio, please take care of yourself. I will pray for your safe journey. Will you write to me?'
'Of course I will. And you write to me. I want to know what's going on in Venice.'
'And I want to know all about London. Farewell, Giorgio.'

Margherita felt her heart collapsing. He had not even suggested she come to London. By now she knew him quite well. In normal circumstances, she would perfectly understand that he could not suggest it because he was not certain it was right even for himself. *So how could he say such a thing?* Margherita was struggling to convince herself. Still, the fact that he had not invited her to come to London hurt her. *It is Vittoria he wants!* The only thing she could do was to try to forget Händel and focus on her career. He was gone now, far away, and there was no point to try to go to London if he would be with Vittoria. *Come on, Margherita, forget about it. Just let it go. He is not the only man. Instead build up your career. Work hard and become famous. You will be rewarded for your effort. Love is not rewarding.*

As soon as Händel was gone, Margherita heard about Prince Ferdinando in Venice looking for him with Vittoria. *So she escaped? Where is she now? Was she intending to join Giorgio in Venice?*

'Grand Prince Ferdinando?' Margherita went pale.
'Yes, apparently, he was after Giorgio. 'Thank God, he escaped just in time,' said Francesca.
'Was the grand prince going to kill him?'
'Well, he does not need to. He can easily hire someone to do the dirty

work and be safe.'

'God...' Margherita clutched her hands to her chest. She realised how much she still cared for him. Yes, after all that, she still loved him, deeply.

'He is lucky, isn't he?'

Margherita did not reply.

'Did you meet Vittoria?' asked Francesca.

'Just once. She was with Cardinal Ottoboni on the way to Bologna. They stopped at Vignanello.'

'How was she?'

'Oh, she looked fine. Very beautiful.'

'She was such a beauty. I really don't understand why she married so young and so low...'

They looked at each other uncomfortably.

Margherita was walking back from the church to her lodging when a threatening-looking man approached her.

'Signorina Margherita?'

She did not reply, and she had turned back to go in the opposite direction when another man stood in front of her.

'Signorina Margherita, we want to ask you a few questions,' the first man said, and he grabbed her wrist firmly. 'Would you follow us, please?'

'Where?' Margherita whispered, frightened.

Seeing her not resisting, the man loosened his grip, letting her rub her wrist. 'We want to ask you a few questions, as I said.'

'You can ask me here,' she said firmly, regaining control.

'Where is the Saxon?'

'Saxon?'

'You know very well who it is, Signorina,' the man got closer, 'just tell us where he is and we'll let you go.'

'I don't know.'

It was in broad daylight, and the passers-by looked at them, slowing down to catch any words.

'That's not the answer. You know where he is.'

'I don't know.'

The man grabbed her wrist again, firmer than before, and said, 'We will make you speak, if you don't tell us.'

Margherita opened her mouth, but no word came out. She was too frightened. People were gathering around them, attracted by the altercation but not daring to interfere.

'Margherita!' A man shouted and approached her. 'What are you doing here? We were looking for you. Quick, we'll be late.' Giuseppe Boschi, feigning confusion, looked at the men, and said, 'Sorry, folks, we are in a rush. We have to sing for the doge.'

The two men were not impressed. One of them sneered, 'Oh, we just want to know the whereabouts of the Saxon.'

'Saxon? You mean Giorgio?'

'Whoever! The Saxon!' the other man hissed.

'You are not from Venice,' said Boschi, with perfect calm, 'or you just arrived. Well, too late. Everyone knows that he is gone. His opera is over now.'

'Where?'

'Back to his country. Sorry you missed his opera.'

'Oh…'

'Let's go, Margherita. We cannot be late. What will you be wearing?' Francesca joined them.

Ignoring the men, they walked away chatting quite merrily. When they were far away from the men, they walked in an awkward silence. Then Boschi broke the silence. He was holding Margherita's arm, leading her gently, when his wife joined them very discreetly.

'Oh my God. Are you all right, Margherita?'

'I am fine. It was scary,' she said, still shocked. She was now shaking.

'Oh, Margherita, poor you!' Francesca stopped and hugged her, 'you are safe now. '

'Are you certain?' Margherita was not convinced.

'I am sure,' said Giuseppe, 'all they wanted to know is where Giorgio is. I think they thought you were hiding him.'

Chapter 12 : Roads to London (1710)

Pratolino, March 1710

> His Highness, Grand Prince Ferdinando de' Medici
>
> Your Highness,
>
> Händel the Saxon, on his way to Hanover, stopped here in Innsbruck with your letter of recommendation.
> I thank Your Highness for sending me such a talented musician. He astonished everybody with his harpsichord playing. However, he showed little interest in staying here. And, he does not seem to need my assistance. He left three days ago, on 9 March 1710.
> He looks civilized, and if he did not play the harpsichord so brilliantly, one could take him for a musically talented travelling gentleman. He looked at ease and his conversation is quite witty.
>
> Your Highness's most devoted and faithful servant,
> Prince Karl of Pfalz-Neuburg

Grand Prince Ferdinand was reading the letter when he heard a voice behind the door. He was alone in is study.
'Yes?'

The door opened, and a maid came in. This was unusual. He did not recognise her. Just one of the servants. However he saw that she was pretty.

'Your Highness, I...' Anna hesitated. Though daring, she was impressed by the grand prince's allure. She collected all her courage and said, 'Your Highness, I want to show you something.'

'What is that?' he asked indifferently. And then he saw a shoe, produced from Anna's apron. It was Vittoria's. He gazed at it. Then he said, looking puzzled, 'So? What is that?'

Anna hesitated. The grand prince did not move a hair seeing the shoe, and calmly went back to the letter. *Is it a mistake?* she wondered. She felt doubts creeping in. But she clearly remembered what she had seen. Pushing back her doubts and gathering all her daring and courage, she said, 'Your Highness, one night I was near that disused well, and... and... I saw...' She looked at the prince, who just kept reading.

Ferdinando was not reading. His mind was racing. *She saw it... What to do now?*

Seeing no reaction from the prince, Anna continued. 'I saw... well, I just want... err... See, Your Highness... I... I am getting married, and you see, to get married, do you understand? I... I...' She was babbling now.

Ferdinando lifted his head from the letter. 'I see, you need permission,' and he smiled.

'Yes, Your Highness.' Anna was relieved. She thought she had done it. Normally when the servants were allowed to marry, it came with a present, a small amount of money. And she was certain to obtain a substantial amount as a price of silence.

Ferdinando looked into her eyes. He got up and approached her slowly. She did not move. They were very close.

'So you are doing it for money,' he said sarcastically. He could see that she was frozen with fear.

Anna swallowed. *How could he read what I was thinking?*

The prince got even closer to her. Then he slowly removed Anna's bonnet, revealing her wavy dark chestnut hair. He ran his finger over her cheek, neck, and down her back in perfect calmness.

Anna gasped but could not move. Then he lowered her shirt to bare her shoulders. Anna was terrified. This was not what she had expected to happen. Clenching her fists was the only thing she could do.

'You can scream if you want to, but nobody will come. I do what I want.' Ferdinando was sneering. He put one hand on her back and drew her against him, while the forefinger of the other hand lifted Anna's chin. 'You have a nasty tongue, Maid.' He could hear her teeth chattering.

The crowd was gathered in the square. They were whispering. Then they heard a scream, a woman's scream, and suddenly it stopped. A man said,

'She fainted.'

'Poor woman,' a woman said.

'She deserved it. She offended the grand prince. Can you imagine?' another said.

'But still...'

'It's over. Let's go home.'

Anna was lying on the pavement, fainted. The blood was flowing from her mouth. The crowd was no longer there. She was alone. A doctor came, accompanied by a servant who held a spoon. It was wrapped in a cloth, and the end was red hot. The servant knelt beside her, handed the spoon to the doctor, and then opened Anna's mouth. The doctor quickly put the spoon in her mouth. It made a sizzling noise, and the smell of burnt human flesh rose. Anna opened her eyes wide open and fainted again. The doctor and his servant disappeared quickly. A shabby looking carriage stopped nearby, and the driver went down to shove Anna inside. Then it was gone.

From behind a column of the square, Paolo was watching everything, trembling. He felt guilty for not being able to help her. He saw Anna before she went to see the grand prince. He was worried, but she was all optimism, bursting with life, as always. He still could hear her saying, 'Don't worry, Paolo. It will go well, and then we can get married. And we'll have enough money. We'll be happy.' She had laughed happily.

That was the last time he saw her, and now she was gone, mutilated. He collapsed to his knees and wept. His handsome and gentle face was distorted in grief and his tall and slender frame was bent, shaking.

Paolo arrived in Leghorn in the early morning. He went into the first inn he found and asked about a woman who had arrived about a week ago. The innkeeper said, 'Are you talking about the tongueless woman?'

'Tongueless?' He feigned surprise.

'The only woman who arrived a week ago is the one with no tongue.'

'Is she quite dark?'

'Brown hair, yes. You are?'

'I am her brother. My sister was working in the household of a merchant near Florence, and then I lost contact. I went to see her there, and they told me she left for Leghorn.'

'Well, I don't know what happened, but if you want to see her, she is working in the inn on the port.'

It was not difficult to find the inn. It was filled with trading people and sailors. He went in, sat at the table in a quiet corner, and waited. Anna came to take his order and froze. Then she composed herself quickly. She stood in front of him and made the sign for a drink. Paolo nodded. She came back with a drink, and as she placed it on the table, Paolo took her hand in his. She shook it quickly and went back to the kitchen. Paolo waited. She did not come out. He ordered another drink and another, but Anna did not come back.

Hanover, Summer 1710

Händel arrived in Hanover after spending some time in his native town of Halle. He had been relieved to see his mother recovered from the death of her daughter the previous year, and happy to be a grandmother. His remaining sister, Dorothea Sophia, had given birth to a daughter recently and both mother and baby were doing well. If he had felt rather perplexed to hold a tiny wriggling baby in his arms, not knowing what to do, he had been more than happy to see his mother delighted.

Hanover in June was hot, but for someone who had just come from Italy, it was rather pleasant, compared to the scorching heat there. As was the custom, the court was in Herrenhausen. Baron Kielmansegg rushed back to Hanover to welcome Händel.

'Händel, just in time. I believe you will be more than happy to see Maestro Steffani?'

Händel hugged the baron and said, 'Is the maestro here in Hanover?'

'Not yet, but he will be here briefly in a few days.'

'Is he busy?'

'Oh, more than busy, I imagine. So, I heard you had a big success in Venice?'

Händel beamed. 'I can still hear the cheers.'

'The elector and the duchess are waiting for you in Herrenhausen. Shall we go?'

'Mother, Händel has arrived. Do you remember him? He came here for a short visit seven years ago.'

'Oh, I do remember him, and I think I know a little of what happened in Italy,' said Duchess Sophia with a witty smile.

'Did he go to Italy? You know a lot, Mother.'

'Yes I do,' she raised her eyebrows, 'are you surprised?'

'I did not see him very much the last time,' said the elector.

'Well, then you'll see him more this time, my son.'

Händel was at the keyboard when he saw the duchess appear, accompanied by her son Elector Georg Ludwig. He stopped playing, stood up and bowed.

'Do continue, Mr Händel. I enjoy it so,' said Duchess Sophia and took a seat.

Händel bowed again and resumed. Her son, Georg Ludwig, was standing by her side. Then he saw Prince Georg August appear, accompanied by his wife. Händel recognised her. He had seen her in Berlin!

'Oh, is that you, Mr Händel, whom I saw in Berlin?' Caroline of Ansbach was delighted. 'Of course I do remember you, Mr Händel. You impressed my aunt and the king.'

Duchess Sophia looked at her granddaughter-in-law and smiled to her tenderly. She saw her grandson gazing at his wife, madly in love, and could not be happier.

Things had evolved in Hanover since Händel's last visit. The duchess was still very healthy and full of life, however her formidable army of heirs was no longer there. On top of losing her second and fourth sons in a battle twenty years earlier, and her third son exiled, her fifth son, Christian Heinrich, was killed soon after Händel left Hanover seven years earlier. Then, unexpectedly, her daughter, Queen Sophia Charlotte had died two years later. Out of seven children, the duchess now had only two: her eldest son the elector, who, after the divorce fifteen years before remained unmarried, and her youngest son Ernst August. However the marriage of her grandson Prince Georg August to her late daughter's protégée, Caroline of Ansbach, brought youth and jolliness much needed to the Hanoverian court. Thus she could fulfil her late daughter's wish to see a happy marriage blessed with children. Nearly eighty now, the duchess thought she would not succeed the British throne, but her eldest son was healthy, as well as her grandson, and an heir born three years earlier. The lineage looked solid. On the other hand, in England, Queen Anne's health was in decline, making the House of Hanover much closer to the British crown.

At dinner, Duchess Sophia kept Händel beside her, enjoying the company of a young and attractive man.

'So, Mr Händel, how was Italy?'

'Excellent, Your Grace. I learned a lot there.'

'Oh, tell me where you went and who you saw.'

'I stayed in Florence, first, and then Rome. And I visited Venice and Naples.'

'How is Grand Prince Ferdinando?'

'He is well.'

'Did you see Grand Princess Violante?'

'Yes, Your Grace. She is the kindest soul I've ever met.'

'Did you see his mistress, the singer?'

'Yes. She is the most beautiful woman I've ever seen.'

'You are lucky, Mr Händel,' Elector Georg Ludwig said, intruding on the conversation. 'It is a pity that the kindest soul and the greatest beauty don't belong to the same woman.'

Duchess Sophia stood up suddenly and left the table. There was silence.

Her son the elector, puzzled, looked at her back and then followed her.

Georg Ludwig found his mother in her room with a casket on her lap and a bunch of letters scattered around.

'Mother...'

She did not answer. She was holding a letter.

'Mother, are you all right?'

She looked up at her son, her cheeks bathed in tears. She handed the letter to her son. Georg Ludwig looked at it. It was one of the numerous correspondences between his mother and his late sister, Sophia Charlotte. It was the letter from Sophia Charlotte talking about a young man full of talent; her husband had wanted to pay for his education in Italy. Händel, from Halle.

'I did not know about that,' said the son.

'I just remembered.'

'Mother...'

'You have to make him Kapellmeister, Görgen.' She called her son by his childhood nickname.

'But—'

'In her memory. You have to do it,' Duchess Sophia continued. 'My Figuelotte, poor Figuelotte. God is unfair to have taken her away so soon.' She was now calling her late daughter also by her nickname. She seemed to have gone back to those happy years where she still had all her children.

Georg Ludwig felt his eyes getting hot. The sad memory was revived. He had been devastated as much as his mother. Still, he composed himself quickly. 'Mother, I do understand, but I think he wants to go to England.'

'Then let him go, but you make him Kapellmeister before he leaves. He will come back.'

For the ageing Duchess Sophia, the sudden death of her only daughter was still a painful memory. Five years earlier, Sophia Charlotte had been visiting her mother in Hanover when she caught pneumonia and succumbed within a few days, leaving her husband, the king *in* Prussia, widowed for the second time and the whole family devastated. She was only thirty-six. The duchess still remembered vividly her daughter lying lifeless on a bitterly cold evening of January.

Elector Georg Ludwig was back in the dining room, smiling.

'Do not worry. She just felt tired. Quite normal for her age. She is sorry to make you all worried. But I can assure you, she is fine.'

The dinner resumed.

Baron Kielmansegg was standing before Duchess Sophia and her eldest son, the elector. The meeting was in the elector's office. The duchess could not stop herself from finding the baron good looking.

'If the information gathered is correct, Händel was in Berlin in 1702, eight years ago, and saw Frederick I in Prussia and Your Grace's late

daughter Sophia Charlotte there,' said Kielmansegg.
'And he refused to be the court musician there?' Georg Ludwig said.
'Apparently so. After that, he spent three years in Hamburg learning opera before going to Italy. I met him in Venice.'
'So he is really talented.'
'I've never seen such a virtuoso, and I've seen a lot of musicians in my life.'
'Is there anything worrying about that man?'
'I could not find anything, apart from...'
'Apart from?'
'Well, he fell in love with a singer in Italy, and the singer in question happened to be the mistress of Grand Prince Ferdinando de' Medici.'
'Oh, I know that!' exclaimed Duchess Sophia.
'There was a rumour that they tried to elope, but apparently it did not happen. He came here on his own, and does not seem to be hiding anyone. I checked,' Kielmansegg continued methodically.
'And the singer in question?' asked Georg Ludwig. 'Who is she?'
'It's Vittoria Tarquini, wife of Farinel,' said the duchess. 'So where is she then?'
'We don't know,' said Kielmansegg.
'You don't know?'
'No. She disappeared.'
The mother and her son looked at each other. Kielmansegg observed them and saw sadness in Duchess Sophia's eyes.
When the baron was out of the office, Duchess Sophia spoke. 'God... Do you remember her? Vittoria Tarquini?'
'Not really.'
'She was so young, and astonishingly beautiful. I really did not understand why she married a man like Farinel.'
'So what do you think, Mother? What happened?'
'It's not a good sign, my son. She tried to escape and disappeared. You can guess what happened... Grand Prince Ferdinando is a powerful man, and he does not have a good reputation. I mean, lovers... Poor girl...' The duchess looked away.

Händel was summoned to Duchess Sophia's boudoir, her private sitting room.
'Madam, you asked for me.'
'Yes, Mr Händel.' The duchess looked at him. 'Would you sit down.' She smiled, tapping the place beside her.
Händel obliged, feeling quite uneasy to be treated with such familiarity.
'Mr Händel?'
'Yes, madam.'

'My grandson Georg Augustus and his wife Caroline are delighted to hear you play.'
'It is my honour, madam,' Händel replied politely.
'It is so nice to see a happy marriage.'
'Yes, madam.'
'Mr Händel?'
'Yes, madam.'
The duchess hesitated, and after a brief pause, said, 'I would like you to tell me everything about Berlin.'
'Madam...'
'You know what I mean. I want to know everything from when you were there. Absolutely everything.'
He looked at her. She seemed sincere. 'Madam, it was a long time ago.'
'Make an effort to remember.'
'Shall I start from the beginning?'
'Do.'
Duchess Sophia listened. She devoured every word Händel told her what he could remember.
'Do you think my daughter was happy there, Mr Händel?'
'There is no doubt, madam.'
'Really?' Her face brightened.
'I was very young then, but still I could see it. I can tell you, madam, that she was happy.' Händel clearly remembered the couple seated side by side, watching him play, smiling to each other, or the king holding his wife's hand affectionately; or going for a walk together, with the king giving his arm to her.
'Was she loved?'
'The king was in love with her, madam. And she loved him. I've never seen such a loving couple.'
'Oh...' the duchess put her hands on her chest.
'Yes. I heard that the king was so much in love with his queen that he forgot about his mistress, madam.'
The duchess laughed.
'Um...' Händel hesitated.
'Yes? What is it?'
Händel straightened himself. 'Madam, I was worried, when I presented myself seven years go, that your daughter the queen's letter mentioned my refusal of the king's offer.'
Duchess Sophia smiled with a hint of sadness. 'I can tell you now, Mr Händel, it did not. But she told me after your departure. Oh, she was a kind soul.'

Georg Ludwig was consulting his trusted friend Baron Kielmansegg.

'So, what do you think? I have no choice. It is mother's order. I have to make Händel Kapellmeister. That's what my late sister wanted, and my mother is adamant. Well I do understand.' The elector looked at the baron. 'The problem is that the post was created especially for Agostino Steffani by my father. In those days, Steffani had a lot to do.'

'I see your point, Your Highness.'

'We can always revive the title for Händel, but what could he do? Not very much.'

'He can give music lessons,' Kielmansegg said no more. But it was obvious he meant the lessons for the elector's three daughters by his mistress.

The opera company had been suspended on the death of Duke Ernst August in 1698, and the post of Kapellmeister had fallen with it. The reason for the sudden decline in operatic enterprise in 1698 was simple, and it had nothing to do with the taste of his son, Georg Ludwig. The opera company had been funded through the income from the Bishopric of Osnabrück, which reverted after Ernst August's death to the Roman Catholic side of the family. With an expensive European war to fight during the next decade, there was no alternative source of money in the budget in Hanover for a revival of the opera, and it was still in abeyance in 1710. The only thing that remained of the splendour, the orchestra, consisted of only seventeen instrumentalists on payroll.

'I think it is a good idea, still,' Baron Kielmansegg said. 'It's an honorific title.'

'For a man willing to go away?'

'Your Highness will have an informer there, if you make him belong to you.'

Silence, then the elector nodded. 'What do you think of him?'

'A genius as a musician. Ambitious as a man. And independent. He does not like to be told what to do.'

'Not appropriate for a Kapellmeister, then.'

'I can find you a man more suitable.'

'My mother, Kielmansegg...'

'Sorry, Your Highness,' the baron made a little smile, 'anyway, do you want him to stay here all the time?'

'No. You are right. I am not a huge music lover, unlike you. Anyway, he cannot do very much here with just a small orchestra and a very limited number of singers. I have no choice but to cut costs for that war... that stupid war.'

'Then use him for what you wish under cover of being your Kapellmeister. I do not expect this young man to be as skilled as Steffani, I mean as a diplomat, but music is an excellent tool to get into the nobility and gentry.'

'How much, then?'

'One thousand thalers?'

'That much only to let him go?'

'It is not too much for a Kapellmeister and an informer combined, I think. But...'

'Tell.'

'We have to be careful to not let Händel know about it.'

'Why, Johann?'

'This is the best way to guard the secret. And Händel is a proud and stubborn man. He does not like to be used.'

'So he is quite perfect.'

'Yes. He will be a visitor representing Hanover as Kapellmeister, and he is not from the electoral family. The queen cannot refuse to receive him.'

'I see.' The elector was becoming convinced and liked the idea. 'How is my half-sister?' he asked, feeling a bit relaxed.

'Expecting.'

'Again?'

'I keep her busy.'

Georg Ludwig laughed. 'Let him come, Kielmansegg. We shall have a talk. No, wait. Let's have lunch with just him, my family, and you – more informal and casual – and I will tell my mother of his nomination. She will be pleased. Oh well, I'll make it the nomination lunch. Your wife is welcome, if she wants to come.'

'I thank you, Your Highness, but I think she will prefer to stay home. How about Steffani? Shall I let him come?'

'Is he back now?'

'Yes. He is back as Pope Clement's apostolic vicar. Travels a lot.'

'Apostolic vicar.' Georg Ludwig raised a hand and nodded. 'Very impressive.'

Alone in his office, the elector contemplated the situation. As his mother, Duchess Sophia, was an heir to the British throne, the big question was, when? That was not only Hanover's concern. A death of a monarch always triggers troubles and political turmoil, and with the ongoing war, many countries were sending spies and informers to watch over Queen Anne's health. He remembered meeting her, his second cousin, in London thirty years ago, sparking rumours of a potential marriage. He was then twenty and Anne fifteen. *We were both young, very young.* He was saddened to think that now he had to track her health closely. This was politics. *A Hanoverian Kapellmeister is a very good idea,* he tried to convince himself, though he doubted that Queen Anne would be easily fooled by that.

The nomination lunch was the most pleasant thing Händel had ever experienced at a court. Duchess Sophia was delighted. Steffani was present. Electoral Prince Georg August was much more interested in music than his father, as was his wife Caroline, both happy with the nomination. With Steffani back from Rome, the conversation was all about music.

'Congratulations, Mr Händel, for your opera in Venice. The news reached Rome quickly,' Steffani said.

'Opera? Oh, tell us about it,' said Caroline, excited.

The elector remembered that the family had permanent boxes at the theatres in Venice. He felt embarrassed about not being able to go there because of the need to save expenses. While Händel was busy explaining his opera, Steffani saw clouds passing though the elector's mind.

Agostino Steffani was an able diplomat, and he knew how to change the conversation. 'Did you know that Cardinal Grimani is deceased?' he asked Händel, and then he turned to the young electoral couple. 'Cardinal Grimani was the one who wrote the libretto for Mr Händel's opera in Venice.'

'Yes, I knew. Margherita Durastante wrote to me about it. Do you know more about his death, Father? He was still young.'

'He died in Naples. He was fifty-five. There was a rumour that he was poisoned by his enemies, but I don't believe it.'

'Poisoned?' said Caroline in horror. 'By whom?'

'Politicians, madam,' said Steffani.

'Oh, Maestro Steffani, no politics, please!' said the duchess. 'We are here today to celebrate the nomination of Mr Händel. Tell me about music in Italy.'

Steffani turned again to Händel. 'You probably knew that Caldara replaced you to work for the Prince of Cerveteri, but your music is very often played in his palace.'

'It was a very nice experience.' Händel remembered the jolly household, full of children. 'I remember you were there for the Easter oratorio, Maestro.'

'Yes, I was. Oh, tell the story of the pope's wrath, Mr Händel,' Steffani beamed, 'such a story, typical Roman!'

So Händel told them of the soprano singer being replaced by a castrato after the first performance, the consequence of panic rehearsing, and also the stage transfer at the last minute, to the delight of all.

'You are going to London, we hear, Kapellmeister,' said Elisabetta.

Händel, Elisabetta Pilotti-Schiavonetti, and her cellist husband, Giovanni Schiavonetti, were rehearsing in a small music room.

'Yes. The elector is generous to let me go.'

'We are going as well,' said Giovanni, tuning his cello.

Händel looked at him and the singer in turn. 'Oh, are you?'

'Yes, we are,' said Elisabetta. 'The music here is getting smaller and smaller, and we got a contract in London, so we are going there on loan. I think it helps the elector to have fewer salaries to pay.'

'You are not the only ones,' said Händel, remembering Giuseppe Boschi and his wife Francesca in Venice.

Händel's duties were light, as opera was in abeyance. The routine music of the Hanover court was in the hands of a Konzertmeister, Jean-Baptiste Farinel, who was in charge of the court musicians. Händel was only expected to provide music for occasional entertainments, mainly as a keyboard player. However, this time, as a Kapellmeister, he was closely associated with the court poet, Mauro. Ortensio Mauro was extremely old, in his late seventies, and he looked it. But he still had an active brain. He used to act as a diplomat, like Steffani who was a close friend of the poet. Taking advantage of the light duties, Händel paid visits to Mauro as often as possible. He wanted to know about the glorious period in which Hanover had been one of the most advanced centres of opera in Europe. Mauro had provided libretti to Steffani, and together they produced eight operas. Händel particularly enjoyed Mauro's descriptions of how the opera *Henrico Leone (Henry the Lion)* was produced to inaugurate the new court theatre in Hanover. Then the conversation turned to the intellectual circle of the court.

'Oh, I have to warn you, Maestro, don't mention Leibniz in front of the elector,' said the poet.

'May I ask why?'

'The elector is quite annoyed with him. His father commissioned Leibniz to write a history of the House of Brunswick from the time of Charlemagne or even earlier, and he has still not finished it.'

'Oh, so it was quite a long time ago?'

'Well, the aim of the book was to justify his candidature to be elector. He was Duke of Brunswick-Lüneburg. The duke died twelve years ago. So…'

'I do understand the elector's frustration,' said Händel.

'Leibniz is an extremely meticulous man, and he took the commission very seriously.'

'Is he still working on it?'

'Yes. He did not abandon it. It will be finished one day, and it will be an enormous work. I personally like him, and Duchess Sophia considers him a friend.' Mauro smiled. 'I forgot to ask you, Maestro. I am getting old. Did you want to talk to me about something?'

Händel had forgotten as well. He nearly jumped. 'Oh, yes, Signor Mauro, if possible. I would like to have a text for a cantata on a small scale. I have a very good soprano here.'

'Elisabetta?'

'Yes.'

'I like her. She is very versatile.'

Händel came back feeling quite tipsy after supper out in town. He quickly undressed himself, dived into his bed, and soon he was drifting away.

It was so dark that Händel could not see anything.
'Oh, I'm so cold, so lonely... please help me, please...'
It was a woman's voice. Then he saw a shadow. It got closer. He thought he had seen that shadow before. Closer and closer, he saw it was a woman. The voice came from her. She was extending her hand towards him.
'Please, please... I am cold... so cold...'
Händel tried to grab her hand, but the more he tried, the more the hand was out of reach.
'Please... please...'
The voice was dying. He tried to tell her to stop, but no voice came from his throat. Then he tripped. He fell but found no ground. He continued to fall and fall into the abyss. He screamed.

Händel woke up, terrified. His chest was moist with sweat. He found himself sitting up in a comfortable bed. He looked around. He recognised the room he was given in Herrenhausen. It was early morning, and the birds were busy outside. He could see the ray of pale light between the shutters. Händel got up and opened the windows. The cool air was refreshing. *I had too much wine last night*, he thought.

Pratolino, Autumn 1710

Marco, the faithful valet to Grand Prince Ferdinando de' Medici was engaged in an animated conversation with his fellow servants.

'I still cannot believe it,' he said.

'Yeah, it is a surprise,' said another.

'I always saw him go to the church rather reluctantly,' said the third, 'he always preferred to stay in the gardens rather than the church.'

'What are you talking about?' said the fourth voice, and they all jumped.

'Your Highness! You scared me!' said Marco.

Grand Prince Ferdinand smiled and repeated, 'So, what are you talking about?'

'Grand Prince, it's Paolo, the gardener.'
'Paolo?'
'Do you know who he is, Your Highness?'
'Not really.'
'Well, Paolo was a gardener here, and he was flirting with A—' Marco stopped himself, just in time, from saying Anna. 'With a girl.'
'And?'
'Well, he entered the monastery, Your Highness, the monastery!'
'And the girl is in tears, right?'
'Er, no, Grand Prince. The girl... the girl eloped. Yes, eloped with another man!'
'Oh, that's why.'
'Yes, Your Highness, but still, to enter a monastery!'
'Well, that's how he found inner peace, I suppose.'

Paolo could not find inner peace. He was tormented. No matter how hard he worked in the fields until he collapsed of exhaustion, his nights were haunted by nightmares. The last time he went to see Anna, he'd realised that she was pregnant, and she'd looked ill. She had still refused to see him, and he'd had to hide himself to observe her. One thing was certain. It was not his child. He had never touched her. He could only guess that it was the grand prince's. The only thing he could do was to blame himself. Because he had not wanted to go to see the grand prince, Anna had decided to do it herself. Because he had been too scared to keep the shoe, Anna had snatched it from him. He had wanted to tell the priest, give the shoe to him, and try to forget, but Anna had been determined.

'Paolo, you don't realise the chance we have,' she had said. 'You are too scared. I will do it if you don't want to.'
'No, Anna, don't do that!' he'd replied.
'Would you do it then?'
Paolo had lowered his head and shook it. 'I can't...'
'Then I have no choice.'
'Yes, there is a choice. We give it to the priest.'
'Oh Paolo, my little Paolo, you are pathetic...'
If he had done it, she would not be there, mutilated, pregnant, and ill. Those were the signs of his guilt. Oh, how he would rather be forever blamed and even belittled by Anna for his cowardice than see her now in that appalling condition. Once slender but fit, his body was like a skeleton, and his straight blond hair was getting thinner and thinner.

Father Pietro was troubled. He was tending Paolo, who had collapsed in the fields again. Paolo was delirious and raging with fever. The monk was sure that the words uttered by the former gardener of Grand Prince Ferdinando meant something.

'Anna, forgive me, forgive me... Was it the grand prince? Was it? No, no, don't go. I'll go to see the grand prince myself. Don't go... The shoe, it's the shoe...'

After some discreet investigation, there was no doubt that Paolo was talking about the girl who was punished in the square for offending the grand prince. Paolo knew something, but Father Pietro decided to keep it to himself.

Paolo opened his eyes. The first thing he saw was the friendly face of Father Pietro.

'You won, Brother Paolo. You won your battle,' he said softly, smiling.

Paolo was still very weak. He looked at Father Pietro, who helped him sit on the bed, placing pillows for support behind his bony back.

The priest took a bowl of broth, and stirred it with a spoon.

'Here, Paolo, make an effort to eat. Just one spoon.'

Paolo swallowed the broth. He could feel the warm soup going down to his empty stomach. Another spoon, and he was feeling the warmth expand from inside. Then, reality struck. Anna. Guilt. Paolo burst into tears.

'Father Pietro, please, please, teach me how to write.'

'Brother Paolo...'

'Please. You know I am suffering. You know I know something. But I cannot tell. It is too terrible... Please, please...'

Father Pietro left Paolo, who had fallen asleep, happy to see that there was still the will to live in the young man. However, Paolo did not recover. His state deteriorated quickly.

'Father Pietro.' Paolo stretched his hand. It was just skin and bone.

Father Pietro took it in his hands. It was cold. 'Paolo, courage. You will get better, like last time.'

'Father Pietro, I will not have enough time to learn how to write. I don't have enough time. I have to tell you...' said Paolo, struggling to breathe.

Father Pietro was shocked. He knew that the grand prince was not all innocent, but such a sin was beyond belief. The grand prince a murderer. He was looking for explanations. Maybe the grand prince had had a heated argument with his mistress and lost control, or perhaps he was insulted. Father Pietro could blame the man's nature. But what about the possible rape of the maid? It was only supposition. Paolo did not witness it. Father Pietro's only hope was that he could find Anna and that she would deliver another version of what happened. He did not have a lot of time. Paolo was dying, and he wanted to assure Paolo that Anna was cared for. And he hoped she would tell him it was not rape.

Father Pietro arrived in Leghorn one early morning. He went straight to the inn on the port. The inn was not open yet. He went to the back door and banged on it.

'It's not open yet!' A young voice shouted from inside. The door opened abruptly, and a young servant girl stood there, looking furious. 'Oh... Father, what can I do for you? Hot soup?' The girl forced herself to smile.

'No, thank you. I want to know about the tongueless woman who works here.'

'Well, I am new here. I don't know very much. I'll have to ask the matron. Do enter, please, Father.'

Father Pietro found himself in the kitchen. An old woman was busy cooking. Seeing a monk, she pulled out a chair for him and offered him a bowl of soup. Father Pietro declined politely and started a conversation with the cook. When the matron arrived, the buxom woman invited the priest to go to the dining room, where the chairs were still up on the tables. Father Pietro helped her to lower two chairs and sat on one. She talked first.

'Father, the girl told me you want to know about Anna, the tongueless woman.'

'Yes. Is she here?'

'Well, no. Not anymore.' She looked at him and continued, 'Father, I don't know how much you know about Anna, but I don't know very much about her. I know her name is Anna – that's the only thing she could write – but I don't even know where she came from.'

'How did she come to you, then?'

'Well, I know a man who provides wine and other stuff for me, and sometimes he asks me a little favour and gives me a bit of money, just to cover the cost. Some time ago, I took in a very young girl who had lost her parents. The man said she needed shelter until she found someone to look after her. I asked about her relatives, and the man said that because her parents left debts, if she were in view, she might be taken and sold to pay for them. So I accepted her. Anyway, that girl did not stay long. One night a couple came to collect her. Apparently they were her relatives, because the little girl ran into the arms of the woman, calling her *aunt*. It was quite touching, because everyone was crying. So I thought I did a good thing.'

'Well, I am sure your action was blessed by God.'

The woman smiled. There was nobody within earshot but, nonetheless, she looked around and lowered her voice. 'Then that same man came back and asked me to take in a woman with no tongue. But not for a short time; he asked me to employ the woman. He said she was all right, young and healthy, and the money he was offering was quite needed. I hesitated, but he insisted, because he knows I am discreet. So I accepted, and Anna arrived. I was surprised, because she was young but not in good shape. At first, I imagined that she was born tongueless, but I could see that was not the case. Something happened and she lost her tongue! She was suffering, and she was very distressed. But she was strong and hard-working. I decided to not question her. Anyway, she could only make gestures, so…'

'So why is she not here anymore?'

'I did not know she was pregnant. Still, as she was hard-working and was quite a help for me, I was ready to help her in return, but…' The woman looked at the monk. 'You know, Father, I have an inn. Lots of people come in here. I cannot keep somebody with a disease.'

'Is she ill?'

'Father, I am really sorry for Anna, but she has syphilis.'

A chill ran down Father Pietro's spine. 'Syphilis…'

'Yes, Father. I had to get rid of her when I discovered it. Well, it was the doctor who told me to do that as soon as possible.'

'I suppose you had no choice…'

'She is in the hospice, but she does not know about her disease. I told her she needs treatment to get rid of the disease and that she could be better soon. Father?'

'Yes?'

'Was I wrong to lie to her? See, she had not known she was pregnant. If you had seen her distress when she realised that… And on top of that, dying of a disease… No, I could not tell her the truth…'

'I do not blame you for not telling the truth to that woman.' Father Pietro's hope collapsed. That was the answer he did not wish to have.

'Oh thank you, Father, I…'

'Yes?'

'I suppose you know better about her than me. If it is not too indiscreet, I would like to know more about her.'

'Unfortunately I don't know very much more than you. I was asked by a dying young man to go to see his sweetheart. Apparently something went terribly wrong.'

'I see.' She turned her head and brushed tears away.

Father Pietro arrived at the hospice with a heavy heart. Anna was already dead and buried, with her child in her belly. Father Pietro stood in front of the communal burial hole in the remotest corner of the graveyard where the diseased people were thrown. All he could do was to pray.

Back in Pratolino, he found that Paolo was dead.

'I am sorry, Father Pietro. I did my best, but Brother Paolo was too weak.'

'Do not blame yourself, Brother Eugenio. Did he suffer?'

'No, it was very peaceful. It looked like he was going to sleep.'

'So finally he found peace.'

'Yes, Father Pietro.'

'Did he say anything?'

'Just before he passed, he said "Anna" softly and smiled, and then he was gone.'

'Poor Paolo...'

Father Pietro could not be at peace. This was murder. Three people were dead. For the first time in his life, he felt anger. The grand duke poured money into the churches and monasteries. It was thanks to him that the monastery could survive relatively well. But his son was living an immoral life and committing murder, without even being tried, and the monastery kept celebrating mass to thank the Medici family.

Florence, Palazzo Pitti, Winter 1710

'He is not well, I know for certain,' Princess Violante said. 'That's why I asked you to come.' She was pale, even paler than usual.

'Princess, could you describe to me what you observed?' Antonio Salvi asked methodically.

'Well, he is mad one day, and then he is normal, perfectly normal, as if he is having waves of madness. And...'

'And?'

'When he is mad, he is really terrifying. He scares me. And those spots that take ages to heal, they are truly disgusting.'

'Do those spots leak?'

'Yes.'

'Does he have a fever sometimes?'

'Yes. But it is not related to his fits of madness.'

'Could you tell me when all that started?'

'Oh, I am not sure...'

'Was it before his trip to Venice?'

Grand Princess Violante considered and said, 'No.'

'Princess.'

'Yes?'

'Do not get offended by my question, please. It is very important that you answer me honestly.'

'Yes.'

'Have you shared a bed with the grand prince recently?'

She stopped, stared at Salvi, and then said firmly, 'No, Doctor Salvi. He lives with his lovers, male and female. I am still his wife, but no, there is not...' She looked down. This was humiliating.

'Grand Princess.'

'Yes?'

'Then continue not to do so. I think it is syphilis.'

Her eyes widened with horror. 'Are you—?'

'Yes, I am quite certain. And I think he contracted it in Venice, which is quite common. Do not worry. It is safe as long as you do not have physical contact with him.'

'So… is he… doomed?'

'Yes. I am sorry.'

'My God…' Her knees gave way. Doctor Salvi was quick enough to support her. Her chambermaid was called, bringing a small glass of liquor.

'Take this, Grand Princess. It will help.'

With her hands shaking, she swallowed the liquid. It was quite strong and sweet, making her feel warm again.

Dr Salvi ordered that Prince Gian Gastone be called to visit the grand princess.

Gian Gastone found his sister-in-law in her boudoir on her daybed.

'Sister, you are so pale.'

'Oh, Gian Gastone. I'm fine. I feel much better now.' She sat up. 'Brother, honestly, you should stop drinking.'

'Can you smell it, Sister?'

'Yes, quite strongly.' She stared at Gian Gastone, who smiled. She then glanced quickly at the maid and said, 'Shall we go for a walk in the garden, just two of us?'

Cosimo III watched two figures going into the garden. One was thin and frail, and the other was tall and fat. No doubt it was Violante and Gian Gastone, as usual. He returned to his desk and did not see his second son stop abruptly.

'Oh God…' Gian Gastone was speechless.

Violante saw her brother-in-law going pale.

'I am sorry, Brother, but I had to tell someone, and you are the only person. I know this is terrible news for you.'

They resumed walking in silence. Gian Gastone's mind was in turmoil. He was even unable to feel compassion for Violante. He was terrified for himself. His older brother was dying, and it was just a question of time. His father, in his late sixties, would not live much longer. Then what happens? Becoming the grand duke was the last thing on earth Gian Gastone wanted. His life was a mess; he felt he was born to be miserable. The only support he could have was his sister-in-law, and he could feel her compassion.

Violante knew too well what he was feeling. She was not as terrified as Gian Gastone, but she was worried. What happens when her husband dies? Would she be expelled from Florence? Where to go then? Go back to Munich? She was quite confident her eldest brother, Elector of Bavaria, would welcome her back. But how about her life she had built in Florence where she'd been living for more than twenty years? It was her affection for her brother-in-law that allowed her to slowly regain herself. She decided not to think beyond now. She knew what to do. She stopped, took Gian Gastone's hands, and looked into his eyes.

'Brother, I will do my best. I will look for the best of the best doctors in Tuscany. Miracles happen.'

'Sister…'

'And I will pray. I will ask all the churches to pray for him. Could you do the same, for me?'

It was not hope but the warmth of Violante that made Gian Gastone feel better, just a little.

Chapter 13 : A Saxon in London : Triumphal début? (1710-1711)

Dear Telemann,

I am writing to you from Düsseldorf.

My opera was well received in Venice. From there I went back to Halle. I really wanted to see my mother and another person dear to me, my teacher Zachow.

My mother is still mourning but happy to be a grandmother. Her eyesight is getting very weak, so she could hardly see the set of silver plates I brought from Italy. They were given to me by Grand Prince Ferdinando.

Then I headed to Hanover, where I was made Kapellmeister with the authorisation to go to London. I am really sorry I could not visit you. I was so near Eisenach, but the appointment and the arrangements to be made to go to London took all my time.

I stopped in Düsseldorf to pay homage to the elector and electress. Maestro Steffani had been there until last year, before going back to Hanover, and he had composed operas for the carnival season. The court poet and librettist Pallavicini talked of Steffani with affection. They knew each other in Padua when the poet was a child and Steffani a treble in the choir. I also had permission to consult scores. There is a possibility I may be able to compose an opera here, thanks to Steffani, who suggested it to the elector and electress. Pallavicini told me he has a few ideas.

After Düsseldorf, I will be off to London. I am to meet Baron Kielmansegg at The Hague, and we will travel to London together. He will be accompanying me to introduce me to the queen. My visit to London will be short, as I will be on my leave, but my goal is to be an opera composer. Unless the ongoing war is over quickly and the elector decides to revive operas in Hanover, there is not much I can do there. However the position of Kapellmeister gives me financial security, and I am grateful for that.

I really like Baron Kielmansegg. He is kind and trustworthy. And he is very supportive.

I am delighted that you will be a father soon. Many congratulations! I wish you all the happiness that you and your delightful wife deserve.

Please write to me. It is with extreme happiness that I receive your letters. I will write to you again from London.

Your most humble, devoted, faithful, and obedient servant, friend, and brother,
Georg Friederich Händel

London, Autumn 1710 – Autumn 1711

The dissolution of parliament took place on 21 September. Many of the nobility and gentry were now busy campaigning for the general election in their constituencies, leaving little room for entertainment.

At the Queen's Theatre in Haymarket, Owen Swiney started the season on 4 October with a play. Now that he had actors as well, he would be busy. His plan was to present different plays until mid-November and then start operas with the revival of *L'Idapse fedele (Hydapses)* from the previous season. This was the first opera sung throughout in Italian with Nicolini in the title role, and was received well. Swiney was confident. Despite the raising of the admission fee and the opposition ridiculing the singers as squeaking Italians, the audience was larger than before. By now the Queen's Theatre was the home of authentic and genuine Italian opera. The only shadow was the overdue fees for the singers. Swiney was counting on this season to allow him to catch up on any payments.

Then the bombshell came in the form of the Lord Chamberlain's order. Owen Swiney was in total shock. He was to go back to Drury Lane with the actors, leaving the Queen's Theatre and the management of operas in the hands of William Collier and Aaron Hill. MP for Truro, William Collier had managed to acquire a licence to operate Drury Lane theatre after its closure. However Collier had no intention of managing the theatre himself, appointing Aaron Hill as his general manager. The publication of *The Ottoman Empire* had made Hill noticed, and it was the young author's impressive social connections rather than any intrinsic managerial ability that let Collier appoint him. Like the previous manager Christopher Rich, Collier just wanted power and money and nothing else. And it did not take long for Collier to realise that the rival Queen's Theatre, with operas, was much more lavish and luxurious. His theatre, reopened now, with just a few actors remaining, was allowed to present plays with musical entertainments - anything apart from operas.

This order was the result of an active manoeuvre by William Collier who used his court influence. The new Lord Chamberlain, Charles Talbot, 1st Duke of Shrewsbury, replacing Henry Grey by order of the queen, was convinced by Collier who exploited cleverly the problems within Queen's Theatre. Collier insinuated the conflict between the English actors and Italian singers in the minds of the Lord Chamberlain, influential nobility, and gentry. Subtly he pointed out that Owen Swiney was friendly with the actors and that Nicolini had filed a suit against him for non-payment.

On 6 November the Lord Chamberlain, Charles Talbot, signed the order. He and his wife were music enthusiasts, and the presence of John Stanley, another music lover, as secretary rather than some political beast was comforting. After consultation, it was agreed that it was a good solution. It would revive Drury Lane theatre again with a capable and hard-working manager. They did not know the true nature of William Collier.

Swiney was more than worried. He was devastated at losing control of the Queen's Theatre. This was not what he'd anticipated would happen. *Why should I go with the actors? Why did the Lord Chamberlain not just transfer the actors to Drury Lane? Collier must have done something*, he thought. *I should stay here for the opera, and Collier should remain at Drury Lane with the actors. That is the way it should be.* The most worrying thing was the contract with Nicolini. Swiney was personally liable for paying the castrato the fabulous sum of eight hundred guineas per annum that he had promised. How? The rent for the theatre of six hundred pounds that he would get from Collier was not enough. Nicolini was getting anxious for his promised salary not being paid. But Swiney had no choice. It was an order. Defeated, Swiney left the Queen's Theatre.

William Collier and Aaron Hill arrived in the Queen's Theatre together, in theory. The reality was that Collier left the theatre in the hands of Hill, as had been the case with Drury Lane. Though inexperienced, the stage became Hill's lifelong passion. It was the excitement and colour of the theatre world that really appealed to him. The scenery, the rich and exotic costumes – it was a whole world that he could create, and he found it irresistible. The company that Hill took over at the Queen's Theatre was headed by the most successful castrato, Nicolini, who was halfway through a three-year contract. Hill could not believe his chance to be the manager of such a prestigious theatre.

What Hill failed to see was that Collier was vicious, just like Christopher Rich. Collier persuaded Hill to pay the rent of six hundred pounds per year for the right to run opera, claiming to be generous and trusting in Hill's ability. With the flattery, Collier also made Hill personally financially responsible. Hill trusted Collier, and did not think of protecting himself. A young man of twenty-five, recently married, with a position as the manager of London's prestigious opera house, Hill's future looked brilliant.

With everything in place, helped by the presence of Nicola Haym, it was a relatively easy start for Aaron Hill. What he noticed first was that opera was extremely expensive to produce. The singers' salaries took up more than half of the whole expense. This, together with the cost of the props, stage sets, costumes, and musicians, all added up to more than twice the cost of ordinary plays. Hill soon realised that he was taking an enormous gamble with Queen's Theatre. However, a true entrepreneur, he enjoyed the thrill of risk-taking, and he was delighted and fascinated by the lavish opera environment. Although signs of friction with the new management appeared immediately, he was not worried. *Nothing can surprise me after what I went through*, he thought. Just a few months before, at Drury Lane theatre, he had been assaulted with swords drawn by supporters of the deposed Rich, trying to take control of the theatre. *Nothing could surpass such violence.*

The frustration was, in fact, caused by Hill's lack of experience. His good looks and polite manners were not enough. The singers were happy to be separated from the actors, who called them Italian squeaks, but they missed Swiney. Hill had no idea how to manage the capricious singers.

'A rehearsal room?' Hill looked up at Nicolini.

'Yes, Mr Hill. I want to have a private rehearsal room, just with *continuo*.'

'Continuo?' Hill was confused. Though quite fluent in Italian, he lacked in musical terms. He did not want to look ignorant. 'No problem, Signor Nicolini. Leave it to me.'

Nicolini was appalled. The rented room, in the back of a coffee house, was too small and too shabby. Standing in the middle of the room, he whispered, 'I will make the musicians' ears bleed with my voice. This is far too small... Well, in that case, I have an idea.'

'In your own house, Signor Nicolini?' asked Hill.

'Yes. The room you rented is too small. Do you know that I have a big voice, Mr Hill?' Nicolini said casually. 'The whole audience can hear me, even the people in the remotest corner of the theatre.'

'Of course I know,' Hill replied.

Of course you don't, ignorant idiot, Nicolini smiled.

'In Nicolini's house? No,' said Nicola Haym. 'It is not good,' the cellist said bluntly.

'Why?'

'Why?' Haym stared at Hill. 'Do you know he is a star? He has his admirers flocking around all the time. It will be impossible to rehearse.' Haym was getting irritated. 'And, everything will be known before we start a new production! There will be no novelty to attract the audience!'

'Oh...What shall I do, then?'

'Rent a bigger room, Mr Hill. Not in a coffee house. A proper room. A proper music room. Do you understand?'

From 22 November 1710, the Queen's Theatre presented operas twice a week, drawing in reasonable audiences. It began with a revival of *L'Idapse fedele (Hydapses),* as had been planned by Swiney. It was during Hill's first month of management that Händel and Baron Kielmansegg arrived in London.

After the stay in Düsseldorf, Händel joined Baron Kielmansegg in The Hague. There he was busy getting ready to go to London. He'd been dressed from top to bottom to make himself presentable to Queen Anne as Hanover's Kapellmeister. Why in The Hague? Because it was cheaper, and there was ample choice there.

'Are you ready, Georg?' the baron asked, watching Händel finish packing.

'Yes, Baron. So, tomorrow morning?' replied the young composer, wrapping carefully the stave-ruler.

'Yes. We are lucky. The wind is favourable.'

'It will be my very first travel on a ship, Baron. I am a little worried.'

'Well, you have to experience it to know if you are fine, or not...'

'Oh...so I might be seasick?'

'That's possible,' the baron grinned, 'never mind. Let's go to have a last stein of ale on solid ground.'

They left the inn, like two brothers. A veiled woman, a Gipsy, watched them from behind a column nearby. She was staring at Händel and murmured, 'You avoided such a destructive love, but you will be blind to the constructive love...' She lowered her head, and disappeared noiselessly.

Händel noticed that the baron became much chattier when they disembarked. The latter was careful not to talk too much in the presence of German-speaking people. Now in the coach approaching London, Baron Kielmansegg felt more relaxed.

'I am sorry that the opera project in Düsseldorf came to nothing,' said the baron, 'but I am rather glad of it, since we were able to arrive early to avoid the bad sea.'

'Could it have been bad?'

'It could have been a shipwreck,' the baron looked at the young man, serious.

Händel stared at the baron. He had taken the smooth crossing for granted. He was impressed to think that all the grand tour people he saw in Italy crossed the sea, risking their lives.

'So, Georg, do you feel ready to go to court?'

'Are we going straight there?'

The baron laughed. 'No. We will spend some time in London to let the noise arrive in the queen's ears, and then we will go.'

'Do you know where I am staying? Am I staying with you?' Händel was not feeling confident. 'Do they speak French?'

'You can speak French at court, but everywhere else you need to have a basic knowledge of English.'

'Oh...'

'Do not worry, Georg. I will find you an English teacher. We shall take a lodging somewhere to begin with, but I will have to find you an accommodation when it is time for me to go back to Hanover.'

'I thank you, Baron.'

'Oh, just a thought. Do you have anything ready to play for the queen?'

'I brought the score of the cantata *Apollo e Dafne* with me, but it will require some changes if it is to be played, depending on the singers. Oh, Baron, I have to tell you. I don't have any spare paper. I completely forgot to get some in The Hague. I was so busy being dressed... sorry...'

'Oh, paper...' The baron thought he had prepared everything, but he was a music enthusiast, not a composer. 'Don't worry, Georg. I will ask to get some paper for you. I am sure it will not be a problem at all. Anything else?'

'Well, I am sure ink will be easy to get. I have the stave ruler with me, just in case I cannot get a copyist, so, yes, I think that's all.'

'Good.' *Hell, where shall I ask for paper? I'll have to contact Kreyenberg as soon as possible.*

'Thank you, Baron. I am glad I came with you.'

And he was. In a completely unknown place where he knew absolutely nobody and with no command of English at all, the presence of such a man who was acting as a moral protector was precious to him. The only way to thank him was to do well, and impress the queen. For that, Händel was quite confident. And he was determined to see as much as he could and enquire about the state of music in London, especially opera. All through the preparation of this trip, Vittoria was always present in his mind. He heard nothing while in Hanover. He was desperately hoping to hear something while in London. *But what if she shows up? How to explain to Baron Kielmansegg? Would he disapprove?* Händel had only just been appointed to the position of Hanoverian Kapellmeister and he did not want to lose it too soon. *But how wonderful it would be if I could perform with her!* Between hope and apprehension, he just kept silence, absolute silence.

Christoph Friederich Kreyenberg had come to live in London that autumn as a Hanoverian resident. To Baron Kielmansegg's relief, he thought of everything.

'Paper? Yes. You get them from the music publishers. There are a few in London, but Walsh is the biggest. Shall I send someone?'

'No. I think it will be better if Händel went there himself. He knows what he wants, but I am quite at a loss.'

'I cannot agree more, Baron. Now, for his accommodation, I've picked up a few music enthusiasts who have court connections but are not too powerful. This is the list.'

Baron Kielmansegg went through the list. 'And are they all politically neutral?'

'That's the most difficult and delicate point, Baron. I did my best, but you cannot penetrate deep into their minds to know what they think.'

'True. So what was your criterion for choosing these people?'

'The degree of their love for music. I believe your Kapellmeister was well received in Italy.'

'He was.'

'Well, you have to love music above religion there to accept a

Protestant.'

'I see.' *This Kreyenberg deserves a good report to the elector*, he thought.

'Baron, I hope your Kapellmeister pleases the queen. She is not an avid music lover.'

'I know. But Händel is young, good looking, and a virtuoso. There is more than enough to impress the queen. And I dressed him. He is flamboyant!'

Händel was impressed by the dynamic of the city. He had seen big cities but nothing quite like London. It was busy and bursting with people. In fact, England's capital was probably the wealthiest, if not the largest, city in Europe at that time. The clear air of the early morning became thick with coal smoke during the day due to the dense population, making the city also one of the most polluted. Coffee houses were not new for Händel, but their number was far greater here than in Venice. And an incredible number of newspapers was available. All kinds of shops were filled with goods. The city looked very prosperous.

Händel attended the revival of *Pirro e Demetrio (Pyrrhus and Demetrius)* at the Queen's Theatre with Baron Kielmansegg. The theatre's façade, rather narrow and plain, did not impress him. However once inside, it was a proper theatre with a big enough foyer and a very decent auditorium. The young composer was impressed by the quality of the orchestra. Then there was a surprise. The aria 'Ho un non so che nel cor' in his oratorio *La Resurrezione* and reused in his opera *Agrippina* was inserted!

'Baron, this is my aria!' Händel could not refrain from whispering in the baron's ear.

Baron Kielmansegg turned to Händel, surprised, and whispered back, 'Really? How?'

'I don't know,' then he forced himself to concentrate again on the opera.

There was a happy reunion afterwards.

'Hey, il Sassone?' said Giuseppe Boschi, seeing a tall figure approaching behind the stage.

'Yes, I am!' said Händel.

Giuseppe Boschi opened his arms. 'How excellent to see you here! Francesca! Come! Il Sassone is here!'

Francesca Vanini-Boschi turned and heard Elisabetta Pilotti-Schiavonetti shout, 'Oh my God, Giorgio! You here!' Elisabetta looked around to find her husband. 'Giovanni, where are you my dear? Come greet Giorgio!'

Johann Adolph von Kielmansegg watched the merry reunion.

'Do you know him, Elisabetta?' Francesca asked.

'Of course I do. He is our Kapellmeister.' Her memory was still fresh with the image of this young, handsome man who played the harpsichord like nobody else.

Baron Kielmansegg saw a young man approaching him, smiling. 'Are you with Mr Handel, sir?' he asked in fluent French.

'I am.'

'I am Aaron Hill, the manager. I am honoured to meet you, sir.'

'Johann Adolph von Kielmansegg. My pleasure.'

There was a big cheer, and Nicolini, still in his costume, appeared. He quickly spotted a group of his fellow singers with a tall man.

'Il Sassone?' Nicolini approached the man.

Händel turned and beamed, 'Signor Grimaldi! It's so good to see you again. You were splendid!'

Nicolini, laughing, opened his arms. 'I've heard about what you've been doing. You had a big success in Venice!'

'So he already knows every singer,' said Hill to Kielmansegg, watching the reunion side by side.

'He stayed three years in Italy. He worked for powerful patrons,' said the baron, looking at Händel with sympathy. 'Some of your singers sang in his opera in Venice.'

Aaron Hill had an idea.

In the coach going back to the lodgings, it was Baron Kielmansegg who spoke first.

'You looked very at ease, Händel.'

'Well, Baron, I know a few of these singers, so yes, it was nice to see them again. Gosh, Nicolini is fantastic, isn't he?'

'He is, but I think he put on weight again. The people here are treating him well.'

Händel just laughed, and then got serious. 'Baron, I think I know how my aria got here.'

'Do you? Tell me.'

'It's the Boschis. Before leaving Venice, they asked for the copy of the score of Agrippina, and they brought it here.'

'I see.'

'I saw it at once. Francesca looked a bit embarrassed. Of course, she could sing it as well as Margherita…'

'Durastante?'

'Yes. In Agrippina it was Margherita who sang it.'

'So they brought the score here, and let the people reuse it. Then why just one aria? If they had the whole opera, they could just play the whole thing,' Kielmansegg asked.

'Expense, Baron, I reckon. The theatre would have to pay quite a lot of

money to get a whole opera score.'
'I see.'
'With just an aria, it costs much less and the audience gets a glimpse of the most recent opera played in Venice, Baron.'
A recently played opera in Venice was something of a coveted novelty. Therefore the score was a precious commodity that provided extra income for singers who travelled extensively.

Since the beginning of the War of the Spanish Succession, London had seen a natural migration of musical talent, impelled by professional or political uncertainties in continental Europe and attracted by the opportunities that seemed to be promised by the development of London's musical life. Composers and instrumentalists were available, and now the operas could be accompanied by a regular orchestra of considerable competence, consisting of a mixture of British and foreign players. The Queen's Theatre also prided itself in having talented Italian scene designers. What was lacking, however, was an opera composer. Until now the Italian operas presented were all pasticcio works converted from pre-existing Italian scores.

Aaron Hill knew he could not miss this chance. He had to have this young composer for his theatre.

'An opera?'

'Yes. Would you?' asked Hill.

'Do you have a libretto ready?' asked Händel, suppressing his excitement.

'No. Can we discuss it?'

Händel was confused. *Discuss what?* 'Do you have a librettist?'

This was not the time to make Händel suspicious. Hill was quick. 'Of course we have, but if you have an idea or preference, I thought that would be more inspiring for you.'

Händel's face lit up at once. 'Oh, in that case, how about the story of *Gerusalemme liberata* by Tasso?'

'Of course.'

'Just one more question. When are you intending to produce the opera?'

'Well, when your music is ready. The sooner the better.'

Händel was quite amazed. One of the very first operas he had seen in Venice was based on Tasso's epic poem *Gerusalemme liberata (Jerusalem Delivered)*, and he had secretly hoped to make his version one day. He still remembered the young castrato in it, called Senesino.

It seemed that London's entertainment world was not really affected by the War of the Spanish Succession. At the Queen's Theatre, Händel found a regular opera company with a permanent orchestra. Italian opera was flourishing, yet all they could do in London was adapt pre-existing operas. The ambience was stimulating though, similar to Hamburg. The big difference was the presence of Nicolini, making the artistic provision in London more lavish.

'A commission?'
'Yes, Baron. I cannot believe it,' said Händel, excited like a child. 'Well, only if you agree, of course.'
Kielmansegg considered, and said, 'Well, why not?' It would be even better - Händel would look like a composer seeking experience, not just an intruder to Queen Anne's court. 'Do you know when?'
'As soon as possible, that's what Mr Hill said.'
Baron Kielmansegg looked at Händel, a little concerned. *As soon as possible* sounded as if the theatre was very poor in repertoire.
'Is it a problem?'
'Well, no, I suppose not. But you have to be introduced to the court. That's more important.'
'I see. Do you have any idea when?'
'I've already asked for an audience. I am just waiting to be summoned with you.'
'An audience?'
'Yes. Then, I will suggest you perform at Her Majesty's birthday celebration. I think that will be the perfect occasion to display your skill. We have to plan it carefully.'
'Birthday celebration... how wonderful...'

At St James's Palace, its main occupant was suffering.
Queen Anne winced. Her gouty legs were particularly painful.
'Is Your Majesty in pain?' asked Abigail Masham, concerned.
'No, Abigail. I am just concerned about my birthday,' she lied, 'don't worry, Abigail.'
Seeing her companion just nod silently, the queen felt relaxed. She was certain that if it were Sarah, Duchess of Marlborough, she would have been subjected to a parade of remarks; that she is in pain because she did not go out for a walk, that it is important to move, that because she does not move, it keeps making her fat and fat, and she eats too many cakes, etc. etc. But there was no abuse. Since last April, she had not seen Sarah, much to her relief. Instead, she now had the sweet and softly spoken Abigail. The queen wished to have Abigail's company and no more Sarah. However, the duchess still held her post as keeper of the privy purse. The queen, with the help of Dr Hamilton, the third physician-in-ordinary to Her Majesty, was preparing the duchess's dismissal. It was a stressful business. Her husband, Duke of Marlborough, had returned from the continent a month earlier to find the political situation completely changed. He was still the captain-general of the forces, but now with the changing situation, there was not too much to do.

His dismissal was just a question of time. The main obstacle remained the duchess as the queen knew she would resist robustly to keep her post.

'Why? Why is Your Majesty concerned?'

The queen woke from the daydream. 'Well, Abigail, I feel no joy at my age in celebrating my birthday. I wish I could get younger; then I would have the reason to celebrate.'

'Oh, Your Majesty, do not be pessimistic. You are still young and—'

'And lame. Don't be ridiculous, Abigail. I am an old woman. You know that.' She was kind enough not to look in her eyes.

Abigail just lowered her head, embarrassed.

Anne looked at her and smiled. She was happy with her presence, but she was not merry. She was constantly in pain, and she missed her husband terribly. The thought of spending the coming Christmas was intolerable. After Christmas, it would be the New Year's celebration with newly composed musical odes and then her birthday celebration in February, and she was not looking forward to all that. Life had no purpose anymore without her husband's presence.

Händel kept himself busy while waiting to be summoned by the queen. He frequented concert halls and private parties. The invitations came quite frequently. Nicolini insisted on having Händel accompany him on harpsichord at those parties. Being with the famous castrato opened doors to many among the nobility and gentry. However Händel struggled to communicate in French.

'They don't really speak French here. And my English is still very poor…' Händel said to Nicolini on the coach heading to one of those receptions.

'I know. I did not expect to be able to speak in Italian here, but I thought French would be sufficient. Well, no! You need to speak English here,' Nicolini said, 'and it's not an easy language.'

'Do you think it better to speak in English at court as well?'

'If you can, that's better, I reckon, much better.'

'I might increase the lessons, then,' Händel said. *I want to be able to introduce myself to the queen in English,* he thought, as he guessed Nicolini was not yet introduced to the court.

Ten-years-old Mary Granville could feel the difference. In the normally quiet and severe household, there was an air of excitement. Her aunt looked busy and conferred often with her husband, Lord Stanley. Sir John Stanley, who married Ann Granville, sister of the politician and author George Granville, was very well connected. Mary was a high-spirited ten-year-old girl and had been living with the Stanleys for two years. Her parents' intention was to groom her to be a maid of honour to the queen, as her aunt had been. Her life was quite close to the court, as Lord Stanley was secretary to the Lord Chamberlain. Because the Stanleys were childless, Mary brought youth to the household, and they felt sometimes overwhelmed by her vivacity. Though under strict discipline, Mary was loved, and they watched carefully over her education, which included English, French, history, music, needlework, and dancing. She was even given her own harpsichord.

'Mary, we are having music, and we have a very special guest this evening,' said Lady Ann.

Mary was used to this. Lord Stanley was a music lover, and she saw him and his wife off to the opera quite often, being told that she was still too small to attend. And they organised music soirées from time to time. At the last one, she saw her uncle and aunt delighted to have a very fat singer who sang in a very high-pitched voice. He was Italian.

'Is it Nicolini again, Aunt?'

'No, Mary. This time we are having a harpsichord player from Saxony.'

'Oh, is he . . .' She looked up. 'Where is Saxony, Aunt?'

Lady Stanley was taken aback by this question but composed herself quickly and replied, 'Mary, I am very busy now. Would you go to the library and look at the globe so you can see where Saxony is?'

That evening, Mary Granville saw a very handsome and tall young man play the harpsichord like nobody else. She sat listening to him play, transfixed. Everybody looked delighted. Then she saw him coming towards her.

'This is my niece Mary, Mr Handel. Mary, this is Mr Handel.'

The young man smiled at her, took her tiny hand, and kissed it, saying in French, 'It is my honour to meet you, Mademoiselle Mary.'

She felt, for the first time in her life, her heart in her throat.

It was late now. Everybody left. Mary was in the drawing-room, staring at the harpsichord. She could still see HIM playing. She sat and tried to play one of the tunes the brilliant guest had played.

'Do you think you can play as well as Mr Handel, Mary?' Lord Stanley said, teasing her.

She jumped up, and outraged, she cried, 'If I did not think I should, I would burn my instrument!' She stormed out of the room, fighting back tears.

Sir Stanley stood there with his eyebrows raised.

'What is the matter?' Lady Stanley asked, coming into the room.

'Well, I think Mr Handel made a big impression on Mary.'

'Then she is a very clever girl, Sir John.' She looked at her husband and smiled.

'It was a very pleasant evening, my dear. Shall we go to bed now? It is quite late.' Sir John Stanley offered his arm to his wife.

It was true. Händel had made a big impression on Mary. She felt as if she had met the God of music. From that day, she practiced more on her harpsichord. She discovered such a beautiful world through Händel's playing, and she now was determined to push herself as far as possible.

If Mary was deeply impressed, Händel was feeling a sort of loss. At each reception he went to, he was called Mr Handel. At first, he had tried to explain his German name, that there were two little dots on top of the *a* and that it was pronounced more like *Hendel*. He saw people getting confused or ignoring his remark completely.

'I feel I lost my name,' he said to Baron Kielmansegg.

'I do understand.' The Baron looked at Händel. 'But don't you think that it's better than being called *the Saxon* or *Mr Endel*?' He saw the young man staring at him. He continued, 'You have to understand, we are in England, and such a thing as an umlaut does not exist in English.'

'You are right, Baron,' Händel smiled. 'It's just two little dots, after all. And I am happy that the English people could pronounce the *h* correctly.'

At St James's Palace, Dr Hamilton found the queen rather well, to his relief.

'A Kapellmeister from Hanover?' Dr Hamilton said.

'Yes. He is with a certain Baron... Ki... Baron something. That baron made a formal request for an audience to introduce that musician,' the queen said, quite annoyed, 'another excuse to intrude into my court.'

Dr Hamilton did not reply.

'Because I don't want anyone from the Hanover family, they keep sending me diplomats and visitors. Do they think I am that stupid?'

'I am sure they know what Your Majesty thinks,' Dr Hamilton said calmly, 'but you cannot refuse them all.'

'I know,' the queen sighed.

'Georg, we are invited to the New Year's Day celebration at the court,' said Baron Kielmansegg, smiling.

'Am I to play?'

'Not officially, but I am sure you will be given a chance to play the harpsichord.'

'Is there any official music, then?'

'Well, it is the tradition for a musical ode to be played.' Kielmansegg scanned the invitation. 'So, the poet laureate, Nahum Tate, wrote the verse, and the music was composed by the master of the queen's music, John Eccles.'

'Oh, is that with the choir of the Chapel Royal?'

'Yes. Are you excited?'

'I am. I heard the choir of St Paul's Cathedral, and I heard William Croft play the organ.'

'You have been busy, then.'

'Baron, do I have to be dressed in the suit you ordered in The Hague?'

'Well, I think not. The queen's birthday is more important, and many people order new suits and dresses for that occasion. So, your second best will do.'

'I see.'

'And let's see how it goes. I hope you will get an invitation to play at the queen's birthday.'

'I'll do my best, Baron.' Händel felt the pressure. Finally, the court! *What shall I play? Shall I compose something special? Would it be better to play something Italian? Would the queen ask me questions? But I am Hanoverian Kapellmeister, so it would be better to present something from there, extract from the operas played there?*

While Händel was busy consulting with himself, Aaron Hill was busy arranging the libretto. Giacomo Rossi, the librettist, felt uneasy. Hill was controlling everything. In fact, Hill was the one who was playing out the plot and writing the libretto, and Rossi was just translating it into Italian and versifying it. What's more, it was quite far from Tasso's poem. Hill was multiplying the love interests and did not hesitate to mutilate the original poem. He invented the character of Almirena to accommodate two female singers. So there were two pairs of lovers, Rinaldo and Almirena, and Armida and Argante. And there is a mix-up, because Argante falls in love with Almirena and Armida with Rinaldo. For Rossi, it was just a cheap love story in Italian.

Händel, receiving the first act of the libretto at the end of the year, was rather disappointed. He had knowledge of Antonio Salvi's libretti, and he had worked on Cardinal Grimani's libretto. In Hanover he set music to the court poet Mauro's text. The difference was staring at him.

'Couldn't your librettist do better than this?' Händel asked bluntly to Aaron Hill.

'I know, Mr Handel,' Hill said, 'but you see, we are in England. It is not easy to find an Italian poet with experience. And we are short of time.'

'I see.'

'Can you manage?'

'I need to see Rossi.'

Giacomo Rossi was surprised to see Händel, and he nearly panicked. 'I am sorry, Mr Andel, but it is not finished yet...'

'Oh, no. I came to ask if you could make some changes. Some passages are really hard to put to music,' Händel said politely, 'would it be possible for me to spend some time with you? I want to go through the text.'

Rossi was relieved and rather satisfied. This time, he felt himself treated as a librettist.

'And, also could you shorten Almirena's part?'

'Yes, of course, Mr Andel. Do you mean fewer arias and recitatives?'

'Exactly.' Händel did not mention that he doubted the ability and the stamina of the singer in the role of Almirena. 'And maybe increase the part for Armida?'

With the New Year's Day celebration over, the nobility was busy ordering expensive coats and dresses for the queen's birthday celebration the following month, which was the occasion to show off and be seen.

The presence of a pair of foreigners at the New Year's Day celebration had diverted the queen's rather gloomy mind. She was pleasantly surprised to see a very handsome middle-aged man with another very handsome young man.

'Händel is my name, Your Majesty.'

His awkward accent was still in her ears. *Handel.*

Their presence was like a fresh breeze amongst the usual boring faces, and that handsome young man was more than brilliant, a true virtuoso. It brightened up the queen's mood, and her interest in music was somehow rekindled. She had had lessons on the harpsichord and lute when a child, and remembered that she loved dancing. She could not dance anymore with her painful legs, but now she wanted more music. She was saddened to be unable to go out unless absolutely necessary. Music had to come to her. She was rather happy at the outcome of not allowing any Hanoverians at court as it led to her meeting the young and dashing composer. For her, a Hanoverian would represent her coffin, counting down the remaining days of her life. Moreover, in this unstable political situation, the last thing she wanted was for the Hanoverians to be used by the opposition. She wanted a smooth succession, and she knew it would be in the near future.

The new year seemed to start well for Queen Anne. Following the parliamentary election, in which the Tories secured a large majority, Anne could count on the Tory government to bring the war to an end. Sarah, Duchess of Marlborough, after a lengthy and bitter attempt to regain her power, finally resigned her court offices. It was her husband, the duke, who brought the gold key to the queen, the symbol of office for the groom of the stole. That meant a huge difference in her daily life. No more authoritative command, no more pressure, and no more that look of superiority upon her. Now Abigail Masham took over as keeper of the privy purse. The queen felt a huge weight lifted. Now she looked forward to her birthday celebration.

'We shall have a nice celebration,' she said merrily to Abigail. Then she muttered to herself, 'This might be my last.'

'Yes, I am Mr Handel,' he said to himself. From the moment he presented himself to the queen, he had made himself known as Mr Handel, without the two little dots. It was rather in a grand manner that he lost his little dots, and he was rather happy about it.

'Mr Handel. Not too bad, after all,' he smiled to himself. Now that the introduction to the court was done, he could concentrate on his opera. He secretly hoped that Vittoria would show up to be part of the cast, but that was now very unlikely. The cast was established and he had to compose according to the singers' ability.

Händel was at Walsh's publishing house to get some paper. He was again invited to the court, this time to play for the queen's birthday celebration with some singers. A cantata with basso continuo was suggested.

He entered the shop and was quite amazed by the number of publications available. An idea came to him to go through some of those scores to see the kind of music played in London. He picked one: not too interesting. Another one: interesting. He might buy it. And the third: he had a shock. It was his music! It was the overture of the opera he composed for Florence. It was credited to 'an unknown master' and had been published six months earlier.

'Are you interested in music, sir?' a voice said behind Händel, who was staring at his music, printed.

'Well, yes. Hmm, this one is…'

'Oh, this one is from the comedy called *The Alchemist*. It was staged in January last year. Yes, just a year ago. And we published it after the season ended.'

'It says "by an Italian master". So you don't know who composed it?'

'We don't know, indeed, sir. I heard that it was brought from Holland.'

Händel came back with paper and his music. He was still intrigued and slightly upset. *Who got my music? It cannot be one of the singers as they were all staying in Florence. Who else got the score? Someone who heard it in Florence? And then it was copied and sold…*

Hill opened the new year with Bononcini's opera *Etearco*, adapted by Haym, on 10 January 1711. It ran six nights on a subscription basis and one night as a regular performance. It was obvious that London did not have an Italian opera composer available. Hill was right to commission Händel to have a proper Italian opera for the theatre, as was usually the case in Italy. The box office receipts for November and December were barely enough to cover salaries and expenditures. Hill needed a big box-office success.

'You are going very fast, Mr Handel. I am amazed,' Hill said.

'I got used to doing so in Italy. Sometimes I had only one day to compose a cantata.'

'One day...' *What is a cantata?*
'I need a copyist, Mr Hill. Could you send me one?'
'Of course. He will come to see you, Mr Handel.'
'One more thing. I don't know if it is the custom here, but I will direct the opera from the harpsichord.'
'Will you? But we have Mr Haym. He can do—'
'Yes, I know. I saw him directing. But I've always directed my operas from the harpsichord, and I intend to do the same here.'
'Oh, but—'
'Mr Haym can join Schiavonetti playing the cello, I suppose.'
Hill saw no room for discussion.

Haym was again dismayed by Hill's ignorance. 'Did you actually suggest to Mr Handel that I direct his opera?' he said, incredulous.
'Well, in a way . . .' Hill felt embarrassed, but it was too late.
'Mr Hill, I thought you went to Italy and saw some operas.'
'I did,' Hill replied.
'And you saw composers conducting their own operas, yes?'
To this he could not answer. He had seen a few operas, but he'd had no idea that the man directing, usually from the harpsichord, was the composer himself.

Haym, seeing Hill embarrassed, did not go further to point out more his ignorance. After all, the new manager was doing his best, and he did the right thing to commission a new opera from Händel. He found, however, Hill's self-confidence mixed with ignorance quite irritating.

The time was going very fast since Händel had arrived in London. Life was busy and fulfilling. Operas, concerts, masses to hear choirs; there was quite a lot to attend, acquaintances to be made, and a commission for an opera and a performance for the queen's birthday. He was doing well, and Baron Kielmansegg felt it was time for him to leave.
'Are you not coming to the queen's birthday, Baron?'
'I cannot. I have to go back to Hanover as soon as possible. I just received a summons from the elector.' A white lie.
Händel, suddenly feeling alone, lowered his head.
'I am sure you will be fine, Georg. You will not be alone here.'
'I know, but...' Then he raised his head again and said, 'Yes, I will be fine, Baron. I will miss you though.'
Baron Kielmansegg's heart nearly melted. It was true. There was chemistry between them. They liked each other instantly when they met for the first time in Venice. There was no summons from Hanover. It was time to go, to avoid making the queen irritated.

Now that Baron Kielmansegg was gone, Händel had been given accommodation in London by a member of the gentry, Mr Henry Andrews of Barn Elms. It was simple but comfortable, far from the lavish lifestyle of his Italian patrons. While with the baron, Händel had a busy life, and it was easy to not think about Vittoria. But now, when he found himself alone, he unintentionally let his heart fill slowly with her. Händel was composing 'Cara sposa'. This was one of the arias for *Rinaldo*, his opera, to be sung by Nicolini. It was the aria from when Rinaldo loses his beloved Almirena and desperately calls for her, 'Where are you? Come back to me!' Händel stopped. He got up from the desk and walked towards the window. It was dark outside. The sky was clear, and he could see the stars. It was too much. He hit the wall with his fists, banged his forehead, and murmured, 'Vittoria, where are you? Why are you not coming?' It was painful. Why this silence? What happened? Rinaldo desperately calling for his beloved was too similar. Where are you? He looked up to the sky. He gazed at the stars, and he saw Vittoria smiling at him. He smiled back and went back to composing.

'I will wait for you, Vittoria,' he said to himself, 'in the meantime, I will work hard and build up my career.' He felt better, and could now pour all his grief into his music.

The festivities on 6 February 1711 to celebrate Queen Anne's birthday at St James's Palace were particularly lavish. The officers of state, foreign ministers, nobility, and gentry went to compliment Her Majesty, all the men clad in their best suits and the ladies in their new dresses and covered with jewels. In the morning, the traditional ode set to music was played. Then, in the afternoon, there was another concert. This was unusual.

Händel, for this occasion, picked up the best of the performers from the Queen's Theatre to perform a cantata. He chose Nicolini and Elisabetta Pilotti-Schiavonetti as singers, Nicola Haym as cellist, and Jean Christian Kytch as oboist. Händel himself played the harpsichord. Among the musicians, Haym was the only one quite at ease attending the royal court, having recognised several faces among the audience. Even Nicolini was quite tense despite him mingling with aristocracy and gentry very often. The presence of the queen was something impressive and somehow overwhelming. Händel was glad to have the court experience, and be able to reassure the musicians. However, as soon as the music started, they were all immersed, enjoying the memorable experience. Händel astonished the court with his flamboyant writing, and Queen Anne was delighted.

Seated, the queen remembered how music could bring such joy. *Since Purcell, I have not had this feeling*, she thought. She was glad to have let the young composer come back to her court, and also to present his own work. She heard that he was now composing an opera. Without the presence of the accompanying baron, he was just a musician, to her. For a second, she believed that the Hanoverian Elector had simply sent her a musical gift, wishing her well. No, nothing was ever that simple.

Nicola Haym, by then, was sure of Händel's ability being far superior to any of the composers, native or foreign, present in London. His musical style, Italian with German influence, was new. Watching him play, Haym could not stop being fascinated by Händel's force that drew the audience into his music.

By this time, Händel was already busy finishing the composition and starting to think about the rehearsals for his opera *Rinaldo*.

'Are you Mr Händel, sir?'

Händel raised his head from the score. He saw a rather small man in front of him.

'Yes, I am, and you are?'

To Händel's astonishment, the man replied in German, 'My name is Lineke, Dietrich Lineke. I am honoured to meet you. I am your copyist.'

Händel was shaking Lineke's hands vigorously before he realised what he was doing. 'God, so nice to meet you! Where are you from, Mr Lineke?' He bombarded the copyist with questions. He could not stop. It was good to be able to communicate in his mother tongue. He was missing it terribly. He ignored Lineke looking overwhelmed.

'Could you first copy the part for the singers, please, so I can do the sing-through?'

'Of course. It will be done quickly.'

It was, and Händel was satisfied with his copying.

From February, Hill started to prepare the costumes for the main characters. Yards and yards of fabric were bought: white and silver satin for Almirena; blue silk, gold satin, and black velvet for the magician; and more satin, cherry-coloured velvet, linings, trims, and sundries for the others. Hill watched the colourful textiles delivered to the theatre with excitement. He loved creating exotic costumes and ideas were pouring out of his brain. However, he had to be careful. The herald, mermaids, spirits, furies, officers, guards, and attendants would be dressed largely from the existing stock to save money. Then the stage set was planned. The timber was provided. Jerusalem besieged, a flying dragon chariot, and an enchanted garden were to be created. Again, Hill delighted in torturing his brain to create breathtaking sets.

Händel arrived at Nicolini's house for a private rehearsal. He felt excited and privileged to compose for the best castrato recognised in Venice. He was determined to enhance the singer's capacity and wanted to see how far he could explore. He was impatient to try two or three arias with the castrato and just popped in without any notice. He knocked on the door and saw it opened by Nicolini's valet.

'Your name, sir?' the valet asked in a rather sulky mood.

'Händel.'

'Endel?'

'Yes.'

Nicolini was in, and normally he would refuse a visit without notice except from powerful patrons. However, he found himself unable to refuse Händel. There was something special in this young, dashing composer, quite pushy without being patronising.

'Giorgio! What brings you here?' Nicolini asked abruptly, still in his gown.

'I composed a few arias, but I want to have your opinion first.' Händel, seeing the singer's expression, thought he had done the right thing. 'I was wondering if they might be too easy for you, so...'

'Oh, let's try then,' Nicolini smiled.

Händel accompanied Nicolini on harpsichord. The castrato finished one aria, turned to Händel, and beamed.

'Giorgio, it is beautiful. I love this aria.'

'Thank you, Signor Nicolini.'

'Would it be with basso continuo?'

'Oh no. You will be accompanied by full orchestra.'

'Splendid. I will make all the ladies weep, believe me.' He grinned. 'What's next?'

'This one is dynamic.' Händel gave him the score. 'Again, you will have the orchestra and trumpets.'

Nicolini sang, and Händel accompanied. When finished, Händel clapped. *'Caro, caro!'*

Nicolini bowed. 'Giorgio, all that is wonderful. With this, I will bring the whole theatre to its feet, clapping and shouting my name!' And he added, 'And yours of course!' Now he looked forward to the opera.

Händel laughed. This was a good start, that the singer liked his arias.

They were interrupted by Nicolini's valet bringing in his costume for *Rinaldo*.

'Oh, is this the costume?' asked Nicolini.

'Yes, Signor, would you like to try it on?'

'Of course!' the castrato turned to Händel, 'perfect timing!'

Nicolini removed his gown. Händel saw something fall on the floor. He picked it up and stared at it. It was a small pouch, very similar to the one he had.

Nicolini turned to Händel, 'So what do you think?' He posed, his hands on his hips, in his mediaeval knight's costume.

'Is this yours?' Händel showed the castrato the pouch, ignoring completely the question.

'Oh yes! Did it fall from my pocket?' Nicolini did not have time to be upset for his ignored costume.

'Yes. What is that, may I ask?'

'Oh, it's just a pouch with some herbs, but I keep it as a lucky charm.'

'Herbs?'

Nicolini kissed the pouch. 'Yes, for my throat.' And he bent near Händel and whispered, 'It is from a witch who helped me recover from *the* operation.'

Händel stared at Nicolini. He slowly put his hand into his inner pocket and retrieved his pouch. He showed it to Nicolini. It was the castrato's turn to stare at Händel.

'May I ask how you got it, Giorgio?'

'It was given to my mother by a Gipsy woman whom my father helped.'

Nicolini, relieved, laughed. 'Oh, I see now. They all have the same habit then!' Then he lowered his voice. 'But it is curious that we both kept those in our pockets. Is it your lucky charm as well?'

'Yes, of sorts.'

Nicolini laughed loudly and slapped Händel's back. 'Maybe we are related!'

Händel laughed. He was relieved to find the singer much easier than he had anticipated, and now looked forward to a friendly working relationship.

Nicolini could not stop admiring the two figures conversing in the theatre. They were both young and tall, one slightly more strongly built and taller. Both were very handsome and well dressed, and they were both hardworking. He wished they could be part of the cast. *They would be such a presence on the stage*, he thought.

Händel was discussing some details with Hill on the stage and felt a gaze. He turned aside and saw Nicolini looking at him. Händel smiled at him, and Nicolini returned the smile.

Dear Telemann,

I just received your letter forwarded from Hanover. I have no words to express my sorrow for you.

Händel stopped. He could not find the words to continue his letter to Telemann. He could not believe it. His friend's letter, just arrived, informed Händel that his wife had died in childbirth, followed shortly after by her baby girl. He clearly remembered the young, charming bride, smiling and very much in love with his friend. And now she was gone. Dead. *Why? He does not deserve it.* This brought him back to his childhood memory. He remembered his father coming back home, exhausted and distressed, and telling his mother about the death of a woman in childbirth. Sometimes the woman was young, and sometimes she was a mother of several children. There was no rule. Every woman was at risk, no matter her social rank or wealth. It was hard on his father, to feel he had failed to save a life. Händel abandoned the letter unfinished.

From 13 February the wordbook of the opera *Rinaldo* was advertised in *The Daily Courant* as being on sale at Rice's coffee house in the Haymarket. It was extravagant for what it was, signed by Hill and dedicated to Queen Anne. The entire Italian text was printed on the left page with its translation in English on the right. Händel was referred to as the 'Orpheus of our century, having completed the whole opera in a fortnight'. In his dedication to Queen Anne, Hill proclaimed his 'endeavour, to see the English Opera more splendid than her mother, the Italian'. This meant a lot to Hill. Händel paid little attention to it and was far from realising the meaning of it and its seriousness. He was just happy to see Hill doing his best to promote the opera, reporting it to Baron Kielmansegg in Hanover.

Hill felt stirred to make full use of the technical resources offered by the theatre. The water effect was unique to the Queen's Theatre. His penchant for the exotic was obvious in his design for the enchanted palace, recalling his publication *Ottoman Empire* two years before. He was also busy advertising for *Rinaldo*. He used *The British Apollo*, a question-and-answer journal created by himself in 1708 and recently sold. The spectacular nature of the opera's staging entailed a fairly long lead-up period of preparation before the performance. Hill used it to build up excitement.

During one rehearsal with the orchestra, Händel recognised Lineke, who smiled at him.

'I did not know you were a viola player.'

'Well, I am, but I earn much more as a copyist.'

'But you are not alone, I suppose?'

'No, of course not, but I am the principal. There is Davies and Smith when I need them. Mr Händel?'

'Yes?'

'You have a very large orchestra. I've never seen four trumpets and kettledrums.'

'What do you think?'

'Oh, splendid. I love it!'

For an epic medieval subject, trumpets and drums gave the military aspect, and Hill was happy about it. However, the extra musicians hired meant extra expense. This was nothing compared to the singer's fees. And Italian singers were much more expensive than the native ones. Hill was doing everything for the opera to be a big hit, but could not stop feeling harassed by the financial tightrope.

Back in Hanover, Baron Kielmansegg felt uneasy. He'd just received a report from Kreyenberg in London. Aaron Hill was a Whig, and the tickets for the opera *Rinaldo* were being sold at the Whig stronghold of White's coffee house. This was rather good news. However, the bad news was that Tories were gaining power, and they were for making peace with France in order to end the War of the Spanish Succession and quit the Austrian Alliance. This situation was irritating for Georg Ludwig, the elector of Hanover, as a key ally of Austria. The baron felt as if dark clouds were gathering far away, and hoped that they would just dissipate, but he knew they would not.

On 23 February 1711, Nicolini organised a small party in his house for just the main cast of the opera and Händel. He was very merry. The singers were all Italian, and the castrato felt at home.

'I thank you all for coming to my modest house,' he said merrily.

'Oh come on, Nicolini, do you call it a modest house?' Giuseppe Boschi teased, looking around.

'And why today? You know very well we cannot get drunk. We cannot mess up the premiere tomorrow,' Elisabetta mourned.

Nicolini just smiled and continued, 'The reason I asked you here is that today is our Giorgio's birthday!'

There was an *oh* from everybody, followed by hugs from male singers and warm kisses from the female singers.

'So, I know it is your birthday today,' said Nicolini, raising a glass, 'but how old are you, Giorgio?'

Händel smiled and said, 'I turned twenty-six today.'

There was another *oh*.

'You are so young, Giorgio.' Valentino Urbani looked at Händel with melancholy. 'It was such a long time ago that I was twenty-six.'

'Not for me,' said Nicolini, 'it was just last year.'

Händel was quite touched by Nicolini's kindness. Despite being quite capricious, the singer had never behaved unfairly to him. He watched the singers. They were all friends, at least friendly to each other, and there was harmony within the cast. If something goes wrong, they will help each other. He was quite confident the premiere the next day would go well.

The very next day, on 24 February 1711, the Queen's Theatre opened its doors to present Händel's first London opera, *Rinaldo*, for the first time.

Händel was nervous. However, it was different from Venice. In Venice, his nervousness was due to the pressure from the audience's reaction, which could make a hero or a wreck of a composer. Here in London, it was the stage operation he was concerned about. He knew he could not really count on Hill, who was not experienced enough. He knew he would have to watch the stage like a hawk. Händel copied all stage directions into his conducting score, which became his habit for the rest of his life.

Among the members of the orchestra, Jean Christian Kytch was particularly enthusiastic. His virtuosity on oboe and other woodwind instruments was recognised by Händel, and he was to shine right from the overture with beautiful solo parts. He was to play almost non-stop, but that was very good publicity for him. The bass singer Giuseppe Boschi was also excited. Though his was not the most important role, his entrance on stage was to be accompanied by four trumpets and kettledrums. He was certain to astonish the audience.

The brilliant appearance of Händel at the queen's birthday celebration shortly before added glamour to the publicity. The theatre was packed with nobility and gentry. Some of them even had to fight for a place in the gallery, normally reserved for the less privileged.

As they waited for the opera to begin, the audience observed and was quite impressed with the large size of the orchestra. Then there was silence, and a tall and very handsome young man entered and bowed to the public. Most of the nobility and gentry recognised Händel. The composer himself conducting was new for the audience.

Act I was filled with stage wonders. The entrance of Nicolini was greeted with clapping and cheers, and the audience was thrilled with the splendidly beautiful Isabella Girardeau in the role of Almirena. Then Giuseppe Boschi made his spectacular entrance as Argante, accompanied by four trumpets and drums. He could see several jaws dropping among the audience. Those following the wordbook raised their heads to stare at the trumpeters stationed on the stage wearing exotic costumes. The loud clapping was still going on when Elisabetta as Armida made another spectacular entrance from above in a chariot in flames. Then the scene changed to a beautiful garden with a fountain where Isabella and Nicolini had an exquisite duet. A flock of live sparrows was let loose. Then Almirena was abducted, and it was Nicolini's turn to sing his aria, 'Cara sposa'.

My dear betrothed, my dear love, Where are you?
Come back at my tears!

This was one of the best arias Händel had created so far. It was the most pathetic song with the richest accompaniment ever heard in England. The powerful expression of Rinaldo's desperation and grief at the loss of his beloved was intense, and it spoke directly to the whole audience. Nicolini saw some women in tears. He could see Händel totally focused on conducting, and not even giving away the smallest drop of emotion. Then Nicolini saw it, just a glimpse but unmistakable. He saw deep grief in Händel's eyes.

The auditorium was in total silence when the aria was over. Nicolini did not move, but managed to look at Händel, who looked frozen, terrified. Then the audience exploded. Nicolini did not smile, still staying in his role in grief, but he could see Händel beaming to him, clapping.

Act I ended with Nicolini's aria vowing to save his love. It was a showpiece to which the audience reacted rapturously. Händel was behind the stage to join the cast. Everybody was smiling. There was a good atmosphere. Händel saw Hill busy directing the change of the stage set, relieved that the first act went well.

In one of the boxes during the interval, James Brydges asked his wife, 'So, what do you think, Mary?'

'Oh, it's wonderful. I've never seen such a wonderful stage. How could they create a fountain? And that chariot descending from above? And the singers!'

'Did you see that young man at the harpsichord directing? He is the composer.'

'Oh, is he Mr Handel?'

'Yes. It is always the composer himself who directs in Italy.'

'He is so young and handsome. He will be feted.'

'I think he will.'

James Brydges, son of Baron Chandos, was a music enthusiast. He played flute, and during his Oxford years he was active in the music club. He was now paymaster general of the forces abroad, and with the ongoing War of the Spanish Succession, he was amassing a great fortune. As the war had dragged on for ten years with no end in sight, his future looked brilliant.

'Signore e signori, get ready for Act II, please!' said Händel merrily. He turned to Isabella Girardeau and smiled. 'I count on you, madam.' Behind her he saw Elisabetta, at whom he winked. He was fully conscious that he had done a better job with the role of Armida, given to Elisabetta. Knowing the singer well he felt at ease to fully explore her capacity, and develop Armida's personality. In fact he liked Armida more than Almirena.

Elisabetta was happy with Händel's score. Despite being in the second role, she could see how carefully her arias had been composed and she could get easily in the skin of the sorceress. She liked Armida's confident personality, in constant control of herself, but with a vulnerability of a woman in love.

Act II started with the departure of Rinaldo by boat, pulled noiselessly and smoothly as if in the water. The enchanted palace of Armida was another visual spectacle to draw muffled oohs from the audience. It showed Hill's penchant for the exotic, with pillars imitating crystal, azur, emeralds, and all sorts of other precious stones.

Isabella Girardeau, in the role of Almirena, was now singing an aria, 'Lascia ch'io pianga', with a slow, simple melody. The audience was very quiet. Isabella was singing 'Let me weep my cruel fate' while in captivity. This aria was recycled from one Händel had composed in Italy, now made slower and more dramatic. He also knew that Isabella was not a strong singer and could not manage technically demanding passages well. But she was beautiful, a good actor, and blessed with a crystal-clear soprano voice. On the stage, she looked splendid, pure, and innocent, captivating the public.

The excitement did not stop there. It was then Elisabetta's turn to show off as Armida, queen and sorceress. 'Vo'far Guerra' was a combination of powerful singing and Händel's harpsichord improvisation. Armida discovers that her lover, King Argante, is in love with Almirena. The aria is about a furious declaration of war, swearing revenge against Argante. This ended Act II with a spectacular effect. The audience was surprised and excited, as it was not the custom for the continuo instrument to shine from the orchestra pit. With Händel's incredible virtuosity, they again went wild.

James Brydges and his wife Mary looked at each other in amazement.

'This is excellent,' said James.

'It is unbelievable. Elisabetta is such a singer, and oh, did you see, Husband, how Mr Handel plays the harpsichord?'

'Incredible.'

Another box was occupied by three women and a very young man. Lady Juliana Noel, Dowager Countess of Burlington, took three of her four children to the Queen's Theatre to see the premiere of Händel's opera. While the youngest of the children, Henrietta, judged too young to attend, was brooding in her room, the party of four was thrilled. Still clapping at the end of Act II, the young Earl of Burlington leaned towards his mother and shouted, 'He is incredible, Mother!' The dowager countess smiled at him and looked at her daughters, who were both transfixed.

'This is going very well!' Hill said, excited. 'Bravo, Maestro!' He hugged Händel spontaneously, leaving the latter astonished.

Nicolini laughed. 'Wait until the end, Mr Hill. It is not finished yet!' the castrato shouted to the back of Hill, disappearing to check the new stage set.

Elisabetta was delighted. 'Oh Giorgio, you were incredible! Can you hear? They are still clapping!'

It was not the time to rejoice. Händel was serious. 'Signore, signori. There is another act to go. Please, stay calm and concentrate.'

As soon as the stage set was ready, Händel shouted, 'Let's go! To the triumphal war!'

Everyone cheered. Haym, looking at Händel lead the cast, recognised his genius and charisma. His music was full of striking invention. The exuberance and variety of the scoring could make anyone feel drunk with the vitality of the rhythms. The whole thing was more than enough to compensate for the weakness of the libretto. *I doubt he will remain in Hanover as Kapellmeister*, Haym thought.

The audience thought the climax was over and that they had seen everything: thunder, lightning, a chariot of fire, a fountain and real birds. They were again surprised in Act III. It started with a dreadfully steep mountain rising from the front of the stage to the utmost height at the very back of the stage. On top appeared the blazing battlements of the enchanted palace, guarded by spirits of various forms and aspects. Then the foot of the mountain opened to reveal the magician's cave. Then the mountain was moved smoothly to disappear.

While hearing the ohs and wows from the audience, Hill sighed in relief to have avoided the ridicule of creaking mountains. He silently thanked Haym for the advice of oiling the wheels once more. His first impression, when he arrived at the Queen's Theatre as manager with Collier, that he was not welcomed just because of who he was, was fading gradually. Sometimes harsh and irritable, Hill did not always appreciate Haym's comments. But now he was realising that the latter was just pointing out his weakness.

Nicolini's singing combined with the trumpet in the aria 'Or la tromba' triggered the audience to go wild again. The castrato was deeply satisfied. Händel knew how to use all his capacities for the best and captivate the audience, but what Nicolini liked most was the tunefulness. Händel could create the most beautiful arias with simple melodies. With all this, plus amazing stage sets, it was easy for him to generate a standing ovation. He just enjoyed it as he knew such opportunities were not available all the time.

Charles Montagu, Earl of Manchester, was in the audience with his friend John Vanbrugh.

'Not bad, is it?' said Charles Montagu.

'That's what I wanted, Charles.' Vanbrugh looked at his friend. 'That's exactly how I was imagining it. Maybe I was too early...'

Vanbrugh was right. In fact, *Rinaldo* was not the first Italian opera composed especially for the Queen's Theatre. It had already been done back in 1705. However, the audience was not ready, and the music by Greber failed to make any impact. This time, with Nicolini, Händel, and the audience being familiar with opera sung in Italian, the timing was perfect.

Rinaldo was a resounding success, much to Hill's delight and relief. Nicolini and Händel received rapturous applause. It was not only the audience who applauded Händel. The orchestra members were happy too. It was a score that satisfied them. Kytch looked quite tired but still happy. The audience was still clapping after the spectacular ending with four trumpets, never heard before. Hill was also exhausted. The technical demands were enormous. Aerial machines, rapid changes of scenery, dancing, smoke operators, lighting changes, and transparencies – all that was under Hill's control with his stagehands. But there was an enormous sense of fulfilment.

Heidegger was in the audience. Born in Zurich, Johann Jakob Heidegger was rather a mysterious figure, arriving in London about five years earlier with apparent experience in the entertainment world. He had been working at the Drury Lane theatre, running the day-to-day management. Tall and ugly, with a mellow voice and polished manners, he started to draw attention and fascination when Owen Swiney came back to the theatre with the actors. Now very much a shadowy figure, he was still at Drury Lane theatre, doing whatever he could, and waiting for the opportunity to move to the Queen's Theatre. He took a modest place at the top of the theatre, and after the opera ended, he was observing the people coming out. They were all smiling, excited, chatting, busy commenting on the singers and the music.

'I've never clapped so much. My hands are sore,' one said.

'I am sure I will lose my voice by tomorrow morning,' said another. 'I shouted too much.'

'I got the sparrow's dropping on my wig! Well, never mind, I enjoyed it so much!'

Heidegger was not the only one. Owen Swiney could not resist attending either, and he managed to squeeze himself in the gallery. He was again convinced of Nicolini's talent. His voice was fantastic, his singing skill was above all the other singers combined, and his acting went with it. Every limb, every finger was part of his extraordinary grace and dignity. *I could bring a deaf man, and he would enjoy it as much as myself. Who can sing and act like him? No one could do it in this country. Therefore he can command such high fees… He is free to ask whatever he wants. Nobody can beat him.*

> My dear sister,
>
> I just came back from the theatre, and cannot wait until tomorrow morning to write to you.
>
> I went to see the premiere of a new opera called Rinaldo at the Queen's Theatre. The composer is Mr Handel, the one we saw at the queen's birthday. You certainly remember him? I've never seen and heard such a beautiful thing in my life. I am sorry you were

> unwell and unable to attend. You have to see it. I'll come with you, because the only thing I want now is to go back there again and again. Nicolini was superb. And when he sang the most beautiful and sad aria, I wept. Rinaldo is grief-stricken at being separated from his love and is desperate to find her. 'My love, where are you? Come back, come back to me!' It starts so softly that you can hardly hear it. It then increases gradually, and when he sang 'come back' with all his voice and heart, it went straight to my heart. Oh, it's so moving and so beautiful! And I was not the only one to be in tears. The theatre was absolutely packed but it was so silent. Nobody moved a hair. When it finished, we all went wild, and I did not realise I was standing like others, clapping and shouting.
>
> Get better soon, my dear sister. I cannot wait to get you out of bed.
>
> Your loving and loyal sister,
> Rachel

Rachel Russell, Duchess of Devonshire, was still living in the world of crusaders, with Nicolini in Knights Templar's costume singing declarations of love, and she was determined to drag her sister Catherine, Duchess of Rutland, to the opera as soon as possible.

The next morning, Händel went to the theatre just to check the result from the previous evening. He found the cast and a few members of the orchestra. As everywhere, after a premiere, there would be a few invitations from the nobility and gentry. Hill was already distributing the letters.

'Here is one for Signor Nicolini. And another one. Oh, a third one…'

After that, there was a conference among the singers. They were all there in a circle. Nicolini presided.

'So, who received the invitation from the Duchess of Devonshire?'

This was to establish if the invitations were to perform as entertainment or just to come for dinner without any formal music involved. Of course, it was also a kind of competition to see who got the most invitations.

Nicolini approached Händel and said, pointing to the invitation, 'The Duchess of Devonshire wants me to sing "Cara sposa" especially. Hey, Giorgio, you did well!'

Händel beamed. 'I am pleased to hear that.'

'She also wants you to accompany me on harpsichord.'

'Just two of us?'

'Apparently so.'

Among the invitations addressed to Händel, there was one from James Brydges, and another one from Richard Boyle, Earl of Burlington.

'Burlington?' said Aaron Hill.

'Yes. Do you know the family?'

'Not personally, but I think it is a very wealthy family.'

'It is,' said Elisabetta. 'I saw them yesterday. The earl was with his mother and his older sisters.' She straightened herself proudly. 'I give singing lessons to the sisters.'

'Do you know the earl personally?' asked Händel.

'Not really. I sometimes came across him. He is still very young.'

Nicolini knew more. 'I was invited several times. The dowager countess has four children, and she lives with them in a mansion on Piccadilly. They are all charming and very musical. You will enjoy it, Giorgio.'

Another invitation came, this one from Pietro Grimani, who was a relative of Cardinal Vincenzo Grimani. Händel had met him in Venice and now he was in London as the ambassador representing the Serene Republic.

Dear Telemann,

Rinaldo is a big success, to my relief. However I am not totally happy with it. First of all, I did not have enough time. I am used to working fast. My training in Italy was good for that. But still, the libretto took time to get ready, so I had to reuse and adapt quite a lot of my previous work. The libretto is weak and the plot hardly convincing. It is mainly the work of Aaron Hill, the manager. He is a very nice and able man, but he has no experience

> in opera management. What he did well was the use of the machinery. The stage was spectacular, and that was one of the reasons for the success. I am happy with the music of war and pageantry, but as for the magic, to be honest, I was at a loss. I did not know what to do! But I hope the audience was convinced by it.
>
> My heart reaches out and joins you in your prayers. In this time of grief, God is the only consolation. I sincerely hope you will find peace soon.
>
> I will return to Hanover in the summer, but I hope I will come back here to London again. It is a dynamic place, and there is a great future here for Italian opera.
>
> Your faithful and loyal servant, friend, and brother,
>
> G.F. Händel

Behind the glittering and glamorous front, there was growing dissatisfaction at the Queen's Theatre. Opera was extremely expensive to produce. From the time Hill took control of the company, receipts had been barely enough to cover salaries and routine expenditures. There was no money for new productions and special expenses. Tradesmen and performers had hardly been paid. Protests were lodged with the Lord Chamberlain, who turned to Collier, who, in turn, asked permission to take control from Hill, which was approved. Collier had been working hard to establish a good relationship with the Lord Chamberlain, the Vice Lord Chamberlain and the secretary. His mask of charm and affection was enough to convince them that Hill was responsible for the mess created.

On 3 March 1711, just after *Rinaldo*'s third performance, William Collier arrived at the theatre, shouting, 'It's the order of the Lord Chamberlain!'

He entered the theatre through the front door and was in the foyer, going towards the auditorium, when Aaron Hill came from the other side. Collier stopped in front of Hill.

'You are dismissed, Hill. Go, now!'
Hill did not understand. 'Mr Collier, what is the matter?'
'I told you. You are dismissed by order of the Lord Chamberlain.' Collier handed Hill the order signed by the Lord Chamberlain.
Hill could only stare at the paper.
'Go, I told you. Go. I own the theatre from now on. Everything in this theatre belongs to me. Everything. Costumes, sceneries, everything.'
'But Mr Collier...'
Hearing a man shout, other people were gathering in the foyer.
'I am the sole master and director of the theatre,' Collier declared, looking around, and then turned to Hill. 'You rascal, I know all about your mismanagement.'
Aaron Hill was speechless. Haym, who happened to be there, witnessed everything in dismay.

'What? Dismissed?' said Händel, staring at the man standing in front him.
'I cannot believe this, but it is the reality. I am nothing now,' said Hill, still in shock.
'But the opera...'
'You shall continue, Mr Handel.' Hill looked in his eyes. 'The subscription. You have to do it at least three more times to honour the subscription,' he said and lowered his head. 'I am sorry.'
Händel watched Hill walk away in disbelief. Could such a thing happen? He rushed to Nicolini's house to report the incident. The singer's reaction was mixed. He was appalled but not totally surprised.
'I thought something was not right with that Collier, and I always wondered why Swiney was sent to Drury Lane.'
'Who is Swiney?'
'He was the manager here before Hill came in with Collier.'
'Why was he sent away?'
'That was the order of the Lord Chamberlain.'
'But why? Was Swiney not good enough?' Händel insisted.
Nicolini smiled. 'He was good, but the problem was those actor-managers.'
'Actor-managers?'
'Yes. Swiney was not alone. He had co-managers. Oh, it's complicated. But I can tell you, Giorgio, that those actor-managers did not like us Italian singers.'
'Oh... I see.' Händel felt he had a glimpse of the reality. 'I've never seen Collier myself. Have you seen him before?'
'Just once, when he came to tell us that he was the new owner. But I knew he was not the owner of the theatre. Again, it's complicated. That was

the only time I saw him. It was Hill who did everything.'

'Well, we have to do with Mr Collier from today. Let's see how it goes,' said Händel, forcing himself to be merry.

'We can sing, and you can conduct. That's fine. Everything is in place. You are probably right, Giorgio. Let's see.'

The devious ways of Collier did not go unnoticed. The new Lord Chamberlain, Charles Talbot, 1st Duke of Shrewsbury, received a report from the Vice-Chamberlain Thomas Coke about Collier's treatment of Aaron Hill. Barely in office for a year, the Vice-Chamberlain was a precious source of information for Charles Talbot.

'Your Grace, I have to tell you,' Thomas Coke said, 'Collier has a taste for violence. I told you about the wretched Christopher Rich. I think Collier is the same kind. And he likes breaking into a theatre to take possession. Your Grace, this is not the first time he's done so.' The Vice-Chamberlain was not, from the beginning, so convinced by William Collier.

'I went to the premiere of *Rinaldo* at the Queen's Theatre. It was splendid. Even my Italian wife was deeply impressed. I cannot believe such ugly things were going on behind the scenes.'

'Well, it started when Mr Vanbrugh decided to build his theatre. It attracted jealousy.'

'Would you please keep watching, Coke. It looks murky.'

They looked at each other, and nodded.

Collier was triumphant to begin with, but the situation soon became a disaster. The opera still drew an audience on subscription for the three remaining performances, but after that, the low nightly receipts reflected clearly Collier's incompetence. The company was losing money at each performance. This pushed Lineke to collect the scores after each performance and keep them with him until he got paid for the copying. He did not trust Collier.

If the situation at the Queen's Theatre looked disastrous behind the façade of success of *Rinaldo*, this was rather an opportunity for John Walsh the publisher. Taking advantage of the chaos, he would skip the usual process of negotiating the terms and paying the composer to publish the opera score.

Hill's distress did not stop there. He soon discovered, to his horror, that the unpaid tradesmen were holding him personally responsible for the debts contracted under his management. He did try to rectify the situation by complaining to the Lord Chamberlain, who was now very suspicious of Collier. Hill regretted bitterly his too casual and optimistic arrangement with Collier. There was no written document to prove his argument. Thus started the bitter lawsuit between Hill and Collier. In the meantime, the unpaid tradesmen continued to pursue Hill in order to collect the debts.

Hill felt drained. For the last eighteen months, he had been oscillating between elation and disaster. Not once but twice he had his management of a theatre violently snatched away from him, the second time when he was at the very height of his success, innovating and experimenting with the future of opera and putting together a dazzling production from scratch within a few weeks. Hill withdrew from the theatre world altogether. He just wanted to concentrate on sorting out his financial problems. He also wanted to provide his wife with a safe environment in which to give birth to their first child.

'Are you all right, Mr Hill?' asked his wife, concerned, 'you look tired.'

'Oh, no, I am not tired, my dear,' Hill forced a smile. 'Do not worry, Margaret, I am fine. I will not be going to the theatre anymore. I resigned.'

'Resigned?'

'Yes. I've had enough. It was taking too much time, and I hardly saw you. I want to spend more time with you.'

'Oh, Husband,' Margaret Hill pressed her hands on her chest. It was true. She hardly saw her husband, since he was so busy with the theatre, and she spent a lot of time alone. Being alone and pregnant at sixteen was hard to bear. She felt warmth flooding her heart. 'I am so happy, Husband, that I will be seeing more of you.' She was now fighting back her tears.

'Yes, my dear, you will.' Hill took her in his arms and tenderly kissed the top of her head.

When the first impact of *Rinaldo* and the enthusiasm it inspired dissipated and all became routine, the critics started to appear. This was London, the world's most developed city in terms of the press. However, there was no vicious attack. The criticisms were based on anti-Italian feelings linked to antipathy to Catholicism. *Rinaldo* was criticised for being performed entirely in Italian, and the extravagant scenery was mocked and ridiculed. But there was no attack on the quality of the music or on the person of Händel.

'Oh, just wait and see, Giorgio,' said Nicolini, 'you are still new, but you will see. They can be quite vicious.'

'How about you, Nicolini?' Händel asked.

'Me? Oh, every kind of criticism was brought against me. The singers are more targeted than composers, obviously.'

'What kind of criticism, exactly?'

'Caricatures are the most popular; then there are articles in newspapers and pamphlets. You know, Giorgio?'

'Yes?'

'Owen Swiney was sensible to go through newspapers to see if there were any critics of the productions, and Hill did the same. I could see they were educated people, but...'

'Collier?'

'Oh, he does not care. He might be educated, but he is just a brute. I'm sure his bible is bound banknotes. Giorgio' – Nicolini looked into Händel's eyes – 'as soon as my contract is over, I will go. This is not a place to stay. This is a place to make money in a short period. I miss Italy. I miss Venice.'

Händel froze. *I miss Venice*. That was exactly what Vittoria had said when they walked together in the gardens of Vignanello. The memory of happy and beautiful days in Italy came back at once.

Nicolini did not miss it. It was very quick, but there was, again, grief in Händel's gaze. This was the confirmation: Händel is in love. But with whom?

'See this, Giorgio,' Haym handed him a folded newspaper.

Händel unfolded it.

'This newspaper is new, just started this month. And it is a daily paper.'

'*The Spectator*,' Händel read.

'This one.' Haym pointed to a small square. 'It's about *Rinaldo*.'

'Who is Joseph Addison? He wrote the article,' Händel said, trying to read it.

'He is one of the founders of the paper, so he has to fill in a lot.' Haym laughed. 'Do you understand what it says?'

'I'm not sure.'

'Don't worry. It's not nasty. He does not like Italian opera.'

'Is there such a thing as English opera?'

'Well, there were a few attempts, but they did not really work.'

'Is Italian opera better?'

'I would not say that, but opera was introduced from Italy, so what they did at first was to translate operas into English.'

'Oh... So was *Camilla* translated?'

'Yes. And I arranged the music. It was a huge success.'

Händel just frowned. *Why? Such a mutilation could not be a success.*

Haym understood and laughed. 'Giorgio, it was the novelty. And then the castrato was brought from Italy, and he could not sing in English, so it became a mixture of English and Italian.'

'What?' Händel stared at Haym in horror.

'*Hydapses* was the first to be sung entirely in Italian. You arrived just in time to avoid seeing such nonsense and fainting, Giorgio.' Haym laughed out loud. Despite his German name, inherited from his father, Nicola Haym was very Italian, born and bred in Rome.

Händel did not reply. The very first opera he saw in London was *Pirro e Demetrio*, and it was sung in English and Italian. He who composed a bilingual opera *Almira* in Hamburg was not appalled. But it was something shocking for the Italians. So *Almira was rubbish, at the point of making the Italians faint?*

Händel accepted the invitation from the Earl of Burlington and was busy deliberating. *Is it better to arrive in style in a coach? But I am not yet paid, and I have to be careful with the expense. Hiring a coach with footmen will be quite expensive, and it could look as if I am trying to be equal to the nobility. So, I will walk, probably.* Then a note arrived telling Händel that the earl was sending him a coach.

Händel arrived in front of a fairly plain, big mansion on Piccadilly. It looked less severe than Italian palaces. He was already imagining the richly decorated, large interior space when he entered the house to find himself in a small entrance hall without any particular decoration.

Händel was received by a very young man, who looked like a boy. Richard Boyle, 3rd Earl of Burlington, was only sixteen years old. His body was still in the process of growing, and his thin and short frame supported a head with a gentle expression. Händel was quite surprised, despite the boy's childish look, to find a quite confident person.

'Thank you for coming, Mr Handel. I am Richard Boyle. Very pleased to meet you.'

'I thank you, my lord.' Händel bowed.

Immediately, two young women burst into the entrance hall followed by their mother, running after them. The two women stood in front of Händel, side by side, smiling, while the mother sighed.

'Let me introduce my sisters, Mr Handel. As you see, they cannot wait,' said the young earl, and smiled, seeing his host not knowing how to react.

Soon Händel realised that the earl's intention was to invite him to come to live in his house.

'I am grateful, and I thank you, my lord. But I have to go back to Hanover when the season ends. That's what I agreed to with the elector.'

Händel saw the two young women's eyes widen with disappointment. The earl's expression was unchanged.

'Is it your intention to return to London, Mr Handel?'

Everybody turned to the voice. It was the dowager countess, who had remained silent until then.

'I will try my best to come back. However, I'll have to negotiate it with the elector.'

'Is the elector interested in music?'

'The war prevented him from having a full cast of singers to perform operas. However, he's always kept an orchestra.'

'Opera? In Hanover?' said the earl, his eyes wide.

'Yes, my lord. The elector's father built an opera house, and some were played there. Agostino Steffani composed nine operas for the theatre.'

'Steffani?' said the earl, bewildered.

'Yes, Steffani.'

'Is he still in Hanover?'

'Well, yes and no. He is based in Hanover, but he is very busy.' Händel saw them gobbling each word he said. 'Oh, he is not composing. His nomination as an apostolic vicar keeps him very much occupied. I was very lucky to meet him when I went to Hanover for the first time.' He heard one of them gasp.

'You... met him?' said one of the sisters dreamily.

Händel could see clearly that Agostino Steffani was venerated and well known in England as a leading composer, but only by his printed music, making him rather a mystic figure. Now they were facing a young man who had met him in the flesh.

Dear Giorgio,

I am now in Bologna. I am singing in Il Giustino, by Albinoni. I am Giustino in trousers. Tamburini is among the cast. You may have heard about him in Florence, as he was under the patronage of Cardinal de' Medici.

I left Venice in November last year. Since the death of Cardinal Grimani, nothing is working properly in San Giovanni Grisostomo, and I got a contract to sing in Bologna. Carli and Diamante are staying in Venice. When things are sorted out, I might go back to Venice. Since you left, I've sung in Lotti's opera. The last one, Isacio tirano, was a big success. I am sending you the wordbook with this letter. As you can see, it is dedicated to the Duke of Marlborough.

My regards and friendship to the Boschis.

Your faithful and loyal friend,
Margherita

Händel stared at the letter. He knew that Cardinal Grimani was dead. Still, it came back as a painful reality. The memory of this man of culture, his love of music, and his generosity in helping musicians was still vivid in Händel's mind. He had not had much direct contact with the cardinal, but he clearly remembered his witty smile, his straightforward way of talking and his warmth. It was the cardinal who enabled Händel to have a Venice debut which he could use as a calling card now. He felt he'd lost a friend.

Margherita did not tell everything to Händel in her letter. In Bologna she had met a man, Count Casimiro Avelloni, an impresario coming from minor nobility. She was not in love, but the count showed interest in her, and she knew it. She had worked hard, not only for her career but to forget her feelings towards Händel. Now he was far away, out of reach and she had little hope to be able to join him. News of his opera's success in London reached her, but Vittoria was not among the cast. *What happened? Do I have still a chance?* Still in love, constant and faithful, and despite getting only friendship from Händel, Margherita could not give up.

At the Queen's Theatre, there was an uneasy atmosphere. Collier ignored the order given by the Lord Chamberlain, on 3 May, to pay the tradesmen and the performers. The tradesmen were left to pursue Aaron Hill. This was not the only payment Collier was ignoring. Dietrich Lineke was getting restless. Collier owed him twenty-six pounds for copying the scores of *Rinaldo*, and despite the agreement of payment by instalments, Lineke saw nothing coming. He missed Owen Swiney, with whom there was no worry for payments. The musicians still performed, hoping to get paid. Händel, without Hill, was conducting and managing the stage manoeuvres. Still, even helped by Haym, he struggled to get everybody together. There was no heart.

Rinaldo was still going on when, on 26 May 1711, Wriothesley Russell, 2nd Duke of Bedford, died at age thirty from smallpox, leaving behind three young children and a pregnant wife. This was particularly painful for his mother, Rachel Wriothesley, Lady Russell, who had seen her husband executed and now had lost her son. For Nicola Haym, this was the end of a generous patronage. However, it was more of an emotional shock for him than a financial one. The duke had been younger than Haym by two years, and from the time he left Italy, the cellist had accompanied the young aristocrat. At the time they had first met in Rome, Russell was Marquess of Tavistock, but by the time they reached London, he had become Duke of Bedford, succeeding his grandfather. Married when he was only fifteen, his real married life started after his return to London. Nicola Haym had observed the young couple with affection. He had shared the grief of the death of their first two sons and the joy of the arrival of a healthy daughter, followed by two more sons. Now the duchess was with her sixth child and was widowed.

Haym saw how money was of little help in grief. He considered quitting everything and returning to Italy. His friend and patron was now gone and the situation at the Queen's Theatre was just a fiasco. He could go back to Rome, to Cardinal Ottoboni's orchestra, where Corelli was still active. But then? He had been living in London for ten years now, and had established his position as cellist, composer-arranger, and promoter of Italian composers. He had a fulfilling life. But above all, there was another reason. Though private and discreet about his private life, he maintained a relationship with a singer, and now she was pregnant.

Saturday 2 June was the last performance of *Rinaldo*, with which the Queen's Theatre ended its season. Händel was growing restless. Vittoria had not come. News of the success of *Rinaldo* must have spread to the continent. Still, she was nowhere to be seen. *Is she waiting for me in Hanover? Why can she not write to me? Margherita wrote to me.* Nothing was working to plan. London was the final meeting point agreed with Vittoria. Her voice still resonated in his heart: *I will meet you in London, Giorgio.* Once reunited with Vittoria, he was ready to abandon the post of Kapellmeister and establish himself in London. She did not come. And his opera's success was considerably deflated by the managerial troubles. He could not stay in London anymore. He had received many invitations from the nobility to go to their country estates for the summer, but he excused himself by saying that he had to go back to Hanover. Then an idea came. *I will stop in Düsseldorf first. The Elector Palatine wrote to me, inviting me to try some new instruments. The electress might know something.* She might have heard something from Florence from her brother, Grand Prince Ferdinando de' Medici. A ray of hope instantly made him merry, and now he could not wait to go back to the continent.

After Händel's departure, the Queen's Theatre started the 1711–1712 season with revivals. Heidegger managed to get in to take the post left vacant by Hill's dismissal, and ran day-to-day operations. Collier, witnessing and foundering under the financially insecure opera, lost interest and wanted to get out. He was now seeking a way to have a guaranteed income and complete freedom from responsibility. The excitement and colour of the theatre world did not appeal to Collier, unlike Swiney or Hill.

Swiney, instead, could not give up the glamorous world of opera. Things were not going so well in Drury Lane. The actor-managers who went back to Drury Lane with him were not getting on well with the rest of the actors. False allegations were made, in which Swiney found himself caught. He had no choice but to fight back. The actor-managers now wanted Swiney removed from an active role; they wanted to be in control of the theatre. When Swiney was offered £100 a year to be a silent partner, he saw a chance. He accepted the arrangement and approached Collier. By now, Swiney's persecutor, Christopher Rich, was out of Drury Lane Theatre and was busy refitting an old theatre in Lincoln's Inn Fields. The coast seemed clear. Owen Swiney traded his silent partnership to William Collier, taking the management of the Queen's Theatre in exchange. Being personally responsible for Nicolini's salary was daunting, but at least, he was back in the Queen's Theatre. Now it was time to prove himself and make his theatre vibrant again. One positive thing was the presence of Heidegger instead of Hill. Swiney saw that he was intelligent, quick and hard working. Confident of making a good team, the manager pushed back the worry and looked forward.

Chapter 14 : Uncertain future (1711-1712)

Dear Margherita,

Your letter gave me much pleasure, but I was saddened to learn the consequences of the cardinal's death.

I am now in Düsseldorf. Thank you very much for the wordbook of Lotti's opera. As I knew I was coming back to the continent, I did not write to you from London. If I did, you would probably have received my letter after this one. The Boschis will not stay in London. Nicolini will finish his contract before going back to Italy, but he is worried he might not get paid.

The Elector Palatine acquired a very nice harpsichord recently, and I am enjoying playing it. The elector and the electress are very kind to me, but they are worried that they are retaining me too long, to the Hanoverian elector's displeasure.

I am going back to Hanover and will think about my future. London seemed good, but I am not sure now. There is a serious management problem in the Queen's Theatre.

Your faithful servant and friend,
Giorgio

Hanover, Summer 1711

Händel felt restless. While in Düsseldorf he had been unable to get any information about Vittoria. The electress had not mentioned Florence or her brother Ferdinando at all. There was an awkward silence about it. Everything was disappointing. Unable to know Vittoria's whereabouts was irritating, and his future as an opera composer seemed compromised now. London seemed an unstable place, and here in Hanover opera was inexistent. He felt powerless.

Back in Hanover, Händel found himself in Herrenhausen, where court was held during summer. Caroline of Ansbach, the electoral princess, had given birth to a healthy girl in June and looked splendid. Dowager Duchess Sophia was healthy and still full of life. The elector, despite welcoming Händel back, looked gloomy. It was a joy to see Baron Kielmansegg.

'The elector? Do you think?' Baron Kielmansegg feigned surprise.

'Yes, Baron. He looks concerned, worried. I don't know.'

'Well, it might be the situation in Britain.'

'Is that the ongoing war?'

'Yes. You probably heard the change of the tide?'

'Vaguely, that the queen wanted peace with France. Is this right, Baron?'

'Yes. She got rid of Whigs little by little to form a Tory government, to negotiate with France.'

'Oh…'

'She even got rid of the Duchess of Marlborough, her long-time friend and confidant, and her husband the duke, a national hero.'

'I heard that the queen was not on good terms with the duchess anymore.'

'That's true, but the duchess was clinging to her post.'

'I see.'

Life in Hanover resumed as before, with little duty and lots of visits to the court poet Mauro and to the library, mainly to consult the scores of Steffani. He also gave music lessons to the three daughters of the elector by his mistress Melusine von der Schulenburg. Elector Georg Ludwig did not attend all of the musical entertainments. When he did, he looked rather distracted.

Dear Telemann,

I am back in Hanover. As before, my duties are quite light.

> *I am taking lessons to improve my English. It is quite subtle, not like Italian, and I sometimes struggle to pronounce things properly. I asked John Hughes, the poet and librettist I met in London, for some text so I can train myself to put English to music.*
>
> *There is some good news and bad news. The good news is, first, that I was paid my first year's salary. Second is that my sister in Halle is expecting her second child, and she asked me to be the godfather. Of course I accepted. The bad news is that my dear teacher, Zachow, died recently. I feel like I lost my second father. He was a good man. I intend to pay his widow a visit as soon as I can. Her son is old enough to support her, but sadly, he is drowned in wine and takes all the money the poor woman has.*

Händel stopped. He was not sure it was a good idea to talk about death to his friend.

One September morning, Baron Kielmansegg was summoned to the elector's office. He found the elector with a messenger.

'Your Highness,' the baron bowed. He could feel the tension.

The elector looked at him and sighed. 'It is done.' He addressed the messenger. 'Go to the kitchen and have some food, and then have a rest.' Then he turned to the valet behind him. 'Mustapha, would you take this gentleman to the kitchen, please?'

The baron watched the messenger bow and follow the elector's Turkish valet.

'He brought this from Kreyenberg.' He handed the letter to Kielmansegg.

The baron went through the letter. 'It seems it is past the point of no return, then.'

'It is going fast. The queen wants peace,' the elector sighed deeply.

The express letter from Kreyenberg informed the elector about the first peace articles agreed to between Britain and France. Both the elector and his confidant knew this was going to happen anyway. They still wished it to drag on and give more time for political manoeuvre. This put Georg Ludwig in a very delicate position. Britain had betrayed its allies, and the Duchy of Hanover was now in the position, legally, to declare war against the traitor. He was upset with Queen Anne for changing sides, but he could not express his feeling too loudly, because of the British succession. It was important to maintain a friendly relationship with the queen. However, not reacting to Britain's behaviour put him in a very uncomfortable position towards his allies. As a soldier and not a diplomat, this dilemma was hard to cope with.

'Your Highness?'

The elector nearly jumped.

'Is it time to go back to Hanover?' the baron just wanted to divert the elector's mind, 'it is getting rather cold.'

Georg Ludwig stared at his friend, and then said, 'Yes, you are right, Johann. I'll have to tell my mother about the move.'

'Would the duchess come with us?'

'She might stay a bit longer here in Herrenhausen. She likes it here.'

On 23 November, Händel stood in front of the Liebfrauenkirche in Halle. He looked up at its twin towers. His memory was sent back to his childhood. He was running towards the side door. Climbing to the organ loft. Playing the violin beside Zachow, who played the organ. Playing the organ on his own. Going down from the organ loft. The priest giving him sweets for shortening Zachow's lengthy cantatas... It was his childhood. It was a happy time, despite the pressure from his father. He was innocent, just wanting to make music and nothing else.

'Georg?' a voice said behind him, making Händel come back from the daydream. He felt a pair of arms around his waist. 'I thought you would come first to the house,' Dorothea Sophia said, hugging her brother from behind.

'I was going to, but I wanted to see the church first.' He turned to see his sister smiling. Then seeing her in black, he did not know what to say. His sister's first daughter died five months before while she was expecting her second child. He remembered holding a tiny baby in his arms and she was now gone.

Dorothea Sophia was thinking the same thing. Fighting back tears, she said, 'I have to go back home first to get changed,' and indicated her mourning dress. 'I'm busy. See you later.' She turned to leave but then came back and took Händel's hand. 'Thank you for coming.'

Händel saw his sister run, then stop and turn and wave to him. Was it just an impression that her cheeks seemed wet? He waved back to her and saw her resume running to reach the house where he had been born. The house where his father had died, where his two sisters had been born; life and death. Though saddened to see his sister in black, he felt peaceful. He smiled to himself and went inside the church, expecting to see the organ packed with memories. There he gasped. To his horror, the small organ above the altar was covered entirely for renovation. That was where he'd had his organ lessons with Zachow. Now his beloved teacher was dead, and the organ was undergoing repair. He desperately gazed at the now invisible organ, trying to remember as much as possible.

'Master Zachow…' he whispered and lowered his head. It was the end of an era.

Hanover, November 1711

Dear Telemann,

I just came back from Halle and found your letter, which made me very happy.

I attended the baptism of my niece, Johanna Frederika, daughter of my sister and Dr Michaelsen. I was one of the godparents. It took place at Liebfrauenkirche, where I played so often with my teacher, Zachow. It made me melancholic to think that he is not there anymore. Now the old organ is under renovation. I wonder who will replace Zachow. I heard a rumour that the city offered the post to an organist of my age, named Bach. Is it the one you talked about?

My mother is totally blind now. Fortunately, my sister lives with her, so she is cared for. I paid a visit to Zachow's widow, who is not very well off.

Agostino Steffani is in Hanover. He is now an apostolic vicar of northern Germany. His task is to protect and expand the Catholic community in northern Germany. As he is a friend of Elector Georg Ludwig, I see him from

> time to time here in Leineschloss, invited for a lunch or supper.
>
> I am sorry to hear that you are not happy in Eisenach. I am, like you, a court musician, so I totally understand why you declined the offer from the Dresden court. You might go to Hamburg or Leipzig, somewhere free from the court. As for myself, I still don't know if I want to go back to London. I am still learning English, because it might be useful, since the English love to travel to the continent, especially in France and Italy. With the War of the Spanish Succession, they go more to Italy, and that's where they buy like mad, everything they can put their hands on, including the musicians.
>
> I will write to you again. Please write to me. I am anxious to know how you are.
>
> Your most devoted servant, friend, and brother,
> G.F. Händel

It was spring of 1712, and the Hanoverian court was looking forward to moving to Herrenhausen. Händel was kept busy by the electoral prince and princess, who admired and valued the Kapellmeister, while the elector was brooding over Queen Anne's change of allegiance in the ongoing War of the Spanish Succession. Händel could see the solid bond between Dowager Duchess Sophia and her granddaughter-in-law, Electoral Princess Caroline, and they brought jolliness to the court. Electoral Prince Georg August was in love with his wife more and more. Now a mother of three, Caroline was able to provide motherlike affection to her husband, who had not seen his mother for the last seventeen years. The mention of his mother, Sophia Dorothea of Celle, still made the elector freeze in horror. It remained a taboo.

A surprise came in the form of a letter from London. It was Owen Swiney writing to Händel, who never saw the man in London. The letter started by the manager introducing himself, explaining that he was now back in the Queen's Theatre. Swiney was asking Händel to come to London to work with him, assuring that there would be no more trouble and that the financial situation in Haymarket was now stable under his management.

'What do you think, Baron?' asked Händel, showing him the letter.
'Well, what is your opinion, Georg?'
'I don't know. London is an interesting place, but... it is quite risky.'
'Is the Queen's Theatre not stable enough?'
'They now have Owen Swiney back, which is a good thing apparently. The main problem is money, Baron. Opera is very expensive to put on. Even a good success will hardly cover the cost.'
'Well, the letter says there are no financial problems.'
'Swiney cannot say otherwise.'
'I see. So you don't know.'
'No, I don't, to be honest.' Händel looked straight into Baron Kielmansegg's eyes. 'I have a salary here. In London, there is no guarantee. Do you think it is worth it to gamble my career?'
'Well, if they guaranteed a salary, would you go?'
'Did you know that Nicolini had to sue Swiney to get paid? He was under contract.'
'Oh...' Kielmansegg did not know what to say.
'Still...' Händel looked away. To him, London was still attractive. It was a new territory to explore, where Italian opera was still quite new. It was not like Venice, a long-established place for operas with its tough competition.

What the baron did not tell Händel was that a letter had been received from Kreyenberg, the Hanoverian resident in London. In his letter, Kreyenberg passed on a request from the Duke of Marlborough. The duke was asking the elector to send Händel to London for a few months, due to the pressure he was receiving from the lords and ladies. London wanted Händel back and the baron sensed that Händel was willing to go despite the uncertainly and hesitation.

'Johann, what is your impression?' the elector asked his confidant.
'I still think it is a good idea to send our Kapellmeister over again.'
'Does he want to go?'
'I think he does. The only thing stopping him is the money problem. But being a Kapellmeister his salary is guaranteed.'
'How long would he be gone?'
'For a season, about eight months?'
'Would that be long enough?'
'Well, he might want to stay longer, but eight months would be the time you would allow him to stay. The queen's health is declining steadily. She will not get better.'

Georg Ludwig felt a pang of guilt. He was going to send the young informer again, to learn exactly the state of the queen's health. As much as he denied he was observing carefully the process of her death, he tried to convince himself that he was not the only one, that the whole of Europe was doing the same. The death of a monarch was a delicate matter, and it often triggered war. There was every reason to observe the situation. Still, he could not stop feeling guilty. At the same time, if Queen Anne died and the succession passed to Hanover, as recognised by parliament, Britain would again be an ally. Or would the succession be contested?

The elector got up abruptly. It was complicated and he felt overwhelmed. He looked at the baron and said, 'Johann, come with me for a walk.'

Summer was approaching. Between London and Hanover, the express messengers and informers were busy, reporting the latest developments. While the Hanoverian court was moving to Herrenhausen, as usual in May, news arrived not from London but from the Imperial court of Vienna. After nearly a decade of concerted action by British, Imperial, and Dutch forces, the military alliance was broken. The commander-in-chief, James Butler, 2nd Duke of Ormonde, ordered the British troops not to engage the French armies. This restraining order left the remaining allied forces vulnerable, open to attack. For the elector, who supported the Imperial cause, Britain was now a declared traitor and enemy. At the same time, the question of the British throne had to be considered. Assuming that there would be no last-minute interruptions from anti-Hanoverians, his mother Duchess Sophia stood next in the succession to the British throne after the death of Queen Anne.

Elector Georg Ludwig spent more and more time shut in his offices, consulting and brooding. He felt humiliated. All that time and effort he'd made was thanked with kicks, and still he had to smile and let Britain kick him harder. *Is it worth it? Why can't I just kick back and abandon the British throne? Shall I talk to mother about it?*

'Georg, are you going to dine with your family? There will be music this evening,' Baron Kielmansegg interrupted his brooding.

'I am not in the mood.'

'Georg, do make an effort. You are making your family worried.'

'They are right to be worried,' said the elector, 'it is a worrying situation.'

'Georg, I do understand, but worrying will not change the situation, even if you worry harder.'

The elector, surprised, looked at his confidant. After a few seconds of silence he burst into laughter.

'Are you going to write to the queen?' Kielmansegg asked, relieved to see the elector more relaxed.

'Well, that's the only thing I can do. I will object in the strongest terms, but that's all.' He shrugged. 'That's all I can do, I suppose, alas.'

'Shall we go for dinner? My wife will be happy to see you.'

'How is she? Expecting? Again?' He laughed. He was glad to have a friend.

> Dear Giorgio,
>
> I am writing to you from Paris. I left London after the last opera of Gasparini, Antico. You might know that Owen Swiney is back in Haymarket, but his English opera was a total flop. He wanted to retain me, assuring me that you would come again. But I left. I had enough. And I am not sure I can trust Swiney. He is a nice man, and he manages the theatre well, but you know what I went through.
>
> I was thinking of coming to see you in Hanover, but I wanted to go back to Italy as soon as possible. As there is a kind of peace between Britain and France now, it is easier to go through France, and that's the quickest way back home.
>
> People were still talking about you and Rinaldo when I left London. I miss it. After you left, there was nothing exciting, and I am glad to go after my four years in London. After all, your opera was the only one I was really satisfied with. It was the only one done properly as an Italian opera. The rest was a joke. I sang in Italian while others sang in English! And if it was all in Italian, it was just a second-hand and badly adapted production. On the whole, my English experience was not very satisfying. So you

understand why I wanted to go back to Italy as quickly as possible.

It is gloomy here in Paris. The king is old, and he lost his heirs one after another. His son, the grand dauphin died last year. His grandson, Duke of Burgundy, died this year in February, and his great-grandson, Duke of Brittany, died in March. So, there is only one surviving heir, his other great-grandson, two-year-old Duke of Anjou, who is now the dauphin.

So, as you can imagine, the whole of France is mourning. Of course, there are no concerts at the court. I gave some small concerts privately, that's all.

The people believe that God is punishing the king for making the war carry on for so long, ruining his country and starving his people. The rumour is that the king's companion, Madame de Maintenon, to whom he is probably secretly married, begged him more than once to stop the war.

I will go directly to Venice, where I hope to get a contract for a season or two. I will write to you again so you can know everything about Venice.

Please write to me and let me know where you are. I am sure you will not stay in Hanover for long.

Your humble and faithful servant – and maybe your distant cousin,
Nicolo Grimaldi

Händel lifted his head from the letter, hearing children laughing outside.

He went to the window facing the gardens of Herrenhausen to see two children running towards the grotto, followed by Dowager Duchess Sophia, Electoral Princess Caroline, and the wet nurse carrying a baby. The sun was high, warm but not hot. It was a beautiful day. Händel decided to join them.

'We need to send Händel to London, Johann. The question is, how and when.' The elector heard children playing and went to the window. He made a sign to Baron Kielmansegg to come.

'When? As soon as possible. How? We have to be careful. It is essential that he is not aware that you are sending him as an informer, so this time, I should not accompany him.' Baron Kielmansegg joined the elector at the window and saw Händel playing with Friedrich and Anne.

'Send him on his own?'

'Yes. On leave. You could tell him that you are giving him the chance to compose operas and accumulate experience, and that when the war is over, Your Highness will have a proper orchestra and singers to bring back the splendour of the Hanoverian court to play opera again.'

'Would it be convincing?'

'To make it convincing, we have to make Händel believe it. To make him believe it, we have to believe it ourselves.'

The elector, watching his grandchildren, whispered, 'They will miss him.' Then he looked far ahead of him. The sky was blue with a few clouds here and there. He wondered what kind of sky Queen Anne was under.

Printed in Great Britain
by Amazon